Adrian McKinty was born and grew up in Carrickfergus, Northern Ireland. He studied philosophy at Oxford University and then moved to New York City in the early 1990s where he found work as a security guard, door-to-door salesman, construction worker, barman, book-store clerk and librarian. In 2000 he moved to Denver, Colorado where he became a high school English teacher and began writing fiction. His first full-length novel *Dead I Well May Be* was shortlisted for the Steel Dagger Award. Serpent's Tail also publishes the second and third parts of the Dead Trilogy: *The Dead Yard* and *The Bloomsday Dead* as well as *Hidden River*. His last novel, *Fifty Grand* won the 2010 Spinetingler Award for best novel. In 2009 Adrian and his family moved to Melbourne, Australia.

Dead I Well May Be

"A darkly thrilling tale of the New York streets with all the hard-boiled charm of Chandler and the down and dirty authenticity of closing time… Evocative dialogue, an acute sense of place and a sardonic sense of humour make McKinty one to watch" *Guardian*

"The story is soaked in the holy trinity of the noir thriller – betrayal, money and murder – but seen through here with a panache and political awareness that gives *Dead I Well May Be* a keen edge over its rivals" *Big Issue*

"Adrian McKinty's main skill is in cleverly managing to evoke someone rising through the ranks and wreaking bloody revenge while making it all seem like an event that could happen to any decent, hardworking Irish chap. A dark, lyrical and gripping voice that will go far" *The List*

"Adrian McKinty is a big new talent – for storytelling, for dialogue and for creating believable characters… *Dead I Well May Be* is a riveting story of revenge and marks the arrival of a distinctive fresh voice" *Sunday Telegraph*

"A pacy, assured and thoroughly engaging debut…this is a hard-boiled crime story written by a gifted man with poetry coursing through his veins and thrilling writing dripping from his fingertips" *Sunday Independent*

"Careens boisterously from Belfast to the Bronx…McKinty is a storyteller with the kind of style and panache that blurs the line between genre and mainstream. Top-drawer" *Kirkus Reviews*

"McKinty's Michael Forsythe is a crook, a deviant, a lover, a fighter, and a thinker. His Irish-tough language of isolation and longing makes us love and trust him despite his oh-so-great and violent flaws. When you finish this book you just might wish you'd lived the life in its pages, and thought its thoughts, both horrible and sublime" Anthony Swofford, author of *Jarhead*

"If Frank McCourt had gone into the leg-breaking business instead of school teaching, he might've written a book like *Dead I Well May Be*. Adrian McKinty's novel is a rollicking, raw, and unsavoury delight – down and dirty but full of love for words. This is hard-boiled crime fiction with a poet's touch" Peter Blauner, author of *The Last Good Day* and *The Intruder*

"McKinty has deftly created a literate, funny and cynical antihero who takes his revenge in bloody and violent twists but at the same time, methodically listens to Tolstoy on tape while on stakeouts. He rounds out the book with a number of incredible fever-dream sequences and then springs an ending that leaves readers shaking their head in satisfied amazement" *San Francisco Chronicle*

The Dead Yard

"Adrian McKinty has once again harnessed the power of poetry, violence, lust and revenge to forge a sequel to his acclaimed *Dead I Well May Be*" *The Irish Post*

"McKinty's literate, expertly crafted third crime novel confirms his place as one of his generation's leading talents…McKinty possesses a talent for pace and plot structure that belies his years. Dennis Lehane fans will definitely be pleased" *Publishers Weekly*

"*The Dead Yard* is a much-anticipated sequel to *Dead I Well May Be* and every bit as good. McKinty crackles with raw talent. His dialogue is superb, his characters rich and his plotting tight and seamless. He also writes with a wonderful (and wonderfully humorous) flair for language, raising his work above most crime-genre offerings and bumping right up against literature" *San Francisco Chronicle*

"Expat Irishman Adrian McKinty has just put out his fourth terrific book…and he keeps getting better. He melds the snap and crackle of the old Mickey Spillane tales with the literary skills of Raymond Chandler and sets it all down in his own artful way. This is a writer going places. Hop aboard" *Rocky Mountain News*

The Bloomsday Dead

"Those who know McKinty will automatically tighten their seatbelts. To newcomers I say: buckle up and get set for a bumpy ride through a very harsh landscape indeed. His antihero Michael Forsythe is as wary, cunning and ruthless as a sewer rat…His journey in some ways parallels that of James Joyce's Leopold Bloom on one day in Dublin, but – trust me – it's a lot more violent and a great deal more exciting" Matthew Lewin, *Guardian*

"A pacey, violent caper…As Forsythe hurtles around the city, McKinty vividly portrays its sleazy, still-menacing underbelly" John Dugdale, *Sunday Times*

"Thoroughly enjoyable…[McKinty] maintains the bloody action all the way from Lima to Larne with panache and economy. His hero, the 'un-f***ing-killable' Michael Forsythe, is a wonderful creation" Hugh Bonar, *Irish Mail on Sunday*

"Packed with sharp dialogue and unremitting action" Marcel Berlins, *The Times*

"Compelling thrillers written in a hard-bitten, muscular style, the novels are given an unconventional twist by virtue of Forsythe's unusually perceptive insights…a fascinating blend of Robert Ludlum's Jason Bourne and Patricia Highsmith's Tom Ripley…McKinty is a rare writer" *Sunday Business Post*

"A tangled and bloody odyssey through Dublin and Belfast…[a] well-paced, edgy thriller" Terence Killeen, *Irish Times*

"A gut-punching gangster story…this illegitimate spawn of a book, with Tony Soprano morality and James Joyce literary weight, ends the Michael Forsythe trilogy" Gerard Brennan, *Belfast Newsletter*

Hidden River

"McKinty is a cross between Mickey Spillane and Damon Runyon – the toughest, the best. Beware of McKinty" Frank McCourt

"A roller-coaster of highs and lows, light humour and dark deeds… Once you step into *Hidden River*, the powerful undercurrent of McKinty's talent will swiftly drag you away. Let's hope this author does not slow down anytime soon" *Irish Examiner*

"[A] terrific read…this is a strong, non-stop story, with attractive characters and fine writing" *Morning Star*

"This is genuinely hard to put down" *Buzz*

"Fast-paced thriller…McKinty's short, sharp delivery manages to make *Hidden River* an engaging read" *Big Issue*

"A dark, lyrical and gripping voice that will go far" *The List*

"An outstanding and complex crime novel that should appeal to fans of hard-boiled Celtic scribes such as Ken Bruen and Ian Rankin…This is not only an expertly crafted suspense novel but also a revealing study of addiction" *Publishers Weekly*

Falling Glass

Adrian McKinty

A complete catalogue record for this book can be obtained
from the British Library on request

The right of Adrian McKinty to be identified as the author of this work has been asserted by
him in accordance with the Copyright, Designs and Patents Act 1988

First published in 2011 by Serpent's Tail,
an imprint of Profile Books Ltd
3A Exmouth House
Pine Street
London EC1R 0JH
website: www.serpentstail.com

ISBN 978 1 84668 782 2
eISBN: 978 184765 322 2

Designed and typeset by folio at Neuadd Bwll, Llanwrtyd Wells

Printed and bound in Great Britain by Clays, Bungay, Suffolk

10 9 8 7 6 5 4 3 2 1

The paper this book is printed on is certified by the © 1996 Forest Stewardship Council A.C.
(FSC). It is ancient-forest friendly. The printer holds FSC chain of custody sgs-coc-2061

FSC
Mixed Sources
Product group from well-managed
forests and other controlled sources
Cert no. SGS-COC-2061
www.fsc.org
© 1996 Forest Stewardship Council

It's no go my honey love, it's no go my poppet;
Work your hands from day to day, the winds will blow the profit.
The glass is falling hour by hour, the glass will fall forever,
But if you break the bloody glass you won't hold up the weather.

Louis MacNeice, "Bagpipe Music" (1937)

prologue
on 238th street

"**M**Y POINT, FRIEND, IS THAT THIS IS NOT AN AFFECTIONATE homage. This is not an interior critique. This is not Jay-Z using, what I advisedly call, the N-word. This is a collection of clichés that actually undermines what it is supposed to be celebrating. This whole ethos is a paradigm in need of shifting. And the fact that it is generated by people, no offence, with only a tangential connection to the ur-source of that culture makes it all the more embarrassing."

The barman nodded. "So do you want another pint then? One without a shamrock on the head?"

Killian sighed. "It's not even about the shamrock is it? It's the entire 'vast moth-eaten musical brocade'. The whole shebang. This entire scene, brother, is, at best, a pastiche. But while we're on the subject of the shamrock, what's with the four leaves? Nothing could be simpler to remember. The Celts are polytheistic, they have many gods, Saint Patrick wants them to worship one god so he employs the shamrock to represent the Trinity: God the Father, the Son and the Holy Ghost. The Trinity. Three leaves. A four-leaf shamrock isn't a shamrock, it's a four-leaf clover. Do you see? I mean, at the bare minimum we should both be able to agree on that?"

The bar man – bar *boy* really – nodded more firmly this time. "I'll get you another pint, without the shamrock. I didn't know you was from the old country itself so to speak."

"Thank you," Killian said.

"Although," the kid added, with a twinkle in his eye which Killian might have caught if he had been paying attention, "You've got to give him credit for the snakes."

"Who?"

"Saint Patrick."

"You're Irish?" a voice asked from behind him, in the blind spot – a dangerous place for anyone to be. Killian flinched and turned, his hand reaching inside his pocket for a ghost piece.

A big guy in a Rangers shirt. NY Rangers that is. Not Glasgow. Different thing all together.

"Yes," Killian said.

"Your accent's not Irish though is it?" the man said sceptically. His voice had a hint of crazy and his eyebrows were madder than Freddie Jones's in David Lynch's *Dune.*

"I'm from Belfast," Killian said slowly.

The man nodded slowly. "Oh, I see, so not Ireland, Ireland. Have you ever been to Dublin? That's a real Irish city."

Killian's fresh pint of the black stuff appeared on the bar in front of him a mere forty-five seconds after he'd been promised it – not a great sign. The barman however must have had concentration or even psychiatric problems because there on the top was another four-leaf clover masquerading as a shamrock.

Killian knew it was time to hit the exit. But before he did: "Dublin's a nice place but you have to remember that it was a Norse settlement for three centuries before it became an English town for seven centuries more. It's been an *Irish* city for ninety years. Are you familiar with the Aboriginal concept of The Dreaming?"

"The Aboriginal what of the what now?"

"The Aboriginals believe that we live two lives. A life here on Earth in what we call the real world and a life in The Dreaming which is really the real world, where everything has a purpose, where we are more than thinking reeds, are part of some great scheme of things. And in The Dreaming certain places are special, certain landscapes, certain settlements. Belfast is one of those places. The neolithic people thought so. To them it was a holy site. Pristine birch woods in a river valley only just freed from a retreating ice sheet a mile thick. The Celts weren't interested in Dublin – it lacked a significance in their cosmology which is why they let the Norwegians have it. Belfast lies at the confluence of three holy rivers. In Irish it means Mouth of the Farset, one of those sacred streams. Do you see what I'm saying?"

The man in the Rangers shirt nodded sagely, "So, you're Australian then?" he asked.

Killian sighed inwardly. Some instinct had told him that this was going to be a mistake. Even before the plane had entered the airspace of Newfoundland he'd begun to have doubts. You can't go home again and the New York of crack wars, quadruple-digit homicide rates, David Dinkins, Mike Forysthe and 50,000 illegal Micks was long, long gone.

He abandoned the pub, the pint and the man and hoofed it downhill to the subway stop on 242nd Street.

He found a *Daily News* that had a picture of Dermaid McCann, Gerry Adams and Peter Robinson having a pint with the President.

They were drinking Guinness.

Obama's grin had *Get me the hell out of here* written all over it.

Killian yawned. He was dog-tired and in the morning he had a job to do in Boston that could well be the death of him.

The train finally came after an epic wait.

It was now after midnight.

"Happy Saint Patrick's Day," the driver said on the intercom.

"Aye, I suppose we'll see about that," Killian muttered to himself.

chapter 1
go down fighting

CURSING THE DOG'S NAME, SHE TOOK THE GUN BARREL FROM HER mouth and set the 9-millimetre on the kitchen table.

The metal had felt good. Like it belonged there. A cold, perfect piece of engineering.

She sat on her trembling right hand and stared at the weapon.

Ice crystals were melting on the Heckler and Koch's polymer grip and running over the magazine as it lay on the yellow and green Formica, *waiting.*

Seconds ticked past in long increments of raw time.

She found herself fixating on the disarmed hammer safety and trigger lock, imagining the terrible power of the chambered round. In an instant it could all be at an end. Click. A chemical reaction. An expanding piece of molten lead. Big Dave would kick in the door and take out her kids, the peelers would arrive from Coleraine and find her note, Tom or Richard's lawyer would wake him with the good news, hacks would drive up from Belfast and someone would put that stock photograph of her with the blonde hair on page one of the bloody *Sunday World.*

But she'd be out of it.

To be dead in the black earth, to be alive only in yesterdays…

The P30 had eight in the magazine, one in the breech – that was the one she could ride into nothingness.

Thresher barked again. If it had still been raining, of course, she wouldn't have heard him at all. Tonight she might really have done it. Wouldn't have thought so long and hard and let the barrel slide off her tongue.

But not now, now she was on alert in case this really was something. *Someone.*

She killed the lights, picked up the gun and went to the door.

She cracked it open and listened.

Surf in the distance, cars on the road, a football match on a distant radio.

"Thresher?" she whispered but he was quiet now. "Thresher, where are ya, ya big eejit?"

She breathed the night air. It was damp, cold. She looked up. The clouds had blown through and the star-field was rich. The Milky Way, the crescent moon, Orion.

She knew about the stars. She'd taken astronomy at Queen's for a year before dropping out. Of course none of Richard's lawyers ever mentioned that in their depositions. They preferred to paint her as the gold-digger, the cultchie, the junkie…

Her nails were digging into her palm. She unclenched her fist.

She closed the caravan door and went inside. Sat back down at the kitchen table. The P30 was still in her hand. A microsecond. That's all it would take.

She reconsidered for one beat, two…

She shook her head. "No," she said aloud. She safetied the weapon, put it in a plastic bag in the freezer, closed the fridge door.

Ended her conversation with death.

She walked the length of the caravan to check on the girls.

The nightlight was casting a pink glow over the buckled aluminum walls. Sue's blanket had fallen to the floor. She picked it up, replaced it. Claire was sleeping like a rabbit, curled on all fours, hunched. The barking dog hadn't woken either of them.

Rachel stared at them, trying to feel love rather than resentment.

But she was so damn tired. Tired of lying, hiding, running.

"Good night," she whispered and went back to the front door.

She opened it and took a last look out. "Go ahead, Richard. Send your men, I don't think I even care anymore," she whispered sadly.

She locked the door and put the chain across.

She tiptoed to her room – the only real bedroom in the caravan – and sat on the fold-out bed. The blankets hadn't been tossed in a week. They gave off an odour.

She reached for her fags, opened the box, discovered that it was empty.

Rain began to fall on the metal roof.

Ding, ding, ding, ding, ding, ding...

"Christ," she muttered.

Surely the girls would be better off without her. Rachel looked about her – *this*, this was madness.

She fished in the ashtray and found a ciggy with an inch left in it.

She flipped Big Dave's Zippo. The tobacco tasted of sand. She blew smoke at a midge and lay back on the sheets.

The roof dissolved.

Pine trees. Constellations. An arrow of cloud intersecting with the moon. There were poppies along the granite wall and a wind bringing the smell of fennel, saffron and boggy emptiness.

She turned off the nightlight and stared through the lace curtains at the caravan park. A green phosphorescence was playing on the TV aerial of Big Dave's caravan. She'd seen it before and she watched while it fizzed there for a moment – if fizzed was the right word – before dissipating into the black air. Most everyone was asleep now. Dave was on earlies and the football match appeared to have finished. Stu and that girl of his were probably the only ones still up, amped out of their minds or cooking blue belly to sell in Derry, or to her.

She finished the smoke, climbed under the sheets.

Darkness.

And when the traffic on the A2 died away, quiet.

She couldn't sleep. Yes, the methamphetamine was still in her system but she hadn't pulled an eight for years.

She was lucky these days to get four.

He wasn't the problem. She no longer thought about Richard or *that* Sunday morning…No, the problem wasn't the past but the present. Money, Claire, truant inspectors, Sue, lawyers, private detectives, the Police Service of Northern Ireland. Drugs.

Rachel tugged the sheet over her face.

Wind.

Rain.

And, finally, at around two, a few hours of erased existence…

Photons from a different star.

Prayers seeping through the bedroom wall.

She stirred. The room was heady, the smell: eucalypt, pine, seaweed. She lifted the sheet from her face. Rubbed her eyes. Her fingertips were soft. Uncalloused. Unworked. She noted this with neither satisfaction nor regret. Work was for workers.

She lowered her legs to the floor. She looked for her watch but remembered that it had fallen off her wrist in town. Always sly, the Rolex had seized its chance to keep forever its knowledge of date and time, second and minute. Perhaps it was even a bold attempt on the watch's part to set her free of such notions. She smiled, she liked that, but it wasn't true – the watch was a present from Richard, it was his ally not hers. And it wasn't even funny. She could have hocked it for five hundred quid in Coleraine.

She yawned, pulled back the curtain.

Blue van, red van, van so old it had lost all its colour, VW Beetle.

She pushed the window open. A cold wind from the Atlantic. She shivered.

The prayers from the Jehovah's Witnesses next door continued. Seven of them crammed into a caravan same size as hers.

She grabbed the dressing gown from the back of her chair and put it on. She opened the window a little wider and listened to the babble.

The chanting was neither a pitch for the Lord's intervention nor even His understanding, but rather a simple plea that the Almighty hear them. That's all they wanted. Just hear us, Jesus, know that we exist.

"Well, I can certainly hear you," she said, getting off the bed.

She slid open her bedroom door and checked on the girls.

Claire was reading *Little House on the Prairie* at the kitchen table; Sue was still out for the count.

"Morning," she whispered.

Claire didn't look up.

"Morning," she repeated.

"What?" Claire said.

"When someone says 'good morning' to you, it's customary to respond," she said.

"Sue's sleeping, I didn't want to wake her," Claire muttered.

Rachel nodded. Always with the answer, that one, but she quickly saw another line of attack. Claire was sipping from a glass of orange juice. There were ice cubes in it.

"I thought I told you never to go in the freezer," she said.

"Mum, please, I'm trying to read," Claire snapped.

Rachel walked the length of the caravan and sat down opposite her daughter. There were two ways to go here: get angry and give her a punishment or ignore it.

She thought for a minute and then picked the latter.

"What's happening in your book?" she asked with a benign smile.

Claire looked up. "They just got Jack back, okay?"

"Who's Jack?"

"Their dog, they thought he was drowned – please, Mum."

"Fine," Rachel muttered and walked to the front door, ruffling Claire's hair a little roughly as she went past. She undid the locks, opened the door, looked between the branches of the Scot's spruce. A sky like irises, low clouds, vapour trails.

The sun had not yet cleared the trees to the east.

Dave's paper was lying on his porch and his car was still there. He was, apparently, sleeping late.

She felt lonely.

Now there weren't even stars. She rubbed her chin, scuffed her flip-flop on and off, on and off. She peered through the line of caravans to catch a glimpse of the ocean but there was only a gluey sea mist down there today.

She sat down in the door opening. At her feet an empty vodka bottle, a half-smoked cigarillo, a wine glass containing rain water and several watermelon rinds now covered with hundreds of black ants.

The prayers to her right suddenly stopped and after a minute the whole clan came out and began manoeuvering their way into the Volvo 240. Four boys, two girls. Eldest nine. Dad run off to England.

Rachel waved. Anna waved back.

"Rachel honey, after I leave the weans off, I'm swinging past the Spar. Need anything?" Anna asked sweetly.

She had a good heart, Anna. Rachel couldn't bring herself to really like her but she had a good heart.

"Nah, I'm okay… Wait, no, I need some fags."

"Sure. Usual?"

"Usual."

The Volvo backed out, wove through the caravans and down the dirt track. A new Toyota Hilux was half blocking the way out, so Anna had to swerve over almost into the ditch.

"Some people, no consideration at all," Rachel said to herself. Probably yuppie scum here to buy blue belly from Stu.

Rachel got up and transferred herself to the deckchair next to her house. She lifted one of last night's wine glasses, plucked out a dead fly and drank.

Perhaps she dozed a little.

She woke with a start. The sun was higher, the mist had burned off. It was March 17 so it was never going to be warm but it was shaping up to be a—

Something was wrong.

"Claire?" she said.

No answer.

She stood. "Claire?"

"What is it?" Claire demanded from inside the caravan.

"Is your sister awake?"

"She's in the bathroom," Claire said with the verbal equivalent of an eye roll.

Rachel nodded to herself but it still didn't feel quite…Something Claire had said, something about a dog.

She turned and looked at Dave's house. The newspaper. The truck. Wasn't Dave supposed to be on earlies?

She walked back to her own caravan. Looked in. Toilet flushing. Claire reading.

"Claire, darling, could you do me a favour and tell me what time it is?" she asked.

"Mother, please!" Claire said.

"What time is it?" Rachel asked more firmly.

"It's eight, okay? Now can I read?"

Eight o'clock. Dave should have left an hour ago. She stared at the new Toyota down the trail. No one in the cab. The thing just sitting there.

And what about Thresher? Where was he?

"Thresher?" she called. "Thresher, boy."

She waited.

Nothing.

"I've got a treat for you. Thresher? Thresher!"

No barking, no running.

"Thresher!"

A chill along her vertebrae.

She dropped the wine glass, tied the robe about her and ran back inside the caravan. She took the book from Claire's hands.

"Mum!" Claire screamed.

She grabbed Claire's wrist, squeezed.

"Mum, you're hurting me."

"Get dressed. Pack a bag. Everything you need. Grab my stuff too and get your sister dressed. Now!"

"What's the matter?" Claire asked. She looked frightened.

"Get dressed, do it now! Tell your sister."

"What is it?"

"Don't argue with me. Go!"

Rachel went to the freezer, took out the Heckler and Koch P30, flipped off the safeties. "Mum, Claire says I have to get dressed," Sue whined.

"Do as your sister says! Do it! Get dressed and pack a bag," Rachel ordered with cold authority. She took a deep breath and exited the trailer. She held the P30 two-handed in front of her, finger next to but not on the trigger. She couldn't shoot a cop. It was twenty-five years minimum if you killed a peeler.

Her flip-flops were onomatopoeing so she kicked them off. She walked barefoot to Dave's, looked in. Blinds down. TV dead. She tried the door. Locked. She crouched down and pushed open the dog flap. She peered inside but she couldn't see anything.

"Dave?"

No answer, but most nights he slept with earplugs.

She walked round the back of the caravan. Here the clayey dirt became sand and the sand showed a russet-coloured blood trail that went off into the woods.

"Jesus," she whispered.

She knelt down and touched it. Dry but not caked.

Swallowing hard she followed it into the trees.

"Thresher?" she tried quietly.

And then she thought of a worse scenario: "Dave?"

She looked back at her caravan. Everything *seemed* okay.

She stepped over a fallen tree and there, about fifteen yards into the big firs, was Thresher covered in ants with a puncture wound in his head.

She bent down. Cold to the touch. Died a few hours ago. He'd gone after whoever had come and they'd killed him.

"Good boy," she whispered. "You did well. Good boy."

She was surprised to see that the blood trail did not abruptly end at Thresher's body but instead went deeper into the wood.

She followed it easily over the dense layer of pine needles on the forest floor. Even if she hadn't been schooled by her scoutmaster da she still could have tracked this guy.

Heavy footprints, a couple of coins, blood, one leg dragging behind the other.

At one point he'd fallen and it had taken him a while to get back up again.

He was crawling now, not walking.

She found him barely a hundred yards from the caravan park.

Thresher had torn him up pretty well. He was about thirty-five, wearing a leather jacket, black jeans, white sneakers. He had two gold earrings, a pale pock-marked face, a thin moustache and a *Mafiya* teardrop under his left eye. Lovely.

He was covered in sweat and he'd contrived to break his leg.

In his left hand was a mobile phone, in the right a handgun.

He was definitely not an Irish cop nor Interpol nor Special Branch.

His eyes were closed but he looked up when she approached.

"*Spacaba*," he said.

Rachel approached carefully. She stepped on his wrist, leaned down and took the gun out of his hand. She threw it into the forest.

"*Spacaba*," the man repeated.

She stepped on his other wrist and picked up the mobile.

"Cigarette," he said.

She scanned the recent calls. Four of them to London.

"Cigarette."

"When are the others coming?" she asked.

"Cigarette, please."

"Are they coming from London?"

"I don't know."

She pointed the P30 at his face. "London or Dublin or Belfast? Tell me!"

"London," he said.

Keeping the gun on him she searched him and found car keys and a wallet. She took a step back.

"You tell your boss…You tell your boss…" she began. She didn't want him to tell Richard anything. She threw away the keys and kept the wallet. She ran back to the caravan park and banged on Big Dave's door until he appeared bleary eyed, confused.

"Rachel, what…what time is it? Jesus, what time is it? Thresher gets me at six, it must be nearly—"

"Dave, I need the Subaru, Richard's found me. His goons are flying in from over the water."

Dave was pushing sixty five and first thing in the morning he looked a lot older than that. His face was greyer than his hair and his eyes seemed far away.

"Dave," she said, looking at him, squeezing his shoulder through his denim shirt.

"What? Oh. The Subaru?"

"Yeah."

He nodded, went inside the caravan, brought the car keys and a roll of money.

"I don't need it," she said.

"Take it."

"No."

"For god's sake, take it, get the girls something."

She put the roll in her pocket. She kissed him on the cheek. "It wasn't peelers, Dave, he sent muscle, bloody Russians or something, they killed Thresher," she said.

Dave staggered a little, recovered, shook his head.

"Guy's a nutcase."

"I know. I better go. I'm sorry about Thresh. He was a good dog."

She kissed him again and ran back to her caravan.

"Girls, are you ready?" Rachel called as she vaulted the cinder block steps.

"Sue won't get dressed," Claire said.

Rachel looked in.

Claire was ready. Standing there with a stuffed suitcase, wearing three shirts and two jackets. Sue was naked.

"Jesus Christ, Sue, you're not even dressed!" Rachel said.

The goon's mobile rang in her hand. She pressed the green button.

"Misha, we're here, where are you?" a voice said in a cockney accent.

She put her finger to her lips so the girls wouldn't speak.

"Misha, where are you? We made it, we're here."

She hung up and looked outside. At the bottom of the dirt road behind the Toyota there was now a black Range Rover. Two men inside, maybe more in the rear.

"Claire, go to Dave's car, get in the back, put your seatbelt on," Rachel said, fighting the panic.

"What's wrong with our car?"

"They might know our car. We're just going to try and drive past them."

"Mum they'll see us."

"Do as I say, Claire, get in Dave's car and put your seatbelt on," Rachel said calmly. It wasn't hard for Claire to see the fear in her mother's eyes. There was only one way in and out of the caravan park and unless they made a desperate run through the woods they were going to have to risk it. Rachel gave her the emergency bag which was always packed with underwear, money, Snickers bars and the laptop, Richard's laptop – the only insurance they had.

"Go!" Rachel said.

Claire ran out and Rachel wiped the tears so Sue wouldn't freak out.

Sue wasn't paying attention anyway, standing there sucking her thumb looking at *Dora the Explorer* on the TV set.

Rachel knew there was no time to do the usual minefield walk with her. She went to the bathroom, grabbed a beach towel and wrapped Sue in it. "Come on, honey," she said. "You can get changed into some of your sister's clothes."

"Wait a minute, where are we going?" Sue asked.

"Don't worry about it."

"I don't want to go!" Sue insisted.

"Honey, it'll be fun, now come on," Rachel said.

"I've got no clothes on!"

"You can wear your sister's."

"I don't want to wear *her* clothes, they won't fit me!" Sue said, wriggling from her mother's grip and falling to the floor.

Rachel could feel a scream welling up inside her. She ran to the door jam. The men had parked and were coming up the dirt path on foot. Two of them, both in T-shirts and aviator sunglasses which definitely meant private muscle not coppers.

Sue had picked up the TV flipper and put on *SpongeBob*.

Rachel grabbed the beach towel from the floor and wrapped it tight around her.

"No!" Sue yelled.

Rachel picked her up and ran outside.

"Mum! Stop it! This is a good one!"

Sue didn't weigh much but she fought all the way, wriggling, scratching, biting.

Rachel opened the rear door of Dave's Subaru Outback and threw her inside.

"Get Sue's seat belt on," she ordered Claire.

Sue was screaming "Noooo!" at the top of her voice.

"Would you just shut up!" Rachel said.

"You better get moving," Dave said. He had pulled on a dressing gown and he was carrying a long-barrelled shotgun.

She nodded, got in the car, put the key in the ignition.

Stick shift, Jesus, Richard had always bought automatics, how did these things work again? Clutch and brake. She turned the key, stalled the car.

Ahead the men coming up the path identified her.

They pulled something out of their pockets and began running.

"I see them," Dave said.

She turned the key, let the clutch out *easy*. Sue leaned over, grabbed a chunk of her hair and tugged hard. Rachel screamed and the car stalled again.

"Stop it!" Rachel shouted. "Claire, hold her down!"

The two men were close, twenty yards, less. They were wearing medallions round their necks and the black T-shirts said "Licenced Bounty Hunter" in yellow letters across their chests – which of course counted for absolutely nothing in Northern Ireland.

"I don't want to go!" Sue yelled.

"Mum, I'm scared," Claire said.

"Come on girl," Rachel told herself. She turned the key. "Clutch out slow, petrol in slow," she muttered. The engine caught. She drove forward. The men were here. Big white guys, moustaches, salt and pepper hair on the first, the second younger, meaner.

The younger one jumped on the bonnet, smashed the driver's side window, leaned in through the broken glass and sprayed her with Mace.

Her retinas burned.

"Aaaahhh!" she yelled.

She slammed down hard on the accelerator. The Subaru leapt forward.

She heard the shotgun tear the air.

She couldn't see.

Thumping on the windscreen.

The kids yelling.

She tried to open her eyes but they were flooded with tears.

She heard Dave shouting.

She grabbed the steering wheel.

It was a straight drive, except, she remembered, for the big Toyota.

"Claire, tell me when to turn so I don't hit the truck!" Rachel yelled.

"Mum there's a man on the windscreen!"

"Tell me when to turn!"

"Now! Now!"

The car went into a pothole, shuddered. She felt Claire's hand on her neck.

"I think he's got a gun!" Claire cried.

Pain from her burnt pupils. She blinked open her eyes, swerved to avoid a caravan, closed her eyes again, grabbed the bottle of water in the cup holder, opened the bottle with one hand and threw it in her face.

Rachel let go of the wheel for a second and rubbed the Mace out of her eyes as best she could. If she squinted she could see a little but what she saw wasn't good. The bounty hunter/private detective was desperately holding onto the windscreen wiper with his right hand and trying to point a Taser at her with his left.

They were at the entrance to the caravan park now near Stu's cabin.

"Give it up bitch!" the man yelled, finally getting a good grip on his Tazer and pointing it through the broken window.

The shotgun blast had brought Stu and Stacey out. Stu was standing there naked, covered in tattoos, holding a hurley stick. She'd never been fond of Stu but when he took a side he took a side and he went all in – especially for his customers.

"Pull over!" the bounty hunter yelled again.

She shook her head.

"I'm authorised to use—" he began before Stu clubbed him in the back.

He bumped off the car and Stu kept hitting him in the rearview.

"Thank you, Stuart," she said and headed east for the crossroads.

They drove to Coleraine, stopped at a petrol station and filled the tank.

A little further along they found a McDonald's.

She wondered how long Big Dave would hold the men before having to let them go. How many hours did she have? It couldn't be too long or he'd be looking at a kidnapping charge.

The girls ate their food. She couldn't touch hers.

It grew cold in the booth by the window. Heavy rain clouds had rolled in from Donegal and lightning was stabbing at ships lost in the immensity of the Atlantic.

The rain turned to hail.

Sue played with the Powerpuff toy from her Happy Meal while Claire, concealing her worry, affected sang-froid and asked: "Mummy, where exactly are we going?"

Not too far with a broken driver's side window.

Rachel stared at the grey water and black clouds and shook her head.

"I really don't know," she said.

chapter 2
back in the life

SOMEONE MUST HAVE BEEN TELLING LIES ABOUT THE SPECIAL K. He wasn't an expert on breakfast cereals, but this stuff, advertised as Kellogg's, was an ersatz concoction of toasted corn shavings injected with flavourings and high fructose corn syrup, and moulded into quarter-sized wedges. He poured half and half into the plastic room-service bowl and ate. A chemical buzz on the roof of his mouth. Shooting pains near his heart.

It actually tasted rather good. He sipped the thin coffee. That didn't.

Killian picked up his luggage, had a final look in the mirror and left a twenty-dollar bill on the dresser. He'd wanted to leave a five but after shepherding it all day he'd foolishly put it into the vending machine last night to get a Kit Kat; now it was either twenty or change.

He walked across the quad of the Union Theological Seminary and skidded to a halt in front of the chapel. A friendly sign said "All Faiths Welcome". The wooden door was locked. The keyhole was iron. He had it open in forty seconds. He took a pew at the back and sat and tried to feel something. This went on for a dispiriting couple of minutes before he finally slipped away.

He left his guest room key with a dozing security guard and stepped out onto Broadway. A shiv attack wind from the Hudson. An empty drinks can blowing along the pavement like a demented xylophone. The sky had a jet-lagged, early-morning-ferry-terminal aspect to it that he didn't like at all. He saw a taxi and hailed it with a fading "Taaaa…" but it cruised on by. Two more did the same and finally a gypsy cab stopped. He got in, heaving his bag into the back seat next to him.

"Which airport?" the driver asked.

"The Logan shuttle."

125 blurred. He name-checked memories from his twenties. M&G, the Manhattanville post office, the A train stop, the boys of Engine Company 37/Ladder 40.

A line of people in business suits was weaving out of La Guardia into the parking lot. From long experience of the misery of human existence the taxi driver said: "I bet this is the Logan shuttle right here."

Killian nodded and rounded the fare up from thirty-six to an even forty dollars. The driver, some kind of Russian or East European, thanked him without sarcasm. He took his place at the rear of the line.

"Excuse me, is this Boston?" he asked the guy in front – a large man in a blue overcoat.

Getting no response, he tried again. "Is this the line for Boston?"

The guy in front twitched but nada surfed. Killian looked beyond him to the airport where planes on their skittery approach down the East River consistently seemed to miss disaster by only a few seconds. A wave of depression hit him. He was tired, off kilter, punchy. The Special K crash was coming and it wasn't just that. It had been a hard week, hard month, hard year. He had three hundred thousand quid negative equity on those Laganside apartments, the Northern Irish property crash typically coming after twelve years of solid growth and just when he had quit The Life and turned the trajectory of his existence in a new direction at the University of Ulster.

To mention that it was raining and he had no coat would have been redundant. Course it was. Drizzly greasy stuff that got you so much wetter than a hard rain because people felt it was okay to stand out in it.

He tilted his head back, let the drops spatter on his cheeks, closed his eyes, listened: trucks on the Cross Bronx, planes at the Marine Terminal and a banshee wind blowing through the car park as if across the mouth of an Absolut bottle.

A raindrop caught him in the left eyelid. He opened his eyes. That sky again. Malevolent, not exactly evil, but certainly not good – the sky of a petty thief, or a drunken, sentimental spousal abuser. He considered poking the man in front between his broad shoulders. What was his problem? He checked for a hearing aid and, seeing none, Killian's fight-or-flight response began to kick in. Adrenalin flooded his endocrine system. His pulmonary artery expanded and his funereal white cheeks became red. He clenched and unclenched his fists, his hands remembering a hundred ways of disabling a man even though that wasn't exactly his métier.

"Hey mate, is this the line for the Boston shuttle or what?" he asked in bass-profundo, old timey West Belfast.

On this iteration the man turned. He was reading the *New Yorker* and without looking up and after a pause which seemed to communicate some deep but inexplicable contempt, he said: "What do you want?"

Killian felt pleased and then irritated by this reaction – really what was so terrific about getting into a fight with a stranger in a damp airport car park? These days they processed you for a thing like that. Central booking, the Island, many hassles. The guy was big and broad, but Killian was bigger if considerably less broad.

"What do you want, asshole?" the man barked.

A 1990 freshly minted Killian, trying to impress Darkey White, might have kicked him in the left kneecap, pulled him down by the hair, taken the man's briefcase and smashed it on his head. But this was not 1990.

"Look at me," Killian said in a voice like the rasp of steel on flint.

The man looked. "Yeah?"

In forty years on planet Earth – twenty-three of them in The Life – Killian's eyes had seen a lot of unpleasantness and he knew that they could convey a frighteningly deep well of seriousness. A person with any expertise in human relations could read them immediately: *This is not a man to be fucked with.*

As it was, Killian's interlocutor took a second or two before he got it.

"Is the queue for Logan?" Killian asked.

Belated recognition, fear, panic.

"Oh…yeah, I'm sorry, yes, this is the shuttle," the man muttered, lips trembling, eyes downcast – a posture Killian had seen a tedious number of times before. It failed to gratify him. It bored him. This whole world bored him which was part of the reason he was at the University of Ulster.

"Thank you," Killian said and released him from the look.

"You're welcome," the man replied and brought the *New Yorker* up to his face like a shield. Killian looked behind him where a dozen more people had joined the line, which hadn't moved an inch.

"How long is this going to be?" he wondered aloud.

The guy in front flinched but sensed Killian was being rhetorical.

How long?

Fifty minutes in the queue.

Forty in the plane.

A grim forty. Middle seat/wedged/talkers/baby/five fucking dollars for a Coke.

Logan looked like an airport failing an audition for the part of Airport. The jetway was on the fritz. The replacement bus took forever. Inside nothing worked. The ceilings were low, flickered, leaked. Cops, state troopers and National Guard milled. Frozen lines snaked across and into one another. Baggage came to the wrong carousel.

Of course because it was St Patrick's Day there was a festive air: bunting, green cardboard things on string, inappropriate drunkenness.

He called Sean. Sean wasn't available so he asked Mary to connect him directly to Michael Forsythe in Park Slope. He worked his way through a couple of flunkies before Michael came on.

"Yes?" Forsythe said.

"It's your mate from Belfast."

"They told me. We were all looking for you last night."

"I didn't want to be found."

"When you're working for us you make yourself available," Michael said coolly.

"With respect, if you'll allow me to correct you, from this morning, I'm working for you. Last night I was on my own clock," Killian said.

Killian and Michael came from the same world: self-improving north Belfast petty criminality. Michael knew the type and the angles. But more than that he knew Killian of old. He wasn't going to out-argue him. Michael decided to let it go. "I just wanted to catch up, not a big deal. Where are you now?" he asked.

"Logan."

"Good. Do you know the Fairmont Hotel?" he asked.

"Yes."

"Go to the concierge, I'll fax you the address."

"Okay."

"You'll need a car."

"It's not in the city?"

"No. The North Shore. You can drive, right?"

"Yes."

"Maybe I can get you someone, we'll see."

"It's not necessary."

"Call me if you have any problems, I'm anxious to get this resolved today."

"I can assure that one way or another this will be resolved in the next few hours."

"Good. The old lady's coming back from Chicago this afternoon for our big Saint Paddy's Day do and I'd hate to have to tell her that this eejit is still giving us shite."

"You won't need to," Killian said.

"My people booked you a room if you want it, unless you're taking the red-eye."

"I'll see."

"Do your lot celebrate Saint Patrick's Day, Killian?" Michael asked in a friendly but borderline racist kind of way.

People had a lot of crazy ideas about tinkers.

"Of course we do," Killian said. "In fact last night I was giving a wee lad in the Bronx your trademark spiel about the Trinity and shamrocks."

"How did that go down?"

"Like talking to a wall."

"Aye. All right. Happy Saint Pat's. Good luck, mate."

Killian hung up, grew thoughtful. He and Mike had met several times. The most memorable, of course, Christmas Eve 1992 when Michael had murdered his employer Darkey White while he and another couple of guards were humiliatingly out of commission.

Killian had been outmatched then by Forsythe, who was his own age and in his own profession, but just so much better at it than he.

Killian had quit New York after that and gone back to Belfast which had turned out to be good timing as the ceasefires had begun by then and the paramilitaries were moving into regular criminality. Everybody needed help for the brand new narco trade and Killian with his "New York experience" was a man in demand. Previously the IRA and UDA had killed drug dealers to prove that they were the legitimate defenders of the community, but after the ceasefires and the end of the Troubles, drugs became the vector for their boredom and ambition and by the mid-2000s narco trafficking and manufacture had become the paramilitaries' primary *raison d'etre*.

Killian had risen and got a reputation, initially as a heavy and then as a persuader, so that even a year after his retirement an "old pal" like Michael Forsythe could put in a call and get him to cross the Atlantic.

Still he wouldn't have come – Mike Forsythe or no Mike Forsythe – but for those bloody apartments. Killian tried Sean again. This time Mary put him through.

"Where were you a minute ago?" he asked.

"Where were you last night?" Sean asked.

"I asked you first," Killian said.

"Crapper, and you?"

"A place I know," Killian said.

"Like that is it?"

"Aye."

"I rang a few of the hotels."

"I knew you would."

"Don't be smart. You bollicksed it ya big eejit. There were a couple of extra clients we could have squeezed in."

"No way. Not my scene. This is a one-off for you know who."

"You weren't staying in Jersey were you?"

"You're not going to get it out of me, Sean. Quiet little spot right in Manhattan. Nobody knows about it but me."

Sean considered pursuing this further, but time was money. "Okay, you're in Boston right now?"

"Aye."

"You know the Fairmont?"

"He already told me. Said I got to rent a car."

"Get a receipt."

"You are such a fucking miser."

"A four-wheel drive but nothing fancy."

"Jesus, it's not Maine is it?"

"No."

"Good."

"Sure you don't want a piece? I can give you a few addresses."

"Nah, you know me. And those people put you off your breakfast."

"What people?"

"Gun sharks."

"Killian, this is a pretty big score, you might have to get epic," Sean said ominously.

"How big a score?"

"Five large."

"Jesus. And he wants it all today?"

"Uh huh, so watch it, when people get backed into a corner like this sometimes it's not pretty."

"I'll be on my toes."

"You watch yourself, okay?"

"Who do you think you're talking to, mate?"

"A burned out, semi-retired, jetlagged old geezer on his first job in over a year."

"Forty's not old," Killian muttered, hung up, turned off the phone, grabbed his bicycle messenger bag, dodged a W. C. Fields lookalike handing out green balloons and walked into the world.

A cab came. The Afghan driver was wearing a paper "Kiss Me I'm Irish" adjustable hat.

Killian thought about the five large. How could anyone come up with a sum like that on short notice?

They rode the Ted Williams. The tunnel led him nicely into existential crisis mode.

What the hell was he doing here?

He'd seen Tony Robbins once at a convention centre in Birmingham. Robbins said you either lived in the past or the future. Course it took him fifty-seven hours to say that.

The future had classrooms and exams and major life changes. It did not have guns or desperate men.

If it wasn't for the bloody apartments…

Out into daylight.

Rain.

A touch of sleet.

Downtown Boston and the beginnings of the Parade: peelers on horses, spectators in leprechaun get-up, dress-uniformed firefighters, shivering, red-cheeked girls in Irish dancing kit.

The Fairmont.

No respite from the Oirishness. The staff were wearing plastic bowler hats and from concealed speakers Celine Dion was singing Mick standards in her dramatic coloratura soprano.

He found the concierge, who was hatless but apparently channelling Vincent Price: "Ye-es? Can I help you?"

"Fax for me. The name's Killian."

"Are you staying at the hotel, Mr Killian?"

"No. The fax is from Erin Realty Investments," he said to short-circuit the chit-chat. Everybody in the Boston–New York corridor knew what that meant.

"Of course, sir," the concierge said.

Killian retired to a comfy chair and read the fax.

It was blank but for one line that said: "Andrew Marcetti, 21 Carpenter Street, Hampton Beach, NH – 500K."

He memorized the name and address and scrunched the sheet. Some lack of confidence made him call Sean. "I'm all set," Killian said.

"What's that awful racket? Are you torturing someone?"

"It's Celine Dion. Listen, I just wanted to, uh…"

"What?"

"Nothing. Call you when it's done." Killian said goodbye and hung up the phone. He was wondering if the hotel could somehow get him a rental car when a shadow appeared in front of him.

He looked up. A big fella standing there looking awkward. A pinched, lanky character, twenty-two or twenty-three, blond, dressed in a hasty shirt and tie.

"Aye?" Killian asked.

"Are you Mr Killian?" the kid asked in a flat, monotonal Southie.

"Who wants to know?"

"Mr Forsythe thought you might need a driver."

Decent of him. Killian liked to work alone, but it was better than the bus or trying to negotiate holiday traffic.

"What's your name?" Killian asked.

"Luke."

"You know mine, where the car?"

"Outside in the—"

"Let's go."

A black Chrysler 3000 up Route 1.

Killian didn't know this part of America so he looked out the window. Clam shacks, cranberry bogs, ice-cream stands, forests, old wooden houses.

The rain stayed off and the sun came out as they caught the bridge over the Merrimac River.

It looked cute.

The kid wasn't a yapper which was something. They crossed the border into New Hampshire and within a few clicks they were at Hampton Beach. It was a typical New England resort town: a big strand, amusement arcades, junk-food stalls, sporting goods shops, and, significantly for Killian, a medium-sized casino.

"Pull in," he said.

The kid parked. Killian got out.

"Wait here," he said. He ducked into a Dunkin Donuts, ordered a coffee and called Sean again.

"What's he do for a living, this client of ours?" Killian asked.

"You know what time it is here?" Sean asked. "I was sitting down to me tea."

"This boy that they've flown me three thousand miles to see, what does he do for a living?"

"I don't know, why?"

"I don't want to get involved in a war. This is strictly per diem for me. I don't need any markers, bad blood."

"What are you talking about?" Sean asked.

"This is a company town."

"Rackets?"

"Legit. A casino. Could be a power play. Wouldn't be the first time my best mate M.F. fucked me up would it? Check it, will you?"

He drank the coffee, watched kids in wetsuits walk across the two-lane with their long boards. Killian was wearing a sports coat jacket, white shirt, dockers, plain blue tie – not exactly dinner with the in-laws but he still felt overdressed for Hampton Beach on an early spring day.

Sean called back. "M.F. says that he doesn't work in the casino business. He's a banker. Married old money. This is his third marker. Hometown, Atlantic City and Foxwoods. Everyone has been very patient. There are no cross tabs, he is not connected in any way."

"Law enforcement?"

"No family links."

"You buy that?"

"Why not?"

"I don't know, if I had a gambling problem, I don't think I'd live in a town with a fucking casino on the boardwalk."

Sean sighed. "Should I call it off?"

Killian rubbed his chin. "Nah. I'll check it and I'll call you when it's done. You should also know this…he sent someone."

"Babysitter?"

"I don't know."

"You just be careful, big man," Sean said in the camp West Belfast tones of BBC TV announcer Julian Simmons.

"You know it," Killian said.

He tossed the coffee, went back to Luke.

They found Carpenter Street four blocks back from the beach.

American dream. Picket fences, sprinklers, kids, cul de sac.

Number 21: big New England Tidewater style, made to look two centuries old but in fact vintage 2002. The irony hit: guy with a gambling problem lives in number 21.

Five- or six-bedroom house with a triple garage. A boy with a wiffle bat trying to play baseball with himself. About thirteen, brown hair, green eyes, *Watchmen* T-shirt. The 3000 wouldn't attract attention in this neighborhood but someone waiting inside would.

"You come with me," Killian said.

"What are you going to do in there?" Luke asked warily.

"What do you do for Mr Forsythe exactly?" Killian wondered.

"I work for Express Cars, I'm a driver."

"What do you think I do, Luke?"

"I really don't know," Luke said but his eyes were telling a different story. He knew, or suspected...

"If you come it'll be worth a couple of thousand experience points," Killian prophesied.

Luke didn't look convinced so Killian changed from the subjunctive to the imperative mood: "Follow me, keep your mouth shut."

Killian got out, straightened his jacket, walked to the front gate. The boy's Red Sox hat was slightly askew and he was doing a baseball commentary to himself just the way he would if this were an early Spielberg movie. Killian looked for a golden retriever to complete the set up but there was no dog.

He swung open the gate.

"Who are you?" the kid asked in a lazy Mainer drawl.

"I'm a friend of your father's. Is he home?"

"He went to Shaw's."

"Is your mother home?"

"She went to Kittery."

"Who's watching you?"

"Nobody. I'm watching me," the kid said.

"Brothers or sisters?"

"Mum took Flannery to Kittery."

"I'm glad she didn't take Kittery to Flannery."

The kid laughed.

"What's your name, son?" Killian asked.

"Toby."

"Toby, I like that, when are you expecting your dad to get back?" he asked.

"I don't know, half an hour?"

Killian reached into his pocket and took out two fifty-dollar bills. "I'm an old friend of your father's. I suppose I owe you a couple of birthday presents."

He gave Toby the money. "Why don't you get yourself a real baseball bat at one of those sporting goods stores on the seafront. A good one," Killian said.

Toby's eyes were wide. "I could get a David Ortiz."

"Yeah. Good idea. Run along now. Surprise your dad."

"Can I take my bike?"

"Sure, you got a helmet?"

"Yeess," the kid groaned.

"Put it on and scat."

Toby got his bike and helmet and pedalled off. Killian walked to the front door, turned the handle, went inside. "Come on," he said to Luke.

A pristine, upscale, well laid out, utterly soulless residence.

Killian did a brace of the bedrooms looking for a safe. He found a loaded .38 in a locked gun case and he took the ammo and left the gun. Under a floorboard in an upstairs spare room he discovered a collection of soft-core pornography and two grand in Canadian dollars. Killian left the mags and the cash. He found nothing else, nothing major. The most interesting room was a ground floor study/library which had about a thousand volumes. Old ones. Some valuable. To his amazement he found a book on Le Corbusier.

He started flipping through it.

He sat down.

"What do we do now?" Luke asked.

"We wait."

Luke pulled out his iPod, plugged in the earphones and lay on an ottoman.

"What are you listening to?" Killian asked, always slightly curious as to what the weans were into.

"What?"

"What are you listening to?"

"Ocean sounds."

Killian nodded casually but his ears were up. He'd seen a snub-nosed Saturday Night Special shoved in the back of Luke's pants. He thought cross and double cross. Insurance. Luke, really an iceman, kills the mark, pins the murder on the shnook from outta town.

Plausible but perhaps not likely. Michael had a rep for straightness and for a complicated play like that you'd need someone with ten years under their belt and this kid was a punk. Furthermore that gun wasn't the weapon of a professional.

"It's nothing," he told himself and went back to his book.

He didn't like Le Corbusier. Le Corbusier didn't understand human nature. Humans were biophilic. Half a million years of living on the Savannah was bound to select for adaptations linked to open plains, grasslands. In his concrete dreamscapes Le Corbusier didn't allow for any kind of spiritual longing for vistas, for greenery, for other mammal species, for space. Like other twentieth-century social engineers Corbusier wanted to remake man in his own image. Hmm, he thought, that was pretty good. He took out a pencil and began to make notes for his term paper and was so engrossed that he didn't hear Marcetti come in. He should have put Luke on point. A mistake. Hopefully not a fatal mistake.

"What the fuck are you doing here?" Marcetti said.

Killian looked up. Marcetti wasn't Italian. At least not New York Italian. White, pale, about thirty-eight, thin, crumpled, with that vacant expression Killian knew all too well from the midnight shift in Atlantic City. He was wearing a Hawaiian shirt, blue jeans, slip-on shoes; his eyes were watery, weak, had a wildness to them. He was balanced on one foot, something Killian didn't like because Marcetti was pointing a sawn-off shotgun at him.

Worse than that, pointing it at him and then at Luke, spinning it to the left and right, all on that one unbalanced leg.

"Well, motherfuckers, what do you want?" Marcetti repeated.

"Hey man, I'm just here to—" Luke began, but Killian put a hand up to stop him.

Killian looked at Marcetti. "You know why we're here," he said dispassionately.

Marcetti nodded. "I don't fucking have it."

Killian set the Le Corbusier and his notebook on the bookcase, smiled. "That's too bad. I had a phone conversation with Mr Forsythe earlier in the day and he made it clear that either I get the money or I send you expeditiously into your next incarnation – if you believe in that kind of thing."

Marcetti was shaking. "What?"

Killian pointed at the chair opposite. "You should probably sit. The gun'll work just as well from a sitting position."

Marcetti blinked.

Those eyes again. Old man eyes. Beaten. Killian didn't like them, Marcetti probably didn't feel that he had a whole lot to lose.

Luke was on the fidgets. Killian gave him the *Do Not Pass Go* he'd perfected over the years. Do not even attempt a play for that gun of yours.

Luke nodded slightly.

"Sit down," Killian insisted.

Marcetti sat.

"How did you know we were here?" Killian wondered.

"I saw Toby on the boardwalk, he told me everything."

Killian nodded. Just a bit of bad luck. Couldn't be helped. He admired Marcetti's cojones, coming here to confront a shark's enforcer instead of run, run, running. Didn't seem a New England move. "Where are you from, originally?" Killian asked.

"You're not playing that game with me. We're not going to fucking jaw like we're old friends. You're fucked, pal, I'm the one with the gun."

Killian nodded. He had enough anyway, the accent was South Jersey. He could imagine the traj: street, or half-street kid, pretty smart, scholarships, college, banking, marries into money, moves to the Boston burbs and gradually migrates north. Perfect until, like some atavistic demon, the grifter comes out: a visit to the local casino, maybe he wins, in any case the hooks are in, he starts playing, starts losing, starts borrowing. In a year, he's under the ocean, deep down, Robert fucking Ballard territory, the Mariana fucking trench.

Marcetti was trembling, sweating, the gun was shaking. Killian knew that unless it was loaded with talcum powder, at this range and at this angle it would decapitate him. Even birdshot could kill him. Wouldn't have to be on purpose, a screen door slamming, a car backfiring, Marcetti reacts. Both triggers. Never get the stain out of the dry wall.

"You carry a sawed-off shotgun in your car. You were expecting me. Someone like me." Killian said.

"Yeah, I was."

"You know why they asked me to come in?" Killian asked.

"No."

"Because I'm from out of town."

Marcetti shook his head. "What does that mean?"

"I'm from out of town. If you're going to kill someone you don't go local. See, if I was just coming to get money out of you, they would have sent up guys from Boston. I've come all the way from Belfast, Northern Ireland. Across the Atlantic."

"Like Forsythe," Marcetti said.

"We're old pals."

Marcetti blinked fast. Sweat beading on his upper lip. He stood up again and pointed the gun "What if I just fucking kill you right now," he said. "Both of you."

"Take a seat, Andrew, you'll be more comfortable and you can still kill us any time you want," Killian insisted.

Convinced by this information Marcetti slumped back into the leather chair.

Killian gave him a reassuring smile. Salesman smile.

"Mind if I smoke?" Killian asked.

"No, Susannah doesn't allow…Sure, go ahead and…no, wait a minute, don't try anything," Marcetti said. "One false move and I'll—"

Killian nodded. He reached into his jacket pocket, took out a pack of cigarettes. Lit one. He offered the pack around, the kid and Marcetti shook their heads.

"Bad habit," Killian agreed. He let the nicotine coat his lungs and drifted for a quarter minute. The world played behind Marcetti's head. Aquamarine sky. A heat transparency to the elms and chestnut trees. Kids on bicycles sailing past the window like extras in a movie.

"How do you think this is going to end, Andrew?" Killian asked.

Marcetti shook his head. "I don't know," he admitted.

"Can I tell you a story?"

"What kind of a story?"

"About the last man I killed."

"I don't want to hear it."

"No, you should hear it, it's interesting. How someone dies is pedagogical."

Marcetti said nothing so Killian cleared his throat.

"I was in Uruguay. Two years ago. I'll give you the coda first. The thing was so bad that when I got back to Ireland I decided that I was going to change everything. I was going to quit The Life, go to college, get married, get some exercise, eat spinach, I had a whole notebook filled with stuff like that. And the funny thing is I more or less did it. I bought a small block of apartments, I gave my gun away, I enrolled at the University of Ulster just outside of Belfast."

"Did you get married?" Luke asked.

"Didn't get hitched but I have incorporated spinach into my diet. Okay, back to my story," Killian said. He took a draw on his cigarette, wondered if the shotgun really was loaded. "Okay, so, there's this guy and he thinks he's pretty smart and he owes. He owes because he steals. Stole. Five of the big M. From friends of friends in London. Escape plan worked in advance, new identity, new face, new everything. But it doesn't work. Someone tracks him down to an obscure little town in Uruguay. Next thing you know there's me sitting on this guy's patio deck on a Sunday morning. I'm watching this line of yachts coming across the Rio de la Plata, the River Plate, coming across in this almost straight line that stretches all the way to the horizon, each boat about fifteen minutes behind the next. The final boats are under the horizon, under the Earth's curve. You get me?"

Marcetti nodded.

"They're coming from Buenos Aires in Argentina. I guess it's a popular Sunday sailing destination for the rich. Up early, pack some booze and sail to little Colonia in Uruguay. Have lunch, have a stroll, back before it gets dark. It's a nice place: beautiful old colonial buildings, shady plazas, cobble stones, lots of cafés. I walked around for a bit, started to get noticed, so I found the house I was looking for, broke in. Of course, he's gone. Bed unmade, coffee still warm. He's just popped out to get a newspaper or croissants or something. While I'm waiting I go out onto his deck and watch the boats. As they get closer you can see the people on board; some of them wave at me as they steer into Colonia's marina but I don't wave back, you know, cos I'm a professional. Twenty little boats come over from Buenos Aires and it's getting warm and even more beautiful and I'm so caught up in this lovely wee moment I almost don't hear our boy come back. He's driven all the way to Montevideo to get his girlfriend. Nothing in the notes about a girlfriend. You can imagine the scene..."

Killian sighed and scratched his neck.

Marcetti was on board. "What happened?"

"They're in kitchen and I go back in through the French windows and get the jump on them. They'd given me a silenced Smith and Wesson .38, but what good is that if she's screaming her head off, you know? I tell him to shut her up. He's crying, begging, flipped. She's hysterical. Gorgeous too and only about nineteen. I can't kill her. Just can't. Wouldn't be right. Now, I know a bit of Spanish from jobs in the Costa del Sol so I tell her straight: she can stay here and die or leave and forget about this. She's a good girl, she wipes her face and walks out. He's begging her not to go. She doesn't look back. He's really bawling now, but it doesn't matter – our boy's wearing his funeral suit – nothing he can say can change the judgement. But you never know though, do you? So I let him talk a little. He tells me he's got money. Millions, he says. We open his safe. It's not millions. It's about twenty grand in euros."

Killian paused, finished his cigarette and stubbed it out on the wooden window sill.

Marcetti was pointing the shotgun at the floor now. Killian let the seconds crawl.

"What happened next?" Marcetti asked.

"While he's spinning some scheme about gold bullion I sidle next to him and shoot him in the head behind the ear, easy, bullet expands in his brain case, exits through his face, kills him instantly. But I have to work fast now. The client demanded torture, a lesson, you know, all that East End cockney geezer bullshit."

"You killed him?"

"Yeah, but listen, that's not the story. The story's coming up. So I'm cutting off his penis—"

"You were what?"

"They wanted me to cut off his penis and make him eat it before I killed him. Not my scene but easy to replicate. Anyway I'm doing that and not really paying attention and guess what happens?"

"He wakes up," Luke said, horrified.

Killian laughed. "Man you've some imagination. No, the girlfriend comes back. And she's got a pair of heavies with her. One of them has a fucking AK-47, another has an Uzi. I'm minding my own business, sawing at this guy's dick with my Swiss Army knife and before I know what's happening – World War Three."

Killian chuckled, shook his head and looked down. He was talking conversationally but he knew he had them now. He was good at this. He was a minstrel. A salesman. A preacher.

"That was a scene, but lucky for me they didn't know what they were doing – jazzing each other, shooting for the rafters. I dive for the sofa, roll behind a wall where they can't see me and then it's tea and crumpets at the Palace. I run to the bathroom, out through the window, back in through the front door behind them."

"What happened next?" Luke asked.

Killian gave him a *shut the fuck up* look.

"I shot both the hoods in the back and checked them in the skull, neat checks, two rounds a piece and I ran over and smacked the girlfriend hard in the face, broke her nose, knocked her clean out. Ran back over to our boy, cut off his dick, put it in his mouth. Then back to the girlfriend. She's the problem."

Marcetti nodded. His lips were purple from holding his breath. Killian blew smoke at him and Marcetti finally sucked in air through his open mouth. "What did you do?" he asked.

"What would you do?" Killian asked.

"I – I don't know."

"I can't kill her, not in the contract. But you can't let her go, not after all this."

Killian nodded at Luke, *now* was the time for him to speak. Kid caught on quick.

"What *did* you do?" Luke asked.

"I went to the kitchen and found a steak knife and cut her throat," Killian said. "Her blood came out crimson. She was young, her heart was beating fast. Frothed out all over the floor and all the way to that wooden patio deck."

He nodded at Luke and then turned his attention on Marcetti. "You see, Andrew, I'm only the advance guard. If you kill me other men will come, wherever you are. Before your eyes they will castrate your son and rape your wife and hurt them until you are begging for their deaths. You need to be made a lesson of. Your story will be legend. It's worth it to them, losing the half mill for that."

Marcetti started crying.

Killian got up, walked to him, put his hand on the barrel of the shotgun and lifted it gently from him. He broke it open and took out the shells. Luke had whipped out his Saturday Night Special but Killian shook his head and Luke put the gun away.

"I don't have any options, I don't know what I'm going to do. I don't know what I can do," Marcetti sobbed.

Killian let him cry for a bit, went to the window, stared out at the street. He did a standing ten-count and still with his back turned said: "When did you buy your house?"

"What?"

"When did you buy this house?"

"2005."

"What's the equity?"

"I don't know, we haven't—"

"You don't know? Guy with your problems, give me a fucking break, you know every penny you've got or can get."

"Things around here haven't been moving."

"What's the base?"

"One, one point two."

"And you bought for?"

"Six hundred and fifty – one hundred and fifty down from me, another hundred down from my parents and a hundred thousand no-interest loan from my bank."

Killian turned to look at him. "Did you refinance? The truth."

"No. Not yet."

"How much do you owe now?"

"Three."

"Who signed the mortgage?"

"I did."

"Need your wife's signature?"

"Yes."

Killian nodded. "Sell me your house right now and you and your family will live. Otherwise, well, you know…Otherwise you're all dead."

Killian walked to him, stuck out his hand. Marcetti looked at the big meat-axe paw in front him. He wiped the tears from his face and after a moment's hesitation he shook it.

"Good, now go to the kitchen, make us some coffee. Mine's black, no sugar, a wee bit of water in the cup."

Marcetti went to the kitchen, stunned, like a car-crash survivor.

Killian called Sean, got patched through.

"Yeah?"

"Sean, can you get lawyers up from Boston, maybe through Charlie Bingham?"

"Why?"

"We're buying the mark's house."

Sean didn't blanche. "We're transferring the escrow to Bridget?"

"You catch on quick. She and her better half will need it today. Can you do it?"

"It's a holiday, but I'll figure something out. We make anything on the house?"

"Fifty K."

"That plus our commission. Profitable twenty-four hours. Sure you don't want to come back to work for me full-time? A dozen scores like this and you're laughing me bucko."

"I'm hanging up, Sean. We need your boys pronto. M.F. will give you the address."

"You tell me."

"We don't leave that spilled over the airwaves."

"Okay, I'll ask him…So, how was it working in the mines after all this time?"

"Bye, Sean."

Marcetti came into the living room with three cups of coffee. He wasn't crying anymore. He was a gambler, he liked the high stakes aspect of all of this. He was digging on the drama.

Killian took a cup, gave one to Luke.

"I wanted cream," Luke started until he saw Killian's eyes.

"Okay, here's the deal, Andrew. We're going to buy your house from you for nine hundred thousand dollars. That's a price we can sell it at immediately. We'll pay off Michael and give you fifty thousand in cash to tide you over."

Marcetti's face was ashen, distant, but still he nodded.

"What'll I tell my wife? What can I tell her?"

Killian put his hands on Marcetti's shoulders. He placed his own cool forehead on Marcetti's sweating furnace of a forehead.

"I'll speak to her," Killian said.

Marcetti closed his eyes. Tears again. They were close now. Like brothers. Closer.

"You'll talk to her?" Marcetti asked.

"Andrew, *paisano*, I'll take care of everything."

Marcetti nodded gratefully.

The wife came back.

The kid came back.

Killian *explained*.

Long shadow.

Highway lights.

Dusk.

Darkness came down like a shroud across the sun.

There would come a time when he'd be dead, when everything would be dead and all the suns were gone and the universe was black. That time would come, but it was not now.

He was alive. Tired but alive.

He took off his jacket and folded it carefully on top of the bike messenger bag.

They drove over some new bridge he hadn't seen before. A white concrete cable-stayed affair with inverted Y-shaped towers. He didn't like it. It was modern, self-important, showy. He preferred slow, incremental change, but the zeitgeist was for revolution.

Luke dropped him outside the Fairmont.

"Cheers," he said, and getting out passed him ten fifties as a tip.

Luke took the money but didn't thank him. "Can I ask you something?" Luke said.

"Sure."

Luke hesitated and found his voice: "That story…Uruguay…did you really have to cut that poor woman's throat?"

Killian slung his bike messenger bag behind his back, tightened the strap, folded his jacket over his arm.

"Son, when I saw your gun, for a second there I thought you were a player that Michael had sent to keep an eye on me or cross me," Killian said.

"I'm not a player," Luke muttered.

"No you're not. Stick to driving."

Killian walked into the hotel. He checked at reception and sure enough Forsythe's people had booked him a room. Big suite on the upper level. Luke came up behind him at the elevator. He was breathless, there was something in his hand. The five hundred bucks. Killian was impressed by his integrity. So was Luke.

"Take your money, I don't want it," Luke said.

Killian pushed the call button, grabbed the five hundred, took Luke's arm in his powerful grip and shoved the money deep into Luke's trouser pocket.

The elevator dinged. The doors opened. Killian went inside. He pressed 6.

"I don't want it," Luke said. His face was shivery, nervous, very young. He was grubbing in his pocket to get the readies back out.

"Let me tell you something, ya stupid wee shite," Killian said.

"What?"

"I've never been to Uruguay in my life."

chapter 3
richard coulter

A KEY. A ROOM. LIKE ALL THE OTHERS. THOUSANDS OF HOTEL rooms over the years. This one was New Orleans themed. Antebellum paintings in pastel shades, fake Victorian lamps, uncomfortable high-backed chairs, fluted light fixtures, four-poster bed. He sat up and walked to the bathroom. He stared at his own face. His tight, narrow mouth. His slate-grey eyes. His iron-heavy black eyebrows. His slab of black hair.

His body was long.

His face was long

And he looked tired. But despite what Sean said he didn't look old. Not yet. Forty in dog and tinker years *was* old but not out there among the civilians.

And so what if he seemed a bit lived in anyway? He wouldn't have minded looking like a mature student, or better yet, a happy middle-aged married professor. Something normal like that.

He turned on the TV news; it was dominated by diabolical herds of local children disguised as leprechauns saying things like "top of the morning to ya," and "where's me gold?" The weather lady's eyes were wide with merriment. "Those are some great kids!" she said.

The hotel room phone rang. Killian found the merciful release of the mute button.

"Hello?"

"Nice work," Michael said. Live music in the background, laughter.

"Thanks."

"So is this you officially unretired?" Michael asked.

"Why?" Killian asked suspiciously.

"No reason," Michael said. "A potential rival on the block, maybe."

"Ha! Me tangle with you, no thanks mate. I'm on the Continental cheapie back to Belfast tomorrow."

"Well, you're impressive, pal. We're different schools of thought you and me."

"How so?"

"I'm the local badass and you're all *softly softly catchee monkey*."

"If you say so."

"I do say so, pity we couldn't have hooked, I gotta go back to the dinner, enjoy your stay in Boston. And thanks."

The phone went dead and Killian looked at it for a long time before it started making that annoying beeping noise that American phones made.

He hung up and went to the bathroom, which was in a different part of the suite and was all brushed titanium and *Star Trek: The Next Generation* flat cabinets.

He had a piss and out of habit took the Fairmont's toothbrush, sewing kit, moisturizer and a hand towel they wouldn't notice and packed them in his messenger bag. Satisfied with this he sat back down in front of the big TV. Through the window he saw that the New York rain had migrated north.

He turned on the telly. He flipped news and movies. Men with guns.

He thought about the day.

It was good to get something like this under your belt. The legit world had shaken his confidence. All his decisions in the last year had been suspect.

He spaced. It was full night outside now.

Night in America. A night that was the absence of love. A night of malls, car parks, chain restaurants, houses. A clumsy washing-line of things strung between aeons of darkness.

He got room-service pizza.

The tomato sauce had been dyed green.

Sometime after midnight he went to the ground-floor exterior courtyard. The piano bar was finished. The night bar closed. Cardboard debris everywhere reminded him of the date. He took a fold-up chair and sat by a fountain with his smokes. It was cold and everything was pretending to be something else. The stars were camp fires. The clouds a naked girl. He wasn't ready to buy into it. For a city so huge it was remarkably quiet. He closed his eyes. Listened to the nothing. Crickets. A faint trickling of water. He wished it were a stream. To take him away. Away from this place, from these people, away from all of it. It didn't matter where. Anywhere. He wanted to lie back and let the current float him out.

He drifted and woke chilled.

Back in the hotel room the light on the phone was blinking.

It was 4.00 a.m. Nine in Belfast.

He played the message: "Killian, something's come up. Call me."

He called Sean. "Well?"

"Richard Coulter."

"What about him?"

"Not a surrogate. Not Tom. Mr C himself. Asked for you by name, wants you to look for his daughters."

"What's the story?"

"Weans were with his ex-wife. She was keeping her end of the visitation agreements until one day she didn't. His lawyers tried to get in contact with her and lo and behold it turns out she's just fucking vanished."

"UFOs I suppose. It's common enough these days."

"What's the matter with you? Have you been drinking?"

"The bars are closed. On Saint Patrick's Day in Boston."

"Look, mate, this is a thing."

"What kind of a thing?"

"A missing persons case."

"Why are you telling me, Sean? You know I'm semi semi. And Dick Coulter? Fuck him. I've flown Coulter Air, the bastards charged me two quid to use the fucking toilet."

"That's an urban myth."

"Not on my flight it wasn't. They're worse than Ryanair! Charged you for water, the bog, they'll be charging you for bloody oxygen next."

"Nice routine but listen, mate, this is a score."

"Okay. I'll bite."

"Fifty thousand for taking the case and the first month's retainer. Four hundred and fifty thousand more if you find her."

"Half a million quid?"

"Half a million quid."

Killian had to sit down. With a half million quid he could clear the debts, sell the apartments, buy a small three-bedroom in Carrick and do the course at Jordy full time.

"Why me, Sean?"

"He's heard things."

"Come on."

"Okay, okay, so your pal told him about you."

"Michael Forsythe?"

"Who else?"

"When?"

"About four hours ago. Michael was evidently impressed by your work."

"So Michael calls Coulter, Coulter calls Tom, Tom calls you, you call me?"

"No. Mr C called me personally."

"It's basically a wandering-daughter job?"

"Coulter's married again. His wife's pregnant. He wants his kids back before the new one comes along. One big fucking happy family."

"How many kids?"

"Two. Look, we're the good guys. The missus is off the deep end. Fucked up. The kids are in genuine danger. It's all true. She's had drug problems. Didn't you read about her last year in the *Sunday World*?"

"I don't read the *Sunday World*."

"You should keep in touch with current events. You know they have a black President now?"

"Why so much money?"

"He's got money to burn."

"Still."

"Ease up on the paranoia. They still want to do this on the hush hush before they have to bring in the peelers."

"Peelers sounds like a good idea."

"It's complicated. Coulter doesn't want the publicity. Not when he's looking shaky."

"Shaky? I thought he was making money hand over fist. I thought he was going to be the first fucking Irishman in space."

"The airline business is in the bog. Coulter Air lost a hundred and fifty million euros last quarter. And after that Iceland volcano they were already in the shitter. They've cut half their routes out of Luton. That's why he's in Macau. Diversifying."

"Macau?"

"Macau, it's a former Portuguese colony in China, next to Hong—"

"I know where it is, Sean. What's he doing there?'

"Opening a casino."

"Aye, sounds like he's really on the skids. That and the half million for finding his wife."

"That's not his money, incidentally, that's coming from the kidnap insurance."

"Oh right, the kidnap insurance, very small time."

"Look, they want a decision immediately. Will I tell him you'll meet him or not?"

"When did this doll go missing?"

"Five weeks ago."

"This thing reeks, Sean. Five weeks and *now* they wanna start looking? They're *considering* contacting the peelers?"

"Okay, okay, so we weren't the first guys they went to. They tried the rest and now they want the best. Believe me this time we're the good guys. Come on, whaddya think? Does it sound like something?"

"It sounds like something," Killian admitted.

"What will I tell him? He wants to meet you ASAP."

Killian thought for a full half minute and then said: "Aye, why not."

"Good. I booked your flights. Non-refundable."

"You booked my flights?"

"Boston to LA, LA to Hong Kong. Coulter wants to talk to you in person."

Killian stared at the phone for a moment. He knew that he should be angry. Sean had gone ahead and the booked the trip?

Was he really so predictable?

"What time do I have to have to be at Logan?"

"Eleven o'clock. UA 323."

"Eleven o'clock this morning?"

"Yes."

"I suppose I better get some kip then."

"Aye, that might be a good idea."

chapter 4
an oyster in the mirror sea

THE AIRPORT CAME FROM THE BOTTOM OF THE OCEAN, DREDGED up Dutch-style and poured into gigantic rectangles from which the water was pumped. It was the newest and flattest part of the Hong Kong Special Administrative Region.

Fans turning overhead, heavies watching the line from behind a partition. Good heavies, really focusing.

Many of the people getting off the planes had that humorless fixation, that manic whiteness about the eyes of the degenerate gambler.

"Purpose of visit to Hong Kong?"

"Tourism."

"How many days will you be staying here?"

"Two days."

"Thank you, sir."

"Thank you."

He walked through the overlit, white, antiseptic Green Channel and nodded to a short young man who was holding up a sign that said "Killian".

Behind him Killian could see sharp, brown hazy mountains.

"Are you waiting for me?" Killian asked.

"Mr Killian?"

"That's me."

The young man bowed slightly and tried to take Killian's bag from off his shoulder. Killian didn't let him.

"This way please," the man said.

"Okay."

"Do you have any objections to taking a boat?" the man asked.

"No," Killian said nervously.

"Excellent. This way."

The man didn't take him to a car or a boat. Instead they rode a train into the city. Killian honed his pitch and spent the rest of the ride watching very pretty Chinese girls on the flat-screen TV explaining the multifarious delights of Disney World Hong Kong.

They got off at Hong Kong Central and took an escalator to the first floor.

"Merely a short walk," the escort said.

Some people might have thrown a huff now, demanded a car, not this subway/walking/boat operation, but Killian couldn't care less. He'd been in a box for fourteen hours, hoofing it was fine.

They yomped an air-conditioned corridor to the Kowloon Ferry Terminal. He caught glimpses of office buildings and apartment blocks dizzyingly perched on terraces cut into the mountains. The streets were full of small Chinese-built taxis and German luxury cars. Few people outside. Most were inside buildings or air-conned walkways. Close to the ferry terminal exit a crowd of sweating Chinese people poured into the corridor, all of them going in the opposite direction, short bustling elbowy people. Killian was six foot four and here he felt like bloody Gulliver.

Coulter's man led him through a set of sliding doors to the outside.

Heat. Humidity. Spain could do 110 but he'd forgotten what 90 per cent relative humidity felt like. It was late in the day, nearly five o'clock in the afternoon, but it probably wasn't going to cool down any time soon.

"Jesus," he muttered to himself and took off his jacket.

"This way," the nameless young man said and led him towards a pier on the water's edge.

Concrete gave way to a boardwalk, glass walls to food stands, newspaper outlets and a ticket office. A western girl standing behind a row of taps in a large, air-conditioned bar caught his eye. She had blonde hair in a short crop. She was pale, wan. The place was empty. He smiled at her. She smiled back.

"Down here," Coulter's man said.

"Where?"

"Down here," the man said pointing to a wooden staircase that led to a jetty on the water.

He looked back at the girl and she was still smiling at him. He nodded and then negotiated the rickety, heaving staircase.

A long speedboat was tied to the jetty. A driver was waiting for them, ominously dressed in a splashcoat and waterproof leggings.

His guide untied the boat from its moorings.

"Would you care to step in?" he asked.

Killian fought the blind panic and made sure that it didn't show on his face.

He shook his head. "Smoke first, okay?"

"Okay."

He lit himself a small cigar and walked back up the steps. He crossed to the bar, went inside and sat down in front of the girl. His hands were shaking. Sean hadn't said anything about boats.

"What would you like?" the girl asked.

"Your name and a glass of cold beer."

"Peggy and a beer's coming up," she said with a generic American accent. She was about twenty-five. Lithe, slender, with green, sylvan eyes. She was wearing a white polo shirt that said "Pier #11 Pub" on it.

"Peggy, now there's a name you don't hear that much these days, I like it."

"It's short for Margaret."

"Yeah, I think I knew that," he said, wondering what year she was born in. 1985? 1986? By '86 Killian's father had drunk himself to death, his mother had killed her boyfriend in a knife fight, four of his nine siblings were in borstal, his younger sister Keira was pregnant and Killian, sixteen years old, had stolen fifty cars, had been the getaway driver on a post-office robbery, couldn't read or write and was in love with a girl called Katie.

"What do you do?" the girl asked and pushed a cold Carlsberg in front of him.

"I'm in human resources – I find people, manage people, you know the kind of thing," he said.

She nodded. "Headhunter. Isn't that what they call it?"

"Yeah, that's it."

He drank half the Carlsberg and grinned at her, but this time she didn't smile back. She was a million miles away. "You look lonely," he thought and found to his annoyance he had actually said it. Too personal too quick.

She shrugged. "I am a bit, but I'm okay. I'm fine."

He drank the rest of the beer in one gulp. He passed her a twenty-dollar bill.

"You take US?" he asked.

She nodded.

"Listen, I have a boat waiting for me. I've got to go, but, uh, you wouldn't want dinner tonight or something? I know this is—"

"Yes."

"When do you get off?"

"Midnight."

"See you back here around then," he said, picked up the jacket he'd left on a bar stool, and made for the door.

"Wait a minute," she said.

"What?"

"What's your name?"

"Killian."

"See you at midnight, Killian."

"Until then Cinderella."

Back at the boat a trim, tall, balding man, with wisps of grey hair, a perma-tan, sunglasses and a linen suit was talking into a mobile phone.

He had a long Gallic nose and under the sunglasses, Killian remembered, grey eyes. "There you are! I thought I was going to miss you," he said, offering Killian his hand.

"Good to see you again, Mr Eichel," Killian replied.

"Have we met?" Tom Eichel asked.

"Yes, but it's been a while," Killian said.

Eichel frowned. He obviously did not remember the encounter, which had been at a party in the Gresham Hotel in Dublin years ago, before Killian had even gone to New York, must have been 1989 or 1990. Killian was still a kid and had been lifting wallets from the coat check and Eichel had had two of Coulter's bodyguards take him out the back and knock the living shite out of him, while Eichel laughed and called him "a thieving wee tinker bastard".

Eichel had been about thirty-five then and he looked much the same. Good doctors or good genes or both.

"I meet so many people," Eichel said apologetically.

"It's okay," Killian said.

"Of course Sean and I go back," Eichel said.

"Aye, I know."

Eichel looked at his watch. "Listen, I was hoping to catch you, I'm afraid I can't join you tonight, but if Richard likes you, I'll have someone leave off the files later, okay?"

"Okay."

"Great. I'm really sorry but I've got to go. Richard's doing the whole ribbon-cutting thing tomorrow and as you can imagine nothing's ready. It was nice meeting you *again*. I'll talk to you for real in Belfast," Eichel said and turned. He was about to walk back to a white BMW which had been waiting for him but instead he took his sunglasses off, turned and looked Killian in the eye.

"You'll consider it won't you? Sean says you're trying to move out of this line of work."

"I'm looking for a change of direction, yes, but Sean says this time we're on the side of the angels."

"He's right. She is a fucking headcase. A druggie. If you found her you'd be doing the girls and her some good. They need to be out of that environment and she needs to be in a clinic somewhere," Eichel said.

Killian nodded, stepped into the boat and put on a brave face as it sped out into the Pearl River Delta. The scene was a mash-up of Canaletto and Ridley Scott: in the Kowloon–Hong Kong harbour area the buildings were on top of one another like a squeezed Manhattan, the architecture functional, a dizzying vertical city that was all about maximizing space with few flourishes, but further out the Pearl River was crammed with junks, cargo boats, ferries, fast ferries, oil tankers, trawlers, yachts.

How many people lived here? Five million, ten? He'd forgotten to do his homework and instead he had spent what time he had available catching up with all the latest news on Dick Coulter. Which actually turned out to be pretty interesting. Sean wasn't kidding about trouble. Coulter Air was slashing routes left and right, had cancelled all their flights out of Derry and Glasgow and Coulter had been complaining in the tabloids that the British Airports Authority was killing his business with their taxes. The Icelandic volcano had cost Coulter Air close to fifteen million dollars and the world recession wasn't helping either. Also nothing, nothing at all in the press about a missing ex-wife and kids, which was impressive. That showed real clout.

Further out from Hong Kong city Killian spotted newer apartment buildings on the mainland marching up and down tropical mountainsides. It reminded him a little of Rio, except there the jungle was being colonised by favelas and there was an organic give and take to the process. This was all take. Hong Kong was owned by man and its sea and earth and mountain were being made to bend to man's will.

Killian wondered if it might make a good dissertation project but before he could think about it Mr Coulter's pilot gunned the big cigarette boat up to twenty and then thirty knots, bouncing it off the waves, beelining for some point on the horizon.

Now all Killian could think about was keeping down his Cathay Pacific breakfast. He stood near a gunwale and gripped a metal rail.

"How long will this take?" he asked, but neither man could hear his plaintive croak over the engine noise.

He closed his eyes and that made things worse. He took deep breaths. For Killian this was far more terrifying than having a loaded shotgun pointed at him.

Like most tinkers he had never learned to swim but for him it was a real phobia. He was terrified of water. When he was thirteen he had ridden a horse over the Bann for a dare and the horse had dumped him mid-stream.

Luck, nothing else, had saved him.

He still had the nightmares.

"How far to Macau?" he shouted again.

"There!" one of the two men said.

He looked ahead and saw the Las Vegas Strip on the South China Sea. Even more vertiginous buildings in parallel blocks on a thin slice of land. The illusion continued all the way to the harbour – what was missing was the desert but it was dusk now and the darkening sea filled that gap; money and geography did the rest.

He couldn't appreciate it. He staggered to the back of the boat and returned the breakfast scampi to its native element.

One of the two men laughed and the other said something in Cantonese which made the first laugh louder.

Bastards, Killian thought half-heartedly.

The boat docked at a wooden pier with tyres bobbing on the side as fenders. A European man wearing a chauffeur's uniform and already speaking into a mobile was waiting for them. Killian wiped his mouth and allowed himself to be helped from the boat. His head was spinning. The jet lag and lack of sleep weren't helping much either.

Mercifully, the car was close. He walked to an open limo and got in the back.

The Strip analogy continued but it was denser than Vegas as land was at more of a premium. The people were Chinese but the names were familiar: the MGM, the Venetian, Caesars Palace.

They pulled into an underground garage. The driver walked him to an elevator, put in a card key and pressed the PH button. He held the door for Killian but didn't get in with him.

The lift doors closed and Killian counted forty floors before the penthouse.

He'd been steeling himself for the chunky, potato-faced Coulter he'd seen on telly and in real life a few times at various things in Dublin and Belfast, but when the doors opened, standing there was a pregnant woman, late twenties, long brown hair, deeply tanned. Very attractive.

"Hello, I'm Helena," she said.

"Hi, I'm Killian."

They shook hands. Her fingers barely touched his, which made Killian think that she shook a lot of hands in any one day. Charity fund-raisers, that kind of thing.

"My husband's running a little late and Tom's in the city," she said.

"I saw Mr Eichel briefly already."

"Oh, I see. Would you like a drink?"

"Yeah I would, thank you, that boat journey..."

"Boat journey? Ah, right. We didn't take the boat. It must have been very beautiful."

The woman had a funny way of speaking English. She was Italian, French, something like that, but with an English boarding-school education. Almost certainly an ex-model or actress or TV presenter. Just the thing Coulter thought might impress everybody back home.

Killian unslung the bicycle messenger bag from his shoulder and let it drop to the floor while she walked to a long bar that was stacked with bottles, cocktail shakers and draft beer taps.

"Let me do that," Killian said.

"No, no, you sit down," she insisted. "Now, what can I get you?"

"Vodka tonic, heavy on the tonic and a lot of ice, please."

She brought him the drink and sat on a complementary black leather sofa opposite his. He removed a plastic stirring stick and looked around the room. South-western motifs. Leather furniture. Animal heads. Brick fireplace and a real chimney. In this locale it was ridiculous.

"You like it?" she asked, following his gaze.

"It's nice."

"It's just our flat for here. We live in Ireland."

"Aye, I know. Me too," Killian said.

"Oh, I didn't recognize the accent – whereabouts in Ireland?"

"You know Carrick?"

Helena shook her head.

"It's near Belfast. You must have driven through it."

"Possibly, I don't know."

"How long have you been married?"

"Six months."

"Congratulations."

He took a sip of the vodka tonic, it was at least half vodka.

"You pour a mean drink," he said.

"Is it too strong?" she asked with a conman smile that immediately got her into his good books.

"How do you get here from Hong Kong if you don't take a boat?" he asked.

She made a little helicopter sign with her fingers which Killian also found adorable.

"Hello?" Coulter called from another part of the flat, his Ballymena accent unmistakable. His brogue had got defiantly stronger the more famous he had become until now it was a parody of itself, sort of a cross between Ian Paisley, Seamus Heaney and Liam Neeson, all of whom grew up in the same general area.

"We're in the living room, darling," Helena said.

"The peeler's with you?" Coulter shouted.

"The man you hired, yes."

"Did you tell him anything?"

"No."

Coulter opened a door and came into the room. He looked sprightly, cheerful, like a demented elf. He was about five-seven, with dyed black hair and a tanned freckled face that had not been untroubled by the knives of gifted surgeons. He looked healthy and good. Killian knew that Coulter put it about that he was in his mid-fifties but actually he was closer to sixty.

In his heyday, four or five years ago, he'd been on the box frequently doing chat shows, variety shows, showing up as a rent-a-quote when there was news about the airline industry.

On the tube he had a stage Irishman, slightly sleazy air about him but in real life he seemed more like a successful ex-footballer or boxer a few years from the ring. There was a sort of rural Mick integrity to him.

Killian stood up. Coulter nodded to him, kissed his wife and got himself a drink from the bar.

"Where's Tom?" he asked Helena.

"Stuck in the city," she replied. He kissed her again, sat down and then leaned forward and offered Killian his hand.

"Tom talked to Sean Byrne about you, Sean says you're the best," Coulter said. Killian nodded. "Sean's my manager, what else is he going to say?"

Coulter ignored this. "And apparently you know Bridget and Michael Forsythe?"

"I've met Michael a couple of times and I've done a few wee jobs for him over the years," Killian said truthfully.

"Well, he speaks highly of your work," Coulter said and then added in an undertone, "and he would know."

Killian winced. It reminded him again of that Christmas Eve when he and a bunch of other guys had fucked up their bodyguarding gig and let Michael make fools of them and top their boss. If he'd been Japanese, no doubt the only honorable course after that would have been bloody suicide. But he wasn't Japanese, he was a Pavee and half of all Pavee were dead before they were forty. Suicide was the luxury of long-lived people.

"How was your trip?" Coulter asked.

"No problems."

"They brought you in a speedboat, right?"

"Aye, it was very Bond villain, I was impressed."

Coulter smiled. "And who did you fly with?"

"Cathay Pacific."

"They're good. Fully horizontal chairs, right?"

"Well there was a bit more room than bloody Coulter Air," Killian just about resisted saying and instead offered the safer: "Very good service. How is the airline business these days?"

Now it was Coulter's turn to wince. "We lurch from crisis to crisis. Passenger numbers are off, fuel's still historically high, taxes are through the roof. They're killing the goose. You know I had to cut half our routes out of Luton? The taxes were three times the cost of the ticket. Bloody BAA. Idiots. The volcano dust! Volcano dust is it? My God. No, no, it's still not good. We're gonna be in the red all this year and probably the first quarter of next."

Killian nodded and the conversation died.

It wasn't Killian's place to revive it but he felt uncomfortable with Helena just sitting there looking awkward.

"So I hear you're going to be the first Irishman in space?" he said, hoping to chance upon a happier topic.

"Not if I have any say in the matter," Helena said with a laugh.

Coulter laughed with her. "Honey, I'm on the first flight with Richard Branson and his kids and Sigourney Weaver and Bill fucking Shatner! It's gonna be safe as houses."

Helena rolled her eyes and Coulter leaned across and kissed her on the cheek. Helena kissed him back on the lips.

Killian smiled. Despite the age and other differences these two clearly adored each other.

Coulter turned to Killian. "And it's mostly for PR, you know? The association with Branson is good for us, and the publicity in the tabloids will be gold. Branson has promised me I will be on the very first flight, so don't believe anything you hear about Michael O'Leary, he's not booked till flight three."

Killian knew the story. He had read that this space race between Coulter and O'Leary – two of Ireland's richest men – was fierce.

"I'm impressed," Killian said and meant it – you wouldn't catch him going up in a rocket and he had nothing to lose, never mind a pregnant Italian model wife.

They talked airlines and flying for a couple of minutes before Coulter turned to Helena and with an apologetic grin said: "Darling, would you possibly excuse us for a moment? I'd like to talk business with Mr Killian, here."

"Of course," she said. Coulter helped her to her feet. Killian stood again and watched her walk to the door.

"You like Helena?" Coulter asked when she was gone.

"She seems nice."

"She's from Arpino," Coulter said and swirled the Scotch in his glass for a second or two before taking a sip.

"I don't know where that is," Killian said.

Coulter unbuttoned the jacket of his immaculately tailored blue suit and leaned forward.

"It's in, uhm, she's from…" Coulter said and his eyes narrowed, his fingers squeezed tighter on the whisky glass and his temple throbbed through the tan.

"Are you okay?" Killian asked.

"Yes. I'm just…This whole thing. It's the last thing I need. She couldn't have picked a better time. Everything's so fragile. You work so hard and it's all so fucking fragile," Coulter said.

Killian nodded. "Aye."

"But then you have to remember that life is short," Coulter went on somewhat absently and with that he relaxed and sat back. His limbs loosened, flopped. He coughed, took another sip of the whisky.

"What are you drinking?" Coulter asked.

"Vodka tonic."

"You should try this," Coulter said jiggling his glass.

"Okay."

"I'll get you one," Coulter said, standing up. He went to the bar and poured him a fifth of Scotch. Killian took it, sniffed it. It smelled peaty, expensive. He sipped it. It tasted good.

"I like it," Killian said.

"1953 Islay. From the Coronation. I have the only case left in the world."

"It's good."

The two men looked at one another.

"So, Michael Forsythe," Coulter said.

"What about him?"

"He said you were good." Killian took another mouthful of whisky and gazed out the window. The sun was sinking into the South China Sea and the sky had turned an unpleasant shade of violet.

"I don't know if I'm good, but if your wife's still in Ireland, I'll find her. If she's hopped the boat across the sheugh it's another story."

Coulter nodded. "You'll do your best," he said.

Killian shook his head. "No, if she's in Ireland, I'll find her."

"That's what I want to hear," Coulter said.

Killian said nothing.

"Arpino is where Cicero came from. Have you heard of Cicero, Mr Killian?" Coulter wondered.

Killian nodded.

"You know how he died?"

Killian shook his head.

"He thought Caesar was a dictator. He applauded his murder and he backed the wrong side after Caesar's death. Mark Antony sent his troops and they dragged him out of his litter and cut off his head. Antony's wife had Cicero's tongue ripped out because of the abuse he had heaped on her. Crazy, huh?"

Killian surmised that Coulter was proud of this connection between his wife and the dead Roman and doubted that he was attempting any kind of threat or metaphor – that of course was Tom's side of the business.

"Crazy," Killian agreed. "Shall we discuss the case?"

"By all means."

"So when did you know that your first wife had gone missing with your kids?"

"Second wife."

"Sorry, second wife."

"My first wife, Karen, lives in Brighton. We're on excellent terms. I see my kids often. All grown up, two girls, Heather and Ruby, at college and doing very well," Coulter said with a trace of irritation.

"I misspoke," Killian said, covering his ass. "Your second wife. Tell me about her."

Coulter sighed. "And as you see Helena is pregnant – it's going to be another girl. Five girls."

"Congratulations," Killian said.

Coulter nodded, sniffed his Scotch.

"If my two girls with that fucking bitch are even still alive. No one knows where they are and that lunatic is crazy enough to try anything. You know she snorted heroin when she was pregnant?"

"I didn't know that."

"Not just once. I put her in The Priory and then Clapton's place. Didn't do any good. Jesus. I should have seen it back then but I loved her."

"You've been trying to find her for how long?"

"Over a month."

"And before that you had what kind of an arrangement?"

"She had primary custody. I got the girls every other weekend and on holidays. This came completely out of the blue. Things were very good between us. I even let her stay at the house in Donegal. She'd met Helena. It was all, it was all…"

"Civilised?"

"Yeah. Civilised. I was in Brussels and Tom calls me and says she's gone. Like a fucking genie. Her and the kids. Gone. Haven't heard tell of them since."

"This was from your house in Donegal?"

"Up past Letterkenny. You know Tarafoe?"

"Aye, I know the place. Did she take anything from the house?"

"No."

"How did you know it wasn't a kidnap? Someone kidnapped them, I mean."

"Well, it is a kidnap, isn't it? She kidnapped my kids. The insurance company is paying your salary, mate. Or will be when Tom sorts it."

"That's not what I meant. How do you know there's not a third party involved?"

"She called her parents and told them that she didn't want to give me custody anymore. Said she was going to hide out with the kids. They pleaded with her but she wouldn't listen. She's a fucking whack job."

Killian took another sip of the Scotch and stroked his chin. "So she wasn't actually in violation of any court orders until when?"

"I was supposed to get the kids the very next weekend. Everything was bloody fine. Normal. And she ups and runs. Crazy."

"Had she given any hint of this before?"

"Nope. And I thought she was over the whole drug thing. I guess not."

Killian nodded.

Coulter stood. "Another Scotch?"

"No, I'm fine, thank you."

Coulter poured himself another glass. It almost brimmed over the top.

"We found out she'd disappeared. Stopped using cash machines, only used payphones. Her solicitor doesn't even know where she is. We thought she'd joined a fucking cult or something. Tom hired detectives and they bugged her parents' phone, started sifting their mail, they got close a couple of times, really close on Saint Patrick's Day, but now she's fucking gone again."

"There's one thing I'm not getting. She was awarded full custody even after you told them about the heroin?"

Coulter snorted. "There was an incident. A domestic incident. Stupid thing. She didn't bring that up, I didn't bring up the heroin."

"You hit her?" Killian asked.

"No, no. Don't go around saying that. Nobody was hit. Blazing row, shoving match and she slipped and went down the stairs, she wasn't hurt. The x-rays came up zero."

"Did she call the police?"

"Look, I know what you're thinking, but believe me it was nothing. That's not my scene. That's not the kind of man I am. It was a moment of stupidity. There was no call for the peelers. Rachel only remembered it when I started wondering if maybe I should have primary custody. We decided to call it even. But even that's making it a bigger deal than it was. The divorce was basically amicable. And in the last year we've actually been getting along better than we ever have. She seemed happy for me. We were getting on like a house on fire."

"Well, now the law's all on your side. She's in violation of the settlement I assume."

"Aye, it's practically a police matter."

"Why don't you call the police?"

"I have consulted with them. Tom has. But I don't want the heavy mob to go in just yet. I thought I'd try the professionals before bringing in the bloody PSNI or the fucking Guarda or, God save us, Interpol. They'll probably spook her into doing something stupid."

Killian nodded. He wasn't the biggest fan of the Guarda or the PSNI either.

"And you've no idea where she might be?"

"I wish I knew. Tom's got a few leads."

"It's always good to have something to work with."

"And I've got proof she's using again. That she's hanging out with pushers and meth addicts. Those little girls. I am seriously worried for their health and well-being. I am at my wit's end."

"That's understandable," Killian said with genuine sympathy. He'd been around serious users – the only subset in his book worse than drunks or gamblers.

"Where was she last?"

"Caravan park outside of Coleraine. Fucking meth-factory caravan park. Can you imagine what the girls have seen? Sue is only five."

"Coleraine? When was this?" Killian asked.

"Couple of days ago."

"They were definitely there?"

"Aye they were. We have a confirmed sighting. I don't know where they are now. Tom's got the dossier, he'll give it to you with your cheque tomorrow."

Coulter finished his Scotch and then suddenly began tearing up.

Killian was a little surprised. All the times he'd seen Coulter on TV, full of outrage, full of bluster. He was the rock of Gibraltar. He had never seen him like this: vulnerable, visibly shaken.

"I'm sorry," Coulter said. "I'm very upset."

"It's okay," Killian said, embarrassed.

"I want those girls here with me. Helena doesn't mind. She's all for it. She'd like Angelika to have big sisters. She knows we're not likely to have any more kids together, you know? This was hard this time. Very hard. Claire is seven years old, she'll forget. I want this to happen, Killian. I want those kids to be happy. We can make a happy family. Obviously we're moving back to Ireland for the birth. But even bloody here would be better. Anywhere's better away from that junkie and her junkie pals. Jesus fucking Christ."

Coulter put his head in his hands. He started making little bobbing movements as if he was actually crying and it wasn't a performance, it was real.

Killian was uncomfortable. He looked out the window but he couldn't see anything through the gathering dark.

"I'm really sorry," Coulter said, still with his head in his hands.

Killian stared at his scalp where the hair dye had stained his skin and muttered "It's okay."

Coulter finally looked up. "You see what this is doing to me?"

"I do and I'm very sorry. I, uh, I have a bairn myself. I can imagine your distress, Mr Coulter."

Coulter nodded and finished his glass.

He stood, stretched.

"Call me Richard. Come downstairs, have dinner with us, let me show you my art."

Killian looked at his watch. "Well, actually Mr Coulter, I have to get back to Hong Kong by twelve and—"

Coulter brushed the tears from his eyes and laughed. "No you don't. I flew you a long way here to get a look at you. Come on, let's go downstairs, tell me about yourself. No, wait here, don't move, let me get Helena."

Helena returned in a flattering off-the-shoulder green evening dress and all three of them took the elevator downstairs to the casino's lobby gallery.

The art was impressive. Monet, Picasso, Manet, Klimt. Small canvasses, tasteful. The gallery was open to the public but the place was empty – everyone was at the tables.

"I talked to Steve Wynn before I opened this place. You know Steve?" Coulter asked.

"No," Killian said.

"His idea. America's money is now China's money. And what do the Chinese like to do more than anything?"

"I don't know," Killian said.

"Gamble! They're complete degenerates. Not like us. A wee tote on the National and the Derby. These guys are all in. Even the women."

"I see."

"Anyway, this is a small casino by Macau standards, but we're attempting to pull in a more select clientele. I tell you, son, when the British Airports Authority kills the goose and the airline business goes belly up this place will still be a cash cow."

They walked through the empty gallery into the contemporary art room which was also deserted about from a couple of uninterested security guards.

"You like art?" Helena asked.

Killian nodded. "I do. I'm trying to expand my horizons."

"Aren't we all. Come on, let's go eat," Coulter said.

The Pearl restaurant in the Coulter Macau was packed. The chef was already gunning for a Michelin Star even though the place had only been open a couple of weeks. It was Portuguese-Catonese food, rich and exotic but because of the boat trip Killian ignored the truffles and strange fish and ordered the steak; he had it well done which scandalised the chef.

Wine flowed.

Convo flowed.

Helena talked about growing up in southern Italy, about her early days modelling, about coming to Dublin for some car show, about meeting Richard. She name checked Paris, LA, Milan, London, New York and, unlike some models he'd met, she actually knew the cities, not just the convention centres or the tented area in Bryant Park. He liked her and Coulter was growing on him too. It was unusual for a high flyer in Coulter's circle to have dinner with such a lowly potential employee as himself and Killian knew that it wasn't because of his dazzling personality. Except when he needed to turn it on for business he wasn't much of a yakker and he didn't have anecdotes to tell. He couldn't talk about his tinker childhood. He couldn't talk about New York. He couldn't talk about his Belfast underworld days. There were a lot of stories but none of them were appropriate. And besides he preferred to listen: to her accent and Richard's tales of the London A-list.

Killian knew he was a good listener. Sean said that that was his best characteristic. And it was a rare one to have in Ireland.

Two tables over Coulter's heavies were trying to be unobtrusive. Killian had spotted them immediately. Chinese goons. Three of them. A tough wee crew. Not that clever looking, maybe, but hard.

They beaded him for a while and one of them lip-curled when he touched Richard on the shoulder, but as time passed everyone relaxed. The restaurant was full, the service impeccable, the meal excellent.

"The Chinese name for Macau is The Oyster in the Mirror Sea," Coulter explained. "It's a gift of the ocean, especially today with so much of it built on reclaimed land."

"I like that," Killian said, and from the best seat in the house he looked out at the blackness of the South China Sea and the occasional lights of container ships passing in the dark like some massive luminescent sea creature.

His gaze slipped back to Richard and Helena. They were holding hands under the table like kids. Helena appeared to really love him and of course he was nuts about her.

He tuned in for the punchline to Coulter's latest story and laughed when she laughed.

Coulter was self-deprecating and funny, but at the back of his stories it was always that *hard-working Presbyterian farm-boy* thing. He never talked about what had really got him going in the seventies – the fact that he had been in the right place at the right time and had somehow been very lucky with his breaks.

Few people wanted to credit luck rather than their own sweat and Killian didn't mind. And not that it mattered now anyway. Rich men could tell it like they saw it. That was their right.

They had two and a half bottles of exquisite wine and Killian was more than a little jazzed. He said goodnight. Coming out of the bog he took the silly risk of bumping into one of the goons who was either coincidentally going in to piss or, more likely, to check up on him.

He took the goon's wallet and as he followed the mental map Coulter had given him back to one of the three Presidential Suites, he looked at the notes which all seemed to have a zero too many.

Some cleaner was going to get the tip of her life tomorrow.

He put the card key in the door and opened it.

They was a brown envelope lying on the floor. He picked it up. It was the full case file on Rachel Coulter along with a personal note from Tom Eichel apologising again that he couldn't have a proper meeting with him.

"It's nothing," he muttered.

"Who are you talking to?"

He flinched but it was only Peggy, the girl from the bar, sitting in a leather armchair eating room-service ribs and flipping between the TV channels.

"What are you doing here?" he asked.

She got up, walked to him and kissed him on the cheek. Her breath smelt of champagne.

"A nice Irishman told me that you were 'indisposed' but if I wanted there was a helicopter waiting that would take me to you. What's a girl to do? How could I say no to an offer like that?"

"Easily – whole thing including me could have been a set up, you could be on your way to some seraglio in the Gulf right now."

She hiccuped and kissed him again and asked: "What's a seraglio?"

"What are you eating?"

"I'm pigging out. Follow me, there's a hot tub on the balcony."

"The balcony?"

"Yeah."

The balcony.

Another stunning *Blade Runner* scape. Casino-hotels. Neon signs. Nightclubs. Shopping malls. Helicopters. He was right, America's money was now China's money and a good chunk of it was being gambled at roulette wheels, poker tables and mah-jong tables within the confines of this pseudo state.

The hot tub was perfect. Peggy had changed into a bikini top. Where had she gotten that?

"Where are you from?" he asked.

"Kansas, what about you?"

"Belfast."

"Ireland, right?"

"Right."

"And they call you Killian?"

"They do."

She waded across the hot tub. "You remind me of someone," she said.

"Oh Jesus, don't say your dad. I'm not that ancient."

She laughed. "Let's go down to the tables."

"Are you kidding? Absolutely not."

"Okay, let's go to the bar on the roof, they have a bar on the roof."

The problem with young people is that they always wanted to move, he thought.

"Okay," he said.

The roof-top bar: rat-pack muzak, low-key neon, a few men in suits making their way through the single malt menu.

"A martini, please," she asked the Cantonese barman.

"I'll have the same," he concurred.

They were underdressed, she in her work polo shirt, he in his suit trousers and shirt. They were still damp from the tub. She drank her martini and slid the empty back across the bar. The barman caught her eye; she nodded and he began making her another.

"Let's get a booth," she said.

Killian followed her. He waited for her to sit. But she pushed him down and sat on his lap. She kissed him. She sat next to him in the curved booth and rummaged in his pocket for his smokes.

"What are you doing here, Killian?" she asked him.

"A job interview with Mr Coulter."

"Did you get it?"

"He wants me to do it and I'm thinking it over."

"He's rich, you should take it."

"I think I might."

They had two more drinks. Killian felt drunk. She pulled him close, lifted his shirt and slid her hand under the waistband of his pants. She felt his dick harden. She kissed him and he pressed his knee against her crotch and through two layers of cloth he could feel the moisture in her pubis.

"Come on!" the barman yelled.

They went back to the room and stripped and kissed and made love and when she came he came and for a fraction of a second, for an intake of breath, for a heartbeat, life was sweet.

Sweet.

While she slept he slipped back onto the balcony, lit a cigar and adjusted the chair so that it was almost flat.

He looked at Tom's file on Rachel.

The firm they'd hired to find Rachel weren't bad at the raw intelligence but they'd rented the heavy mob to bring her in. Russians resident in England. He skimmed their report which was half-arsed and full of excuses.

He thumbed the 10 x 8s. She was an attractive woman. Thirty with curly, reddish hair, a retrousse nose, green eyes. A little like Helena. Coulter had a type.

He read the lawyers' brief. A lot of claims, but a lot of evidence to back those claims. He skimmed the bio. She too was from the Ballymena area. She'd gone to Queen's for a year. She'd taken astronomy. That was about the only interesting thing about her. The rest was boilerplate. Of course she'd quit and drifted, eventually moving to Dublin, getting a hostess job in Temple Bar. He yawned. There was a lot of information and he was very tired. He set down the folder and looked at the Southern Hemisphere stars. He'd liked astronomy too when he'd been a kid. Astrology, to be more strictly accurate.

"Killian, where are you?" the girl asked from the bedroom.

He picked up the briefing notes and put the photograph of Rachel Coulter back in the folder. He had told himself that he wasn't going to take the case until after he'd met Coulter but now there really wasn't any alternative: to turn down this much money would be obnoxious. And he liked Richard and he liked Helena.

He back went to bed and they fell asleep in each other's arms but when she woke early the next morning Killian had already gone.

chapter 5
lawyers, guns and money

I T TOOK HER AN HOUR TO FIND A PAYPHONE THAT WORKED. IT wasn't that they'd been vandalised, it was just that no one used them anymore and gradually they'd all been taken away. In the end she had to go Derry City Hall.

Her head was throbbing.

She hadn't had meth, or indeed anything, for three days. This was the cold turkey.

But this was not the way to quit. She was not in "a place of healing", she did not "love herself", she was not "submitting to a higher power".

Her head felt like it was going to split in half.

She dialled Ballymena first. She was praying that she'd get the answer-phone but her stepmum picked up.

"Hello?"

"Hello, Gillian."

"Oh my God, where are you?"

"Gillian, I can't tell you."

"Rachel, what are you doing?"

"Gillian, I'm doing what I have to do."

"There was a reporter. A reporter in this street. I'm sure Mrs McAtamney saw."

"What did you tell them?"

"Your father told them to buzz off. They'll find you, Rachel. And the police will be next. Where are you?"

"Gillian, I just wanted to let you know that I'm fine and the girls are fine and I love you."

"Rachel, this has gone on long enough."

"Is Dad there?"

"You have brought disgrace to this family, you need to turn yourself—"

"I want to talk to Dad."

"Rachel, it's not too late to—"

"I want to talk to Dad!"

"Fine."

There was a brief pause before her father came on.

"Hello?"

"Dad, I miss you, I'm going to send you a postcard."

"Okay sweetie, I'll look out for it."

"I love you."

"Love you too, honey. How are my girls?"

"The girls are good."

"You're looking after yourself?"

"Of course. I gotta go."

"Bye darling."

She hung up, pleased with herself. She'd already bought a postcard from Belfast to throw any peelers or private eyes off the scent, but her dad knew that her real letter was going to come care of the lodge.

She rummaged in her bag of fifty pees and called Tony next. He wasn't home so she left a message: "Tony honey, I'm okay, we're all okay and we miss you, love to Sandra."

Next she called Saoirse.

"Hello, McKinney, Benson and Thomas, how may I direct your call?"

"Saoirse Thomas please."

"Who shall I say is calling?"

"Rachel Anderson."

"I'll put you right through, Ms Anderson."

"Hello?"

"It's Rachel."

"Rachel, where are you?"

"You know I can't tell you that."

"You can tell me. I cannot be compelled to give the court that information, it's attorney–client priv—"

"That's not really true, is it? Under child protection statutes you can be compelled and you know it."

"Rachel, I wouldn't do that. I would never—"

"Listen, I don't have a lot of money in the phone, I just wanted to ask how you're getting along with those decrees or whatever they are."

"Rachel, you're in a great deal of trouble. The best thing for you to do at this stage is to turn yourself in – I can't get any orders set aside with an outstanding warrant against you. The judge wouldn't even look at it. You know they're considering a charge of double kidnapping. That's fifteen to life, Rachel."

"How can I kidnap my own kids?"

"It's very complicated, but believe me they can do it. Please, for your sake and the sake of your kids just turn yourself in. I'm trying to keep everyone calm. Coulter's lawyers want the court to throw the book at you."

"Let those fuckers do what they like. I'll go to the press."

"Good, do that. Tell your story. I'm sure you'll get a great deal of sympathy in certain quarters but you've got to turn yourself in first."

"I don't have to do anything. Why am I not front page news now? Richard's got the money."

"You did this to get in the newspapers?"

"No. I'm asking you why Richard hasn't splashed my picture everywhere already? Newspapers, the TV. Why do you think that is?"

"They've told me that they don't want to spook you, they don't want to panic you into doing something stupid."

"That's not the reason."

"What do you think's going on?"

"A conspiracy."

"A conspiracy? Rachel, do you even hear yourself? A conspiracy?"

"He knows I know too much."

"Tell me what you know," Saoirse said, suddenly interested.

Rachel hesitated.

"I – I can't. If I tell you then my leverage is gone."

Saoirse sighed. "Okay Rachel, look, this isn't about you or Coulter. This is about your kids. You've got to do what's best for them. And once the police start formally investigating the jig is up; eventually they *will* splash your picture on the TV news and someone will find you. It's inevitable. What kind of a life is this for the girls? It's better by far to turn yourself in now and explain yourself to the court."

"I've come too far for that!" Rachel said, losing her temper.

The pressure behind her eyes…

She felt like screaming.

"Rachel, you sound cra— Look, just trust me, please trust me, turn yourself in, it'll be okay."

"This is your professional advice to me? Turn myself in, let Richard get the girls?"

"When you're in a hole you have to stop digging."

"You know I was even thinking about killing myself – why don't I just do fucking that?"

"Rachel, come on, don't even say something like that."

"I'm hanging up now, I'll call you when I can."

"Rachel, don't hang up, please don't hang—"

She hung up. She had half a dozen fifty pees left.

Who to call? Who to call?

"Fuck it," she said and dialled Tom at his office in Belfast.

"Tom Eichel's office."

"I want to speak to Tom."

"Mr Eichel is out of the country, can I take a message?"

"Yeah, tell him Rachel Anderson called. Rachel Coulter. I'll try him again another time."

She gathered her remaining change and was about to walk back to the Volvo when the phone rang.

"Hello?" she said.

"It *is* you," Tom said.

"It's me."

"Jesus, Rachel."

"What?"

"You know what."

"I'm in the centre of a shit typhoon."

"Entirely of your own making. Have you lost your fucking mind?"

"I don't think so, Tom."

"We almost got you."

"Aye, that was plenty close. One of your heroes killed a dog," Rachel said.

"Heard about that. It could have been you."

"I suppose it could have been."

She bit her fingernails.

This conversation was pointless but she had to tell someone. "Tom, you know that gun you gave Richard? The pistol. The one we all shot that time in Donegal."

"Yeah? What about it?"

"I took it and I put it in my mouth. I was thinking about blowing my brains out."

"Oh, Rachel."

"And that wasn't the first time either."

"Don't say that, honey. You're smarter than that."

"I'm so tired, Tom."

"I know. I know what you're going through. I've been there, remember?"

"I know, Tom."

"Let me help you, darling. Tell me where you are and I can have someone there in half an hour."

"I'm at the top of The Empire State Building."

Tom laughed. "Great, I'll come myself, I'll be the one carrying red carnations."

"Get roses at least, you cheap bastard."

"How are you living? I suppose you've hocked your jewellery."

She was glad that he'd said "your" jewellery and not "Richard's jewellery". Tom had an old-world courtliness about him. She liked that.

"I'm living off the grid, it's easy," she said.

"I don't even know what that means."

"Tom, I should go."

"Wait, Rachel, I feel I should warn you, cos nobody else is going to. We've hired a pro to find you now. Scary guy. He's good. I don't want you to get hurt. Why don't you do me a big fat favour and walk to the nearest police station and turn yourself in. You'll get your one phone call. Call me and I'll come with a whole army of star lawyers. We'll get this straightened out in no time."

"I'm not going to do that and you know it."

"I don't understand it. You and Richard were getting along so well. *So* well. I mean, I know you've had problems in the past, Rachel, but we've always got through them together."

"This isn't about me, Tom. I'm hanging up."

"Wait, Rachel, I got one more idea."

"Fast."

"Leave Sue with Claire. She's pretty responsible, right? Get in your car and drive for a couple of hours until you're well away. Then call the cops, let them know where the kids are and you just keep on driving. Love, it's not *you* we want. It's the kids; you can do whatever you like. Give us the kids and we'll leave you alone."

Rachel was surprised.

She stared at the phone.

Really?

Richard hadn't told Tom about the laptop?

Tom was his oldest friend. His lawyer. His *consigliere*. Who *did* Richard trust?

Or…

Or was Tom just being coy because of a potential wire on the line.

Rachel didn't know what to say now.

It was probably best to say nothing.

"I like you Rachel, you know I've always liked you. That's why we haven't called the cops. Richard wants this taken care of in as low key a way as possible," Tom said.

No, that's not the reason.

You don't know, Tom.

You don't even know!

The pain in her head was almost unbearable now. "But you gotta understand we're going to win. You can't steal a guy's kids. Not a guy like Richard. You've lost the legal battle and you're probably going to go to jail. Why not just do everyone a favour and end this now. For the sake of the girls at least."

"That's why I'm out here, Tom. For them. I don't want them near that psychopath."

"What are you talking about? Richard's a good man. I mean we're all really sorry about that one time; he's changed and he loves the girls. And you know Helena's pregnant, right? All he wants is his family. He doesn't even bear you a grudge. He just wants the girls to be safe."

"Is that what he says?"

"He's serious about this, very serious. He's determined to find you. He's pulling out all the stops."

"I'll bet he is. I'll bet he's keeking his fucking whips. He doesn't scare me, Tom – I'll go to the papers. I've heard they've been snooping around."

"With what? Honey, you've got nothing and the stuff we have on you under lock and key, believe me you don't want in general circulation. Think of your ma and da in Ballymena. What would they say?"

He shouldn't have mentioned her da.

That's what tore it, she thought later.

Much later.

That and maybe the fact that her mind wasn't exactly *balanced*.

"I guess you don't know about the laptop," she said.

There was a long period of static before Tom said: "What laptop?"

"I have a feeling you and Richard are about to have a fun conversation," Rachel said and hung up.

She walked back to the Volvo. They'd given her a ticket. *Just try and collect that, motherfuckers*, she thought.

She put the key in the ignition and after a worrying couple of stalls the engine finally caught. It was a 1983 240 Turbo she'd bought in Derry, but apart from ten square feet of rust it actually ran pretty well.

She drove along the N56. It wasn't rush hour so it was easy. It was, however, raining hard. Only one wiper worked and it made a draggy, scraping sound as it moved.

She had to slow to twenty-five. Fog had drifted down from Malin Head and the lights on the Volvo gave off a discouraging yellow glow.

She looked at her watch. The girls had been alone for over three hours. That was about as long as she felt she could leave them. Boredom could incite a lot of mischief, and then there was Eric.

Eric came on Big Dave's rep, but Big Dave hadn't seen him for years and you just never knew with people who were seasoned by isolation in the middle of nowhere…

When she reached Gartha the rain and lough spray and fog had commingled to produce a cold, seething blanket of unpleasantness.

She eased along the road until she hit the BP station.

The pumps were closed and although the general store's light was on Kelly was nowhere to be seen. She went inside, lifted a Mars bar and left 50p.

She started the Volvo and again it complained about it.

She switched down to first gear and avoided puddles and potholes as best she could and finally after an even slower than usual drive she parked outside the cabin.

The surf was pounding the beach in huge, close-rolling breakers. The rain was coming in horizontally from the Atlantic.

She walked up the steps and knocked on the cabin door.

"Who is it?" Claire asked.

"It's me," she said.

"What's the password?"

"I don't know, darling."

"You can't come in without the password," Sue chipped in.

"Just unlock the bloody door, I'm getting soaked out here."

She heard the bolt unclick. She pushed on the door and went inside. The metal bucket she'd set up under the drip was overflowing.

"You didn't think to empty the bucket?" she scolded Claire.

"Never told me to."

"You know what initiative is?"

"Yeah," Claire said glumly.

"What is it?" Sue piped up.

Rachel grabbed the bucket and carried it to the front door. She threw out the water and put the bucket back under the drip.

"I'm hungry," Sue said.

Her cheeks were red and her eyes blue and faraway. She was pale. Beautiful. She almost looked like a normal kid. In fact she was a normal kid, physically at least. She just had what the social workers called "learning difficulties", and what the day-care people in Belfast had called "challenges".

"Well, sweetie, I got some hot dogs and I thought I'd boil up a coup—"

RAP RAP RAP on the front door.

"Fuck," she muttered under her breath.

"You said the F-word," Sue sang.

"You don't even know what an F is," Claire taunted her.

Rachel put her finger to her lips and got the 9-millimeter from the fridge.

RAP RAP RAP.

"Who is it?" Rachel asked and turning to Claire, she whispered, "Get your sister! Go to the back door, open it."

Claire picked up Sue and ran to the rear of the cabin.

She took the semi-automatic out of the plastic bag.

The rain had come on harder and once Claire had opened the door she could feel the breeze blow through.

RAP RAP RAP.

She held the Heckler and Koch two-handed and pointed it dead ahead.

"Who is it?" she asked again.

RAP RAP RAP.

"Who is it?" Rachel demanded in a louder voice.

"What?"

"Who is it?"

"It's Eric."

"Oh...Eric. Hold on. I'm coming!" she said. She went to the back door and brought in Claire and Sue. Sue had stuck her face out into the rain and her hair was already soaked. Rachel put the gun back in the freezer bag and closed the fridge.

She slid back the bolt on the front door.

Eric was standing there in a sou'wester and tarpaulin hat.

"Come in, come in," Rachel said, faking concern as best she could. Eric was forty-five, with a thick beard, a barrel chest, salt and pepper hair. He drank. He'd inherited the main house and the "guest house" – as he called it – when his father died. He didn't appear to *do* anything; apart from the rent he got on the cabin and the campsite in summer he didn't have an income.

Rachel didn't like him. She got a vibe. It was true that she got a vibe from most people, but he creeped her out big time. Dave had known him when they were both in the navy. Dave had been a twenty-year man, but Eric had called it a day after five.

"You got a letter," Eric said, holding up a sodden envelope.

Rachel took it. There was a Ballymena postmark.

"Thanks," she said.

"Who do you know in Ballymena?" Eric asked.

"Mummy, can we play Snakes and Ladders?" Claire asked.

"Yes, play with your sister, I'm talking to Mr Brantley," Rachel said and gave Eric a smile.

The lightbulb flickered and a few moments later thunder crashed in the distance. "Well," Eric said, rubbing his grey stubble with the back of his hand. "Don't let me keep you from what you're at."

"I'd ask you to dinner, but I just got back from Derry...*we* just got back from Derry."

Never let him ever know that you leave the girls here alone, she thought.

"Dinner would be nice," Eric said, looking at the girls over Rachel's shoulder. She turned round. Sue had taken off her wet clothes. She was standing there naked.

"Claire! Get your sister dressed this instant!"

"She's all wet," Eric observed.

"Put a blanket around her, she'll catch her death," Rachel told Claire.

"You do it," Claire said.

"I'm talking to Mr Brantley. Do it this instant, young lady!" Rachel barked. Groaning, Claire got up, went to the bedroom and came back with a blanket which she draped over her sister's back.

The fixed smile returned to Rachel's face.

"Must be a handful," Eric said in a kind of drawl, like he was Cornish or something, except that she knew he was from Ulster – it was an affectation he'd picked up in the navy and now was stuck with.

"Oh, no, they're pretty easy," she replied quickly.

"You were talking about a wee bite of dinner," Eric said.

"Yes, yes, how about Friday? How would you like to come over on Friday?" she asked.

"What's Friday?"

"It's nothing special, but if you give me a couple of days I can really prepare something. I can make a Chicken Kiev. Do you like chicken?"

"Ach, I'm not choosy. Why not right now? Whatever you're having would be fine by me," he said and swayed a little toward her.

His breath smelled of whisky. He was gazing right through her and when she turned again she saw that the blanket had again fallen off Sue's back.

"No, no, no," she laughed nervously. "I'll give you something to look forward to. A real treat. Chicken, potatoes, a real home-cooked meal and an apple tart; when was the last time you had a home-cooked apple tart, Mr Brantley?"

"It's been a wee while," he admitted.

"Shall we say Friday at seven?"

"What's today?"

"Today's Tuesday, Mr Brantley."

"Ach shite, that's the whole week."

He blinked so slowly that she thought for a moment he'd taken a micro sleep. He made a fist and banged it into his leg. It made her jump. He wasn't tall, but he had long, sinewy, powerful arms.

"Love, just let me sit down for a wee minute," he said and lurched further into the room. He grabbed the top of a chair, steadied himself. "I could have opened that letter, you know, it came to my house," he continued and looked over at the girls for a third time.

"I'm glad you didn't."

"You have a nice family," he muttered.

Rachel walked to the fridge and took out the bag. She set it on the counter next to the sink. She walked back to Eric, steadied him and leaned him back from the chair. Touching him sent a chill along her spine. He was burning up.

"So are you on for Friday?" she asked as calmly as she could.

"I dunno."

"I'll get wine, or beer if you prefer."

"Definitely prefer beer," he said and wiped his arm across his nose.

He wasn't that drunk, she concluded, not paralytic, just enough to plane off a little of his caution and reveal the inner psyche. She wondered if his name would come up under one of those paedophile checks at a public library.

"So are we on for Friday?" she attempted again.

He blinked, shook himself.

"Friday? Oh. Yes. Of course."

She saw him to the door, opened it, gently pushed him out into the rain.

"Goodbye, goodnight," she said. "We'll see you on Friday then."

"Huh, okay," he muttered.

She closed the door and put the gun back in the freezer.

She opened the envelope.

A letter from her father and four fifties.

It wasn't necessary. She'd been doing okay for cash; if it wasn't for the problems with the Volvo…She had an idea. She went back to the front door, opened it. The rain had turned to drizzle and the wind had dropped. Out in the Atlantic she could hear white caps breaking on the reef.

"Oh – Mr Brantley, what's that boy called who does the tune-ups?" she yelled.

He turned, looked at her for a second, processed what she'd said to him.

"That's Reese Piper. Sometimes we call him Rowdy. Fair special with his hands that boy."

"You couldn't ask him to come over tomorrow morning to look at my car?"

"Ask him yourself."

She mimed not having a phone.

"Oh, aye," he said. "I forgot about that. Well, if I remember I'll give him a call."

"Oh, please do – and you're definitely on for Friday?"

"I'll be there. Friday night, sounds good," he said.

She closed the cabin door, heard him trip on something and swear.

Friday was good. She'd bought seventy-two hours. They'd be gone in twenty-four.

She gave the girls hot dogs and put them to bed.

She destroyed receipts and began packing suitcases.

She slept well.

In the morning the sun was shining, the sky an eggshell blue.

She let the girls run out onto the sand. The cabin faced dunes and the long wide beach that hardly anyone ever came to because it was usually wet, windy and cold.

"Keep an eye on your sister," she told Claire and watched them from the porch, thumbing through a *Vogue* magazine she'd taken from the bin at the library.

"Morning, love, what can I do for you?"

Reese was six-three, blond, skinny as anything but he was only seventeen and wouldn't fill out for a couple of years yet. He was wearing tight, old-style blue jeans, wrecked Converse hi-tops and a loose black T-shirt. His accent was a Sligo variety that could make him a small fortune as a barman in London.

"The Volvo wouldn't start yesterday. I have to go to Fermanagh tomorrow – you couldn't look it over for me could ya?"

"Not a problem," he said.

He popped the hood, did his thing.

"Well?" she asked.

"Where do you want me to start?" he asked.

"It's that bad?"

"Aye," he said grinning.

"What do you need to fix just to get me to Enniskillen?"

He thought for a minute, scratched under an armpit, grinned.

"Sparks, belt," he said.

"Do it."

"Need to go to the garage to get sparks if you want to wait."

"I'll wait."

She called the girls and gave them cheese and pickle sandwiches and orange lollies.

She sent them back onto the beach. Spring was coming, it could be lovely – she'd be sorry to leave. This was one of the places they'd all enjoyed together. Maybe it reminded the kids of Richard's beach house, not a million miles away.

She saw Reese driving back along the shore road with the supplies.

She went inside the cabin and looked in the bathroom mirror at her hair. It was long and straggled and a lot of the natural copper had bleached blonde. The wind and elements had brought out her freckles. A huge line of them across the bridge of her nose looked like scar tissue. Still she knew she was an attractive woman. She brushed her hair and changed into a denim shirt and left the top three buttons undone so that her black bra showed. She disciplined the freckles with powder and applied a little dusky eyeshadow.

She waved to him through the window. He nodded and went to work on the truck.

She wanted him. Badly. Two birds with one stone. What did it matter what that made her? At least she wasn't doing it for drugs.

"Well love, I suppose that about does it," he said after forty-five minutes.

"What do I owe you?"

"Forty euros would cover it."

She checked on the girls. The tide was two miles out and not due to turn for a couple of hours. Eric's Ford Sierra was gone.

She opened her purse, pretended to look inside. "I may be a little short," she said.

"Whatever you've got," he said.

He didn't know his lines. She sighed. She found her purse and gave him the money, leaving him with a vague sense of disappointment.

She watched his truck kick dust and called the girls and got them ready.

It was hard to tell Claire that they were moving on again. She went to the bathroom to secretly cry. Sue didn't really get it at all.

Rachel packed the suitcases, made sandwiches, looked out the puzzles and games from the Coleraine drive.

"Where this time?" Claire asked wearily.

There was only one place left.

"Well we can't go east cos that's the way we came."

"We can't go west cos that's the Atlantic," Claire said, playing along.

"We can't go north because that's the edge of the world," Rachel said.

Claire smiled, that little toothed double-dimpled grin of hers. "So, it's south then."

"Yeah, south, south-east really."

I have one place left that's off the grid, Tom, she added to herself.

She loaded the Volvo and belted the girls in the back seat. She put the 9-millimetre in the passenger's seat, safetied and trigger-locked, just like Tom had shown her.

"Take a last look at Donegal, girls," she said.

"It's too misty to see anything," Claire muttered.

"Look anyway."

She drove up the private road until it looped back and joined the N58.

"South," she said and turned the clunky dial that flipped the lights as a small spell against a fog.

Rachel had good instincts. She was right about Tom.

As soon as he'd finished speaking to her he'd gone to see his boss, who was packing for the return trip to Ireland.

Helena was downstairs swimming a couple of laps.

They'd talked about the laptop.

The conversation grew heated.

Tom was flabbergasted. Angry. Amazed.

But then his temper cooled and he sat down to think.

He thought for several hours.

Killian was the wrong man for this job.

He had read Killian's CV. He was a thieving tinker's brat from some shitehole north of Belfast. Unfortunately he and Coulter had hit it off, which was fine when all that was at stake was a couple of brats. Bints at that.

But now *everything* was at stake.

It would have to be someone from outside.

No Irish or English sandman could risk the heat.

The flight from Hong Kong to London was due to leave in an hour.

Tom wanted it settled before they got into the air.

He called Michael Forsythe in New York.

"What is it?" Michael asked.

"You sent us a fucking gyppo," Tom said.

"Jesus, don't tell me you're prejudiced."

"So you knew?"

"Of course I knew. Listen, Killian's one of the best."

"His name's not even Killian is it? He's one of the fucking Cleary Clan isn't he? Fucking north Belfast fucking tinkers, the fucking worst."

"Tom, what is it? I did Richard a favour here. As a friend. I don't normally deal with this kind of stuff. I'm up on a whole other level these days."

"Aye, I know, sorry – look Mike, I'm in the red zone here. There's been a wee complication."

"Oh aye?"

"Aye, nothing I can talk about over the phone even on this line, but Killian's not the boy I want on this case. Pity of it is that he and fucking Coulter hit it off. Dick likes him."

"He's good, he's very good, Tom. Nearly as good as me back in the day," Michael assured him.

"It's not that. It's not just finding the bints. With this particular wrinkle I'm going to need an iceman."

"Oh yeah?"

"A real piece of work. He'll do what he's told, no questions, take the pay cheque and vanish. It's not just that Killian's a tinker, I need someone who isn't squeamish. Someone who is not connected in any way to Belfast. Someone from your side of the sheugh."

"Outsider. That makes me think it – whatever *it* is – is very bad."

"It is. I'm thinking Killian stays in to find the hoor, but someone at a whole other level does the rest."

Michael didn't hesitate. "You'll be wanting the Starshyna then. I'll have one of my boys give him a call."

And with that the last of the pieces fell into place.

chapter 6
starshyna

THE PLACE STANK OF DEAD MEXICANS AND NOBODY WAS EVEN dead yet. He found a sports store at a strip mall outside of Nogales and bought himself a set of swimmer's nostril clamps and a pair of golf gloves. At first they overcharged him thinking that he was a tourist but a moment later the manager followed him out into the street to give him his real change.

Stuff like that happened to Markov all the time.

He took the money and stood there on a sort of boardwalk.

From his pocket he removed a hard rubber ball and bounced it into his left hand ten times and then put it away.

The sports store was next to a shop selling cheap, crudely figured statues of the Virgin Mary, the pietas looking like a Finnish bog monster with its victim. They depressed him and he wondered if he'd made a mistake coming here. It was hot, you couldn't get Coke Zero, and his phone didn't work even after he'd pushed the + key. And the heat really was bothering him. In Vegas you could live in air-conditioning; but then again that was the kind of living that had made him soft.

The gloves were good. Kid skin with hand-stitched evap holes.

He might even use them for golf some day.

He got back in the car, looked at the bottle of tequila he'd bought for

Daniel, wondered how it would taste, shook his head. That was the way of fuck-up officers.

The road murdered the BMW's suspension for ten Ks until the GPS said something in German and he saw the taverna.

He stayed in the car with the engine running, the air pumping and the music playing until they showed.

They were driving an old Toyota pick-up and wearing plaid shirts, crumpled cowboy hats and cowboy boots.

They flashed their lights. He flashed his.

Everyone got out.

Good morning, they said and in English asked to see his ID.

He showed them his American passport. They nodded and told him to ride in the back of the truck.

"What about my car?" he asked and they told him that they would look after it. The one with one eye pointed a grubby finger at the tailgate.

"I don't do the back of trucks," Markov said.

He sat next to the driver for half an hour on dirt roads in a cab stinking of aftershave until they came to a big house in a guava cactus plantation.

Men with AKs gave him the once-over and waved them into a shady interior courtyard with a fountain.

Kids playing. Women talking. A washing line.

Markov stretched his back. He counted guards until a man he recognised from Bernie's info pack got up from a chair and shook his hand.

His count showed a dozen heavies and as many gardeners, maids, butlers and other auxiliaries. Hard to fight your way in or out of here.

The hand shaking his was covered with rings, the man was short and his breath had liquor on it.

"This way," the man said and they went out a side gate into the plantation.

They walked a few hundred metres through the cacti until they came to a long shed with mud brick walls and an aluminium roof.

"In here," the man said and they went into an empty barn.

Markov tensed as four men got up from a card table and walked towards him. Four ahead, one behind, in this nothing place. He didn't like it. The men weren't toting guns though, just beer cans covered with condensation. He was thirsty but he wasn't going to say a word until they offered him a drink, which he knew they wouldn't.

"He's the one they brought from America?" one of the new men asked in Spanish.

"Yes," the man with the rings said.

The card players looked at him sceptically for a beat but Markov didn't have anything to prove to these *putas*.

"We should have got a retarded kid to do it for nothing," another of the men said.

"Kids talk," the man with the rings said.

"Where now?" Markov asked in English.

"This is it," the man with the rings muttered.

Markov looked about him. The fuck was this? Some kind of cross? Where were the clients? "I don't get it," Markov said.

The Mex with the rings laughed, spat and pointed underground.

"The basement?" Markov asked.

"Is not okay?" the man with the rings asked.

"I need light. Can we work outside?" Markov asked.

The man with the rings pointed at the sky and shook his head.

"Planes?" Markov wondered.

"Satellites."

They kicked straw and pulled the trap door.

The smell of shit was a trip back to the day. Ten thousand miles and ten years.

Down the ladder.

Flashlights.

The prisoners were chained up against a concrete wall. Some naked, some not. All of them lying in their own filth. All of them had been tortured, most castrated, the wounds cauterised with welding gear.

Markov had seen worse. But not recently.

"All of them?" Markov asked.

The man with the rings shook his head.

"Just one."

"How?" Markov asked.

"Watch us."

They went to a metal cupboard and unlocked it. They took out a chainsaw. This also was not a novelty, but again it had been a while. The man with the rings pulled the rip cord and the brand new machine snarled into life like a demon in a samovar.

One of the Mexes produced a video camera.

He'd known it was coming. "Keep that thing away from my face. Film me from the back only," Markov said, pulling his hat down over his eyes just to be on the safe side.

There were half a dozen witnesses now and everyone was drinking. Tequila, but not from the plantation, home-brewed firewater that they passed around in a plastic milk jug.

They grabbed the first guy on the line, unchained him, shoved him to the ground and sat on him.

He began to scream.

The man with the rings applied the tip of the chainsaw to the back of the man's neck and pushed it through the second and third cervical vertebrae, severing his venal arteries. He was killed almost instantly.

Almost.

The rest of the men, even the ones who had been blinded, began to yell. It was a terrible, desperate screaming that also fucked with Markov and sent him reeling back across the years to February 2000.

Maybe that's why he'd come here. To trip on the sense memory. Bodies. Fear. Blood.

But this wasn't the moment.

This was the moment to focus on the now. To build *this* memory.

"I'll take a shot of that," Markov said and drank while they held down the second man. He was a skinny, older character of some spirit who struggled and fought them and when the chainsaw entered his writhing neck it veered into his skull making a noise like steel grinding on a lathe. The man with the rings rings looked at him and shook his head. They were losing face in front of the Yankee. He barked orders and one of the others ran upstairs and came back with a cattle prod.

Markov remembered his nostril clamps. He fished them out of his pocket and put them on.

They electrocuted and pistol-whipped all the rest of the men to render them meek and it was easy after that. The last two victims had begged for their lives on their knees, crying, saying things about how they "were really sorry" and that they had "wives and children, beautiful children" but it didn't do any good, they beheaded them just the same.

Eight people were dead.

All the prisoners.

All except one.

A formerly well-dressed young man, in a now filthy suit, chained separately from the others in the far corner. Markov hadn't even noticed him until now.

They handed him the chain saw.

"This one's yours," the man with the rings said.

"What's special about him?" Markov asked.

The man with the rings touched his nose.

Markov took the cattle prod and the chain saw and walked to the young man. The man looked at him; he had deep, intelligent brown eyes and a little smile. Markov knew immediately that he was a priest.

In Markov's slum in Volgograd there were few Catholics. Even after the fall of communism it was the orthodox who'd had the power in that town. Fatherless Markov had a lot of respect for his local priest, a Pole called Korchnow, who had impressively survived every regime from Khrushchev to Yeltsin.

"Excuse me, Padre," Markov said in Spanish.

"Is there any possibility that I could be released from here?" the priest asked in a whisper.

Markov shook his head. "Even if I wanted to there are too many."

The priest nodded. "Well then, you must do what you do," he said.

Markov took a breath and pulled the rip on the chainsaw.

It buzzed into life and before the priest had time to panic Markov swiped it sideways into his carotid artery, through his neck and out the other side. It was over in three seconds.

For a horrifying moment the beheaded priest blinked but then the life went out of his eyes.

Markov turned off the saw and set it on the straw.

The Mexicans crossed themselves and muttered and spat. Death was all around but it was a hell of a thing to murder a priest.

The Mexicans gathered the bloody heads in a pile perhaps the way their Aztec ancestors would have done half a millennium before.

They videoed the pyramid of heads and since Markov's work was done he went back up the ladder. He walked out into the guava plantation to get air.

The sun was setting and it was quiet. Someone in the house was playing on the piano. He stared at the blue flowers of the cacti and the dust whirls and the sky which had turned a deep desert magenta.

He breathed deep.

His arms felt weak and the new golf gloves were soaked with blood. He took them off and dropped them in the dirt.

The man with the rings patted him on the back.

He didn't like to be touched by men but he was too fatigued to object.

"You'll need to take a shower," the man said.

"Yes," he agreed.

"This way," they said and led him back to the house and showed him to a stand-pipe near a stable.

"Here?" he asked. "Fucking forget it. I need a shower."

"You can't go in looking like that," they told him. And there were six of them and they were adamant.

He stripped and showered under the cold water and he heard the men muttering about his scars and tattoos. They gave him a change of shirt and jeans and finally he went inside to meet Don Ramon.

Ramon had a fully serviced bar set up in the dining room with a barkeep and a cocktail waitress. He ordered a double vodka and a freshly squeezed orange juice and ice. He mixed them following a formula of his own devising and drank.

He waited and waited until the sky was the colour of a black bull and the old paranoia and suspicion had risen to the surface again.

He drummed his fingers on the bar and refused the offer of more liquor.

The barman looked uneasy.

This, Markov told himself, was what happened to you as an independent operator. Without a crew or a family to back you up there was no possibility of retaliation. No possibility of a war. Anyone at any time could decide that you were expendable.

Markov began thinking of ways he could get out of here. Surely he could lose them in the desert at night. The barkeep was a kid, about nineteen. He could kill him in a heartbeat and—

The man with the rings came back and told him that with regret Don Ramon could not meet him personally but he had asked him to give him this.

Markov took the envelope and didn't count it.

They took him to the truck and he rode in the back where he hoped the stink would be less. He looked at the stars and smoked.

They left him at his own car and he had to drive for forty-five minutes before he stopped shaking.

It was nine by the time he arrived at the Nogales Days Inn.

He just made the last meal service. He got the enchiladas and a pitcher of beer and tequila. He asked around at the bar and he was able to score a gram of coke. He snorted it in his room and lit a cigarette and sat on the balcony chair. The view was over the parking lot and the highway and the smell was of kerosene cooking fires and cheap corn oil.

When the coke started wearing off the memories came and now he realised he didn't want them after all.

But it was too late. The smell of blood. The screaming…

He only ever flashbacked to three events in the whole Chechen War: the parachute drop, the OMON guy between the lines and this one: the two hours that followed the phosphorous shells hitting the municipal hall.

He went to the minibar and got couple of Modelos and drank and remembered it all with crystal clarity. The flames burning bright yellow through the grey rubble, Dmitri, the platoon sniper shooting at anyone trying to get out. The victims trapped inside, yelling at them in Russian as the wooden ceiling caught and the roof beams burned. Finally, of course, the women who had taken to hurling babies and children out the windows. Not that that did them any good. Their orders were clear. No survivors. No witnesses. Perversely too, of course, it had all been so lovely: the bear mother in her sky, the phosphorous fire burning gold, red tracer from the AKs arcing like fireworks. When Captain Kutzo said it was sufficiently safe for their platoon to go in they went in. There were half a dozen still alive. They killed four and saved two women to rape. Two women who ultimately survived the entire war and ended up telling their story to a disbelieving foreign media. Yeltsin could get away with anything.

Markov clutched at the crucifix round his neck. A phantom crucifix that he had lost long before on his very first days in New York in Brighton Beach.

He was drooling. He had fallen asleep. The hotel phone was ringing.

He went back inside the hotel room, found his leather jacket and took out the red rubber ball he always kept there. He squeezed it and bounced it once off the carpet.

He picked up the phone.

"How was your day?" Bernie asked.

"Okay," he said.

"I won't ask you about money."

"I tell you, anyway," he said like some goddamn yuk just off the boat. He corrected himself. "I *will* tell you anyway. It was okay."

"You're wasted down there, brother. Marina called, I didn't know whether you wanted me to tell you the hotel number or not, so I didn't."

"I will talk to her later," Markov said.

"Anyway, bro, I got a real money job for you," Bernie said.

"How much?"

"You heard of Michael Forsythe?"

"Yes."

"He'll give you the rec. Fifty thousand. There's a catch, though."

"What's the catch?"

"It's in Ireland. You ever been to Ireland?"

"No."

"You object to the travel?"

"For fifty thousand I'll go to fucking Mars."

"That's my boy. When can you get back to Vegas?"

Markov felt the car keys in his trouser pocket. He had a flight booked for tomorrow afternoon but if he drove the rental non-stop...

"Let's talk at breakfast," he said.

chapter 7
the tail

WHEN HE ARRIVED IN CARRICK HE WAS SO TIRED HE HAD just one pint at the Jordy Arms and went home and slept for thirteen hours straight.

He didn't know what day it was when he woke up. It was raining and the halyards were clanging off the aluminium masts on every boat in the marina.

He lay in bed for a long time and thought about the forty thousand quid he had made in the New York trip. Rent on this place for two years or mortgage payment on the apartments for four months. Either way it was sweet.

And there was more money coming.

A fifty-thousand-pound retainer.

Four hundred and fifty for finding some wee lassie on the mitch. A wee lassie and bairns.

He lay and the longer he lay there the more claustrophobic he felt.

He sat up, walked to the window and swung it open. Gulped the sea air.

Sometimes the house felt a prison. Every house he had ever stayed in had, at times, felt like a prison.

But he couldn't go back to a caravan, not now, not ever.

He stared through the open window at the rain and the boats in the marina and Carrickfergus Castle which was a grey presence through the mist.

Nah, he couldn't go back to tinker life and he was trying to leave The Life too. *Would* leave The Life after this.

The rain was pouring on his head. It was mixed with sea spray and snow.

He let it all hit him.

"I'm a tough guy, see?" he said and closed the window and went to the bathroom. He had to bend down to reach the mirror. He was tall and pale and with a four-day beard he looked like the survivor of a long-term kidnapping. Some people said that they could tell that he was a tinker, but others said there was no tinker look, except that tinkers seldom had grey hair: the oldest Pavee he'd ever known was Declan McQuarrie's granny and she died at fifty-nine.

The cat came. How did it know that he was back? He'd have to write off a letter to the *Fortean Times*.

At least he knew how it got in now. Through the basement window and up the basement stairs and through the crack in the kitchen door.

He sat on the toilet, put the cat on his lap and continued to look at himself.

He looked harassed, stressed. He'd been keeking it for over a year now since Ireland's economy had gone completely down the bog. In six months the unemployment rate had gone from five per cent to eleven and all over the island builders were dumping property. He was stuck with two luxury apartments overlooking the Lagan in Belfast. Half a million each was what he wanted, but the last offer he'd gotten was four hundred K for both, which would leave him at least three hundred thousand in debt.

Of course this money from bloody Dick Coulter would free him. He could sell the apartments, buy this house. Jesus. He could actually start living.

He didn't like to think about it too much.

He feared the jinx.

"Let's just see what happens, I mean you never know, eh, cat?"

The cat wasn't used to long sentences. The old bird next door never talked to it and it stared at him oddly and cocked its head like a dog.

"You're know where I've been? I've been all the way around the world, so I have, Kitty," he said.

He called it Kitty, because when the old lady had told him its name a year ago, it had been something so dull he had forgotten it. Not that "Kitty" was a display of creative genius.

He got up and gave it some tuna from the fridge and ran the bath.

He read Rachel Coulter's case notes and shaved. He dressed and went outside. He inspected the front of the house, a couple of times there'd been graffiti on the wall or the fence, once a wee mucker had even scrawled "Tinkers Out" but Killian had had a word with the local UVF commander and not only had the graffiti stopped but now someone came along and did his gardening when he was away.

The house looked fine. There was a letter in the hall. When he opened it he found a credit card statement that included a charge from the Fairmont Hotel for a missing hand towel.

He had breakfast at the Jordy: Guinness pie and a coffee instead of a pint.

He walked to the car rental place on Cornmarket Street.

He wasn't sure how he'd ended up in this town. He'd never liked it. It was the young people. Even the nineteen-year-old douchebag giving him the rental car was way too cool for school. There was more attitude in Carrick than Belfast or Dublin. First the kid said the place didn't open until half past seven and then the car itself turned out to be a white Ford Fiesta when he'd specifically ordered a Land Rover over the web. He kicked a pro forma stink and the douchebag pretended to look for another vehicle on his screen.

"Sorry, nothing else," he said.

"Okay," Killian muttered.

The Fiesta was parked at the far end of the lot, under a tree, covered in squirrel shit. Inside it smelled of aftershave.

"Thanks for nothing," Killian mouthed as he drove out of the car park.

"Bye, and why don't you go fuck yourself," the douchebag mouthed from his booth.

Killian, who'd been taught to read lips by Kev McDonnell in the pit at the Trump Atlantic City gave him the finger; the kid responded in kind, and at exactly the same time both of them laughed.

"Carrickfergus," Killian said, and suspected that he was only pretending not to like it.

He drove north up the coast.

The radio was no good. Politics, country, soft rock.

There were mountains, glens, trees, cute wee towns and across the North Channel a fair of chunk of Scotland spectacular in the morning light.

For a while it looked a little like there was a tail on him, a kid in a big SUV, but when he hit the Causeway Coast the tail was gone.

Coleraine was students, civil servants and more students.

Rachel Coulter's last known address was a caravan park a little down the coast from the centre of town, not too far from the surfing and tourist spot of Portrush. Coulter's boys had found her there but they had fucked up the get. Three of them on her and she'd got clean away and they didn't even write down a licence plate. Well, as Sean would say, amateur hour was over.

He hit the caravan park, knocked at a few doors until he was pointed in the direction of Anna, the next-door neighbour. He could tell straight away that money wasn't going to be an incentive for her. She was poor and a Jehovah's Witness, with a glint of eternity in the white of her eyeballs.

There were a lot of kids running around; two of them were singing some kind of hymnal that would have sent Alan Lomax running for the tape recorder and the rest were playing a complex game that seemed to involve a lot of violent disputes about the rules. Consequently he had to give her the rap between screaming matches.

Ten questions in he saw that she didn't know anything. Rachel hadn't trusted her, which was pretty smart.

"You should ask Dave," Anne said. "Him over there. She took his car."

Dave was the other next-door neighbour, the man who'd owned the trailer she'd rented and, yes, whose car she'd borrowed and sold.

Coulter's men had got nothing out of Dave which was only to be expected.

Dave was sitting in a lawn chair drinking a beer and watching him while pretending to read *Top Gear Magazine*.

"Mr Reynolds?" Killian asked.

"That's me."

"My name's Killian," Killian said.

Killian reached over and offered Dave his hand. Dave left the hand hanging there.

"What can I do for you?" Dave wondered. He was a tubby guy with a russet beard and an RN tattoo on an exposed forearm.

"Navy, eh?" Killian asked.

"What? Oh, aye, what of it?"

"I was up on *Caroline* once," Killian said.

"Is that so?" Dave said, interested.

"Very nice ship," Killian said.

Killian had indeed been on *HMS Caroline* once – the Royal Navy's reserve headquarters in Belfast – when he was eighteen and him and a mate had paddled over there in a stolen rowboat, thrown a grappling rope over the side, climbed up, broken in and stolen five thousand quid's worth of silver plate.

"Ach, she's a great oul girl," Dave said. "The last of her class, the last commissioned vessel from World War One."

"Is that a fact? I did not know that," Killian said with the appropriate amazement.

Dave grinned. "She was in the Battle of Jutland was *HMS Caroline*."

More amazed nods. When Dave smiled he became a different guy, good-looking, with a pleasant face under the beard and the easy confidence of an ex-serviceman.

He was drinking himself to death of course, but who wasn't?

"Were you in the forces then?" Dave asked

"Nah, not me. Me ma's da was a Yank soldier though. Passing through, you know? He was at The Bulge. Dentist, if you can believe it."

Dave nodded. "I can believe it. The fucking Bulge. I've read about it. Yon was a bad one. He and your gran not hook up after?"

Killian laughed. "Are you joking? He had a whole other family Stateside. He sent me ma money, though, till she was eighteen, course by then she had two weans of her own, you know how it is."

Dave nodded. He did indeed know how it was.

"So, what can I do for you Mr Killian?" Dave asked.

"I'm looking for Rachel Coulter," Killian said.

Dave went all cold front and stroked his beard like he was trying to make a fucking genie come out of it.

"Aye, you and everybody else."

"She sold the car you lent her in Derry," Killian said.

"I gave her the car. She didn't do anything wrong," Dave said, his eyes narrowing as his right hand crumpled his magazine into a tube.

"Well, I think the cops have it now. You might even get it back," Killian said.

"I don't want it back, I gave it to her," Dave muttered.

"Mind if I sit?" Killian asked.

"Free country."

Killian unfolded a chair and positioned it next to Dave. He closed his eyes and breathed the air in through his nose. "Suppose you don't know where she was going?" he asked after a minute.

Dave shook his head. "Don't know. Don't want to know."

"Is that her caravan, there?" Killian asked, pointing to the only one in the place with its windows closed.

"We prefer 'trailer' and yes that's it yonder."

"Mind if I take a look inside?"

"You got a warrant?"

"I'm not a peeler."

"Then that's a no."

Killian smiled and leaned back and contemplated the woods for a while. He liked it here. The ocean in the distance, big Scots pine trees that sloped up the hill, fresh air.

"I'll probably just break in when you're gone some day, so why don't we save ourselves the trouble? You already destroyed all the incriminating materials, right? Letters, maps, phone books with numbers circled on 'em, that kind of thing?" Killian said, after another pause.

Dave said nothing, careful not to incriminate himself just in case.

"You didn't forget the phone books did you? Some of the best stuff is in the yellow pages," Killian said.

Dave looked uncomfortable. Killian yawned and Dave perhaps sensed that Killian's patience was boundless and that if he wanted to he could sit out here all day. "Look mate, what is it you want, exactly?" he asked brusquely.

"You see the thing is, Mr Reynolds, I want to help her," Killian said.

"You want to help her?" Dave said with obvious scepticism. "I work for her lawyers," Killian said and handed Dave his card which was just a name, phone number and email address.

Dave took the card, examined it and put it in his shirt pocket.

"What we're trying to do is establish contact with her before Coulter's people bring her in, or before, god forbid, she harms the kids. I suppose you know she's about one jump ahead of a kidnapping rap," Killian said.

Dave nodded. "I heard that."

"It's Interpol, and believe me they are cold characters. They'll stop at nothing. They could charge you with being an accessory. It was your car, and from the report I read you weren't exactly cooperative were you?"

"I didn't do nothing. Those bastards killed my dog. I'm putting together a lawsuit. Coulter's fucking loaded so he is and I want compensation for Thresher. I loved that stupid dog. I've got a solicitor."

"I hear you, brother, I hear you," Killian said, shaking his head.

A minute crept by and they sat in the chairs, listening to the surf booming in the far distance.

Killian felt himself relax. This was nice. Like old Boston Luke he really should put some ocean sounds on his iPod.

Dave obviously appreciated the silence too because it was another full minute before he cleared his throat and asked: "What's going to happen to her?"

Killian shook his head. "I don't know. Coulter'll probably find her. If he doesn't the peels will. I suppose Coulter gets the kids, she goes to jail. It's not complicated."

"She says that Coulter hit her. That he can't be trusted with the kids."

"Really? What did she tell you?" Killian asked, intrigued.

Dave shook his head. "She didn't spell it out. But she said that and she was afraid of him. You could see it in her eyes. And those guys he sent, Jesus…"

Killian nodded. "He's a first-class arsehole, that's for sure."

After another silence Dave got up, went inside the trailer, came back with two cans of Harp. He offered one to Killian.

"Don't mind if I do," Killian said.

When the can was a third drained Dave looked at him. "If you guys get to her first what the fuck can you do?"

Killian shrugged like it wasn't a big deal to him. "Truth be told I don't know if we can really do anything much. The whole situation is pretty far gone."

He finished the Harp and then as if the thought was just occurring to him he added, "I suppose if we get her to turn herself in we could put the kids in the custody of her mother and father in Ballymena, throw in a domestic violence complaint and the court will probably let them stay there until custody gets resolved."

"She talked about her da, said he was good people."

"Aye. Her da was an engineer for Hughes, her mum, her stepmum actually I think, played hockey for Ireland."

Dave smiled. "No kidding?"

"Nope. Montreal Olympics."

Dave laughed. "That is wild. Montreal Olympics? She never told me that."

"Don't think she would have been born would she?"

Dave shook his head. "No, I suppose not."

Killian crushed his can and stood.

He smoothed his jacket.

He was wearing a suit for this gig. Blue suit, tie, black raincoat, black loafers. It was a nice ensemble. Throwback. If only fedoras had been in…

"Thanks for the beer, partner," he said. "I was kidding about breaking in by the way, and I'm sorry about your dog. Just another one of the things that eejit is going to have to pay for. You know what I told my bosses? I told them we should get her to turn herself in to *Oprah*. Coulter's a pretty famous guy, this story isn't getting the play it should. You gotta wonder about that." He gave a bitter laugh.

"Aye, you do," Dave concurred.

Killian offered Dave his hand again and this time Dave shook it.

"And if you think of anything you give me a call, okay?" Killian said. It was canned dialogue and it stuck going out but adding to it would have made it worse, so he just started walking.

Killian thought there was about a thirty per cent chance of a flip but when he'd gone almost to the Ford he'd diminished those odds to close to zero.

He was wrong though.

"Mister, hey mister!" Dave called.

Killian turned. "Yeah?"

Dave walked over. "Look, I don't know if it's any help but I told her about this sort of cabin my navy mate rents out near Letterkenny. You know, if the car showed up in Derry, she might have been heading out that way…"

Big Dave handed Killian a piece of paper with an address on it.

Killian nodded. "This is good."

They shook hands again. "I hope we get to her before he does," Killian added.

"If you see her, tell her I was asking about her," Dave said. "And the weans."

Killian nodded and walked Dave back to his caravan. "Hey, you wouldn't happen to have a recent photo would you? I'm working off wedding pics."

Dave nodded and came with a picture of her and the kids outside the caravan.

Rachel looked nothing like the wedding picture. She was aged and pale – hollow. Her eyes were deep-set and dark. Her face had a faraway Dorothea Lange look. No, bad analogy. She was a modern girl, she looked modern. She was a beauty that had faded fast, "like Julia Roberts after the kids", that eejit Sean would have said.

"*Ada ah roisin*," Killian said, much to his own surprise.

It was thank you in Shelta. A language he hadn't spoken for nearly twenty years. Now, why he had done that? What was his brain cooking up. What memories were fighting their way to the surface. Not the reference to his grandfather the army dentist? No, something else. Probably the caravans.

Killian got back in his car and drove out of the caravan park and onto the A2 near Coleraine. He didn't pick up the tail again until he'd been on the Derry road for nearly an hour.

"Man, that boy is good," Killian said to himself with a whistle. Good but not great. Item #1: Killian had seen him twice now. Item #2: he'd rented a honking big white Range Rover – maybe the only thing they had available, but even so.

Killian drove for an hour and stopped for lunch at a McDonald's. Killian was old enough to remember when this road had wee cafés and local chippies, but now it was all McDonald's and KFC. Thirty years of low-level civil war had kept out the chains, but the peace dividend had brought them in with a vengeance. Drugs, new houses and McDonald's – that was post ceasefire Northern Ireland.

He ordered the Big Mac meal.

It was years since he'd eaten at a Mickey D and he'd forgotten that he didn't like the sauce on a Big Mac.

He drank the Coke and did the crossword in someone's copy of the *Guardian* and eventually the Range Rover driver came in to get food and take a piss. He was about thirty to thirty-five, a shaven bullet-shaped head, grey eyes, a paper-white, scarred face. Neck and knuckle blue-ink tattoos. Probably prison tattoos. You only got that pale and muscled on the inside.

He was a scary dude.

Either paramilitary thug or...

Or what? Killian couldn't place it.

Killian watched him as he ordered a cheeseburger. He watched him still as he found a seat as far from Killian as you could possibly get in this restaurant. He was a pro – didn't look once in Killian's direction, not even by "accident".

Killian took a couple of photographs of him with his camera phone and sent them to Sean.

"Urgent," he texted as his subject line and added:

TAIL – FRM CRRCK WHO?

"Excuse me, sir, can we sit?" a woman asked Markov.

She was with her son.

It was his own fault, he was hogging a corner table for six. Markov glanced at Killian, but that old fool was still reading his newspaper, totally oblivious to the fact that there was anyone on him.

Markov grunted and the woman sat down.

The boy had red hair and a gap-toothed smile like a comic-book character. He didn't eat his food, instead he played with the freebie, which was a plastic paratrooper with a working chute.

Parachute.

Markov flinched.

He could see it coming: another voyage down into the dark of the lizard brain.

Perhaps Mexico had been a mistake.

Getting soft was all right. Soft was good. Soft was the future. Marina wanted to get married and move to Henderson. He *should* marry her. He should marry her and get her pregnant and have kids and wait until the property market completely bottomed out and then buy in Henderson.

He closed his eyes and thought about Marina riding her bike to UNLV in her pink T-shirt.

Pink T-shirt.

Marina smiling.

Pink...

Eventually the boy and the woman left.

Killian was still reading his newspaper. Markov shook his head. How could a man like that who had never lived ever hope to outwit him?

Killian's phone rang.

It was Sean.

"Tell me about our boy," Killian said.

"Mary thinks she knows him from somewhere, I sort of think so too. He's got that sort of face."

"Paramilitary?"

"Definitely not Irish. Mary's saying she knows him from the sheets. From America."

"Fucking Forsythe. This is him, I'll bet you a ton. A tail on me. A fucking double cross."

"Relax Yojimbo, you don't know anything."

"I know Forysthe, I know his ways. He's tailing me to get an angle. I find the girl, our boy over there takes her in."

"I doubt it...however, if that's the worst-case scenario, what are you going to do about him?"

"Who knows? Keep an eye on him. For now."

"Do you have any leads on our girl?"

"It's not as cold as I thought it was going to be. A trail to Donegal."

"Coulter's bound to have checked Donegal of all places."

"I don't know. That's why he came to us, isn't it? He digs pyrites, we dig gold."

"Yeah. Okay. And if I can come up with a name I'll call you back."

"Sure thing."

Killian hit the red button and folded the *Guardian*. He window-peeped. On the other side of the glass it was raining and grey and everything was falling back into the pattern. That oh-so-predictable pattern he'd left behind. Divorce work, missing persons, heavying. Him on a case in a McDonald's on a highway in the rain with a girl at the end of it and some Aryan Nation nutcase on his ass. Where was this new life he'd promised himself? This new era that was supposed to be well in place before the time he turned forty? This? This was bullshit. Of course it wasn't entirely his fault. No one could have foreseen the crash. What he needed was an older brother in the legit world or friends in the legit world, people who read the *FT*, people who could analyse trends, see ahead. Sean was connected but he knew shit about the world outside the racing pages of the *Daily Mirror*. You needed to spread yourself out.

The skinhead had finished his food now and still wasn't looking in Killian's direction at all which showed patience. Killian turned the phone on its side and zoomed in on him. He was only about five-nine but big-shouldered, wiry, strong. His lips formed two little rose hips and his cheeks and eyebrows were scarred. He wasn't bad looking though and he was still young – if he let the hair grow he could pass for a civilian. Poor sap. A decent mentor would have told him. I'll bet he *is* a foreigner, Killian thought. He looks like a goddamn Kraut.

The tail's face vibrated and a moment later the phone rang. It was Mary asking if he wanted her to book a hotel room in Donegal. He said no. He'd play it by ear. He hung up, cleared his table and went to the bathroom. Went he got back out to the restaurant the skinhead still wasn't looking at him but he'd put his jacket back on and had his car key in his hand.

Nice.

Killian walked out to the car park and drove to the motorway.

Traffic was bad and it was nearly seven by the time he hit Letterkenny

– too late to go to that address along the coast. He called Sean and asked if he could get Mary to book him a hotel after all. In two minutes she got him a room at the Quality Inn and the satnav took him there.

He parked the Ford underground and checked in. They gave him room number 505, which was far from the street noise and had a view of the water.

He asked the concierge for a decent fish restaurant and was directed to the Silver Kettle on Francis Street. It was a huge, popular joint with excellent food and he was halfway through a dinner of sea bass and sautéed spuds when he noticed the tail, sitting at a corner table reading a newspaper.

Not too shabby.

Killian ignored him for the rest of the meal, took an Ambien with the last of his wine, paid, went back to his room, locked the door and asked for a 7.00 a.m. alarm call.

He set the bedside radio alarm and the alarm on his phone for five.

He knew what the tail would do. It's what he would do:

"Hi, this is room number 505, I forgot what time I asked for an alarm call."

"Oh yes, of course sir, let me see…7.00 a.m."

"Thank you."

The Ambien kicked in and he was asleep by nine. He didn't dream and he woke before the alarm on a cold, foggy, rainy morning feeling refreshed. He cracked his door and saw no one. He went down the fire-escape stairs and by five-twenty he'd checked out and was on the N45 west.

He pulled in for petrol at a truck stop where the N56 met the R257. He got a coffee and did a lengthy spot check for tails. Nothing. He entered Dave's buddy's address in the satnav and followed the 257 into a bleak rainy country of new forest, slippery roads, and tiny wee places filled with fishermen, artists, German architects and nutcase survivalists.

The 257 became a local road, curving through big wet pine forests that were spiderwebby and dark and elemental and appealed to him. He wound the window down. The air was good. There was moisture in it and it was filled with ions and oxygen. The smell was tree fern and seaweed and a hint of mountain ash. Moss was growing in the petrol-station toilet where he stopped to get a Snickers bar and a coffee. He checked his directions with the petrol-station attendant, but the guy was from Belfast and before that, nine months ago, a delta city in Bangladesh.

But the satnav didn't let him down and he'd made it to Dave's buddy's cabin by 9.30.

A long stony beach, breaking surf, white caps dissolving into the sort of gentle haze Impressionists painted when they went to Normandy. The cabin itself was a box rough hewn from a dark hardwood with big windows facing the cold, Prussian-blue Atlantic which was minding its business and rolling by just a few hundred yards away. She liked the ocean did this girl, Killian thought. He killed the engine and got out of the car.

He rubbed his hands. Jesus, it was colder than it looked. It looked cold but it was colder than that. This goddamn wind was probably coming all the way from Greenland.

He walked across the cement car park to the cabin. He knew she was gone. No car. No sign of life. The cabin was locked, the lights off.

He lifted the lid off the garbage can.

Cans, a milk carton, cereal boxes. Nappies. Nappies? How old was that youngest kid? Five? What age did you stop wearing nappies? Killian knew that he should know the answer to that question but he didn't. He had a vague painful stab of guilt that he crushed by slamming the lid back on the garbage can.

He did a circuit of the cabin and peered in through the glass.

That stuff he thought was sea spray was really rain. He turned up the collar on his coat.

He banged on the wooden door.

"Hello?" he tried. The haar fog that was smothering the littoral part of the beach took his voice and flattened so that it sounded unfamiliar and alien. It weirded him out. He had the feeling he was being watched. He looked back up the road for the tail but there wasn't a ghost of a car up there.

He examined the lock on the cabin door.

A rusted iron affair that he could have open in a minute.

"Hello?" he tried again.

He took out his pick kit and smiled as the tines moved and the lock turned. He pushed open the door and attempted a third "hello".

The pen flashlight revealed a twenty-four-hour/two-day dust layer. Not much more. He found kids' clothes in a bottom drawer and a meticulous read-through of the yellow pages revealed nothing.

He went back to the garbage can and dumped it.

Zilch.

The place was a bust. He closed the door, locked it, went back to his car.

He sat in the Ford and got hungry waiting for the tail to come round the bend but the tail didn't come. No one came.

It was raining hard now. He flipped on the heat, tuned the radio but all he could get was Radio Iceland. In Icelandic.

He buttoned his coat and checked the passenger's seat for a hat he knew wasn't there.

"Stuff this," he said. He got out of the car and ran across the beach to the only other house here, which was a little further down the beach. He banged on the rickety door. There was no answer and he was examining the lock and thinking *one good kick* when a man peeked his head round a wood pile.

"Who are you?" the man asked. He was wearing an anorak and a Man City hat. His nose was red and his eyes yellow, watery. He had obviously seen the car in the car park and maybe he'd even seen Killian break into the cabin. He was a toting an ancient-looking air rifle and although it was early yet he had been drinking.

"Put that fucking thing down," Killian said.

"Asked you a question," the man persisted.

"Put that fucking thing down now!"

The man broke open the air rifle and showed Killian that it was empty.

"I'm looking for Rachel Coulter."

The man shook his head.

"Never heard of her."

"Thirty, brown hair, two kids, she was probably calling herself something else," Killian said.

The man nodded and walked over.

"Oh aye. Said she was called Julie."

"Two kids, brown hair, thirty-ish?"

"That's her."

"When she cut out?"

"Wednesday."

Two days ago. Could be anywhere by now.

"Say where she was going?"

"Are you a peeler?"

"No."

"Who are you?" the man asked with a cunning leer on his face. Killian handed him his card. The man leaned in. His breath was bad and yes there was booze on it. Those yellow eyes could be the early signs of renal failure.

"Did she say where she was going?" Killian repeated.

"What's it worth to you?" the man asked.

"Can we go inside?" Killian asked.

The house was shite. Boards had sprung from the floor. The roof leaked. There were pictures ruined by moisture in antique frames. The TV was covered with a plastic sheet.

Killian sat in an armchair that smelled. An old blind poodle-cross came over and started sniffing around him.

"Sorry about the place. I might move over to the rental – this place is, this place...isn't so great," the man said, as if becoming aware of it for the first time in a long time.

"So – Rachel Coulter."

"We were talking money."

They did the dance and the man took Killian's fifty without much of a fight.

"She told Reese she was driving to Fermanagh. To Enniskillen. That's not a lie, that's what she told him."

He was a sleekit wee drunk and Killian could tell that was only a part of it. "What else have you got? You've got something?" Killian asked.

"She told Reese she was going to Fermanagh. That's worth fifty. But that isn't all I got."

Killian nodded. "Okay, what else is there?" he asked.

The man went to a back room and came back with a letter that he had steamed open. The envelope was addressed to her and had a return address. Killian could easily have taken it. One light push and this character would have fallen over.

"She was bad news. Reese says she was all over him. She was after me too. I wouldn't fuck her though, probably all poxed up."

"How much?" Killian demanded.

"Hundred euros in my hand," the man said.

Killian gave him the money. "You got anything else?" Killian asked.

The man shook his head.

Killian went back into the rain and read the letter in the car.

It was short:

Honey I hope you and the girls are well. We're doing just fine and you know I'll support you whatever you decide. I'm sure you have got your reasons. I never trusted that man in the first place. Anyways keep in touch and remember that I love you. Hope you can use this fifty. Get the girls something fun, Dad.

But like a good citizen, Rachel's father had filled in his return address on the back. It was from his RAOB lodge in Ballymena. That's where she wrote to him, that's how they avoided a peeler or private eye mail tap on their house.

And it had been two days now.

There was a pretty good chance that her father would have already received a postcard with her new address.

"Guess I'm going to the arsehole of the universe," Killian said to himself.

He left this scene, went outside, and called Sean.

"News."

"What?"

"Can't say over the phone, but I got a letter that's going to give us the next step."

"You know where she is?" Sean asked.

"I know a man who does and he's not too far from the old home base."

"Good stuff. What about our boy? The tail?"

"He was a punk, I lost him."

"Great work. You still got it, brother. You want Mary to book a hotel somewhere?"

"Nah, I'll go home tonight and hit my lead in the morning."

"Where are you now, Letterkenny? That's a long oul drive to Carrick. You should take it easy mate."

"Thanks, Sean. I'll be fine."

It took Killian four hours to get to Carrickfergus.

It took Markov three and a half.

He was impressed by the town. There was a castle and sail boats and the air was pleasantly moist and cool. Marina would love it. He booked into a place called the Coast Road Hotel and phoned Marina in case it all went wrong.

"Hello?" she said.

He smiled. Unlike him she instinctively answered the phone in English. She read English novels, she watched American TV. She had even forgotten some of her Russian. He'd actually met her in English class at the North Las Vegas Community College. She'd been two grades above, but now even he was reasonably proficient.

"It's me," he said.

"Oh, darling. Where are you?"

"I'm still in Ireland."

"I have never been to Ireland, is it good?"

"It's okay," Markov said. "It's better than Mexico."

Marina's voice sank to an embarrassed whisper and she said in Russian: "I miss you."

Markov grinned and switched to Russian too. "I miss you more than anything. I will be home soon."

"You got a cheque."

"Oh yeah? Who from?"

"The IRS."

Markov laughed. "That's a first. How much?"

"Fifteen hundred dollars."

"Great."

"When will you be back?" Marina asked.

"I don't know. I'm on a case. It's important. It could be a lot of money."

Marina said nothing. She was worried about him. "Look, I wasn't expecting that fifteen hundred, why don't you go to the mall and get yourself something. Don't get crazy on me, but, you know, get something special."

"I could get something for the nursery," Marina said brightly.

"No, no, no, get something for you, you deserve it," Markov said.

Marina gushed and Markov told her he loved her and she said that she loved him. He hung up feeling good and he went for a walk to a local pub called the Jordanstown Arms and had good food and whisky.

Back to his room.

He surveyed his equipment. He'd been sceptical at the Crime Con in Vegas but the man had been right on. Plastic strip cuffs disguised as luggage locks, pepper spray disguised as deodorant, a glass cutting tool disguised as a pen. A pen flashlight disguised as nothing. All that gear he'd taken through airline security twenty or thirty times and not once had anyone asked him about it. It was a beautiful thing.

Of course the baseball bat he'd had to buy in Belfast and that had been a chore because they didn't play baseball in Ireland. The Colt .45 ACP had been bought from a gun shark in the easiest fashion imaginable.

He watched TV until it was one in the morning and then loaded the gear in his pockets and tucked the nub of the aluminium baseball bat under his armpit, beneath his raincoat. He buttoned it up and exited.

Carrickfergus at one in the morning was ghostville. No people. Drizzle. Lights illuminating a power station along the coast to the left and the old castle to the right.

He took the red rubber ball from the pocket of his leather jacket and bounced it off the sidewalk ten times. He put it back in the pocket and walked to Killian's house.

Lights off, no sound. Markov's mouth was dry. He dabbed sweat from his forehead with his sleeve. There was a chance that Killian hadn't taken the Ambien tonight or that he was in there with a prostitute or something. Anything really. A one-man tail ran such risks. You needed a team to be really safe. But of course that meant splitting the greenbacks.

He unbuttoned his jacket, walked down the path and listened outside the door.

Nothing.

He stepped into the garden and cut a circle of glass from above the window handle. He turned the handle, pushed opened the window and climbed into the living room. He turned on the flashlight and went upstairs.

First bedroom nothing.

Second bedroom, a person in the bed snoring.

He had to go fast now. Markov closed the door behind him and carefully took off his jacket. Some people you could cuff while they were asleep, especially if they were in a drug sleep, but Killian was a dangerous customer. It was better to go in heavy.

He took the lid off the pepper spray and gave him a five-second burst in the face from a foot away.

"Aaaghhh, what the fuck!" Killian gasped and as he tried to suck air, Markov smashed the baseball bat into his ribs and ankles. He pulled

Killian off the bed by the hair, give him another burst of the pepper spray and kicked him hard in the balls. Killian doubled over in pain and Markov smacked the baseball bat into him again and again.

When Killian came to everything hurt and he had been tied with plastic handcuff strips and dumped naked in the bath.

Markov had gagged him with two of his own ties and was pouring water on him from the shower.

"Wake up," Markov said with a blunt and scary lack of emotion.

The gag made Killian panic.

You didn't gag people that you needed information from. You gagged people you were going to torture or kill.

Killian opened his eyes but his vision was blurred, his head spinning.

"Can you hear me?" Markov said.

Killian fought the panic, grunted.

"I want you to know who I am. Who it is that does this to you."

If he could have talked Killian might have gone for a mistaken ID rap but all he could do was grunt again.

"They call me Starshyna, old man. It means sergeant. I am what you can never be. I kill you, but you are very old man. I take pity on you. I let you live. You hear what I am saying to you? This is business matter, do you understand? I now have letter from Rachel Coulter's father. I reach him first, I reach her first. I not kill you. I let you live. This is how civilised men behave. We beat you at your game. You are old man! You retire now. You are Jay Leno. I am Conan O'Brien. I respect age. I don't break legs, I don't cut off dick. I think you understand. I kill you if I want to. Kill you like pig. Yes. You are lucky man. Very lucky man."

Killian felt duct tape cover his eyes and mouth.

The Russian leaned in and Killian could feel his breath on his cheek. He stank of the same aftershave he had smelt in the Ford yesterday morning.

"Not bad for punk, eh?" the Russian said.

Laughter. Footsteps.

Killian heard the door close.

His head span.

He felt sick.

He knew that if he threw up in his mouth he could choke to death.

Everything really hurt. His nerve endings were overloading his brain with messages of pain and destruction.

And his mind was torturing him with questions.

How had he tracked him? What was he going to do next?

That punk line.

It had to be the car.

He'd hacked his phone or his email and gone ahead of him to the car rental place. He'd moved fucking fast. He'd bugged the Ford and bribed the kid to make him take it.

He hadn't needed to be close.

He'd installed a GPS tracker and a voice-activated transmitter.

Perhaps he'd let Killian see him. Perhaps he'd wanted to be seen. But all along he'd been a step ahead. And he was right. I am too old for this, Killian thought.

He fought the nausea and the heaves.

He felt the clammy cold of the bathtub against his face.

He started to cry under the duct tape. For the second time in a day and in years he thought of Katie. He thought of her pale face, her pretty brown eyes. He knew that she'd had six or seven or maybe even more kids since the separation. In the only life she had ever known she was probably happy. That could have been him. Maybe it all went back to that. Maybe there was a good fucking reason for not taking the road less travelled. It was quiet now.

Just the wind playing on the halyards in the marina.

Spirals of sound. Atonal variations on a pair of notes. An Irish Ramayana.

Spirals and labyrinths.

Boats floating in and out of the void.

Every boat a soul in the immense night.

And every boat, lost.

Blood lapped his face from the contusion above his ear.

The spinning world grew distant.

The ringing in his ears stopped and he knew that the pain had gotten so much that his mind was closing up shop.

No, he protested, no, but it didn't do any good.

Killian heard a car door slam and a plane fading in the distance. Yeah, he thought, you're right mate, it's not bad for a punk.

chapter 8
an island in the stream

THE CABINS WERE ON AN ISLAND IN THE LOWER REACHES OF Lough Erne, which wasn't really a lough at all, more a wide part of the Erne river. They were expensive because you in effect rented the whole island, not just the cabin. Andrew hadn't offered her a discount, even with no other residents, and he was super-gay so there was no possibility of using feminine charms. And, to be honest, she hadn't been that nice to him in high school anyway. She hadn't kept in touch, she only knew he had this place from the Academy newsletter. He'd been friendly enough when she showed up, of course, but she knew she could expect no favours.

The unit Andrew had put her in overlooked the lough and it was clean and isolated. Few people came here at the best of times and the main channel to the east didn't really start becoming a tourist road until July.

There was yet another beach for the girls to play on.

They were almost used to it now.

Making sandcastles in the rain. They were hardy. Even Sue who, it had to be said, was doing a little better. Richard, if she could have told him, would have been pleased.

She watched them through the window and counted her money. She had two thousand euros and about a thousand quid left which was a considerable amount but which would only delay the inevitable. Ten weeks at the most, although the back channel to her father might give her more time.

The cabin, bungalow really, was quite large – two bedrooms, a bathroom and a kitchen/lounge. Big windows with views of the beach and beyond that to swans on the misty lough. It was a Tourist Board version of Ireland.

"That's mine!" Sue said.

"No, it's mine!" Claire yelled.

She closed the window so she couldn't hear the ensuing fight.

She watched the herring gulls soar over the water. She watched the gentle waves on the beach turn oleander white.

She thought about mistakes: quitting Queen's, getting into the big H, marrying Richard, running off with the weans, telling Tom about the laptop.

Jesus, she could go on all day.

And then there was the good.

A week of cold turkey.

She'd given up drugs on four previous occasions but something about this time felt different. Maybe because this time she had finally realised that this wasn't just about her.

She thought about options. There were four.

#1 Suicide: she'd be out of it, the girls would probably be safe; however she had proved again and again that she didn't have the bottle for it.

#2 Tom's plan: leave the laptop, leave the girls, call the peelers and try to vanish. But Tom would certainly come after her now. Why had she opened her big mouth? She'd be hunted, alone, and they might even use the girls against her. Richard might do that, Tom certainly would.

#3 Go to the peelers/media: that might actually be the best option. Richard would be fucked and would never get the girls, she'd be protected by the tabloids, but Tom would no doubt unleash the details of her heroin use and the fucking tabs loved building you up to knock you down again. She might not get the girls either. They might get taken into care! She might never see them again. And then of course there was McCann. The

IRA would be thrown into chaos, she'd become a hate figure – some faction or other might try to assassinate her. She was terrified of that. She'd become the centre of some awful media vortex. That would even be worse than this…

Probably, eventually, when the money ran out she'd pick #3 but for now it would have to be:

#4 The status quo. Staying here, one step ahead. At the very least it would give her time to think.

And it was beautiful. Here where Europe ended in lakes and sea spray and slate beaches and forest.

There was a knock at the door.

Her heart missed a beat but it could only be Andrew. Richard's men wouldn't knock and the peelers weren't randomly coming out here on a rainy day in March.

"Come in," she said.

Andrew came in. He was completely bald with half-moon glasses over a strange figure-eight face. He wore a red ascot and a tweed suit with yellow checks in it. He was a little plump now and you could tell that he was cultivating eccentricity. In the village they no doubt talked about the poof with the English accent.

He should be across the water auditioning for a BBC mystery series, he'd be a good minor character – the nosey vicar or the retired colonel.

"Hello," Rachel said.

Andrew took out his handkerchief and dabbed the back of his neck. He did this with his left hand because he was holding something in his right behind his back. He pocketed the handkerchief, fumbled behind his back and again with his left hand put a letter on the Ikea kitchen table.

"Oh, thank you," she said. It was from her da, posted yesterday.

"Didn't know they did deliveries on a Sunday," she said.

"They do when there's enough to justify a run out here. Might have taken another week if they hadn't had a bunch."

"Mind if I sit?" Andrew asked.

Rachel smiled. She could feel notes inside the letter. He really shouldn't do that. She didn't need the money. It was the contact she craved.

"Mind if I sit down?" Andrew asked a little louder.

"Oh, sorry. Yes. Sure."

"Thank you."

He sat and attempted a smile and said nothing.

He had left the door open and Rachel could hear the girls laughing. The fight had resolved itself.

"What's the matter, Andrew?" Rachel asked.

He coughed and shook his head. "Are you in some kind of trouble or something?" he asked.

"No. Why?"

"Only, you see, the thing is, I haven't exactly been, you know. You see, the thing is, I haven't really paid any corporation tax. Do you know what I mean? They don't know that I've reopened the place. Who was going to tell them? We're so out of the way here. And as you can see, things are precarious. I need every penny. Ten thousand quid tax would sink me. And then what? Go back to Ballymena? No chance. They wrote 'Kill the Queer' on my garage, except they spelt it wrong. Kill with one L."

If he'd been straight Rachel might have taken his hand but she didn't know if he'd like that or not so she kept her hands to herself.

"What's the matter, Andrew?"

He avoided eye contact and continued. "What I'm saying is, Rachel, I can't afford an investigation here. You appreciate that don't you?"

"Aye. But I'm missing the point. What is it that you're not telling me?"

"The point is total economic collapse. The point is the Republic's worst unemployment rate in twenty-five years. The point is tourism off by seventy per cent. The point is my business on a bloody knife edge. If they think I'm mixed up in this and look into my books, I'm finished."

"Mixed up in what?"

With a little bit of a flourish, from behind his back, Andrew put the *Sunday World* on the table. "Page four," he said. Rachel turned to page four and saw the story, a gossip piece:

Where In The World Is Rachel Coulter?

Sunday World sources are telling that us that beefy, tyrannical, Coulter Air boss Richard Coulter is having wife problems. Which wife you'll want to know, for of course Sir Richard (he wishes) has been married three times. Not wifey number 1, Annie Baxter, who is safe as houses in her millionaire mansion in Brighton. Not wifey number 3, hot (preggie or just reacting to hubbie's Irish cooking?) Italian TV presenter Helena Visconti. No, wifey number 2, Rachel Anderson, who apparently isn't keeping up with her end of the kiddie sharing arrangements and is off somewhere, destination unknown, much to Mr C's fury (and we all know what that can be like). What kind of a pickle has Rach got herself into this time? Rumours have been circulating for years that she runs with a fast crowd. Other rumours hint of darker secrets which have not been confirmed by your *Sunday World* and until they are we will keep them under wraps. Intriguing, eh? We have however confirmed that the Police Service of Northern Ireland is examining a "possible child custody order violation" and that Richard Coulter has hired a private investigator to look into his wife's whereabouts. Poor old Dick. Maybe he can spot her next year when he's orbiting the Earth from mate Sir (definitely Sir) Richard Branson's space shuttle.

She passed the paper back across the table. "I can't believe you buy into this rubbish," she said.

Andrew shook his head. "I want you out of here. Today if possible. Tomorrow at the latest."

"Andrew, I've paid for the week."

Andrew put two hundred euros on the table. "Take it, I don't want any trouble, Rachel."

"I can't move the girls again so soon and they like it here."

Andrew got up from the table. "If you're not gone by tomorrow, I'll, I'll..."

"You'll what? Call the police? You wouldn't."

He shook his head. His cheeks were crimson from the stress of all this. "I would."

"If you fucking did, first thing I'd do is make sure everybody knows about your little tax dodge operation," Rachel said.

Andrew looked shocked. "You wouldn't. I just told you that. I told you that in confidence."

"Oh, I fucking would, mate."

Andrew stood there, sweating for a moment. The moment was grim for both of them: a trip back to sixth form when everybody had bullied him. No one had thought he was gay back then – you couldn't be gay in Ballymena – but they knew he was something.

She felt bad about it but she wasn't going to give in.

"I don't want any trouble. I just want you to go, okay? If the police or the *Sunday World* start snooping around here, I'm fucked. You can imagine what business has been like, here," Andrew said.

"How about a week? Will you give me a week? I can't move the girls again, Andrew, not so soon. Not too much to ask, one week."

Andrew shook his head. "The hacks will be here in a week. They have snoops everywhere. Old man McConkey on the ferry is bored out of his mind. What do you think he talks about down the pub? Us."

"I'm not moving the girls."

"How about forty-eight hours, two days?" he said.

"I can't do it."

Andrew smiled. "I like you, Rachel, I really do, but you have to do this for me. Threats, uh, threats can, er, go two ways you know."

Rachel shook her head. "No, I don't think you want to try that line, Andrew, I really don't."

"I didn't mean anything by it," he said quickly.

Rachel could feel the moral pressure of his chubby cheeks and desperate eyes.

"I'm going to see my mother until Thursday. Could you be gone by then? By the time I get back?"

Rachel sighed. She couldn't take this. "Okay, Thursday it is," she said.

"You have to be gone," Andrew insisted.

Rachel nodded. "Then gone we'll be, Andrew, and fuck alone knows where."

Andrew left the cabin. He got the ferry off the island later that day, leaving her alone with the girls. Alone in their own private kingdom. She made the girls Heinz tomato soup with white bread and from Andrew's cabin she borrowed a bottle of Gordon's gin and had G&Ts after she put the girls to bed.

She dozed and heard a noise. It was Sue. Sleepwalking. Trying to lift the deadbolt to get outside. "Where are you going, honey?" she asked.

"To see the ducks," Sue said drowsily.

"You can't go outside, it's dangerous," she said.

"What does dangerous mean?" Sue asked.

"Dangerous is bad, sweetie."

"Oh."

She lifted Sue back to her bed and climbed in beside her, stroking her forehead until Sue fell asleep. She went back to her own bed. Tried to sleep. Tossed, turned, finally drifted off.

The murmur of the lough water invaded her dreams.

The king of the lake was singing. An old song in the old tongue. Melancholy. The meaning eluded her.

She woke with a start, feeling that things were going horribly amiss. At this moment. Right now.

She checked that the house was locked and the girls were safe.

She still wasn't satisfied. She tried conjuring life into her mobile phone but that was a lost cause. She wanted to shout a warning but she didn't know who to warn or what to warn them about.

chapter 9
twenty miles to slemish

THE SECRET OF TIR NA NOG IS NO SECRET. THE LAND TO THE WEST is here. Ireland is the holy place. Every field and meadow teems with significance. Every hill and brook and lough has its Platonic counterpoint in the dreamscape. It's like what you said to that guy in the bar in the Bronx. It was the Dreaming that took out us of Africa. The Dreaming named us and called us across the ocean. The birds had kept the secret of the land but the song of birds grew wearisome and casting out the Dreaming found us on the great savannah. The Dreaming sang to us in its loneliness. It summoned us and so began the march of man. A few made it to Ireland and the rest dispersed upon the world, perplexed forever by the necessity of the journey. That's why we wander. We Pavee. We travellers. We tinkers. We follow the ghost cattle of our ancestors. Ireland is our Promised Land. At the confluence of our histories. We live in the sacred. We live in mythology.

Do you see?

Killian.

If that is your name.

Do you see?

Wake up, I'm talking to you.

A breeze.

A breeze on your face from the open window.

The wind's long fingers cooling your lips.

You hear halyards. You smell salt water. You taste blood. You feel a dull heavy pain.

You bite into the duct tape that's been put clumsily over your mouth. You bite right through it and yell.

A nightjar pauses in its hunt.

"Help!" you croak. "Help, me! For god's sake!"

Like Homer you sing blind. "Help me! Help me!"

You try this for a minute and thirty seconds and black out.

Ellipses.

Moments.

The what in the mirror sea? The pearl. The sky is a mirror. The sky is a giant grey mirror reflecting pain back to Earth.

It is night.

And again everything pretending to be something else: those camp-fire stars, those clouds in the shape of a naked girl.

That river under your feet. A forgotten river, now part of greater Belfast's underworld of tunnels and storm drains, but previously a welcome stream for pilgrims, merchants going to the holy well at Carrick.

The holy well of Fergus Mor mac Erc. Fergus who drank from this same stream before setting out to found the kingdom of Scotland.

You know things like that because of who you are. What you are.

The water is emerald, filled with gold and chlorophyll.

Water.

Wind.

Thoughts.

You don't do well with your own thoughts. Your own thoughts hurt you in this world of nothingness. This world from the other side of the mirror. Here where the shadows fall inversely, where entropy reverses itself, where you watch yourself...

And there's something else: none of these thoughts have been in English. You have been thinking in Shelta.

You get to your knees.

Clear your throat, spit blood.

"You should have killed me, punk, whatever your orders were," you say in the language of the Saxon.

You struggle to your feet in the bathtub and step out onto the kitchen floor. The duct tape is still across your eyes and your hands are in the plastic cuffs behind your back.

You know what to do.

You walk to the sink, lean over it and grab the bathroom cabinet handle with your teeth. You pull open the cabinet, shove in your face, knock everything to the floor. You make sure the cabinet's empty and then you lie down on the floor and smoosh your face into every object that was in there: shaving foam, safety razor, soap, until you find the sewing kit from the Fairmont. You sit up, grab the sewing kit box in your fingers, slide across the plastic lid, tilt it. The needles come out. You grab one, hold it between thumb and finger and wedge it into the saw-socket lock of the plastic cuff. You wedge it carefully between the teeth.

Gently does it.

That's it.

Perfect.

Using the needle as a lever, you slide out one plastic rim of the cuff with your thumb. Centimetre by centimetre.

If the needle snaps and gets stuck in there…

But you've done this before.

A hundred times.

Your father taught it to you and the other boys.

Escape from handcuffs, the picking of locks, the untripping of alarms… tools of the trade.

Plastic handcuffs were after his time, but you'd learned their secret in an hour and a half from your Uncle Patrick: you create a lever, run the plastic tie over the lever and it slides completely out…

You have the lever and all you need now is patience.

A quarter inch, half an inch, an inch, an inch and a half…

You manoeuvre out the strip and wriggle your wrist loose until it's free.

"Yes!"

You stand, rip off the duct tape covering your eyes, run to the bedroom, call Sean.

Ring. Ring. Ring. Ring.

"Hello?"

"Mary, put Sean on, this is an emergency."

"Who is this?"

"Put Sean on now!"

Pause.

"Hello?"

"It's Killian. The tail got me. Russian kid. Beat the shit out of me, tied me up. And now he's gone to Ballymena to brace Rachel's parents."

"What? Fuck. Okay. Okay. Well, that won't do any good. They don't know where she is. Tom's operatives have been tapping their phone, intercepting their mail, following them and she's wise to it. Doesn't even bother trying."

"Nope. She's been sending postcards to her da at the RAOB, the fucking Buffs lodge, in Ballymena. I found a letter from him to a place she was staying at in Donegal. She's skipped, gone somewhere new, but odds are that he knows her new address and now our tail knows he knows. He'll fucking brace them, get her location, get the drop on us and our fucking half mill."

"Jesus! How in the name of god did he get to you?"

"I don't know. He followed me. He's good, okay? He's must be Forsythe's. I told you something was fucking fishy about this operation. He's a fucking Russian. I'm playing with – at least – fractured ribs. He went easy on me. Could have killed me."

"Shit."

"What time is it?"

"Two-thirty."

"Who do we know in Ballymena? UVF, UDA, must be somebody?"

"Rocky McGlinn, old stager for the UFF, I think he's up that way."

"Okay, find out the Andersons' address and tell Rocky to get over there right away. Ivan might not have found it yet. If he has we're fucked. Regardless I'll be there in twenty minutes."

"From Carrick? No chance."

"Call me with the address on the road."

"I can believe this bollocks," Sean muttered.

"I told you it was too good to be true. You know we could call the peelers. They'd be over in ten minutes and if the bastard's in there torturing them they'd get him."

"Last resort, Killian. Get the peelers involved and there goes our dough."

"You're right. Okay, bye."

Action stations.

Second person to third.

Killian hung up and pulled on a jumper, jeans and sneakers. He grabbed a coat and ran outside. He got in the Ford Fiesta and turned the key.

The phone rang.

"Aye?"

"Are you sure about this, Killian? He sounds like a bad bastard."

"Mary giving you the old eggy?"

"It's not about Mary, it's about you."

Just then Killian got a stab of pain from his left eye down to his toes. If he'd been driving he might have ended up in the bloody sheugh.

"Christ!" he said to himself and groaned.

He surfed the wave again.

Let the pain disperse.

"Killian?"

"Ugh."

"Killian!"

"I'm okay."

"I'm worried about you. Maybe this was a mistake. This is too big for the likes of us."

"No. It's fine. Look, I'm hanging up. Find me that address. Call Rocky."

"Okay. If you say so."

He killed the phone and set it on his seat.

Ballymena?

Beltoy Road to Kilwaughter and then the A36. Twenty miles of single-lane country roads through bog and hill. Closer to twenty-five if he was being honest with himself.

He flipped the lights, found Classic FM, and drove off. There was probably still that bug of Ivan's in the car but he could do fuck all about that.

Two miles later on a bleak stretch of the Tongue Loanen Sean called.

"The address is 3 Slemish View Lane, Carnalbanagh Sheddings."

"Was that in English? Where the fuck is that?"

"Near Broughshane. Satnav it."

"I'll need to, never heard of it."

"Rocky's on his way over. I promised him a grand."

"Tell him to be careful, the guy's good."

"Ach, you know Rock. He'll be fine."

"Aye that's what I thought till Ivan fucked me up."

"Second thoughts, mate? Maybe we should let him take it if he wants it so badly?"

"Are you fucking kidding me? Coulter hired *me*. I had dinner with him and his wife. I flew to fucking China for this gig. This is mine. I will fuck that skinhead up so bad he'll wish his hoor ma aborted him."

He hung up, turned off the music, wound the window down.

Muggy air had wafted up from Larne Lough into the boglands. The hard rain was over now and a drizzly warm front was hanging over the Antrim Plateau like a sculpture.

A mile further down the road he saw a car ahead of him. Ivan?

He took the Fiesta up to a hundred through the village of Glenoe and passed it but it was a Vauxhall Astra, not a Range Rover.

The phone.

"Bad news?" he asked.

"Is there any other kind?" Sean said.

"Okay, what?"

"Rocky can't find the house. He's says it's in the arsehole end of nowhere up near Slemish."

"Fucking hell. Tell him to keep on it."

"Did it come up your satnav?"

"Haven't done it yet, was waiting till I got to Broughshane."

"Aye well, hopefully one of you will find it. Where are you? How far are you away?"

"I'm bombing it. I'm doing a ton on the A36."

"How long?"

"Fifteen minutes."

"What's his start?"

"Hours. Maybe three."

"Jesus fuck. Who do we call? Tom?"

"Tom? Bollocks. This is his play. This is his boy."

"What then?"

"Tell Rocky to get his head out of his arse."

"Okay."

"Tell him to look out for a big white Range Rover – big honking thing, won't be able to miss it."

"Watch where you're going. Don't fucking kill yourself."

"I won't."

The warm rain was coming sideways from the mountains now and he had to flip the wipers. He turned on the radio again but the reception up here in the wilds was shite. All he could get was accordion music from Radio Scotland.

He nixed it when the phone rang again.

"Did you get Rocky?" he asked.

"Aye, I did," Sean said.

"Says he wants two grand now."

"Cheeky bugger. What did you say?"

"What could I say?"

"Good man. So, what's the story?"

"He found the house, he was right, it's on a country road, right out in the arse end of nowhere."

"That's bad for us. No witnesses."

"It is. And there's worse."

"Spill."

"Ivan's already there."

"How does he know?"

"He sees the car. Yon big white Range Rover."

"Damn it! I'm hanging up, tell him to call me."

"Okay."

The phone rang a few seconds later.

"Hi," Killian said.

"This is Rocky, is that you, Killian?"

"Aye."

"Thought you were retired? Off at college or something?"

"You heard wrong. What's going on, mate?"

"I see your boy's car."

"You're at the house?"

"Am I born daft? Good bit down the road, so I am."

"Nice. Now this house, lights are on or off?"

"Off."

"Is he in the car?"

"I don't think so."

"Hmm."

"Look, I'm going to go a wee bit closer and take a look. I'll call you back."

"Wait a minute! Hold the fucking phone, Rock. This is only a scouting op, okay? You'll do nothing until I get there? Understand?"

"I got ya."

"Make yourself useful. Write down that licence number and check the car. Fucking approach with caution, mind? Our man's a hard case from Yak Central. Be careful."

"Where am I from, Tickletown?"

"Seriously Rock."

"Okay, okay, so do a scout and then what? Go in the house?"

"No, no, no! Wait for me. If he drives off, follow him at a distance and I'll meet you on the road, okay?"

"Okay."

"And mate, please proceed with caution. This character already did a number on me. I'll be along in ten."

"Dead on mate. I will. Over and out."

Killian had reached Ballymena now. Traffic was non-existent. Ballymena was the capital of Free Presbyterian Ulster, it was Paisley Country, Ireland's most conservative town by a country mile and come midnight all good Presbies were long abed. By 1.00 a.m. you could have walked down the high street naked playing the tuba and not a curtain would have twitched.

Killian kept his kit on but he hit 105 mph on the bypass to Broughshane.

The only people who saw him at all were a couple of smack dealers who were in the middle of a moan about the collapse in prices of real estate, stolen cars and brown tar heroin.

He finally plugged the address into the satnav and a Welsh voice took him through Broughshane, to a spot on the map where there didn't appear to be anything at all – merely green blankness and dotted lines instead of roads.

The windscreen told him the same story: rolling hills, boggy sheep farms, cottages abandoned since the famine and not much else. In the starlight you could see the looming presence of Slemish Mountain, which dominated this part of Country Antrim. St Patrick had been a slave on Slemish for seven years and it had a reputation among Killian's folk as a haunted and unlucky place. Killian, who'd never quite got over his superstitious-in-fucking-spades childhood, shivered.

The satnav was all Catherine Zeta Jones in the nineties. "You are approaching your destination. You are approaching your destination. You have reached your destination."

"I have?" Killian said and peered out into the gloom.

Nothing.

He was wondering if he'd programmed the thing correctly when he saw a car parked ahead. Not a white Range Rover.

He flipped the Fiesta's headlines to full beam.

Aye, definitely not a Range Rover – a grey Renault Espace, a big family car.

"Rocky's wheels," Killian said to himself.

It unnerved him.

He called Sean.

"Sean, did Rock ever ring you back?"

"Nope. I thought he was calling you."

"He didn't."

"Is there something wrong?"

"I don't know. I see his car but I don't see the Range Rover. Can you give him a buzz while I park."

"Sure."

Killian pulled the Fiesta into the sheugh two hundred yards back from the Renault. He still couldn't see the house from here but it must be just over the dip in the road.

He killed the lights, got out, listened.

Nothing.

It was so quiet in fact that you could actually hear the sea, ten or fifteen miles away.

His phone rang and he switched it to vibrate before answering it.

"Yes?" he whispered.

"Rocky's not answering."

A chill went through him. He thought and said the same thing: "That can't be good."

"No," Sean agreed. "Killian, are you armed?"

"Nope."

"You don't have a gun?"

"I don't have anything. I'm retired, remember."

"What did you do with your shooter?"

"I give it to Carly McAleese, 'member she was having a domestic with her ex?"

"Well, that was a fucking buck eejit move wasn't it? What are you going to do now without a piece?"

"I'll be okay, Sean. Look, I'm going in. Don't call me back. I'll call you."

"Son, I know you need the money, but this doesn't seem like a brilliant plan – why don't we abort and call the peelers like you said."

"Sean, I'm going in. I'll call you in ten."

Killian hung up and walked along the boggy sheugh to the Renault. When he got there he looked inside. Nobody. A couple of school bags and a stuffed elephant.

He looked back at the hill.

The rain had stopped.

The clouds had blown through and the moon was shining right down the road. If someone was up there by the hedges and they were a half decent shot at all they could take him out easy.

He had to get off the street.

He climbed out of the sheugh and up over the fence. He started hiking through a boggy meadow. The moon and the Milky Way had really turned it up a notch and he could see down into a flooded valley on the windward side and back to the town on the lee. It was a part of the country he didn't recognise, he hadn't been out here before, even in all his wanderings.

He struggled to make out the main road to see if a distant car was driving away but another band of rain was coming in from the west and swallowing up virtually everything else in the valley.

Ivan might indeed be down there legging it but he couldn't tell.

He had nothing else. He was all in on this plan.

He ducked low and walked through the squelching waterlogged ground approaching the Andersons' place from the back. He jumped a stone wall between the fields and on a rise he finally saw the house.

No lights.

No noise.

No sign of the Range Rover.

"Damn it," he whispered.

He walked on, wading through little mounds of sheep shit and sinkholes filled with water. He came to the edge of their field which was bordered by a river and it was either cross it or go back to the road.

The road was out of the question with the situation unknown.

The river was deep, fast moving, black. A barbed-wire fence had been stretched across it a little further up at another field boundary. That would do.

He ran to the fence and with his Nikes on the bottom wire and his hands grasping at the gaps on the top strand of metal he made his way gingerly across. It vibrated with every movement and he had to lean in to compress it.

Of course he got cut; in the darkness he couldn't avoid it and at the end he nearly sliced his thumb on a barb and almost slipped down into the water.

Blind panic.

He closed his eyes and made it to the far bank.

He stepped off the wire onto the tyre and sucked his thumb.

The moon was moving slowly back behind the rain clouds – darkness would have been nice but he couldn't wait for it.

He cut through a crude path in the heather worn by stray sheep and reached the back gate of the Andersons' house.

He peered through the iron bars. A two-storey farm lodge in white stone. Nice wee spot. Picture postcard scene in the daylight with Slemish and the sea in the background.

Killian scanned the driveway next to the house. An old farm Land Rover, no Range Rover, no other cars, no nothing.

The hairs on the back of his neck were standing up.

The gate was locked but he climbed it easily. He stood in the garden among rows of cabbages and clothes on a washing line. The house was still. Curtains drawn, back door closed, silent.

Killian walked down the path. Net curtains over a dining-room window. He looked through but saw nothing. He tried the back door. Closed. It was a Northern Ireland Yale Standard. By the age of ten he could open those in two minutes. Every boy in his clan could.

He took out his pick and was about to put the two ends in the lock when he remembered Ivan's glass-cutting proclivities.

He walked around the side of the house.

Footprints in a rose garden and the kitchen window wide open with a circular cut in the glass next to the handle.

Killian's hands were shaking now.

No gun.

No clue about what to expect.

This wasn't a pathetic gambling addict in a beach town in New Hampshire. This was a pro doing what pros do. Sitting in there, quiet, waiting for him.

Killian climbed onto the window ledge and noiselessly went through into the kitchen.

No gun and no flashlight either.

There was nothing else for it.

He turned on the kitchen light.

A tidy little Ulster kitchen: cooker, kettle, fox-hunting prints on the wall, chequered floor, a stack of crossword-puzzle books on a breakfast bar.

The kitchen door was open and Killian could see into the hallway beyond.

Something was on the ground.

Someone.

He turned on the hall light.

Rocky McGlinn was lying there face up with the top of his head blown off and the exit wound sprayed all over the Fleur de Lys wallpaper. He'd been shot twice. Once in the gut and then that kill-shot in the temple. There was a lot of blood from the belly slug, which meant that Ivan had questioned him first before checking him in the brain.

Killian knew what he'd find upstairs.

His head was throbbing.

He went back into the kitchen and poured himself a glass of water.

He called Sean.

"Sean boy, send someone to my house in Carrickfergus will you? There's a chance Ivan will wait for me there to come back. I don't think he will, but he might. He knows we set Rocky on him anyway."

"What's going on, Killian?" Sean asked.

"Everybody's dead. He killed them. He got the info and killed them."

"He knows where Rachel is?"

"If her da knew, now he knows."

"Do you know?"

"No."

"He killed Rocky?"

"Aye."

"Ach, for Jesus sake."

"I know, poor Rock."

"Doesn't make any sense. Why kill them? I mean he let you live? What the fuck could have happened?"

"It's bloody obvious what happened. Rocky came in to play hero. Ivan shot him in the gut, disarmed him, questioned him, topped him. After killing Rock he had no choice but to ice the parents."

"Jesus Christ, I've got chills, man, fucking time-tunnel back to the bad old days."

"Aye and you're not alone here. Christ, Sean, it's a gigantic cluster fuck. I ballsed it. I'm sorry."

"It's not your fault. It's a cross. How could you know there'd be a man on the man."

"For half a million. Should have seen it. Also half a million? Who pays that for their weans? Even for Coulter, it was dodgy. I'm sorry mate. I should have stayed retired, declared bankruptcy, got a fucking job."

"Okay. That's enough. Don't beat yourself up. We did our best. It's over. Time to move on. You better get out of there."

"Aye, I will. I'm gone. One thing to do first," Killian said.

"No. No things to do. Just go. Are you sure our boy's gone?"

"He's away."

"Rock had three bairns. Remember to take his mobile, we can't have this coming back to us."

"Ivan may already have it," Killian said, but when he looked inside Rocky's raincoat pocket there was the phone. And something else. A piece of paper.

He unfolded it.

"JGI 3245," Rocky had written. The licence plate from Ivan's Range Rover.

"I have the phone," Killian said.

"Dump it in a deep dark place."

"I will."

"Now get out of there."

"I'm hanging up, I still have that one thing to do."

The one thing to do was go upstairs.

He took the stairs two a time and he was breathless when he made it to the landing. He turned on the light. Blood had oozed out from one of the bedrooms and was pooling in the varnished pine floor. There was an acrid burnt aroma to go with the sweet smell of a kerosene heater and all that coagulating blood.

He caught his breath and licked his dry lips parrot fashion.

He walked along the skirting and went to the murder bedroom and turned on the light.

Both of them were naked from the waist up. They were younger than

Killian had been expecting. The man was late fifties, the wife slightly younger than that.

She had blonde hair, his was black with only a few grey traces.

They were on the bedroom floor.

She'd had her hands cuffed behind her back. Her face had not been smacked about but her ghostly, pale, still lithe body was covered with cigarette burns. The mortal wound was a single gunshot to the forehead. He was untouched except for the gunshot wound above his ear. Ivan had tortured her to get the information from him.

The father had talked.

The thing about it was that as bad as the wounds were, clearly Ivan had been dialling it down. He hadn't raped her, he hadn't sawn anything off. He probably would have let them live if Rocky hadn't come in. Ivan didn't want trouble. He wanted the pay day and his instructions were to go easy – this case involved a millionaire who owned an airline and a casino, who hobnobbed with Richard Branson and who was going to be the first potato-eating Mick in space.

"Go easy," Killian thought as he looked at the dead woman with only half a brain.

Dick Coulter's former mother-in-law. This level of violence made no sense.

But it was Rocky who had caused this. Ivan might have been happy enough to tie them up in the basement to give him time to find Rachel.

He was heavy mob, yes, but Forsythe wouldn't have recommended him if he was a total loon. Killian examined the wife. The cigarette burns were fresh. In the last half hour.

He sat on the edge of the bed and recapitulated everything up to two minutes ago: Ivan flies to Ireland, follows him, breaks in to his house, knocks stupid old Killian for six, gets Rachel's da's letter, drives up here and ties up the two old folks, starts bracing them in a fairly scarily conventional way until Rock comes blundering in with a six-shooter and then it all goes to fucking shit.

Aye.

Something like that. He kills Rock and then, pressed for time, strips Mrs Anderson and burns her till her husband talks.

"Probably missed them by a matter of minutes," Killian said out loud. He looked into the lifeless face of Mrs A.

What he'd actually missed was being killed along with them by a matter of minutes, for with no gun or weapon of any kind Ivan would have taken him down too.

The phone rang.

"Aye?"

"You're still there aren't you?"

"Yes."

"Get the fuck out. Go. It's not your fault. Get in your car and go."

Killian shook his head. "Something's not right about this, Sean. This can't be about custody. It can't be about the kids. I've been thinking about it. Forsythe wouldn't have sent a guy like Ivan for a wandering-daughter job."

"Half a million dollars."

"Forsythe gets a finder's fee? Twenty-five grand. Chicken feed to him. Bridget's worth millions. All legit too. No. This is something else. Something we haven't clocked to yet."

"What then?"

"I don't know."

"Think about it in the car."

"Okay, Sean," Killian said, utterly defeated. He hung up, took out his handkerchief and wiped his prints from the light switch. He walked back downstairs past Rocky and back to the kitchen. He wiped the hall light switch, the kitchen light switch and the water glass.

He wiped his prints from the kitchen window and slipped outside.

He scuffed over the footprints in the roses and wiped his prints from the gate.

When he reached the Ford Fiesta the first hint of sun was rising over Scotland. He got in, stuck the gear stick in first and drove past the Renault and the death house in the direction of unlucky Slemish.

Sean called.

"Please tell me you've left."

"I'm in the car driving to Larne."

"Good. We'll forget this ever happened. I'll tell Tom that you were the victim of a break-in and you've been shook up and we're dropping the case. Okay?"

"Well, there's no way we can go on is there?"

"No."

"We'll have to return the retainer."

"That's okay."

"I don't see how Tom keeps this out of the papers."

"Oh, they'll blame the paramilitaries. They always do."

"Aye I suppose you're right."

"Are you okay, mate?"

"It's funny I was feeling so good after New Hampshire. I handled that well. Not a drop of blood. Everybody happy. I thought I was getting my groove back. I'm too old, Sean. I don't have the stomach for it."

"Aye, I know. Don't worry about it. Circumstances beyond your control. Go to bed and try and get some sleep and get that window fixed if you can."

"There's one other thing though, isn't there?"

"What?"

"Well, he'll probably kill Rachel now, won't he? Now that he's off down this road he's got nothing to lose."

"That's someone else's problem, mate, not ours. Come and see me in Belfast tomorrow, okay?"

"I will."

"Get some sleep if you can."

Killian hung up.

The Larne road was deserted but there ahead of him was the North Channel and all of Galloway. He could see the ferries and blue mountains and even the lights of planes on the approach to Glasgow.

He drove through a whitewashed traditional village he didn't know existed, through chimneys curling peat smoke over thatched roofs. There were horses in fields. Big hunters and fine racing mares.

Of course because it was early morning he got caught behind a herd of cows on their way to milking. A kid driving them about eleven years old in jeans and Barbour jacket and a flat cap.

The kid was smoking. Killian was time travelling. To cattle markets and horse fairs of his youth. He still didn't know where he was, except that Slemish was in the rearview now. The satnav was showing blankness and even the Welsh girl was suspiciously quiet.

The cows were going slow and Killian stalled the Ford Fiesta.

Of course Sean was right. Go to bed. Sleep. Forget about it.

Sean was older than him by fifteen years. Killian had gone to work for him when he was twenty-one after he'd returned from America.

Sean had become a kind of surrogate dad.

His real father, of course, would have given him completely opposite advice to Sean: *The tinker code did not rely on paper. Your word was everything. Your name was everything. Duty was more important than right. You fulfilled your obligations above all else. Even unto death…*

Killian had read a thousand books since Sean had taught him his letters. He had tried to transcend that code.

But he knew better.

You are where you came from.

There are no disembodied selves. There are only humans embedded in practices, places, cultures. The man without a culture is a myth. No such being exists.

In the Pavee code of honour a life is given meaning by the narrative each narrator imposes on himself within the story.

Killian's journey could not end at this place. It just wasn't possible.

He called Sean.

"Yes?"

"I want you to do something for me."

"What?"

"I've got the licence plate of the Range Rover: JGI 3245. I'll bet it would be pretty easy to get the guy's credit-card details through the hire-car company. Find out who he is."

"Aye, probably."

"And it's bound to have satnav, isn't it?

"Aye."

"If he's running it, which as a stranger to Ireland, he probably is, the car rental company can trace the car through it, can't they? We can find exactly who he is and where he's heading."

"Killian, you're not thinking of—" Sean began but Killian cut him off.

"Aye I am *thinking of.* Call me back when you've got a bead on this motherfucker."

"It'll cost us. I'll have to lay out a couple of grand."

"Lay it out."

"You can't let it go mate, can you?"

"No, I can't."

"Is this some sort of fucking tinker thing?"

"Yeah. It is some sort of tinker thing."

A long pause.

"I'll call you back when I have anything."

The Fiesta had reached the edge of Antrim Plateau now and beneath him was the ferry port of Larne. The sea had white caps and a navy helicopter was flying close to the water churning spray as it searched low for some lost comrade or missing boat or dog walker swept out to sea.

Up here in the high country, however, everything was calm.

chapter 10
the high window

THE PHONE RANG IN APARTMENT 14D OF 1738 EAST TROPICANA. Marina was on the balcony watching the planes carve big ellipses in the azure air above McCarran. It had been a full morning. She had ridden her bike to her class at UNLV and on the way back had bought fruit at the Safeway. As usual she was the only cyclist in any direction. When she got back to her apartment building a bus had collided with a jeep right outside the Liberace Museum. No one was hurt and the cops were just standing around. Broken glass had made it to the sidewalk on the north side of Tropicana and she'd gotten off the bike and carried it gingerly into the lobby.

In the elevator Greghri, the Lithuanian dealer from the MGM, hit on her a little, asking about her bike and telling her that he liked her with short hair. She was feeling lonely and enjoyed the compliments. Sasha knew that Greghri often talked to her but for some reason Sasha had gotten it into his head that Greghri was gay and he didn't mind.

She'd spread cream cheese on rye bread and made tea and gone up to the balcony to watch the accident but gradually had been drawn to the aircraft in their holding patterns. She knew Sasha wouldn't be in any of them, not for a while yet, but she still wondered. Often he surprised her, coming home unexpectedly. She used to think he did this to try and catch her in the throes of an affair, but now she knew that he did it because he missed her and because Las Vegas was home.

At the first ring of the telephone she ran to the living room. She picked up on the second.

"Hi," Sasha said.

"Oh, hi, darling!"

"I miss you very much," Sasha said.

She knew he was upset because he was speaking in Russian and he was trying to hide the slur in his voice.

"What happened?" she asked.

"Nothing," he lied.

"Are you okay?" she asked.

"I'm fine. Everything is fine. How are you?"

"I'm okay. It's morning here. I had my class. Are you still in Ireland?"

"Yes."

"Where are you?"

"It is place called En-nis-kill-en," he said, sounding the difficult word in increments.

"What time is it there?"

"Night," he said and lapsed into silence.

A Boeing 777 air-braked on its final approach.

A police radio crackled.

Sun glinted off the pyramid at the Luxor a mile to the west on the Strip.

"Do you want me to call you back?" Marina asked.

"No. No. I will go to sleep now. I have an early start in the morning. I am so tried," he said.

Marina waited for the other shoe to drop. The confession. The tears. Sasha was an emotional man and Marina was his only outlet for these emotions. To everyone else he was Starshyna – the Sergeant – but to her he was Alexi Alexander, little Sasha of the golden hair.

Of course now he almost always shaved that hair "for the job".

A fire truck pulled noisily up outside to deal with the accident and she closed the balcony door.

"What's going on there?" he wondered.

"Nothing. It's paramedics. There was a car accident."

"Did you wear your bike helmet to the college?"

"Of course. And I always ride on the sidewalk anyway."

"Tropicana is bad street, many drunks," Sasha said in English.

She switched to English too. "Are you all right?" she asked.

There was another long pause.

"Yes, it was just, little tense."

"Have you been doing your stress ball? Remember Dr Keene, Sasha. Do your stress ball."

"I have been doing stress ball!" Markov snapped.

Marina said nothing and waited. She didn't have to wait long.

"There was an incident. An unpleasant incident," he said back in that Volgograd dialect of his.

"Are you hurt?"

Sasha muttered something that she couldn't get.

"Are you sure you're all right?"

"I'm fine. Other people are hurt when they deal with me," he said. "Old fuck, old, interfering fuck. I should have cut his throat."

"But you didn't – you didn't hurt anyone that badly did you?" Marina asked.

Five thousand miles away in the Quality Hotel, in Enniskillen, Fermanagh, Northern Ireland, Sasha looked at the phone as if it had just bitten him. Did she really know? Was she still buying into this denial? She, who was so clever that she had graduated first in her English language class and was now studying at the University of Nevada. Was he such a monster that she had to do this in order to live with him?

He smiled at the mirror above the writing desk in his hotel room.

Yeah, she did.

And worse, he had to play the game too when he was back with her. And no, not for her. For himself.

He shuddered, frowned, sat down on the edge of bed.

He bounced his rubber ball off the wall, but it didn't help.

The old woman had screamed so sickeningly.

The man had begged him.

He hadn't wanted to kill them.

Their daughter's fuck up was nothing to do with them.

No good deed went unpunished. He had let the old fuck in Carrickfergus live and because of that he had to kill three people.

It wasn't necessary. He would have made the husband talk eventually. If he'd been given the time. If the old fuck had only given him the time. That fool he had sent to do his dirty work for him. Barging through the door. Was that really the best they could do in this country? It was bullshit. This country was bullshit.

They thought they were tough? They thought they had had it hard?

They were spoiled.

"If you want to see the aftermath of a real civil war visit fucking Grozny sometime, assholes," he muttered inaudibly.

He thought of the boy with the parachute in the McDonald's.

And this time it came.

This time he didn't suppress it.

"Sasha?"

But he was there. Being herded out of the Tupelov by an officer with a drawn side arm. Jumping from 2000 metres with no live jump training because they always took the strips now or landed you in helicopters. A dozen of them falling from the sky. Screams, frantic pulling at cords. The ground coming to meet him, green and brown like a wet, lethal family dog. Accelerating towards him so fast, so eager to hug him, so eager to smash him to bits, to send his tibias through his kneecaps and into his skull.

Free fall. Open your eyes maggot, open your fucking eyes.

Clouds, apartment buildings, grey evil.

Yuri face's covered with blood. Yuri – his buddy. Falling with him. What the fuck had he done to himself?

Buildings.

Screams.

"The orange toggle," he remembered somebody somewhere saying once. A slurred voice, a drunken voice. He pulled the orange cord and the yelling next to him ceased, the drama around him displacing itself into a silent world.

They lost a quarter of the platoon.

Pancaked.

Worthless dead conscripts that nobody would ever miss.

The corporal, high on moonshine he'd brewed from boot polish, lived. The officer who'd "saved" the plane from Chechen AAA got promoted.

"Sasha?"

"I am still here."

"And you're sure that you're okay?"

"Yes," he said impatiently.

"You're not in any kind of trouble? Should I call Bernie?"

Sasha laughed. "No! You worry too much. Don't call Bernie. I just called because I wanted to hear your voice," he added.

"Well, here it is," she said.

"Tell me about your day, how was your class?" he asked.

In Las Vegas Marina smiled. She told him about the class, about who hadn't showed up, about what the professor had been wearing, about his talk on the tensile strength of I bars and how disappointed he had been that none of the Americans had understood calculus.

"But you understood it, didn't you?" Sasha said.

"Of course."

"What else?"

"Nothing else. I came home. I saw the accident. I saw Greghri."

"I like him, he is a good man, for a Lithuanian."

"Yes."

Sasha yawned. "I must go darling," he said.

"I love you."

"I love you too."

He blew a kiss down the phone and hung up.

Marina walked back out to the balcony and set the phone on the glass coffee table.

The accident in front of the Liberace Museum had finally been cleared away, much to the disappointment of a camera crew from Channel 7 who now had nothing to shoot.

He hadn't sounded *that* intoxicated, she told herself.

She sat down, sipped her tea and closed her eyes.

She crossed herself and prayed to St Andrew that Sasha wouldn't drink himself into oblivion and that he wouldn't do anything stupid, and finally that he would come home safe.

chapter 11
the big sleep

KILLIAN WATCHED FROM THE CAR PARK UNTIL THE HOTEL LIGHT went off. Earlier than he'd been expecting. The phone said 10.33 and the Fiesta clock said 10.42 which was probably more or less the same thing. He figured Ivan for a night owl, but he'd seen him knock back five bottles of Bud and five double vodkas in the hotel bar.

He'd seen him go outside and bounce a rubber ball up and down ten times and then go back inside and get two more double vodkas.

A lot of booze and the fella was skinny...

He'd give him half an hour to toss and turn and take a piss before he'd try anything.

The rain had stopped. Rivers and seas boiling. Forty years of darkness. Earthquakes, volcanoes. The dead rising from their graves. The fucking rain had stopped.

He called Sean. "It's gonna be a piece of piss," he said.

"That's right, just jinx it why don't you," Sean said.

"Any blowback yet?"

"None."

"When do you think they're going to find them?"

"I don't know. We could call it in. But why would we."

"Aye, we're not doing that."

"So you're going to give this scheme a go?"

"Aye."

"I don't need to say it, do I?"

"No, once bitten and all that."

"You should have put something in his drink."

"Amateur hour. Patience is all you need."

"Call me if there's trouble."

"I won't."

He hung up.

He got out of the car. His heart was racing. Adrenalin pumping. He wasn't going to do anything for at least thirty minutes, but Ivan had clearly gotten under his skin, spooked him.

He lit a match. The phosphorous ignited with a white flare, fire kicking staccato backwards along the wood pulp and turning yellow as it cooled. He watched it, oddly fascinated. The damp air caught the smell of burning and smothered it in the stagnant earthy smells of the wet evening. With only a few seconds left in the match he pressed the hand-rolled joint reluctantly into the flame. It was his last one and it was too late now even to get a packet of ciggies. In a few seconds the cannabis was already dissolving in his blood. His hand stopped shaking, his head cleared, his eyes learned how to focus again. The match dropped out of his hands taking a long second to fall and die in the black leaves that had collected in the gutter. He crushed what was left under the heel of his shoe and took another drag on the Virginia tobacco, mixed with a touch of Moroccan hash.

Ivan's hotel room was still dark.

A breeze was blowing off Lough Erne.

Nice place Enniskillen.

All traces of the big IRA bombing in '89 were long since gone.

Nice place. But cold.

There was a pub on the other side of the car park which had a lot of empty seats. Some in the window.

And he felt cold inside too.

He wished just once he could have a real conversation with Sean, instead of business or blather. He wished again there was someone he could talk to, who would listen to the thoughts he overheard himself thinking.

But there was no one.

"It's the path you've chosen, ya eejit," he said and spat.

Keeping his eye on the window he walked to the lake shore.

His stomach was rumbling.

He hadn't eaten in a day and his head still hurt from the beating.

Oil and beer cans were jigging in and out between the tied-up boats. It was quiet, the yachts making the only music, clanging those familiar halyards and shaking their booms into discordant notes which resonated uncomfortably off the water. He grimaced, even with the dope mellowing him it was irritating – like a hundred school kids playing some warped modernist triangle symphony. Sort of thing you'd see on BBC4.

A kid came by. A short sleekit looking boy with freckles. Mouth open and closing. Clearly itching for a convo. Either that or a poofter. Nah, there weren't any poofters in Fermanagh or if there were they kept bloody quiet about it, poor sods.

The kid sidled.

Stood there.

"Evening," he said finally, in a cautious country voice.

Killian said nothing.

"Is that grass you've got in your fag?" the kid asked.

"What are you, a peeler?" Killian asked.

The kid laughed. "No, but you are, or something," he said.

Killian liked that. "How long have you been watching me?"

"Since the hotel bar," the kid said. "Who are you after? I couldn't tell which one. Was it the Chink? Are you gonna lift him?"

"I'm not a cop. It's a divorce case. Most tedious fucking thing in the world," Killian said.

The wean's face fell.

Killian was freezing and hungry. "Hey, you want to earn twenty quid?" he asked.

"Aye."

Killian pointed at the hotel. "Keep an eye on that second floor for me, if a light comes on, come in the pub and get me. Okay? Think you can handle it?"

"What about the joint?"

Killian threw it in Lough Erne. "Stunts your growth, doesn't it?" Killian said.

The pub was called The Boatsman's Arms. Enniskillen saw a lot of pleasure traffic between lower and upper Lough Erne and all the way over to the Ulster canal and the Irish internal waterways. Narrowboating was a popular holiday for some people. Other people even lived on their barges, travelling from place to place. Of course *they* never got called tinkers or gyppos or pikeys.

"What are you having?" the barman asked.

They had two taps. Guinness and Harp.

"Guinness, I suppose," Killian said. "And do you have any food?"

The barman nodded. He was about fifty with a moustache that curled at the edges. Killian was a wee bit worried that he might be a "character" and a talker. He still needed to concentrate on the window.

"Nuke ya a shepherds pie, aye?" the barman asked.

"That would hit the spot," Killian agreed.

He sat in the window seat where he could see Ivan's hotel room. The barman disappeared into a back room. It would be okay. Between him and the kid Ivan would have to be sharp. And that wean might come in useful for part two of the plan if he was what Killian thought he was.

The Guinness and the pie came together. The black stuff was well poured: black to the brim, the head above the glass, no fucking trace of a shamrock.

He sipped the pint, drowning everything out in the hoppy taste of the black liquid.

"Five even," the barman said.

Killian gave him a fiver.

The pub was empty now. Killian wondered when closing time was.

"How long have I got to eat this?" he asked.

"Ach, you're okay," the barman said and went back to the counter to clean glasses. Killian started on the pie. Pretty good. Meaty, warm.

"It's all right is it?" the barman wondered.

"Aye, it hits the spot," Killian said.

"The wee woman makes it, so she does. So where are you off to, if you don't mind me asking?" the barman asked.

"Sligo," Killian said off the top of his head.

"Oh aye? Lovely there. Go there a lot?"

"No."

Killian finished the pie and the pint.

No light had come on in the hotel room. No light was going to come on. Ivan had spent all day driving and then all evening drinking.

He had about six or seven hours…

"Toilet?" he asked and was pointed to the left. He walked through the public bar to the bathroom at the back. It was really only a wall with a metal trough at the bottom, angling into a ditch that ran outside. There were big holes in the whitewashed walls that he could see out of, and a hole in the felt ceiling through which he could see the sky. Clouds were moving silently across the constellations like vast alien ships. He pulled down his fly and pissed into the soap ball stuck in the bottom of the drain. It fizzed and bubbled and he shook the last of the yellow urine onto the soap and pulled up his fly again. There was no water for the washbasin so he wiped his hands on the back of his black jeans.

The graffiti here was a time warp back to the nineties: Up the IRA, Fuck the IRA, Fuck The Pope, Fuck The Queen, UVF, UDA, INLA, PIRA, CIRA, No Pope Here, with the occasional Man United, Liverpool and there in a corner: Tinkers Out!

They'd never grow out of that would they?

He looked at his watch.

11.20.

Ivan had been down for nearly an hour.

Suddenly his legs gave way. Heart hammering, breath shallow. He leaned up against the wall and pinched the top of his nose. It was a panic attack, not a heart attack. "Fuck," he said and slammed his fist hard in the whitewash. Plaster crumbling under the blow. "What's all this about, Killian? Tinkers out? The dead woman? Tangling with a big boy like Ivan?"

Through a hole in the outer wall he could see the car park and the lough beyond. It was pitch black beyond the arc light. Like a friggin' coal mine. Like the friggin' grave. He focused on the dark until his breathing was normal.

"Okay now, is that it?" he asked himself.

Apparently it was. He took his car key and scratched a line through the graffiti about the tinkers, digging it until it was illegible.

He bent down to look in the piece of glass that was almost a mirror but with the tain scraped to a few flakes. He was like a ghost in the glass.

He walked back out into the lounge and said goodnight to the barman.

He found the kid in the car park and gave him twenty quid.

"Thanks, mister," the kid said.

"You want to earn a hundred more?" Killian asked.

"Aye!"

"I need a car."

The kid didn't baulk but merely asked, "What's the matter with yours? Or is that nicked too?"

"No, it's not nicked. It's mine, but it's been fitted with a tracking device by the guy upstairs. He's a rival investigator and we're both on the same divorce case. It sounds exciting but it's not. It's a fairly common practice."

The kid looked at him. Killian had pegged him as a sleekit wee so-and-so, probably joyriding since he was about thirteen. Of course he could get the car himself, but it had been a while and it would take *time*.

"Aye, I can get you a car, easy," the kid said, "but it'll cost ya more than a hundred quid."

"How much?"

"Let's say five."

"Let's say two."

"Two-fifty."

"Two."

"Aye, okay. What sort do you want? It's Enniskillen so you're not going to get a Porsche."

"No, nothing like that. Nothing flashy."

"I'll go to the side street, better chance of an unlocked wee job," the kid said.

"How long will it take?" Killian asked.

"No time at all."

"Meet me back here in ten minutes?"

"Aye, nay probs."

"One more thing," Killian said.

"Aye?"

"I am not a man to be fucked with."

"I can tell," the kid said a bit cheekily and sloped off into the shadows.

The car park had one CCTV camera on a pole near the emergency exit of the hotel. Killian walked back to the water's edge, fished out a shopping bag, dandered to the hotel wall and made his way behind the pole. He shinnied up without difficulty and put the shopping bag over the camera.

He dropped to the ground and ran to Ivan's white Range Rover and took out his skeleton key. He was lucky this was an old model. The new ones sometimes confounded him. Stealing cars was a young man's game. He put the key in, toggled it, pressed on the tines and heard a click.

It was all about the alarm now. He opened the hood and disabled the battery.

He tugged on the door handle and flinched but no alarm sounded.

He looked inside the Range Rover just to give it a once-over but there was no guard dog or fucking booby trap, just a dense, expensive aftershave smell.

He sat on the driver's seat and tried a couple of the skeleton keys on his key ring until he found one that turned the ignition. He reconnected the battery, flinched, turned the key and the Range Rover roared into life. No alarm sounded this time either.

The put the car in neutral and turned on the satnav.

He thumbed through the menu until he found the last programmed address:

3 The Holiday Cottages
Dervish Island
Fermanagh

He wrote it down in his notebook and then cleared the satnav's memory just on the off chance that Ivan hadn't written it down somewhere else. He rummaged in the glove compartment for money or IDs but Ivan had been scrupulous about taking everything to his room. That was okay. This was already a good night's work. He shut down the satnav, turned off the engine and pressed the bonnet release button.

The hood popped up.

He got out of the car, closed the passenger door and locked it again. He took out a penknife and mini flashlight he'd bought on the road.

He held the flashlight between his teeth.

He lifted the hood and propped it on its stand and then leaning carefully over the engine cut the spark-plug wires with his penknife where they went into the cylinder heads.

He stood back and examined his work with the flashlight. If you took a casual look you wouldn't see anything wrong. Even an experienced mechanic might not twig it for an hour or so.

He closed the hood just as the kid was pulling into the car park with a black Mercedes W112, which wasn't exactly the most discreet vehicle in the world with all that chrome, tail jets and lacquered bodywork.

"What do you think?" the kid asked.

Joyriders and professional car thieves had completely different sensibilities, Killian reflected.

"Well, it's a bit fucking shiny and there's no satnav," he said.

The kid's face fell. "You want me to get something else?"

"Nah, it'll do. Where's there a garage I can get a map of Fermanagh?"

"Twenty-four-hour garage just down the road," the kid said.

"Aye well, a deal's a deal," Killian said and gave him two hundred quid. He was secretly pleased. His uncle Garbhan had had a W112 for years, stolen of course. He was much less of a drunk than his da and Garbhan had taught him to drive in that car, which was nerve-racking because it was an attention getter – not only nicked and a bloody classic but Garbhan regularly painted it with green gloss house paint so that it stood out a mile.

Finally Uncle G traded it for a couple of horses who were supposed to be goers on the flat but both of them failed miserably at Down Royal. And Garbhan himself had died in an infirmary in Glasgow at the ripe old age of forty-four. Poor bastard.

"Here's another fifty for doing it quick," Killian said and counted out two twenties and a ten.

"Thanks!" the kid said, beaming, the sleekit gone from his face. He wouldn't make a serious player. Too big a heart that wee mucker, Killian reckoned, but thought of another task the wee mucker might be able to handle.

"You want to double your money?" he asked.

"Maybe," the kid said.

"You'll need to get a few hours sleep and come back here early. Can you do that?"

"Aye, I think so."

"I'll want to know when the owner of this here Range Rover finally gets his car going. I've slowed him a wee bit and he'll need to call a mechanic."

"You've knackered his car?" the kid said. "Why didn't you just drive it in the lough?"

"I don't want him to catch on straight away. If you nick his car he just hires another one, doesn't he? But fuck with it a bit and he'll spend hours trying to sort it, see?"

The wean nodded. "Ohhh, aye," he said.

Killian and the kid were both enjoying the pedagogical aspect of this relationship. But it couldn't last. Killian had to get moving. "I'll give you a phone number and you'll need to tell my associate the exact moment he gets back on the road, okay? Have you a mobile?"

"Aye."

"And you think you can handle it?"

"Aye. I can do that," the kid said.

Killian give him five more fifties.

"And in case you're thinking about just sleeping in and giving my mate any old shite, remember what I said before: I am not someone to be fucked with," Killian added.

In Ulster there were at least two or three hundred convicted murderers walking the streets these days – paramilitaries who had been released under the Good Friday Agreement. Killian wasn't one of them but the kid didn't know that.

"Look, I'm in it for the money, and maybe if you're down this way again, you could use me?" the kid said.

"Maybe," Killian nodded and gave him Sean's number.

"Name's Bobby," the kid said. Killian shook his hand but did not offer his own name.

He got in the Mercedes.

Everything was familiar.

He put it in first, wound down the window and said thanks to the wean.

He drove to the BP garage and bought a map of Fermanagh and some smokes.

"Can you tell me where Dervish Island is on this?" he asked the man behind the desk.

"Dervish Island?" the man said and rubbed his chin. "I think that's down on the upper lough."

The man got out his glasses, took the map and showed him. It was an actual island island – which might prove interesting – on upper Lough Erne almost over the border in the Republic.

It looked miles away on the map, but that was only because the scale was massive on a county map.

"How far of a drive is that?" Killian asked.

The man considered.

"Well now, hard to say, maybe a two-hour drive depending on the state of the roads." Killian nodded. Unless he completely fucked up he could certainly be there by first light.

He didn't fuck up.

He was there by 4.00 a.m.

Or at least the car park at the ferry.

The island itself was a mile out into the lough. A sign said "Ferry Operational from 8 till 8".

Killian parked the Mercedes, got out and looked across the water. He lit himself a cigarette.

She must have thought that that would give her security.

Being on an island.

An island on an island.

But it wouldn't do her any good.

Not from Ivan. Not from him.

He smoked the Marlboro Light. Sean had told him to call any time day or night when he had solid info.

The poor bugger would get a thumping from Mary but he called him anyway.

"I found her," he said.

"Jesus! That was good. It was on Ivan's satnav?"

"Aye, just like I thought."

It was the hire-car company's satnav tracker that had told them where the Range Rover was in the first place, after a few pennies had greased the wheels; now Ivan's programming had told them where to go next.

"And Ivan himself, did you have to get heavy?'

"No, no, I just let him sleep."

"Good work, mate. So where is she?"

"Place called Dervish Island on Fermanagh. I'll go over there when the ferry starts running in the morning."

"Great. Unless you want to go over there now. You know, middle of the night, element of surprise and all that."

"What? Fucking swim it?"

"No, no, there must be a rowing boat around somewhere."

"I'm not going out there in the dark."

"So what *are* you going to do now?" Sean asked.

"Probably just have a smoke."

"Get some kip," Sean suggested.

"Oh, I paid a wee mucker to keep an eye on Ivan's car, he'll call you when he gets moving and you'll call me."

"Can you trust him?"

"Aye. Wee joyrider shite. Oh and one more thing."

"What?"

"I fucked with Ivan's Range Rover. Cut the sparks."

Sean was impressed. "You've done a good night's work, mate. Get some kip. And remember she's no bloody picnic either. Just confirm that she's there and I'll tell Tom and we'll get further instructions. Half a million! Jesus, what a week!"

"I'm hanging up. Apologies to the missus."

"None necessary if this pans out."

Killian threw his cigarette butt into the water.

He got back in the Merc and leaned the driver's seat back as far as it would go.

He took off his jacket and draped it over himself.

Killian was very tall but the W112 was a big car back when that actually meant something.

He closed his eyes.

It was quiet here save for a few geese and the pitter-patter of rain which was back on again of course. Killian wasn't the world's best sleeper, but he had done a good night's work. And he was shattered.

He drifted…

On the edge of sleep. On the edge of the Dreaming.

Over the water.

This was another important place in the Pavee mythology. Site of the first Neolithic settlement in Ireland. More ancient even than Newgrange or the Giant's Ring. It was here that Badhbha, Goddess of crows and war, made her home. His ma and even cynical old Uncle Garbhan wouldn't have come here.

Rain clouds came and passed above. Stars moved in a giant circle around his head, strange constellations brushing against his cheeks.

It was a dream of old Ireland. In the old speak. He heard the Ernai on the water and he spoke their true name. He talked in his sleep and his thoughts were weird and when the light woke him at seven he knew that this day wasn't going to go the way he or Sean or Dick Coulter or Tom or Ivan or anyone else could possibly have foreseen.

chapter 12
farewell my lovely

TOM EICHEL DROVE FROM HIS APARTMENT IN CENTRAL BELFAST to Dick Coulter's house in Knocknagulla in a speedy twenty minutes. If it had been rush hour it might have taken him an hour but at this time of the morning all the traffic was going the other way.

He zipped through Carrickfergus and Kilroot and turned left at the big No Entry sign just before the Bla Hole turn.

Viv nodded to him at the gate and lifted the barrier.

Security had been tightened at what the locals called Castle Coulter since 2006 when a Continuity IRA abduction scheme had to come to light. CIRA had planned to kidnap one or both of Coulter's two daughters and ransom them back to him for a million each.

With an estimated worth of twenty million and triple that in shares of Coulter Air he could have paid easy. But the CIRA were fuck-ups and the peelers had heard about it and the whole thing had come to nothing.

But now Coulter's place here on the shores of Belfast Lough and the house in Donegal and the house in Tenerife were guarded by ex-SAS.

Of course, Tom reflected, as he drove up the gravel driveway, no one had expected the girls to be kidnapped by their own mother.

The early rain had passed and the sun was shining and the house looked particularly lovely today. It was an art deco affair, very unusual in Northern Ireland, where tastes in country piles were primarily for the

Gothic and the Georgian. It was pink and long and arched and fluted. Someone doing a profile years ago had compared it to the Hoover Building on the A40. Dick had been incensed by that of course until Tom had shown him a picture of the Hoover Building and explained that it was the finest art deco structure in England.

What really set Castle Coulter apart from other Irish country homes, discreetly hidden away in valleys or forest estates, was its cliff-top location. Set above Whitehead it commanded 360-degree views of Belfast, County Down, County Antrim, the entire Galloway peninsula in Scotland and on clear days the Isle of Man and the Mull of Kintyre further up the Scottish coast. Coulter even claimed that you could see England through a telescope but Tom knew that the curvature of the Earth made this materially impossible.

Not that the house needed additional superlatives: fourteen bedrooms, an indoor and outdoor pool, a squash court, a stable, a snooker room and the piece de resistance – an airstrip that could accommodate Coulter's six-seat Gulfstream 270.

As places to doss went, it would do.

Tom parked in his usual spot and walked up the marble steps to the front door.

He rang the bell and since Paul was at the hospital visiting his brother Mrs Lavery answered it.

"'Tis yourself, Mr E," she said, somewhat startled to see him at 7.20 in the morning.

"It is I, Mrs Lavery," Tom agreed with a forced grin.

"I believe he's not even up yet, Mr E, and neither is the Mrs for that matter."

"Really?" Tom asked, surprised, for Dick was an early bird.

"They were watching the telly last night till after two, so they were. Come in now, don't be standing there," Mrs Lavery said.

Tom walked into the spacious entryway. Here the marble gave way to Portland stone and little alcoves filled with beautiful statuary from eclectic corners of the world where heritage laws either did not preclude export or could be suspended for the right price.

To the left was the billiards room, to the right was a lounge; the upstairs could be reached by a gently curving deco staircase. That was where Tom needed to go. Dick's living quarters were on the first floor but Tom felt uneasy about going up to his boss's domain with him apparently still out for the count. Not even the domestics or the bodyguards went up there without a direct invitation.

"Do you want to wait with me in the kitchen? The living room's freezing, so it is. I'll make you a wee cup of tea," Mrs Lavery said.

"Make it coffee and it's a deal," he said with another fake smile.

Fake because smiling had become impossible since he had learned about the laptop.

"Aye, all right now, but I won't be making any of that Italian rubbish, it'll be Irish coffee or none at all," Mrs Lavery said, before turning bright pink with embarrassment. Her mouth opened and closed like the rainbow trout Tom had tickled on the Bann only last week before the trip to China.

Mrs Lavery's voice descended to a whisper: "By 'Italian rubbish' I wasn't casting dispersions on the new Mistress. You know that Mr E, I was, you know, attempting to be jovial about your good self, sir, so I was."

Tom touched one of Mrs Lavery's ham-hock arms, "I knew that. And before the thought even enters your head, let me tell you that Dick has said he wants you to stay after the birth of the little one because – and this is a direct quote – a growing reed needs a good feed for breakfast and Mrs Lavery does the best Ulster fry in the nine counties."

"Did he really say that?" Mrs Lavery asked, her eyes watering a little.

"He did indeed," Tom lied through his teeth.

They walked into the ante-room where Tom threw his raincoat on a leather sofa and tied his tie in the Tiffany mirror.

"Okay, let's get some of that coffee and we'll wait for himself to wake up," Tom said and followed Mrs Lavery into the large, spotless, modern kitchen.

Almost directly behind them in the kitchen garden on the other side of the cypresses, the old bugger was not only awake but now completely cognizant of the pair of them as their voices carried through the open window.

Although he had indeed stayed up until 2.00 a.m. showing Helena *Lawrence of Arabia* after it came to light that she not only had not seen the film but had never heard of it, he had tossed and turned all night before finally getting up, with zero sleep, at six, his normal waking hour.

When the dark behind the bedroom shutters had changed from black to brown to grey he had slipped out of the bed, padded onto the back stairs and down to the kitchen garden to have a smoke.

Mrs Lavery might not have known Coulter's whereabouts, but Bill, one of the two night guards, certainly did, and had informed Viv on the gate, who was just this second texting the information to Mr Eichel in case he was looking for him.

"There you go, Mr E," said Mrs Lavery, giving Tom a Nescafé with condensed milk and brown sugar, the way he took it. It was about the only taste he had acquired from his father. Tom's dad was a German who had come to Ireland at the end of the forties to help set up textile factories and who had then become an administrator in Ulsterbus. He had a married a local girl, had two kids and stayed until the Troubles really kicked off in the seventies when he had moved back to the peaceful life in Germany. Tom seldom visited his parents, or his sister who had gone with them.

Tom had been pressured to go into law and it was at Queen's that he had met Richard Coulter who, after knocking around South Africa and Australia for a few years, was studying business administration. Tom graduated with a first and became a junior solicitor but Coulter had got an even better first and was headhunted to join the prison service, the only booming industry in the mid-seventies.

Coulter had become the governor of a halfway house for wayward youth, getting the kids to stick to the straight and narrow and parlaying the publicity of that rare good-news story into meetings with government ministers. Coulter became one of Belfast's few entrepreneurs of the

Troubles, dipping his finger into many pies but especially bomb-damage contracting work, which was the pie to have in seventies Belfast.

The rest of Coulter's trajectory was a well-known and oft repeated tale: his construction firm had branched into the hotel business and the package holiday trade. He had then acquired a small start-up airline operating out of Belfast Harbour Airport and Glasgow's Prestwick: ten pilots, three Shorts 330s and a DC-10. Of course no one back in 1986 could have foreseen the monster which Coulter Air would become; by 2011 CA had a ninety-plane fleet, it serviced forty European airports, had three million passengers a year and had flights starting at nine quid, plus fees.

Tom hadn't been quite there at the beginning, but almost the beginning. When Richard was getting out of prisons and into construction Tom had come on board and agreed to become Richard's fixer.

None of it had really been legal work.

It was all dealing with paramilitaries.

A paramilitary negotiator was vitally important. No one could do business in Northern Ireland without making deals with (in order of importance): the IRA, the UDA, the INLA and the UVF. And after you'd paid off the paramilitaries, next you greased the union wheels and finally you grafted the cops. It was hard work and you had to creatively account for the revenue. (Not that the tax men ever pressed that hard – with businesses closing left and right Richard Coulter was one of the few people in the bleak north Belfast catchment area who could provide non-government jobs, and no one wanted to fuck with the golden goose.)

Tom had been Richard's man in Belfast and, until a few days ago, Tom thought that Richard confided everything to him.

That obviously was not the case.

Tom sipped his coffee, received Viv's text and texted Richard:

I AM HR. I KNW U R AWAKE.

Richard read the text and frowned. If Tom was here it was bound to be terrible news.

"Just give me a minute," he said to himself and then added: "I wonder how those limes are doing?" He slid open the glass door and stepped inside the closer of the two greenhouses. The smell in here was comforting: compost and expensive fertiliser. He turned on the mister and walked among the lime trees, looking with satisfaction at the budding fruit on all of them. They were hardy trees from the Basque country and next season if he wasn't dead or in prison he was going to have them transplanted outside to the dell next to the oak grove. Northern Ireland got few days of frost and up here on the very mouth of Belfast Lough the Gulf Stream came right in. Jack, his gardener, said they had a good shot at surviving and what Jack didn't know about horticulture wasn't worth knowing.

He gave a wee squeeze to the biggest fruit on the biggest tree.

"A thing of beauty," he said to himself.

He sat on the wicker chair he had set up in the corner, wiped condensation from the glass and looked out at the ashy North Channel, ashier Irish Sea and the blue waters of the Atlantic far to the north. The phone in his pocket was vibrating. It was another text from Tom.

"Fuck," Coulter said to himself. The guy was going to keep after him and Tom knew he liked to come out here.

Richard scurried to the west door of the greenhouse, opened it, bolted into the kitchen garden and, keeping low, ran to the protection of the hedge that separated the house from the airstrip.

He walked along the hedge and slipped behind the Gulfstream's hanger to the estate's high stone exterior wall now topped with razor wire since the CIRA's interest in him had become apparent.

He unlocked a steel gate and went into the sheep meadow behind his house – still technically his property but outside the grounds proper.

He walked along the salt trail to Bla Hole Lane.

It was windy and gulls were hovering over the cliff face, unbending and motionless in the stiff breeze coming off the sea. The clouds were scudding through the sky but in Scotland it looked clear. He looked back at the house and saw Tom's car parked in his usual spot.

Fucking Tom, what fresh nightmare was he bringing news of now?

As if on cue the phone vibrated a third time.

He ignored it and kept walking along the lane. He was dressed in his pyjamas, dressing gown, slippers and he hadn't any money but since he was de facto lord of the manor in these parts none of that mattered.

And his watch alone could be pawned for a plane ticket anywhere. With his millions in secure accounts in the Bahamas and Switzerland, he could bugger off right now if he wanted. He didn't need the publicity. He didn't need the notoriety. He didn't need Northern Ireland or his family. The thing that no one understood was that basically he was a loner and actually a bit shy. He had grown up in conservative, backwater 1940s Ulster. His da had been a teetotal, Gospel Hall attending, evangelistic, Paisley voting, dairy farmer. His ma was a sectarian nut who believed that the Bible was literally true and that everyone not of the Free Presbyterian Church of Scotland was going to hell, with a special place reserved for followers of the Bishop of Rome. Richard had five older brothers (three of whom had become missionaries in Africa) and no sisters, which meant that he had all the usual sibling hang-ups and quite a few idiosyncratic extras. And they were hardy stock, the Coulters – border warriors in Scotland and Ulster who had survived Flodden, Glencoe, Culloden, World War One and the Belfast Blitz during World War Two when a Luftwaffe Heinkel 111, miles off course, had dropped a bomb on their dairy.

Both of Dick's parents were still alive and of course they and all his siblings believed everything they heard and read about their youngest son and brother. One of the reasons he often had to go on those ghastly morning shows in person was to defend his good name. He'd even promised his ninety-two-year-old ma that he, a Free Presbyterian, would beat Michael O'Leary, a Roman Catholic, to become the first Irishman in space.

ND TO TALK, Tom texted.

"In a minute!" Richard muttered to the phone.

The lane next to his estate wall was muddy and the tractor divots were filled with rain water and it was some job not to get his slippers drenched. However after five minutes of careful manoeuvring he reached the main road and the village of Knocknagulla itself which was precisely six houses and a shop.

The shop wasn't yet open and the newspapers were piled up outside in bundles. He slipped a copy of the *Daily Mirror* from its pile. There was nothing about him in it, or the airline. Nothing in the *Express* or the *Star* and it wasn't until he got to the *Daily Mail* that he found his own name mentioned in an editorial from Peter Hitchens, something about how travel narrowed the mind rather than broadening it and how Coulter Air was responsible for British people seeing how rotten Europe was and how lucky they actually were to live in glorious Albion. Coulter read it twice and really it was almost a kind of compliment.

He put the *Mail* back on its pile.

His phone was vibrating yet again. He called Tom back. "Okay, okay, can you come and get me? I'm at the newsagents just down the road," he said.

The soles of his slippers were soaked in mud so he scraped them clean while he waited. He sat on the pile of newspapers, putting his slippers up on the Scouser- and Coulter-Air-bashing *Sun*.

Tom pulled in. He was driving the VW Touareg.

Richard got in the passenger's side. "What were you doing out here?" Tom asked.

"Reading the papers," Richard said. "Let's go for a drive. I don't want to go home just yet."

"Okay," Tom replied and turned left on the A2 which would take them north along the coast.

"So what's up?" Richard asked.

"Got a call from Sean this morning. His bloodhound has found your girl."

"Has he now?" Richard said, excited.

"Aye. I suppose yon boy knew what he was about after all."

"Of course he did. I liked him."

"Aye, well, I didn't. Fucking tinker."

"Would you listen to you. You're worse than Mrs Lavery," Richard said.

"It's not racism, it's fucking experience, mate. I've been crossed once too often."

"Okay, so where is she?"

"In a lake."

"Drowned?"

"No, no. Sean won't say exactly, which is sleekit of him, but our boy's got her trapped on one of those islands in Lough Erne. He's getting the ferry over at eight and whenever he makes a positive ID, he's gonna call Sean to inquire about further instructions."

Richard stroked his chin thoughtfully and looked furtively at Tom as they drove along the Larne Road through the village of Magheramorne.

"'Further instructions'," Richard muttered and looked at Tom, whose eyes were firmly on the road. Was Tom speaking in euphemisms?

"The instructions are easy. Get the laptop and the girls. One less problem to worry about. Two less problems. Tell him that. Get the computer, get the girls, give her something to remember us by so she keeps her big fucking mouth shut," Richard said.

Tom said nothing.

"Alex says you're doing the Radio 4 *Today* show tomorrow?" Tom said conversationally.

"Oh, I didn't know," Richard said. Alex was always scheduling things like that. He didn't mind as long as he could do them over the phone, he hated flying to London for these things. It was just more bullshit.

They drove south and began to hit the Belfast traffic.

"You know, we should discuss how this is all going to go down," Tom said.

"With Rachel?" Richard said, surprised that they were back to this again.

"At the very least we'll have to pay her a vast sum of money," Tom said.

"Pay her? Pay her what? She's lost. We found her. Her play's over. We're already paying the tinker half a million. Half a million. Jesus. Thank God for insurance."

Tom looked at Richard and shook his head. "For one thing, I'm almost certainly not going to claim this from the insurance company. The last thing we need is an investigation."

Richard looked at Tom incredulously for a moment before he conceded the point.

"Okay, so half a million of my money for my own kids. And you want us to pay more?"

They drove through Knocknagulla and Kilroot before Tom continued with his point.

"Richard, we both know that we can't let things end here. We're going to have to discuss how we keep Rachel quiet."

"What are you talking about? She'll be quiet. She keeps quiet about the laptop or we release the fact that she used heroin when pregnant with Sue."

Tom shook his head.

"She told me she'd thought about killing herself. She's erratic. Unbalanced. She's probably using drugs again. You really think we should bet our entire future on Rachel's continuing good will? It's luck and luck alone that she hasn't gone to the press already. The *Sunday World* is clearly gunning for you, mate. Did you read last Sunday's?"

"Of course I fucking did," Richard said, irritated.

"So there's that. And it's also lucky that she didn't, in fact, top herself."

"Why?"

"Because when you shoot yourself in the head someone generally calls the peelers and the peelers would have come and found the laptop and you my friend would be in a white-celled interrogation room right about now."

Richard's eyes narrowed.

"So you want to pay her off?"

Tom didn't answer.

Richard looked at him. Tom felt the look but kept his eyes on the road.

Richard shuddered. They'd been dirty over the years.

Very dirty.

But pay-offs were one thing. Doling out cash to paramilitaries, bullying unions, dealing with protection rackets and the worst political class in western Europe.

This though...

They sat in silence while Tom took them up the M5, across Belfast and onto the Bangor road.

They still hadn't said a word when they reached the Bangor marina, the biggest one in the north of Ireland.

There was a shirt and shoes rule but the security guard knew Richard of old and let him down onto the pontoon.

They went onboard and down below to the chart room.

His yacht, *White Elephant*, was modest. A fifty-five-foot twin masted ketch without a lot of prettying. Below decks was spacious enough and it was fully automated so that in theory you could sail her across the Atlantic solo. Not that Richard had. He'd gotten it for Rachel and they'd only ever been as far as Belfast Lough on calm days.

The last time he'd been out in it had been with her. Were the kids with him?

No, no kids. Just him and her.

It was late winter or maybe early spring, it was cold anyway.

Two, maybe three years ago.

They'd sailed over to the Copeland Islands. A big Russian tanker was anchored at the mouth of the Lough. "*Lena* – St Petersberg" it said on the stern. He remembered that. That and the trace of a hammer and sickle still painted on the ship's funnel. They'd put up the jib and the main and sailed past the massive anchor chain and sad men in wool caps had waved to them and she'd waved back and they'd given her some kind of intercourse symbol with their hands.

She'd laughed but when he'd launched the dingy, she'd been nervous. It's going to be okay, he told her and it was. The water dark and moody and the sky as blue as it ever gets out here. They'd rowed to one of the forbidden Copeland islands, off limits to people, and the fat seals had howled at them from the shore. The whole island was a nature reserve.

You had to have express permission before landing, but there was no one there to enforce the rule. They'd pulled the dingy up onto the shingle beach and everywhere there were birds and grass and wildness.

This is wonderful, she'd said and kissed him. And he had held her and thought that moments like these would be happening his whole life.

His whole life.

Richard fished in the *White Elephant*'s chart locker and produced a bottle of Glenfiddich. He looked around the interior of the forecabin until he found a couple of coffee mugs.

He poured two stiff measures and slid a mug across the chart table to Tom.

Richard drank and then Tom drank.

The boat rocked gently on the pontoon and the smell was sail cloth, paraffin and beeswax. Not unpleasant.

Tom looked at the time on his phone. It was nearly eight now. The ferry on Lough Erne would be up and running. They'd be hearing from Sean very soon. They had to make a decision.

Tom knew what that decision was going to have to be because he was on the laptop too.

If Richard was unable to get this done, then Richard was going to have to be bypassed…

There was no choice.

"That's why we brought Michael's man in, Richard, the Starshyna. You know why he's here," Tom insisted.

Richard poured them another measure and drank his at a gulp, but his friend and advisor left his drink alone.

"Well?" Tom asked after a minute.

"The girls are my number one priority. I love them, more than life itself."

I do not, Tom thought, but merely said: "He understands that."

Richard sighed and nodded. "Aye, okay, then," he said. "Do whatever you have to do."

chapter 13
the lady in the lake

I N THE BLUE LIGHT OF MACHINES, IN HOUSING ESTATES, IN GRIM flats and new apartments, in cottages, caravans, cars, faerie rings and sacred groves, Ulster was waking up.

Killian stood on the ferry, waiting. He had paid his pound and the ferryman was hoping for another customer to make this journey at least a little more economical.

The two of them stood there together.

Not talking.

Killian lit a cigarette.

The man lit a pipe.

Swans lifted into the air, disturbed by a noise to the south.

Joog, joog, joog, joog, joog, joog. A helicopter thudding over the bogland and the lake. The twin rotors of a Chinook, carving up the landscape and sending shivers through the sheep as it flew low along the border at a demented pace. A claw of blades and points, roaring under the thin saliva-coloured clouds. It was a throwback. It was rare to see an army chopper these days and the men instinctively ducked as it passed overhead showing its wide bottom that curved up in a slug of antennae and projectile flares. Well that's Rachel and everyone else on the island awake, you eejits, Killian said to himself.

But it was clipping so quickly that before the thought had barely jumped across his neurons, the chopper was gone, the double rotors singing and revolving in a lazy edit of diminishing noise and fuss and leaving behind a flap of birds and an embryonic stillness.

"Hey, you wanna get cracking?" Killian asked the man.

There were no other distractions and clearly no other passengers so the ferryman muttered: "Well, I suppose we'll give this a wee go."

He was a balding ginger bap in his late fifties. Pale with big orange freckles all over his face. He was dressed in heavy tweeds and a wool hat and he was sweating like a bastard.

He pressed a red button, a motor whirred, he turned a small wheel and the large flat-bottomed boat putted into the lough.

The fickle rain was easing now and compacting everything in front of Killian into a fine residue of comfort-drizzle. He stood there by a guard rail and drank from the ferryman's thermos filled with coffee, taking a sip from the thin plastic mug to quench his thirst. It tasted foully of the flaked pieces of white dye on the lid.

"Ta," he said and passed the cup back.

Out of the reeds a curlew rose and flapped into the air.

It was calm, lovely, like being inside a frickin' Yeats poem.

The ferryman started fiddling with a radio but he couldn't get anything and the hissing noise was upsetting the ducks.

"Could you cut that out, mate, I'm having a wee moment here," Killian said.

"No, I've got it. It's a geographic thing. A quirk. There's an array of cosmic forces that works through the exact way you position the aerial, only I can do it," the ginger bap said.

"Array of cosmic forces," Killian muttered to himself before Radio 3 came in clear as bell. He didn't know classical music but this was definitely Mozart or one of the biggies and Killian had to admit it actually improved the "moment".

The ferryman steered them around the swans, who had landed again, and after only a few minutes brought them to a rickety wooden jetty that could have done with a nail or two and a couple more tyres along its side.

The boat touched and Killian got off.

He had been expecting to immediately see the settlement but instead he found himself in a field with a deciduous wood beyond.

"Where do I go?" Killian asked.

"Ach, there's a wee path, follow it for about five minutes and you'll come to the village if you can call it that. Here, you wouldn't mind asking if there's anyone who wants to go back to the mainland would ya? I'll wait here a quarter of an hour and then I'll go back."

"No problem," Killian said and set off along a not terribly worn-looking trail through the grass.

Starlings flitted among the dandelions and bluebells, and red hawks were hovering in the air above the woods. There were butterflies everywhere: purple hairstreaks, dingy skippers, essex skippers, gatekeepers, clouded yellows.

It took him back to childhood walks with his da and uncle: apple scrumping, blackberrying, mushrooming. Of course they'd had the lore and knew every type of medicinal and edible plant.

All that knowledge that had gone with that generation – few traveller kids these days were interested and Killian wondered if any of them could even tell a chanterelle from a death's cap.

He entered the wood and was surprised to find himself in an old growth forest among ash, oak trees and giants ferns. Moss was growing on fallen trunks and the smell was close and heady. He hadn't gone a minute before he saw a deer staring at him from a hillock between the trees.

"Good morning," he said.

The deer watched him and when he passed by she bent her head and began nibbling at a wet mound of grass.

Through the trees he could see houses now, or rather wooden cabins, four of them close to one another with a cement block toilet and washhouse near the shore.

In one of the cabins a curl of blue smoke was drifting from the chimney stack.

He could hear children's voices.

They were fighting and then one of the children began to cry.

"You're bad!" a girl exclaimed. There was fistling ahead and a girl ran into the trees and stopped in front of him, open-mouthed.

She was about five with reddish curly hair, small pointy ears and greyish otherworldly eyes. She was wearing a grubby yellow dress and no shoes. She could have passed for Pavee easily.

"Who are you?" she asked.

"I'm Killian," he replied.

She nodded and then, remembering why she was running in the first place, she started to cry.

"What's wrong?" he asked, getting down on one knee in front of her.

"Everyone's always cross with me," she said with little sobs gultering out.

"Who's everyone?" Killian asked.

"Mum and Claire. Claire says I'm stupid, that I don't know anything. Not even the alphabet," the girl said.

"What's your name honey child?"

"Sue."

"How old are you?"

"Five."

Killian stood. He vaguely remembered something in the notes about "learning difficulties" for this one. Richard had also said that Rachel had taken heroin while pregnant with Sue.

She seemed fine to him though. Were kids in the straight world supposed to know their letters by five? It hardly seemed possible. Five?

"Come now, wipe those cheeks and I'll take you back to your mummy," Killian said.

"I don't want to go back, I want to go with you," Sue said, "you're the only one who's ever nice to me."

"I'll tell you what, I'll take you back but we'll go the long way round, is that okay?"

"Aye, okay," she said.

Killian offered her his big oversized paw and she slipped her fingers into it. From the outside this scene must have looked like that bit in Frankenstein when the girl goes walking with the monster. Of course, thought Killian, the monster brained her.

He led her back through the woods.

The deer unfortunately had gone but when they got to the meadow the butterflies were all still there.

"Do you see these butterflies?" Killian asked.

"Of course, I'm not blind!" the girl said, all eggy with him which he liked.

"Do you know any of their names?"

"They're just butterflies, so they are."

"No, no, no, they all have names. Three names. An English name, a Latin name, an Irish name. Would you like to know some of them?"

For the first time a little smile appeared on the girl's face. "Maybe," she said.

"Okay, see that big orange one with the white and black underside? Normally they don't survive the winter, can you guess what that one's called?"

"No."

"It's called a painted lady. What's it called?"

"A painted lady," Sue said.

"That's a funny name isn't it? Okay, now you see those wee pale blue ones?"

"Aye."

"They're called holly blues."

"That's easy. Holly blues. What's that white one?" Sue asked.

"That's called a wood white, it's not very interesting," Killian said.

"I like it!" Sue insisted.

"Ooh, now, look at that lemony yellow coloured one. I've only ever seen one of those once before. That's called a brimstone butterfly. In Irish we call it a *buiog ruibheach*, in France they call it the *le citron* which means the lemon. That's a good one to see, it's lucky."

Claire's eyes widened. "Lucky?"

"Uh huh."

"Now," Killian said briskly. "Tell me them all back."

"Painted lady, holly blue, a wood white and a brimstone butterfly which is the lucky one."

"Very good. Now you know something your sister doesn't. Let's go find them, shall we?"

Sue shook her head. "Tell me one more thing first."

Killian rubbed his chin. "You drive a hard bargain," he said, "Okay, you see that little bird in the tree. The one making all that racket?"

"Yes!" Sue said enthusiastically.

"That's a wheatear. It's a very special bird. Tough little guy. It flies further than any other small bird. All the way across the mountains and the ocean and the desert. Just a few weeks ago that cheerful little chap was in the middle of Africa. What do you think about that?"

"Cool! What's he called? A wet ear?"

"Wheatear. He's got a nice song too hasn't he? He's happy to be alive after all that perilous flying. Okay now young lady, let's go."

They held hands back through the wood until they came out once more at the cabins. The older girl was down by the water launching driftwood into the gentle current.

"Go play with your sister now, be careful of the water, and I'll talk to your ma," Killian said.

"I'll tell Claire about the butterflies and the wheatear."

"Do that but don't tease her with something you know and she doesn't."

"She does it to me," Sue said.

"Ach, you be the better'un now, run along bairn," Killian said.

Sue ran to her sister and Claire gave her a hug and they began to play with the wood together.

Their ma was further up the shingle beach having a fag and gazing out at the lough. Rachel hadn't seen him yet and he framed her in the TV set of his fingers to get a bead. Aye, she looked a good bit like her photo. Wilder now, thinner, but still very attractive. He took a picture of her with his camera phone to send to Sean later. She was wearing jeans and a baggy green jumper and black wellington boots.

He walked to the beach so she'd see him in her lateral vision and wouldn't be startled.

At the first crunch of his shoes on the shingle she turned.

"Morning," he said.

"Morning," she replied suspiciously.

"Is this an all-female preserve?"

"No," she said suspiciously. "Are you looking for Andrew? He's not here. He's down in Enniskillen for a couple of nights."

You shouldn't have told me that, Killian thought. Better to let me think that you've got allies everywhere.

She threw the cigarette into the lake. He walked closer. She had freckles on her cheeks and the scarlet traces in her hair were glinting in the sunlight. Her hands were very white against the green of her sweater, fretting with nowhere to go once the cigarette was done.

Her head turned and looked at the cabin. To late to run for your gun or your phone, Killian thought. He stopped a few feet from her and shifted position so that he was balanced on his back foot and more relaxed.

Her arms were crossed.

"What can I do for you, Mr...?"

"Killian," Killian said offering his hand.

She shook it limply and put the offending palm under her armpit.

"So what's this about?" she asked.

"Your husband hired me to find you, Mrs Coulter."

Her eyes widened momentarily.

"There must be some mistake, I'm not Mrs..." she began, but the words died on her lips.

She bent down and picked up her box of cigarettes. Her hands were shaking and when she put the fag in her mouth she couldn't get it lit. Killian cupped his hands over the end and lit it with his own lighter.

"How did you find me?" she asked.

Part of him wanted to tell her about her parents in Ballymena, but since the cops were undoubtedly going to blame that little episode on a mysterious burglar it wouldn't be wise. Sean would keep his mouth shut, Ivan would certainly keep his mouth shut and everyone else who knew the truth of the matter was dead.

"I intercepted a letter to your ma with this address on it," he said.

"I haven't written to my mum in years, I don't even know where she is. She's in England somewhere," she said triumphantly.

"I'm sorry. Not your ma. Your da. You were communicating with your father through his lodge in Ballymena. The RAOB. The Royal and Ancient Order of Buffaloes, I believe."

She shook her head and muttered "fuck" to herself.

She looked at him. "How much is Richard paying you? I've got money. I could pay you to go away for twenty-four hours," she said.

Killian nodded grimly. "How much?"

"Five grand."

"Mr Coulter is paying me half a million for finding you and the girls," Killian said.

"Half a million!"

"Half a million."

She shook her head and then she nodded again. "Ah, I see, it's not about the girls is it? It's about the laptop now, isn't it? I should have kept my stupid mouth shut. My bloody bake is always getting me in trouble. Richard hadn't even told Tom."

Now it was Killian's turn to look confused. "What laptop?"

She smiled and blew smoke into the air.

"He didn't tell you either?"

"Tell me what?"

"You think he'd pay half a mill to get these two wee skitters back? No way. Hardly spent any time with them when we were together. This isn't about that."

Killian's mobile rang.

"Excuse me, I have to take this," he said. "Hello?"

"Killian, it's Sean. What's cooking in the fair Lough Erne?"

"I'm getting everything sorted. Any word on Ivan? Is he on the road yet?"

"Not yet, no word. What about Rachel? Did you find her?"

"I found her."

"And the girls?'

"Aye."

"Excellent! What's your next move?'

"I'm working on it. I'll call you back, okay?"

"Keep me informed."

"I will."

Killian hung up.

"You told him that you'd found us," Rachel said.

Killian nodded. "Well I have, haven't I?"

Rachel smiled and squinted into the sun. "So the game's up, eh?"

"The game's up," Killian agreed.

"You're not the first he's sent."

"I know."

"He sent creeps the last time. You look okay. I'm actually relieved in a way. I was beginning to think I'd bitten off a bit more than I could chew, you know?"

Killian didn't understand. "You did bite off more than you could chew."

"No, that's not what I meant, I was beginning to think...well to tell the truth, I was beginning to think that he'd send someone to top all of us, you know?"

"What?" Killian said.

"I thought maybe he would just send someone to kill us. After I had spilled the beans to Tom about the Dell. That was a stupid move. My head wasn't straight. But who would have thought Richard would be such a control freak that he wouldn't even tell Tom."

Killian frowned. "What exactly was on this computer?"

"Would you like a cup of tea?" Rachel asked.

"No."

"Okay, no tea. Do you want to go for a wee walk and talk?"

Killian looked at his watch. It was 8.20. Ivan wasn't on the road yet, apparently, but there was no point taking any unnecessary risks.

"It'll have to be a *wee* walk."

"Just dander down the beach a bit."

"The girls?"

"They'll be fine. Both of them can swim and they know better than to go in the water," Rachel said. Killian nodded. "Girls! This is Mr Killian. I'm going to go for a wee walk with him, okay?"

"Mummy!" Sue shouted and came running over.

"What is it?" Rachel asked.

"He told me all about the butterflies and the wheatear bird that flies across the desert. But the butterflies are the best. There's the painted lady and the holly blue and the French one, the citron, except in Ireland we call it the brimstone butterfly," Sue said proudly.

"You've got a good noggin, well done," Killian said.

"Come on, we're ready!" Claire called and Sue ran back to her sister.

"You told her about butterflies?" Rachel asked.

"Aye, she saw me before the rest of you did and we had a wee chat about butterflies. Smart as a whip that wean."

"Sue's got learning difficulties. She doesn't even know the alphabet," Rachel said.

"I didn't learn the alphabet till I was twenty," Killian said.

"Are you serious?"

"Aye."

Rachel studied his face. Who was this big eejit? She bit her lip and offered him the cigarette box. They were Marlboro Lights too. He took one and lit it.

"Okay, so let's go for that dander and I'll talk you out of turning us in," Rachel said.

"Talk me out of half a million? It'll have to be good."

They walked along the beach, Rachel turning every few feet to check on the girls.

It was nice here. No boat traffic. Only birds. On the far shore it was bogland with a line of white heather like strands of grey hairs. They smoked and didn't speak.

Killian looked at the phone clock again. 8.30. Ivan was bound to be awake by now. Time to speed things up. "Love, if you're going to say something you better say it now, because I have to go; we have to go," Killian said allowing in some of the menace he'd been keeping back. After all, a man he knew was dead because of this woman, her parents were dead because of her, and he himself had had the shit knocked out of him because of her.

She was a junkie. She was a fuck up.

"Where are you from? If you don't mind me inquiring," she asked.

"All over," he said.

"What does that mean?"

"I'm Pavee."

"What?

"A tinker."

"Oh, you don't look it." she said.

They crossed a little stream by going over some stepping stones. She had trouble getting up the bank on the other side. "Give us a hand," she asked. He pulled her up onto the other side, their hands in each other's grip for a second. Rachel's knuckles were calloused but her fingers were strong. It was a small surprise.

"I know what I'll do. I'll take you back to the day I fled. I'll tell you the whole story, how does that sound?" she said, releasing her grip from his.

He nodded. "Just make it quick."

"What's the hurry? You've won, I've lost."

"I'm on my own schedule. I'm a busy man. Let's walk back and you can tell me what you like."

"Okay," she said, staring into his face with lovely green eyes that weren't going to work their magic with him, he told himself. "Okay, so we're in Donegal. That's where it happened. Richard was very generous with the divorce settlement. A hundred thousand a month and we could use the house in Donegal anytime he wasn't there."

"That is decent."

"I mean he'd bought us a wee place up in Cushendun, but we still liked to go to Donegal."

"Why? Cushendun's nice."

"The place in Donegal had its own beach, fields, the girls loved it. So we'd go there at the weekends when he wasn't using it."

They strolled past Claire and Sue, and Rachel rubbed Claire's head.

Killian's phone rang.

"Your boy says that Ivan just left," Sean said.

Killian looked at the phone clock. It was exactly nine. Earlier than he'd been expecting, but that would still give him a couple of hours.

"Okay," he said and hung up.

They walked to the cabin. It was a small, clean affair, much better than the places she'd recently been staying, Killian noted. On an island like this, in a nice place, she should never have sent that letter to her da. Could have holed up here indefinitely. Rachel put the kettle on and started cleaning a couple of mugs. "You were saying?" he insisted.

"About what?"

"Donegal."

"Oh yes, so we were in Donegal and the divorce was amicable and the sun was shining and Richard was great. Feeling guilty no doubt. He'd even sent flowers to the house for us, you know? All the latest DVDs for the girls."

"And then what happened?"

"Well, it was raining and the DVD player wasn't working and the girls were desperate to see *Toy Story 3*."

"Right."

"But the DVD player just wouldn't go. And Sue's screaming, as she does. Basket case that wee girl. So I start rummaging around looking for a DVD player and up in Richard's office I'm hoking through the drawers and I see this old laptop. I look at the side of it and sure enough there's a DVD slot."

Killian sat on the edge of the kitchen table. Outside the girls were laughing. Steam was pouring from the kettle. The hairs on the back of his neck were standing up. His skin was tingling. The old Pavee ladies would tell you that that's what happened when you could feel the future coming.

That was when you had to be on your guard and pay special attention.

Events from tomorrow were leaking back into today.

"And then what happened?" he asked slowly.

"Well," she began and he watched carefully as she poured the scalding hot water into a tea pot. "I brought the computer downstairs and plugged it in. Milk, sugar?"

"Both."

She poured milk and a teaspoon of sugar into the mug and handed the tea to him. She sat down on the sofa.

"Go on," Killian said.

"We watched *Toy Story 3*," she said.

Killian waited for her to sip her tea and when she did so, he sipped his. "That's it? That's some fucking anecdote," he said.

She put down the mug, went into a back room and returned with an old Dell 2800 laptop. She put it on the table and turned it on.

"After I put the girls to bed, I was tootling around on the laptop looking for Solitaire when I found this."

She dragged the mouse pointer onto an avi file. "I'm going to leave. You can watch it. Let me know when it's over."

She clicked on it and went outside. It was Super 8 footage that had been converted into a video file. It was a sex tape. Shaky camera. Roughly cut.

Men having sex with children. Girls, about thirteen or fourteen years old.

Something not quite right about them. He couldn't put his finger on it before finally noticing that they all had 1970s haircuts.

"What is this?" he asked her.

"Keep watching," she said from the cabin door.

The film continued and half a dozen men appeared in a scene with a blonde, vacant-eyed but enthusiastic teenage girl. Someone held up a card that said "Gang Bang Special!"

Killian recognised several of the men. The first was Dermaid McCann, *the* Dermaid McCann: famous paramilitary chieftain, ex-commander of the IRA and now a minister in the Northern Ireland devolved government; Dermaid was important, he had met President Obama and Prime Minister Cameron, he had condemned 2009's Real IRA bombings, thus preventing loyalist retaliation and saving the Northern Ireland peace process from going off the rails into civil war. Another of the men was now a well-known High Court judge. Another read the news for the BBC. The man holding the camera and whose face was caught briefly in a mirror was Richard Coulter. The very last shot in the footage was an even briefer glimpse of Tom Eichel.

chapter 14
the long goodbye

MARKOV WAS FEELING PLEASED WITH HIMSELF. IT WAS CLEAR that Killian – Bernie had found out his name from Michael Forsythe – was not going to call the police over the incident at the farmhouse. It wouldn't be in anyone's interest to get Mr Coulter mixed up in that, so clearly they were going to let the cops believe it was a robbery gone wrong or some such thing.

In a way he should be thankful to Killian for that.

He also should be thankful for the fact that his plays were so obvious.

Bush league stuff from twenty years ago.

His scheme had failed almost from the outset.

Markov had checked out of his hotel and gone to his car at six-thirty in the morning. He'd known as soon as he turned the key in the ignition that it had been sabotaged. He'd checked the exhaust pipe for obstructions and after an engine inspection he'd found the cut spark plugs in about twenty seconds.

What was more the skinny red-haired kid who was hanging around the parking lot and looking at him was transparently something to do with it.

He'd walked over to the kid and pointed the .45 ACP at his forehead and without even asking a question the whole thing had spilled.

Markov had tried not to yawn during the kid's story:

Private detective/stolen car/wait for you/spy on you/call him when you left.

The kid would have turned even without a financial incentive but Markov gave him two hundred pounds sterling anyway.

"Come with me," he said to the kid.

The rest was a picnic.

This country was easy. It was open territory. Not like the US where people were armed, cars alarmed and cops and cameras lurked everywhere.

He felt like a time traveller from the 2000s unleashed in the 1950s.

He found a 2008 Toyota Camry in the lot that he liked the look of. He cut glass from the window, opened the door, climbed inside, ripped the plastic cover from underneath the steering column, hot-wired it and went back to the kid.

"How long to drive to Dervish Island?" he asked.

"An hour and a half," the kid guessed.

"Okay, this is what you will do. Wait until nine o'clock and then make phone call as originally planned. Tell Killian I have just left."

"Okay."

"What time?"

"Nine o'clock."

"Perfect. If you fuck up, or try to cross me, I will search four corners of Earth until I find you. Your death will be long. It will be famous."

It was now seven in the morning, plenty of time to get to the island and take Killian by surprise. Plenty of time. And the money and the prospect of a .45 slug in the temple would keep the little shit honest.

Poor old Killian.

But that's the price you paid for being old and slow and stupid.

Markov drove the Camry to a gas station, bought a map, a sandwich and a Coke Zero.

It was a full service station and while the man pumped the gas for him, he bounced his rubber stress ball up and down into his left hand. It was cold and a little drizzly but he was wearing a leather jacket and his jeans and a thick T-shirt. He was okay.

He was feeling good.

He tipped the guy pumping gas five pounds and drove south out of Enniskillen into a boggy sort of woodland.

The rain came on and Markov flipped the window wipers and later he had to hit the fog lights as a mist rolled in from the shores of Lough Erne.

He found it quite pleasant.

He wound the window down, turned off the radio and his phone and breathed the air.

He liked it here. Las Vegas dried you out, wearied you, and after the initial excitement neither he nor Marina nor any of the locals ever went anywhere near the Strip.

This might be a good place to retire to.

Marina's father was a Volga German who had recently migrated to Berlin. They could probably get German citizenship through him and with German citizenship they could live anywhere in the European Union.

Maybe.

He'd see.

He drove on.

He had to consult the map a few times but he didn't get lost and he found first Upper Lough Erne and then Dervish Island easily.

When he pulled into the ferry parking lot he saw that the car Killian had stolen was still there.

An old Mercedes the kid had said.

Da.

He parked the Camry next to it.

There were no others cars. No people.

There was a small flat-bottomed boat which was obviously a ferry, but no attendant. If it had been Russia, he would have said that that ferryman was lying drunk somewhere and in America it would have been one of those holidays they were so fond of.

Markov pulled apart the starter wires and the Toyota's engine died.

He got out of the car and stretched.

He sucked the cool, moist, oxygenated air.

It felt good.

He walked over to the ferry.

There was a sign on a steering wheel that said "Back in 15 Minutes".

Markov nodded. He'd already been here at least ten minutes.

But what did it matter?

Killian and the girls weren't going anywhere. Not unless they all decided to swim for it.

He walked back to the Toyota, got inside, turned the phone back on, calculated the time in Vegas and called Bernie.

"Hi," Markov said.

"I've been trying to reach you, man," Bernie said, sounding annoyed.

"I turned the phone off."

"No, really, dude, you can't do that, this is serious."

Markov immediately thought of the bodies in the farmhouse.

"Is it the police?" he asked in Russian.

"Do you have a landline where we can talk?" Bernie said, continuing the conversation in Russian.

"No. Just tell me what it is."

"They got translators in Ireland. Let me email you."

"I don't have a terminal."

"What about your iPhone?"

"Didn't bring it. You told me it wouldn't work. You told me to buy a phone at the airport."

"Fuck.

"What is it? Is it about Marina? Is she okay?"

"She's fine. It's about the job. Jesus Christ. You need a partner or an assistant or something, you know? You do the job, they do all the fucking admin," Bernie said, still in Russian.

"Will you tell me what's going on?" Markov said.

Bernie gathered his thoughts. "Okay, where are you?"

"At the island. She's on an island in a lake. I'm at the ferry terminal. I'm here."

"How big is this island?"

"Small."

"And she's definitely there?"

"She is. That's the good news. The bad news is that so is our friend."

"He beat you?"

"Yes. It doesn't matter. There's only one way off the island and I'm standing at it."

"Okay, okay, brother, take it easy, relax."

"You're the one who needs to take it easy."

"Look, everything's changed. Let me get confirmation and call you right back, okay? Keep your fucking phone turned on."

"What's going on?"

"I'll call you in two minutes."

Bernie hung up.

Markov lit himself a cigarette.

A red Mazda pulled into the parking lot. The ferryman got out and walked over to the flat-bottomed boat and sat under an awning on the deck. He was a red-headed guy of about fifty. He had his raincoat on and a tweed cap pulled low over his head. He must have noticed Markov standing next to the Toyota but he didn't pay him any attention or say hello. He didn't seem interested in soliciting custom, which meant that he was obviously some kind of civil servant.

Markov's phone rang again.

"Are you there?"

"I'm here," Markov said.

"Okay, now listen to me. The job has changed. We're getting a lot more money, okay?" Bernie continued in Russian, just on the off chance that it might indeed help obscure things if the police ever did get a recording of this.

"Okay."

"This is what I want you to do. I want you to care of the wife. I want her to go on a trip? Okay? You understand me?"

"I understand you."

"You think you can do that?"

"Yes, I think so, I will have to take care of our friend too."

"Okay, then do that."

"Okay."

"Now listen, old friend. The kids are not to join those two on the trip. They are going to stay at home, do you understand?"

Markov nodded. Kill Mrs Coulter and Killian but spare the kids. Made sense. "I understand, take care of the wife and her friend, but not the children," Markov said.

"Exactly. Now the most important part of all of this is the computer. You must get the laptop. That's crucial."

"I know that already."

"I don't have all the information about their location or who they are with. I'll call you back in five minutes."

"Do that."

"One final question."

"Yes?"

"How much more money?"

"A lot more money, but you must get the computer, and you gotta leave the kids."

"Wait a minute, you don't want me to bring the children with me?"

"You can't bring them with you after you've just taken care of their mother, can you? Just take care of her and her friend and get the computer. Someone will leave an anonymous tip about the kids."

"Okay. I'll call you back when I've done my assessment."

"Do that."

Markov put the heroin syringes in one of his jacket pockets and the ski mask in the other. Kill the wife, kill Killian, leave the drugs paraphernalia in the cabin, get the laptop, leave the island, call the police. Some kind of drug deal gone wrong. A tragedy but not completely unexpected with her family history.

He got out of the car and walked over to the ferryman.

"Good morning," Markov said.

"Morning," the ferryman replied. "Will you be wanting a ride over now?"

"How many on island?" Markov asked.

"I'm sorry?"

"How many people on the island?" Markov repeated.

"At the moment?"

"Yes."

"Who are you after?" the ferryman asked suspiciously.

"I am supposed to meet friend. Tall man, you must see him?" Markov said with a grin.

The ferryman nodded. "Aye, I know the very bloke. Aye, he's over there."

"He is alone?"

"No. Andy's gone for a couple days but there's a woman over there too. Your mate and some doll with her two bairns. You just missed your mate by the way, I only just let the big fella over a wee while ago."

"On the island, only two adults, two children?"

"Aye."

Markov looked at the ferryman. Unfortunately he was a complication. He reached into his jacket, took out the Colt and shot the ferryman in the heart. The ferryman's eyes widened, blood foamed at his lips, he tried to speak and then he fell sideways to the deck, dead.

Markov called Bernie "It's on," he said.

"Good. I'll call you-know-who."

"No, don't call anyone until it's done. More professional that way."

"Absolutely. Of course. You just give me the nod."

"I will."

Markov bounced the rubber stress ball and pulled on the ski mask.

He got onto the odd, flat little boat, slid off the mooring ropes and pressed the red button which started the motor. It putted into life and he steered it away from the dock. When he was a good bit out into the lough, he shoved the ferryman's body into the water.

A thick fog was rolling down the lough from the sea, which suited Markov perfectly. If someone was on shore and looking out at the ferry they wouldn't notice something amiss until he was close to shore.

What was obviously the dock was looming out of the mist. Markov would need one hand on the steering wheel and one on his gun. He took out the ACP and pointed it at the shore and steered the boat towards a wooden jetty bedecked with tyres.

When the ferry was a few metres away, he killed the engine and let it drift. It bumped up against the dock with a dull concussion. He jumped off, tied the boat to a bollard and crouched with the gun perpendicular to his body.

He breathed, waited, stared into the fog.

No one was here.

He looked down the jetty into a sort of meadow. A path led through it towards a wood, but because of the mist he couldn't see anything beyond that.

No sign of houses or people.

Still, it was a small island, they couldn't be too far away.

He looked at his watch. It was 9.16.

Killian would only just have gotten the phone call from the kid. He wouldn't be expecting him for another two hours. What an asshole.

He listened and thought that he could just make out children's voices in the distance. Maybe he couldn't see the family but he'd certainly hear them.

He stood there for a moment and thought and checked the Colt and put it back in his trousers.

A lot more money, Bernie had said.

It was obvious why the laptop was worth "a lot more money".

Blackmail material.

It had to be blackmail material on Richard Coulter, one of the richest men in Ireland.

If they'd pay "a lot more money" as a finder's fee, they'd pay ten times that to get it back. Millions.

Maybe the smart move would be to take *everyone* out, get the computer, fly to Nevada and look at it with Bernie. They could cook up a completely new play together.

Markov took out his rubber ball and bounced it off the deck, catching it in his left hand ten times.

He thought about the incident in February 2000 in Grozny when the insurgents had captured an OMON officer and crucified him between the Chechen and Russian lines. He was a fucking OMON whose motto famously is "we give no mercy and expect none" so nobody wanted to risk their lives trying to save him, but his screams had gone on all night and he was young. He was yelling for his mother and begging his comrades to come and save him, but even in the dark they knew he was sniper bait and he'd probably been booby-trapped too. It took Captain Zhiganov's arrival just after dawn for anything to get done. Zhiganov had assessed the situation in fifteen seconds, asked for a bolt action rifle and killed the OMON with one shot. Nothing in the entire Battle of Grozny had impressed Markov quite like that. Hesitation was the enemy. Boldness was the key. Captain Zhiganov had been one of the few competent officers in that whole theatre and, of course, later he'd been recalled to Moscow and subsequently court-martialled for some ridiculous offence. But Markov never forgot the lesson. You acted fast. You took a decision and you acted on it. You didn't prolong suffering.

He nodded and put the ball away.

He would know what to do when the occasion arose. He would act and act decisively. He looked at his watch again. 9.18. Yes. It was time. He turned off the phone and holding the ACP one-handed in front of him he walked along a trail that he assumed led to the cabins.

Markov's instincts were correct.

Killian was not expecting him.

Far from it.

At precisely that moment four hundred yards away on the other side of the island Killian was looking at the blurry, cheap, disturbing images on Richard Coulter's laptop and having an epiphany.

Now it all made sense.

And not just about this case.

Cosmically.

The big picture.

Everything that had happened in the last twenty years.

Coulter's career.

Even the whole Peace Process.

In the 1970s the Northern Ireland Housing Executive was the biggest landlord in Europe. Huge contracts were being given out to build new houses, flats, apartment blocks – it was money in the bank. During the Troubles it was the only sector that was growing.

How had someone like Coulter who had run a halfway house – a fucking borstal – suddenly become a player in that racket?

How? Because he'd been part of a circle of paedophiles. *The* secret society of secret societies. More exclusive than the Masons, the Orange Order, the Order of Buffaloes or the Hibernians.

Secret men who protected one another and who knew it would never come out.

Not here.

Not in darkest Ulster.

Of course there had been scandals before, but this was Ireland, where everything was hushed up and the various tortures children had undergone in Catholic orphanages hadn't been revealed until 2008.

And in the north where secrets went to the grave...

Killian understood why Rachel had run.

Coulter was a twist. An evil man. And she couldn't let her kids near him. He had prostituted the kids in his care, not for money, but for access. Access to power, access to contracts, access to protection.

And he had taken part in the fun and games too, maybe as a willing participant, or perhaps to prove his bona fides, as a mutual protection against blackmail.

The four-minute film on the laptop was universal acid. It was the *Malleus Maleficarum*. It was poison.

It would destroy Coulter.

It would destroy Dermaid McCann. It would cripple Sinn Fein.

It would be a want-of-a-nail thing. A butterfly effect. McCann's whole wing of the party, the pro-ceasefire IRA, would have their limbs cut out from underneath them.

There were already dark conspiracy theories about McCann and why the IRA had embraced peace after twenty years of struggle. Some said that McCann was a British agent or that he had been bought off by the Americans. Maybe that was true, maybe not, but this, this would destroy his credibility. If this came out Sinn Fein would fall apart, the power-sharing executive would collapse, the Assembly would fail, Ulster would stagger back into the abattoir.

And Coulter? He'd be looking at several years and the loss of everything.

And then there was Tom of course.

Tom would be disbarred, disgraced.

Tom might be real engine behind all of this.

Killian's head was pounding.

This is why we shrink from people. We Pavee. Why we don't want their talk. Their hypocrisy and lies. We don't want them breathing near us. Humans were never meant to be this close to one another. We weren't meant to be in buildings. Architecture is based on a gigantic lie. Cities. We huddle for security, closer and closer until, like now, we are on top of one another. Stuck in these glass and steel and brick structures with all these other confused, unhappy people.

Rachel came back into the room. Her face was white. She was crying.

Killian put his arm around her. Coulter, you fuck. It had never really been about the kids had it? It had always been about this. That was why Tom had hired Ivan. Coulter had finally told him the truth.

"You see?" Rachel said. "You see?"

Her voice sounded like it was coming from the bottom of a ravine.

Killian nodded and closed the laptop.

"Did you watch the whole thing?" he asked.

"No. When I saw McCann and Richard that was enough. I had to get out of that house, I had to get the girls away from him, you see that, don't you?"

"Aye."

"I mean, what else could I do?" Rachel said.

Killian stood and took big gulps of air. "I don't know. Go to the newspapers? Go to the *Sunday World*? The British tabs?"

"Are you kidding me? I'd be on an IRA death list immediately. You see who that was?"

"I saw."

"They'd kill me. This is big. They've been protecting him this whole time," Rachel said.

Killian shook his head. "They've been protecting each other, haven't they? McCann and Coulter. Catholic and Protestant. Player and politician."

"It's fucking sick. It's sick. I wasn't crazy, was I? That is Dermaid McCann, isn't it?"

Killian nodded. "Oh aye. Without question."

"And then there's Richard himself."

"Did you watch the whole thing?"

"No. Why?"

"At the very end, I think that's Tom Eichel on there too."

She gasped.

Tom.

"If Tom went down he'd make sure I'd never see the kids again. He'd use the drugs against me. He'd destroy me."

"How did you get mixed up in drugs?"

She shook her head. "I'm just a wee girl from Ballymena. I didn't know that world. Richard's world. That lifestyle."

"Smack wasn't it?" Killian said trying to recall the notes.

"It was just marijuana at first, then cocaine, then the bad stuff. That's the way of it. We had so many fucking hangers on. It was like Michael Jackson when Richard became a media star. Of course Richard found out and hit the roof. I was pregnant. He went fucking mental at first but then he got the job done. He got me into Crossroads in Antigua. Eric Clapton's place. It worked. I went off everything for a while. But then you relapse. I made terrible decisions. Look at poor Sue. Learning difficulties, behaviour problems, you name it, it's my fault."

Killian looked at Sue and Claire playing together by the water. Both of them were happy and Sue, at least to him, seemed fine.

"I don't believe there's anything wrong with that girl except perhaps overly high expectations," he said.

"It doesn't matter, does it? Social services would never give me custody if they found out what I had done. I'd lose the kids and the IRA would put me on their fucking death list. What else could I do but run? Get them away from him and run."

Killian shook his head. "No, a better play would have been to leave the laptop where it was. Pretend you'd never found it. Or, if you'd wanted the evidence, copy the files onto a disk. He didn't need to know that you knew."

"But then I'd have to go on sharing custody with him! I'd have to see him! I'd have to pretend!" Rachel said indignantly.

Killian looked at the hut and the beach and the mist rolling down the lough shore.

"But you wouldn't have to live like this, you'd be safe and your kids would be safe..." *and your parents would still be alive*, he almost added.

"Besides, I wasn't thinking straight. I'm clean now. I've been clean since those men came for me. This time it's for real."

Killian nodded. He hoped that was the case. A corrupt father, a junkie mother, dead grandparents, the kids didn't have much hope, did they?

"What would you have done?" Rachel asked.

"You should never have taken the computer," Killian said dourly. "You grew up in Northern Ireland, you know the rules: you don't talk, you leave secrets well alone."

"I panicked. I had to get out of there. To think, that man did those things – I just got the kids and I ran."

Killian shook his head, smiled at her compassionately. "You didn't panic. You took it on purpose. You were thinking blackmail. You were thinking you could use it as a chip. It was stupid. You should never have done it. It was proof that you knew. Richard tried to play it close for the first few weeks but now he's told Tom."

"I told Tom. I called him. I wasn't thinking straight."

"Regardless, now Tom knows and Tom's ruthless. He sees right through all the bullshit. He has sent a man to silence you."

Rachel look frightened. "You?"

Killian shook his head. "Not me. My job was to find you. What time do you have?"

"Nine-fifteen."

"We've got about an hour. We better get moving."

"Where?"

Killian walked to the water's edge and examined the still, green water. What are you talking about, mate? he asked the reflection. *Go somewhere?* There's no going anywhere. Your job is to find the kids and make a phone call. Sit back, do not pass Go, collect half a million quid.

The reflection looked uneasy. But Ivan was going to kill her and where was there to go?

Not a hotel. Not a motel. Credit cards, traces. Certainly not Carrick. Ivan had been there once already.

It didn't seem doable. He'd be jumping off this island, but still be trapped on the big island of Ireland.

The whole situation was bollocks.

Killian looked at the phone clock again: 9.16. Ivan was getting closer by the minute.

In the distance he could hear a tapping sound.

His head was throbbing.

What was that noise?

A woodpecker? No. There never was such a thing in Ireland. Someone chopping a tree. Nah. The bilge of the ferry? Not that either.

He looked across the lough at the little car park beyond. Three cars over there now. The Merc and two others. He squinted. And the ferry wasn't there. And it wasn't on the water either.

It had brought someone over.

And then he knew.

Ivan had stroked him.

He'd turned the kid.

Paid him more money or put the fear in him.

He was here, right now, on this island, "Bouncing his rubber ball up and down on the dock at the terminal stop," Killian said, recognising the sound.

He was here and he was going to kill everyone. He was going to kill everyone and make it look like he – Killian – had done it before turning the weapon on himself.

"No Sean, I'll be fine, I don't need a gun for a wandering-daughter job," Killian said ironically to himself.

He ran to the girls and pulled them to their feet.

"Come on lasses, we're leaving," he whispered.

"Where are we going?" Sue said loudly

"Ssshh!" he said.

Rachel looked at him "What is it? What's wrong?"

Killian put his finger to his lips.

"There's someone coming," he hissed. "Very dangerous, I don't have a gun."

"I do," Rachel said. She ran into the cabin and returned with the laptop and a Heckler and Koch 9-millimetre wrapped in a freezer bag.

Killian took the gun, checked the mechanism and bent down to talk to Sue.

"Sweetie, you're going to have to be very quiet. What's the highest you can count to?"

"Fifty," Sue said.

"That's brilliant. I want you to count to fifty in your head, okay, sweetie?"

Sue nodded enthusiastically.

Killian turned to Rachel and Claire. "He's coming to kill us. We have to get out of here now."

"Do as he says," Rachel added and they ran to the woods keeping low to the ground. They hadn't got twenty feet when they saw Markov walking down the trail.

He was wearing a balaclava, holding his pistol in front of him and walking cautiously towards the cabin. If he had looked to his right just then he would have seen them, despite the trees and the mist.

"Everybody down," Killian hissed and they ducked behind an elm tree.

They lay on the ground until Markov had passed their spot.

Killian peeked above a low branch and saw Markov's back entering the campsite.

He was a pro. It would take him only seconds to scope it.

"Now we run," he said and picked up Sue.

She was heavier than he'd been expecting but Killian was a big man. He could carry two of her without much difficulty.

They ran through the woods and got to the butterfly meadow before they heard Markov yell behind them.

Killian turned, Markov was running, but they had a hundred yards on him.

"Keep going!" Killian yelled.

Branches were cracking under their feet.

"He's shooting!" Sue said.

"It's just the tree branches!" Killian assured her.

"He has a gun. We're sitting ducks!" Rachel said.

"He'll never hit us at this range and he knows it," Killian said and hoped that that was the case.

They ran through the meadow and reached the jetty.

"Everybody get on board," Killian said.

He loosed the ropes and pressed the start button. The engine sputtered into life. He looked at Rachel. "Head for the shore. Don't wait for me."

"What are you going to do?" Rachel asked.

"I'll give our Russian friend something to think about."

He boomed off the little boat with his foot and it started moving into the water.

Killian crouched behind an oak tree and waited for Ivan.

One gut shot would take that motherfucker out.

He wait and lined the sight along the barrel.

But Markov was a paratrooper who had fought the Chechen mujahideen.

That was a school where you learned or died.

Frontal assaults got people killed.

He didn't know if Killian was armed or not, but he had to assume that he was. And Markov had risked too much and had too much to live for.

Killian looked into the gathering mist and saw no one.

"Where is he?" Killian muttered.

His nerves were jangled.

He was tense.

Fog was still drifting across the meadow but visibility wasn't that bad.

He counted out seconds and made it to 30 Mississippi.

"Where are you, dickhead?" Killian shouted.

Nothing.

"Come on, I'm waiting for you," Killian said.

Markov wasn't interested in Killian.

The personal was the realm of the amateur.

The computer, the wife, were on the boat. Killian was nothing to him. Less than nothing.

He ran to the left, off the meadow, into the bog grass and then the reeds that led to the lough. He took off his leather jacket, zipped it and ripped the laces out of his sneakers. He tied off the jacket arms and folded it in on itself. He shoved the gun down the back of his jeans. It would get wet, but it was a Colt .45 ACP, a mother of a gun, blowing people's heads off since 1911. It would work.

He waded into the reeds and pushing the jacket in front of him he launched himself into the lough using the jacket as a float and kicking with his feet.

The water was warm, calm, the distance to shore wasn't a kilometre.

They had a start on him, but the lady couldn't steer for shit. The ferry was zigzagging across the gap and every time she corrected her mistake it cost her more time and distance.

Markov was eating up the metres in a straight line.

He felt a little sad. It was just going to cost him time, it was going to cost her her life.

"Where are you, eejit?" Killian said and couldn't escape the feeling that he'd been made a monkey of yet again.

He walked back into the meadow.

Butterflies, mist, no fucking Ivan.

Aye, he'd been stroked.

Twice in one day.

He turned and stared at the lough water and there he was, sure enough, two hundred yards from the shore.

"Christ!" Killian said.

Ivan was like swimming like a bloody torpedo.

Like someone who'd been in the friggin' Olympics – or who'd had special forces training.

He was going to catch her. He was going to climb up on the ferry and shoot her and he had taken her only defence, her pistol.

"Rachel!" Killian screamed, his voice carrying all the way down Lough Erne.

She turned to look at him.

"The Russian, he's in the water behind you!"

He pointed to where the assassin was swimming.

He was now more than a third of the way across the lough.

And she was still halfway to the shore.

Killian not only couldn't swim but didn't know the first thing about it.

He was damned if that was going to stop him. He ripped a tyre from the side of jetty, threw it into the water, jumped on top of it and started kicking with his feet. As long as the tyre was underneath him he was pretty sure he couldn't drown.

The tyre was steady, the water still, but even so he was terrified.

On the ferry Rachel saw Killian launch himself into the lough.

It was too late.

The Russian was going to catch them.

After all this. "No," she sobbed.

Claire started to cry.

"Is he going to kill us?" Sue asked calmly.

"Help us! Somebody help us!" Rachel screamed at the car park, but there was no traffic on the water or on the road.

"Somebody help us! Help us! Please!" she screamed till her lungs were burning.

She urged the boat faster but it was at the limit of its capacity.

"Somebody help us! Please!"

"Mummy, what's happening?" Sue was asking. "Mummy!"

The ferry was barely over halfway to the mainland and the Russian was fifty metres away. He'd be here in seconds.

She could see the assassin's face.

He was in his thirties with blue eyes.

There was a coldness in those eyes.

He'd be clinical, emotionless, like a surgeon.

She turned to Claire. "Take the wheel and keep steering for the shore. Don't stop."

She pulled off her sweater and grabbed one of the orange life rings from its hook and shoved it inside the sweater. She tied the arms underneath the life ring so that it was taut.

She went to the back of the little ferry and waved at the Russian.

"Hey you! You!" she yelled.

Markov looked up at her.

"You don't want us. You want the money? Right?"

She picked the laptop from off the deck.

"This is what you want, isn't it? It's all here. This is what he's paying you to get. Right? Look what I'm doing."

She put the life ring with the sweater stretched across it in the water. She placed the laptop on top and launched it off into the lough like one of the girls' homemade rafts. The eddy took it immediately, spinning it away into the current.

"There it goes!" she said to Markov.

Markov watched the life ring separate from the ferry almost as if it had a motor. Killian watched too. He wasn't surprised at the speed. Upper Lough Erne rises in the high bog of central Ireland and flows north into Lower Lough Erne and finally to the Atlantic and when the tide was on the turn, the current could be very fast.

Markov swam in place for a beat, two, three...

It was absurd.

Farcical.

His orders had been to kill the woman and take the computer. He had not been instructed regarding the priorities of the mission. And like an idiot he had not asked.

He looked at the woman on the ferry.

He looked at the life ring.

Further clarifications would be not be forthcoming. In any case his phone by now was soaked. Undoubtedly ruined.

He had to make a split-second decision.

The ferry with the wife and kids was reachable.

The laptop, drifting north at a surprising velocity was also reachable.

But he could only make a play for one.

Which one?

What would Bernie do?

What would Marina want him to do?

The wife and kids would probably cause him nightmares down the road.

As the wife herself said, it was the computer that contained the incriminating evidence.

That's where the money lay.

He abandoned his pursuit of the ferry and started swimming for the laptop.

It was moving fast, but now he that he too embraced the current instead of swimming across it he moved just as quickly.

In ten strokes he had cut the distance between it and himself in half.

Killian watched him give up the pursuit.

Ivan had out-thought him and she had out-thought Ivan.

She was a woman of rare quality was Rachel Coulter.

She had quit drugs. She had protected her weans. She was smart. She was fast.

She was worth saving.

He kicked out after Rachel and the kids, moving his legs up and down in the water. He kicked and he went forward. It wasn't rocket science. He wasn't sure how you were supposed to stay afloat without a tyre, but people obviously did it. Dogs did it. Even cats did it and they hated water more than Pavee.

Rachel saw him. She grabbed the wheel from Sue and steered the ferry back towards him.

"Go to shore!" he yelled at her for Markov wasn't far enough away yet for his liking.

"No, I'm coming for you," she said.

He and the ferry converged and then bumped into one another. For a horrifying second he thought that she'd inadvertently killed him, dislodging him from his tyre, sending him without a buoyancy aid into the terrifying briney, but it was only for a second. Three pairs of hands pulled him sputtering onto the deck.

He stood and smiled.

"Thank you," he said.

"You're welcome," Rachel said.

Killian caught his breath, reached behind Sue's ear and produced a gold two-pound coin.

"Where did that come from?" Sue asked.

"Your ear," he said.

He did the same with Claire, who took it with a good deal more scepticism.

"What now?" Rachel said.

"Shore," he said.

"I think Claire steers better than I do," Rachel said.

Claire took over and did indeed do it better than her mother. "The jetty?" she asked.

"Aye, keep going love, you're doing great."

"You launched the laptop on a life ring?" Killian asked Rachel, impressed.

"It worked. He chased it, not us."

Killian grinned. The Russian was a bobbing presence four hundred yards to the north. The laptop was an orange blob fifty yards beyond that, almost out of sight.

"Let him have it," Killian said.

He could already foresee the double cross coming and smiled at the complications that this would cause Tom Eichel and Richard Coulter.

But it was not to be.

A fast moving cigarette boat was gunning up from the Lower to the Upper Lough probably on its way to the Shannon canal. The big purple-painted, high-sided boat, was easily clipping twenty-five knots.

It missed Markov by ten boat lengths but the wake knocked him about a bit and of course overturned the life ring.

The laptop and all its secrets joined all the other secrets at the bottom of Ireland's holiest lake. Markov screamed in frustration just as the ferry touched the jetty on the mainland side.

"That's a crying shame," Killian said with a grin.

They piled into the Mercedes just as rain began to pour heavy and cold out of the low clouds.

He flipped on the windscreen wipers and the lights and drove onto the B127.

"I can't believe we made it," Rachel said.

Killian safetied the Heckler and Koch and passed it back to her. She put it in the Mercedes' spacious glove compartment.

"And all without a single shot being fired," he said with satisfaction.

At the junction of the B127 and the A34, he took the A34 road east.

"Where are you taking us?" Rachel asked, a furrow of suspicion forming between her eyebrows.

"Somewhere you'll be safe," he said.

She looked at him and she looked at the girls and then back at him. This is my whole universe and I'm giving it to you, she seemed to be saying.

"I give you my word," Killian said. She looked into his slate-grey eyes, which told her that where he was from, this actually meant something.

"How are you doing back there, girls?" Killian asked.

"We're doing okay," Claire said bravely.

"Where are we going now?" Sue asked.

"Do youse like animals?" Killian wondered.

"What sort of animals?" Sue asked.

"Horses, goats, dogs, cats, chickens, donkeys," Killian explained.

"I like horses," Claire said.

"I like horses too," Sue added.

"And I like horses," Rachel echoed.

"Well then ladies, I think you're really going to like this place," Killian said.

chapter 15
after the equinox

KILLIAN KNEW ABOUT ISLANDMAGEE OF COURSE, BUT FOR SOME reason in his forty years walking the old sod he had never been there. It was an isolated part of Northern Ireland but they weren't that far from the ferry port Larne or from Belfast, or indeed from Coulter's main house in Knocknagulla.

The best that you could hope for was that Tom Eichel and Dick Coulter wouldn't think of looking right under their noses.

The Pavee weren't exactly in the business of concealing their movements either. It had only taken him two phone calls from a hotel lobby in Enniskillen to find out where the travelling clan had moved to now, although the last phone call had been entirely in Shelta, a language neither Coulter nor his agents would have any knowledge of.

Islandmagee was one of a dozen campsites in Ulster that the diminished band of the Cleary-McKentee Pavee shifted to when they had either exhausted the resources and patience of the locals in their last camp or when everyone just felt that it was time to move on to somewhere new. This was never done by a vote or a meeting, just a growing sense that the time was right to go.

Islandmagee, like the other places in the Pavee Dreaming, was a holy place: in Irish it was known as *Oilean MhicAodha*, Aodh being one of the many sea gods of the Ulaidh. It was a particularly resonant holy site, not unlike Newgrange or Tara or Emain Macha; in the *Annals of the Four Masters* it was recorded that Neimhid of the Long Arm led the very first colony into Ireland through Islandmagee in the year of the world 2859, founding a settlement there called Rath Cimbaeitchn Seimhne.

In popular mythology too Islandmagee was a haven for the ancient peoples and the Wee People and it also had a reputation for witchcraft – in 1711 a local woman was pilloried in the last such witch trial in Irish history. You could see why the Pavee would be attracted to such a place and when a sympathetic farmer had let them camp on his land at Brown's Bay in the northern part of the peninsula, it had become a new stop on their travelling route.

Killian hadn't been to this particular part of the Pavee sacred way, but as a boy he had spent much of his time on the road, mostly in the South of Ireland and England. Indeed he always remembered with a shudder the two unpleasant years in the early eighties when he and his clan family had been forced to live on a bombsite in north Belfast, as a way of making sure the children went to a local school and the adults claimed unemployment benefit from only one dole office.

Of course none of the children ever had gone to a school and the adults still claimed dole from two or three offices, and finally after a couple of sectarian/racist attacks that got mentioned in the English newspapers the government had relented, offering those Pavee who wanted council houses a place at the top of the list and those who wanted to move on in their caravans a chance to move on.

Neither option had appealed to Killian, who had by then reached his seventeenth birthday and who went first to London and then New York to offer his expert car thieving and chop-shop skills to people who would appreciate them.

But over the years, more and more of the Pavee had taken the offer of council homes and as the older population died the number of travellers who actually travelled shrank.

Of the 15,000 Pavee in Ireland, perhaps only two or three thousand nowadays were truly nomadic.

Killian had no idea what to expect when he arrived at Brown's Bay. Would there be five caravans or fifty? Would there be young people or just oldsters? Would anyone remember him? Would they welcome him or turn him away? Would *she* be there? Or had she long since moved to England or America?

The drive from Fermanagh to the coast of County Antrim had taken all day and as they arrived the sun was setting on the vernal equinox which marked the beginning of the quarterly horse fair.

Killian had forgotten about that.

But he had promised horses and although in the old days you might have seen hundreds, now that meant, at the very least, a few dozen, which was more than enough to excite both girls as they pulled up the B560 and parked in the large car park at Brown's Bay.

There were hunters and ponies aplenty in muddy fields and the auction ring and some even on the beach where they were getting a free fetlock bath in the surf. The actual horse auction was only one part of the fair, there was also a chip van, an ice-cream van, a couple of stalls selling handicrafts, a fortune teller and a mini carousel for the kids.

The traveller settlement itself was a line of small white caravans facing the beach. Fourteen caravans, he counted, which was a couple fewer than he'd been expecting.

Killian drove through the car park and parked the Mercedes in the field where the Pavee camp was located.

"Are we here? Is this it?" Rachel asked.

"This is it," he said.

He got out of the Merc, opened the back door, and gave Claire and Sue two more pound coins each.

He looked at Rachel.

"Okay for them to get an ice cream each?" he asked.

"I don't see why not," she said.

"Can we go see the horses?" Claire asked excitedly.

"Yes, but be careful of them and don't touch them and stay where I can see you," Rachel said.

"Okay," Claire said.

"Keep an eye on your sister, and stay where I can keep a direct eye on you," Rachel emphasised.

The girls ran off.

Rachel turned to Killian. "What is all this?" she asked with a little smile on her face.

"A horse fair."

"I can see that, I mean, where are we? What are we doing here?"

"We're on Islandmagee. We're among my people. I'm going to see if we can stay for a few days. We'll be safe here," he said.

"Oh," she said and nodded absently.

"We'll be safe here," Killian said again.

"Yes," she said.

Her eyes were red, distant.

"Are you okay? Are you hungry?"

On the journey they had only stopped once at a Kentucky Fried Chicken and Rachel had eaten nothing.

"I'm okay," she said.

"Look, it's been a traumatic day for all of us, we need food and rest. You should try and eat something."

Rachel nodded. "I could do with a cup of tea," she said.

"That's the spirit," Killian said. "Now, I'm going to see if there's a spare caravan where we can stay."

Rachel nodded. "I'll go down to the beach. I'll keep an eye on the girls from down there," she said.

"Okay."

She walked over the field and onto the Brown's Bay beach. It was a nice beach, sandy and long and protected from the swells on two sides by the headlands.

She took off her shoes and rolled up her jeans and let the water coat her toes.

Killian grinned. He was right about her. Search for her near the sea, boys, that's where she's happiest.

Rachel looked back at Killian and smiled at him.

She was grateful that he had done this. That he had taken over. She was so tired of all it.

She needed someone to confide in. Someone who would carry her burden for a while. Killian seemed to be that man.

They had a built a small bonfire on the beach and were burning driftwood and kelp. It smelt good and she walked over to it to keep herself warm and to be nearer the girls who were in the queue at the ice-cream van.

The sun had set over the Antrim hills and the sky had turned scarlet and persimmon. Scotland was already in silhouette and she could see the many lighthouses that ran along the Ayrshire coast and each of the glens along the Antrim coast was a different colour.

Blue. Indigo. Violet. Green.

And the water between the kingdoms glass. A silver grey cistern on which no ships moved.

Rachel looked at the sky and spaces between the stars – into that deep forever – and cried with relief.

She let the tears flow and flow and went over to the girls and joined them in the queue.

"What do you want, love?" the ice-cream man asked.

"What you recommend for these two?" she said.

"Ach, there's only one thing. A 99 with chocolate sprinkles," the ice-cream man said with finality.

"Okay, three of those."

She watched him make it.

Soft-serve ice cream in a cone with a Cadbury's chocolate flake shoved down the middle and then the ice cream dipped in chocolate sprinkles.

All three of them walked to the beach. A man with a donkey appeared beside them and asked Claire if she wanted a "toty wee ride on it". Claire stared at her mum with a guilt-inducing tremble in her lower lip.

"Can I, Mum?" Claire asked.

"Ach, she's a quare aul girl, easy with the bairns," the man said, patting the donkey on the forehead.

"Okay," Rachel said.

"And me next," Sue demanded.

"Sure," Rachel agreed.

Killian walked along the line of caravans, negotiating his way among stray dogs and cats and even chickens who you would have thought would have been in their run by this time of the evening.

There were kids running around and although most of the men would be having a barney over at the horse auction, Killian knew that he was being watched by several pairs of adult eyes from behind net curtains.

Five hundred years of prejudice had taught the Pavee to be on their guard against strangers.

He walked to the first caravan and knocked on the door.

A girl of about twelve answered it. She was dirty and holding a screwdriver in one hand and the air-intake of a motorcycle in the other.

"Hello," Killian said.

"Hi," the wean replied.

"What's that, a two-stroke?"

"Look, I'm busy, what do you want ya big yin?" the girl demanded in a Glasgow accent so broad that it would have made Colonel Pickering think twice about a wager with Professor Higgins.

"I'm looking for the camp boss," Killian said.

"That would be me," a voice said behind Killian.

He turned.

A young man wearing a green trench coat covered with badges and wild flowers. Underneath he had on a navy blue jumper, brown corduroy trousers, combat boots and a long striped scarf. He was pale-skinned with unruly black hair and a pointed beard. He was about twenty-four or twenty-five which would be about right.

"Who are you?" Killian asked in Shelta.

"I'm Donal. I'm the clan chief," Donal replied in the same tongue.

"You're the king?" Killian wondered.

"We don't use that terminology anymore," Donal said.

"Okay. What happened to Dokey McConnell?"

"Dokey's been dead three years now, and the chief before me was topped down on Muck Island a while back. It was an incident. Made the TV. You may have heard about it."

Killian hadn't heard about it, but it didn't surprise him. Travellers died early and usually in violent ways.

"Now, friend. Who are you?" Donal asked.

"I am Aidh Mac an tSaoi of the Light Hands of the Clan of the North," Killian said.

Donal stroked his beard and nodded. "Aye, I know ya. Or of ya. You'll be wanting Katie then?"

"She's here?"

"Yes."

"I'll talk to her presently, no doubt, but I wanted to ask you for your help."

Donal's eyes narrowed. "What sort of help?"

"I've got a woman with me and two kids; we're on the run from the peelers, we need a place to stay for a few days."

Donal didn't hesitate. "You can stay in my rig, I'll bunk with Dovey Carmichael."

"It's only for a few days, mind, until we get things figured out."

Donal laughed. "It doesn't matter. Stay a year and a day if you like. You need money?"

Killian shook his head.

"Third one in, give me fifteen minutes to move my stuff. Weans ya say? Boys, girls, both?"

"Two girls, Seven and five."

"Okay. Give me a few minutes. It's that bluey white one over there."

"I'm really grateful," Killian said, touched by the easy hospitality of this world that he had left so long ago.

"Nay worries mate. If you need any grub, Granny Sheila just made some stew, it's wild good, fresh lamb, if you know what I'm saying, two down there on the right. It'll set you up powerfully. Girls was it, you said?"

"Yes."

"Okay, gimme ten minutes."

Donal offered his hand. Killian shook it.

"I had a feeling someone or something was going to turn up today," Donal said. Like all Pavee Donal reckoned that he was in touch with invisible forces whose power, alas, never somehow extended to racecourses or the dog track.

"Where's Katie's house?" Killian asked.

"The very end, with the best view of the bay," Donal said with a wink.

"I'll say hello while I'm waiting," Killian muttered, oddly embarrassed.

"Do that. She's got Tommy but she's still a bit lonely now that all the weans have flied the coop. I'll get this caravan sorted for you."

Donal went into his caravan and turned on the light.

Killian walked along the caravans and trailers until he reached the last one. It was a standard Ace Ambassador from about 1989. The aluminum had buckled and the paint was chipping. It had seen better days.

He hesitated for a moment, then knocked on the door.

"Who is it?" a voice asked.

"An old friend," Killian said.

There was a significant pause and the sound of a glass clinking before the door opened.

Her hair was long and brown with only a few streaks of grey. Her face was sunburned and her lips thin. She was skinny. Too skinny, but her eyes were clear and she was still very beautiful. You wouldn't have thought that she'd had six kids. Six that he knew about it.

She looked at him. Shook her head. Smiled.

They hadn't seen each other in a dozen years. More.

"You want a drink?" she asked.

"Sure," he said.

He ducked his head and followed her inside the caravan and sat down on a wicker chair. The inside was better than the out. The foam furniture had been reupholstered in leather and the stove and mini fridge looked new.

And the view indeed was spectacular.

All of Brown's Bay, the glens of Antrim, Scotland.

Katie handed him a glass of clear liquid.

"Thank you," he said and sniffed it.

There was no smell.

"It'll have to be a quick one. Tommy is wild jealous."

"Who's Tommy?"

"You know Tommy Trainer? Betty Trainer's boy?"

Killian shook his head. "Doesn't ring a bell."

"He's a bit, shall we say, boisterous, you know what those Trainers are like, they hung his great granda during the war."

Killian shook his head. "I don't remember them. Is he a bother? Does he hit you?"

"Ach, he's just a boy. I can handle him, but he might do something stupid if he barged in here and then he found out about you and me. He might want to give you a going over."

"You think he could?" Killian asked with a twinkle.

"You're no spring chicken," Katie said and laughed.

"I'm only forty," Killian protested and took a sip of the poteen.

It was a pleasant little moonshine as moonshine went, but still it wasn't made for sipping. He knocked it back and it burned his throat.

"So how are you?" Killian asked.

"I can't complain. The kids are all in one piece."

Killian smiled. "Six of them, I heard."

She nodded. "Three boys, three girls, perfect eh?"

"Perfect," Killian agreed.

"Let me fill that wee mug."

She poured him another healthy measure from an old Smirnoff Vodka bottle and he swirled the poteen around in his glass.

"So what are you doing here?" Katie said.

"I'm in a spot of bother," Killian replied.

"Why does that not surprise me?"

Killian leaned back in the sofa and shook his head happily. "I don't know," he said, getting a little buzzed.

"What happened to your clothes?" Katie asked.

"I went for a wee swim in Lough Erne this morning," Killian said.

"I'll bet there's a woman at the back of this," Katie tutted.

"That's a bet you'd win, as usual," Killian said.

Katie pulled the hair from her face and clipped it back. She got up from her seat and sat next to him on the sofa. She took his hand in hers.

"How long has it been, Aidh?"

Killian shook his head. "I don't know," he said. "You haven't changed much."

She laughed again. It was the same lilting, girlish laugh that he'd loved when he'd only been a snapper.

She squeezed his hand a bit harder.

"Are you still in America?" she asked.

"No, no, I've been back a few years now. England for a while, but back here for good I think."

"And you're in trouble?" she asked, with concern in those hazel eyes.

With her forehead knitting like that, she looked older. Old.

"A wee bit of bother, nothing for you to concern yourself with."

"Ha!" she said and pinched him. "I stopped worrying about you, last century. The nerve of ya!"

Killian's grin broadened.

There was a bang outside and he flinched, but when he looked out the window he saw that it was only fireworks they were letting off after the conclusion of the fair.

"Where do you live?" she asked. "Are you on the road?"

"No, I've got a wee place down in Carrick. I actually have some flats up in Belfast too. Can't get rid of them. You know what the property market's like."

"Is that the bother you're in?"

"No. It's a different kind of bother."

She nodded, drank her glass and dragged the bottle across the coffee table with her foot. She filled two more glasses.

"How's Karen?" he asked after a deep breath.

She beamed. A big easy smile with no recrimination in it.

"She's doing well. You know how hard it is for the first year."

"First year of what?"

"She has twins."

Killian's heart skipped a beat.

"Twins?"

"You hadn't heard? No, how would ya?"

She stood. "Hold on a wee minute. I've got a picture. Hold on there sunshine." She went to the back room of the caravan and came back a moment later with a small picture of two baby girls in pink nightgowns. They were about six months old in the photograph and both had a shock of red hair.

"Oh my God," Killian said, delighted.

His hand was shaking and he could feel the tears.

"You can keep that if you want," Katie said, moved. "They look like a couple of wee trolls don't they?"

Killian shook his head. "No. They look beautiful. I can really keep this?"

Katie leaned forward and kissed him on the cheek. "Of course you can, love," she said.

It was the waterworks now and Killian sniffed and dabbed his face with his sleeve.

Rachel and her weans. And now these two little gangsters.

He turned his head from her.

It was almost too much.

He took his sodden wallet out of his back pocket and carefully put the photograph under the clear plastic where his driving licence should be.

The wallet gave him an idea.

He looked between the notes and found a slightly damp cheque.

"Have you got a pen?" he asked.

Katie looked at the cheque and shook her head. "Don't be doing that now," she muttered.

"I want to," he insisted. "It's okay. My problems aren't financial. It's the right thing to do and I want to."

"She's doing great. She's with this guy. Regular guy. Civilian. Not in The Life. English."

"She's married?"

"Not as such. But, you know, it's a steady thing. He's called Trevor. Works for the Civil Service. He has a goatee."

Killian laughed. "That's the clincher is it?"

"You can mock. I've met him. He's good. You'd like him."

"I like him already. Gimme a pen, woman."

After a wee bit more poking she found a biro and he wrote a cheque for ten thousand pounds and gave it to her. He knew he could trust Katie to give Karen the bulk of it.

"This is too much," she said.

"Take it."

Katie took the cheque and of course by now she was crying too.

"Have you seen Donal?" she asked by way of changing the subject.

Killian nodded. "Aye, he's fixing me a place. His place in fact."

"He's a good 'un too."

Killian sighed and got to his feet. "Well, I suppose I better…"

They stood there and looked at one another. The years and the mistakes and everything else seemed to evaporate and there they were two weans again, sort of, but not really, in love.

"How are the rest of your kids?" Killian said, remembering his manners.

"Everyone's fine," Katie said. "Now, look, the fireworks are reaching their climax which means that everything's gonna be over and my old man will be along in a wee minute."

Killian nodded and went to the door.

Katie hid the cheque under a coffee jar. "I won't cash this until you're free of your present difficulties," she said.

"No, no, cash it now, please, it'll make me feel better knowing that you're sending something to her. And really I'm fine for money."

"Okay," she said.

He put his hand on the door handle, but before he could leave she gave him a hug and a kiss and then pushed him outside into the dusk.

She waved to him from the living-room window and then pulled over the curtains.

He hoped she really would cash it.

He coughed and wiped the tears from his face and touched the wallet with the picture in it.

He couldn't resist another look.

Two wee gangsters indeed.

Donal saw him from the other side of the campsite and waved. Killian put the photograph away.

"You're all set, mate," Donal said. "It's a fairly big caravan as you can see, you and your lady friend will have a twin and the girls can share the double, unless you want it the other way around?"

"No, that sounds fine," Killian said. He'd probably sleep on the sofa anyway.

He shook Donal's hand. "You're a real lifesaver, mate," he said.

Donal shrugged. "Don't even mention it. Remember there's stew if you want it."

"I forgot about that, I'll ask the girls."

They shook hands again and Killian walked down to the beach.

Word had gotten round about him already and a skinny character, almost as tall as he was, intercepted him in the car park.

He was gangly and bearded with a sleekit wee player grin.

"I'm Tommy Trainer," Tommy said.

"Aye, I thought so," Killian said.

"Just to let you know, Katie's with me," he said.

"How old are you, son?" Killian asked.

"Twenty-two," Tommy said.

Killian nodded. "You take care of her, okay? She's a good woman and I wouldn't want to hear anything bad about ya."

Tommy blinked. "Why what would you do about it, pal?" he said.

Killian stroked his chin and thought about it. "I think with you I'd geld you like a horse, with hot wire, so there'd be no significant blood loss. Aye, I think that's what I'd do."

Killian grinned and held Tommy's stare until Tommy grinned and then both of them laughed. "You're a case, so you are, old man," Tommy said.

"Aye, that's right, I'm a case," Killian replied and walked down to the beach.

There was a still a small crowd watching the last of the rockets shoot into the air and burst in a display of green and golden sparkles.

The smell was cordite and seaweed and home-made ice cream and beer.

He found Rachel and the girls sitting on a tree trunk.

Rachel was smoking a cigarette and there were four other butts beside her. It had been a hell of a day.

He sat next to her. "Hey," he said.

"Hey," she replied and passed him the ciggie.

He shook his head.

"How are we doing, girls?" he asked.

"We got ice cream and we rode a donkey and we patted the horses and we even went to the water and a man gave us a necklace that he'd made and then there was fireworks!" Sue said breathlessly.

Their eyes were wide and excited and sleepy.

Killian smiled. "There's food if you want it, some sort of stew," he said.

Rachel shook her head. "I think we'll just put the girls to bed, it's been an emotional twenty-four hours."

"That it has," he agreed.

They sat there and watched the very last rockets and as it began to grow cold Killian took Claire in his arms and Rachel led Sue by the hand up to Donal's caravan.

They walked a little apart now as the beach narrowed. She went ahead and his footsteps splayed into her smaller footsteps, distorting them and turning them into his own. He did it on purpose, noticing as he did her unusual gait: the tiny spaces between the steps and the wide leg stance. She'd ridden horses as a kid. Their worlds weren't so distant…

They laid the girls together in the double bed.

Donal had changed the sheets so that they were pink with flowers on them and he had put a stuffed Tigger and Pooh on the pillows.

"I'll take the Pooh," Claire said sleepily.

Donal had also got a bunch of children's books – picture books and Roald Dahls – which was a nice touch from someone who probably couldn't read himself, Killian thought.

Claire was excited by the books and immediately grabbed *Danny the Champion of the World*.

Killian left Rachel to get the girls undressed and went into the living room.

There was a note on the small foldaway table.

It was a picture of a bowl of stew and a picture of a fridge. Another picture showed a roll-up in the ashtray.

He sniffed the roll-up and it smelled pretty good. He opened the fridge door and saw a Tupperware bowl full of stew.

"Well, I'm hungry even if no one else is," Killian said.

He dished some of the stew into a pot and heated it up.

"What are you cooking?" Rachel asked coming into the kitchen area.

Killian put some on a wooden spoon and offered it to her.

She took a bite. She hadn't tasted anything so fresh and delicious in a while. The lamb was succulent and melted on your tongue and the vegetables were young, tender, perfect.

"My God, that's awesome. I'll go tell the girls."

She came back a minute later.

"They're out for the count," Rachel said. "The poor wee lasses. Probably be in psychotherapy for the rest of their lives after today."

"I don't know about that," Killian said. He had seen plenty of horrifying things by the time he was Claire's age: a man kicked to a death by a horse, a man burned in a paraffin heater explosion, a woman stabbed in the belly…"Kids are resilient," he added. "Let's eat."

They sat at the fold-out table by the window. The horse fair was over and the Islandmagee locals were gone, leaving only the travellers and their animals. It was quiet. The sky was filled with stars.

They ate the lamb stew and had a couple of cans of Harp from the fridge.

They cleared the table and turned on the portable TV but the only thing they could was get was *The Flintstones* from BBC Scotland's Gaelic service. Killian discovered that he could understand almost all of it.

"What's happening?" Rachel asked.

"Wilma thinks Fred treats her badly and she's leaving him," Killian said.

"It's Betty I feel sorry for. Barney's no catch," Rachel said.

Killian laughed and when the episode ended they wrapped themselves in blankets and went outside and sat on a couple of ratty deckchairs.

The bonfire on the beach was a mass of embers being dispersed by the surf breaking on the shore. They sat for a while looking at the fire on the water.

"Let me check on the girls," Rachel said.

Killian lit a cigarette and Rachel rejoined him two minutes later.

"The girls are asleep," she said. "What time is it?"

Killian shrugged. "I don't have a watch and my phone's dead."

"I'm shattered," she said.

"Go to bed," Killian said.

Rachel nodded. "I will."

"I'll sleep on the sofa," Killian added.

"There are two beds in that room."

"I know. I'm restless though and you need your sleep."

"Have you got any smokes?"

Killian lit her a ciggie.

"The sea's nice," she said.

"Yeah, it is."

"It's mild for March."

Killian nodded.

They sat and smoked and Killian counted the lighthouses. Eight of them, the one furthest north maybe fifty miles from here.

"So these are your people, eh? Gypsies."

"Not gypsies. Pavee."

"That's a new word on me."

"Not to us. You can call us tinkers or travellers if you like."

"No, Pavee is good. But, if it's not a stupid question, what is the difference between Pavee and gypsies?"

"Gypsies are *Roma* people. Originally, I think, from India. They speak an Indo-European language, which I've been told is quite similar to Sanskrit."

"And Pavee?"

"No one's really sure where we came from. I've heard and read about dozens of theories over the years."

"What are the theories?"

"Oh, that we were the original inhabitants of Ireland before the Celts came, or that we were the survivors of Cromwell's land clearances, some even say that we didn't come from Ireland at all, but an Atlantis-like island that used to exist between Ireland and Scotland."

"What do you believe?"

"I like the *we were here first* theory."

"Are there many of you?"

"Not many. A few thousand in Ireland, couple of thousand in England and America."

"Never really gave you lot much thought before, you know? In Northern Ireland, you don't. It's all about Prods and Catholics."

"Most people don't."

"You speak what, Irish?"

"It's kind of an Irish dialect, we don't like to talk about it with outsiders, it's an argot."

"How come you never learnt to read until your twenties?"

Killian shrugged. "Just never got around to it. We were so busy learning other things."

"What things?"

"Fixing motors, chopping cars, picking locks, learning to care for horses, that kind of stuff."

She nodded, looked at the water.

"What's going to happen to us? Me and the girls?"

"You'll be safe here, for a while at least. I'll get a phone and make some calls. Losing the laptop changes things. It changes the whole game. If I can't get through to Richard I'll get through to Tom."

"It's going to be okay?"

"It is. I promise."

She smiled at him. "So is this what you do for a living? All this madness."

"I used to. I've retired. Semi-retired. I'm doing architecture at the University of Ulster. BA. Mature student kind of deal."

"Architecture? That stuff interests you?"

"Very much. Not you?"

"Not really. One building's pretty much like another isn't it?"

Killian put the ciggie on a breeze block between the two chairs. "You see for me, houses are mysterious and fascinating places. You have to understand I lived in a caravan until I was seventeen. And then hotel rooms for the next ten years. I didn't actually live in a house until my late twenties. They still seem weird and exotic. I've got a whole theory about it."

"Aye?"

"Aye," he said with a smile.

Rachel considered him. You wouldn't exactly call him handsome, he was too tall and ungainly for that. But you could see how certain women could fall for him. His eyes in particular had an odd grey glint to them that she liked.

"Go on then," she said. "You know you're itching to."

"Well, architecture is the art and science of permanent structures, but

I think humans aren't supposed to live in permanent structures. It's not natural. So that's why the whole thing is weird."

"What are you talking about?"

"Homo sapiens came from Africa. For a million years we and our ancestors lived in the savannah of the Great Rift Valley following the herds. Our life for the last fifty thousand generations has been about motion. There were no buildings because there were no settlements. We followed the grazing animals, hunting them, gathering fruit and wild grasses. This whole idea of living in cities is completely alien to the human species. It's a blip in our history. We've only been doing it for the last few hundred generations. Wanderlust is programmed in, you see? It's in our DNA, we're supposed to move. We're supposed to see new vistas with each new dawn. Man was not meant for a sedentary lifestyle and that's why most of feel unhappy and anxious living in these boxes in towns and cities. Architecture, good architecture, tries its best to alleviate some of these problems, but it's a losing battle. The problem isn't with the buildings. It's with us."

Rachel nodded in the darkness and watched a little night-fishing boat chug out of Larne Harbor. "So you, the tinkers, uh, I mean…what did you just call them?"

"Pavee."

"Sorry. So you think Pavee are happier than the rest of us?"

"I don't know. I had a happy childhood. Even though my da died, it was happy, you know? And go out there among those men and their horses at the fair and I don't think you'll find much angst."

He thought again about the photograph in his wallet and wondered if his grin was lighting up the beach. And the truth was, that right now, in these chairs, among his own people, with this woman, he was happier than he had been in decades.

"I suppose not," Rachel said and laughed and coughed. She threw away her cigarette.

"Want another?" Killian asked, offering her the pack.

"Nah, I'm giving those up too. I'm trying to be more careful about what

I put into my body these days. I've gone straight before. But this time…
this time I mean it. It's different."

Killian liked to hear that.

He smiled at her.

"You know I went to university too. I studied astronomy for a year. I
loved that guy Patrick Moore. Ever see him?" Rachel said.

Killian shook his head.

"I loved all that stuff. It's not just looking in telescopes. There's a lot of
maths and forumulas."

"Why did you quit?"

"Ach. I met Richard in the Beaten Docket. That was when he was just
coming on the TV, you know? Completely fell for his act. The patter, the
persona. He was still married then."

Killian concealed a yawn behind his hand.

He was tired. He enjoyed talking to her, he was liking that cold breeze
off the water, now, but it had been an exhausting few days.

"What did you like about astronomy?" he asked out of politeness.

She began talking.

She talked stars and Doppler shifts and planets and the expanding
universe and the possibility of life on Mars or on the frozen moons of
Titan or Europa.

Her voice was losing that neutral Anglo-Irish cadence it had acquired
in the years with Richard and slipping back into pure Ballymena.

He enjoyed that.

She kept going and he found himself drifting.

"Let's go to bed," she said.

He nodded and followed her inside.

"You go on, I'll sleep out here," he said.

"No. Let's go to bed," she said.

She took his hand and led him to the bedroom.

They pushed the twin beds next to each other and stripped naked and
lay together under the skylight.

She showed him the constellations and she told him the Latin names and he told her the Shelta names, the Irish names, the real names.

And they lay under Orion and Mars and Saturn's spouse, King Jupiter.

"I forgot to tell you something," she whispered.

"What?"

"Thank you."

"For what?"

"For saving our lives."

"You saved yourself."

"No. It was you."

Their hands touched.

Her fingers in his big paw.

Maybe he's the one, she thought.

And if he wasn't it didn't matter.

They made love.

And the planets turned in the Keplerian clockwork of their ellipses.

And the moons about the planets.

Their mouths meeting over the frozen oceans of Europa.

She kissed his furrowed brow and his strong jaw and his hard lips.

He kissed her back.

And she said: "I'm afraid, Killian…it's been a long time."

And he said: "I'll show you."

And her legs wrapped about him and they showed each other.

More increments of that raw time…

And this time the seconds weren't long enough.

And then, when it was over, they lay in each others arms and slept.

chapter 16
ceilidh night

KILLIAN WAS SITTING ON THE BEACH WATCHING THE OCEAN traffic and listening to the surf break along the shore. It was March in eastern Ulster which normally meant permanent drizzle but although it was grey and overcast, the rain appeared to be over – at least for now. Scotland was invisible this morning behind a line of magenta haze that hadn't stopped the passenger ferries confidently heading in its general direction from the port of Larne.

It was their third day on Islandmagee and Killian was relaxed but not at ease.

He waved to Donal, who was making his way along the dunes towards him.

The Pavee had given all of them a change of clothes so that now he and Donal looked similar, an elder and older brother perhaps, dressed in long German army surplus trench coats, boots and working jeans.

Donal stopped next to him and took a pipe from his pocket. "*Nus a dhabjon dhuilsha*," he said in Belfast Shelta and then in Irish: "*Go mbeanna Dia is Muire duit.*"

"And to you," Killian replied in English.

Donal rubbed some uncut tobacco in his palm, filled the pipe and sat down next to him.

"I got that phone you wanted," Donal said.

"Thank you," Killian said. "Untraceable?"

"It was only stolen this morning, it'll take them a working day to switch off the service," Donal replied.

"Where'd you get it? They might be able to deduce my whereabouts if it was somewhere close."

Donal shook his head. "We got it in Belfast. You're fine. But they might be able to triangulate you if they're really clever."

"I won't stay on that long," Killian said.

"Well, here you go," Donal said.

Killian took the phone. A shiny little red thing with a picture of Hello Kitty on it.

"You've no idea how much I appreciate this," Killian said. "Can I give you some dough? All I'm doing here is eating your food and sleeping in your house."

Donal shook his head. "Nah, you're fine. You're the Prodigal, it's our job to take you in."

Killian tried to hand him a fifty-pound note but Donal wouldn't countenance it.

"Your money's no good here, mate," he said.

Killian rubbed his chin and considered for a moment. "Can I at least give you a hand at the cemetery? I heard that's what you were doing for cash."

Donal shrugged. "It's not necessary."

"I'd feel better about staying here if I was doing something," Killian said.

"If you want to. I'm going out this afternoon. It's just me and a spade, it's tedious stuff. They'd get Poles for it if they could afford Poles."

"I'm not shy of a wee bit of sweat. Okay if I tag?"

"Aye, if you want. Gimme someone to talk to."

"And me too, it's an oestrogen fest at my house."

Donal yawned, wiped the sand off his bum and stood. "Well, things to do mate. We're having a ceilidh tonight. Can you play an instrument?"

Killian shook his head. "Not me."

"I'd make your calls now and toss it just to be on the safe side," Donal said.

"Aye, I'll do that," Killian replied.

"*Slainte.*"

"*Slainte.*"

Donal wandered back to the camp puffing his pipe.

A gang of kids and dogs came running along the beach in front of him. They were playing Kick a Tin, a complex hide and seek game Killian had played as a wean. Rachel's girls were among them.

In a couple of days they'd gone completely native. Their hair was braided, they'd swapped jeans and T-shirts for dresses and home-made wool sweaters, and shoes were an alien item of clothing. The big gang of Pavee children had taken the girls and made them wee sisters. Rachel of course still kept an eye on them, especially little Sue; not that Sue wanted her ma keeping tabs since this was her first chance to be a big lass with lassies younger than herself.

Still, Killian mused, Rachel was right to be watchful, there was the sea after all and no Pavee could ever forget that the watery element was a dodgy place.

Although Rachel tried to keep a discreet distance Killian could see her in front of the caravan, sitting in a deckchair, reading a novel. She too was shoeless and her hair was blowing about her face.

"Hello Mr Killian," Sue said breathlessly as she ran past.

"Hi," Killian said.

"I've got the best place in the world to hide," Sue shouted.

"Where?"

"In the old phone box!" Sue exclaimed.

"Good idea," Killian said, although that was the first place he would have looked.

"I'm hiding in the phone box," Sue said again, this time even more loudly.

"Good idea," Killian said again and now everybody knows it, he thought.

Sue looked at him as if he was a great big eejit.

"If anyone asks that's where I'll be," she said ridiculously loudly.

"Okay," Killian said, still not catching on.

"I'll really be behind the skip in the car park, but when Tara goes to the phone box, I'll run to the den, kick the tin and get in free!" Sue whispered.

Killian grinned and slapped his thigh. "Genius!" he said.

"Aye, I know," said Sue, who not only looked healthy and happy but also appeared to have grown an inch over the last three days.

"*Olann an cat cluin bainne leis!*" Killian said.

"*Meaow!*" Sue agreed and off she ran.

Picked up some of the lingo too, Killian thought. But his grin flatlined as he realised it was now time for his own phone shenanigans.

He called Sean.

"Hello?" Sean said.

"It's Killian," he said.

There was a long pause. A very long pause.

"Where are you?" Sean asked.

"I'd rather not say, mate," Killian said.

"You can tell me," Sean insisted.

"Better not."

"You're with her now, right? Her and the weans. She fucking turned you, didn't she?"

"It's not like that, Sean."

"What is it like, Killian?" Sean said, seething.

"There's a lot of information you don't know."

"Try me."

"Like the fact that our *friend* pimped out kids in his care in the 1970s, like the fact that he's got a collection of homemade pornographic images of children."

There was another long pause.

"Can I ask you a question, Killian?" Sean asked.

"Ask."

"Have you lost your fucking mind?"

"No."

"You know who came to see me at my home yesterday?"

"I'm guessing it wasn't Cardinal Brady."

"Tom E and his new pal Ivan. In my house. In my fucking house with Mary in the back kitchen making tea for everyone," Sean said, dripping poison.

"I'm sorry, Sean."

"They explained how high up this goes. It's not just Mr C, is it? It's people just a wee toty bit scarier than that. And Ivan's a pretty scary motherfucker himself isn't he? Mate."

"Sean, listen, I'm sorry they've got you involved in all this but—"

"You're sorry? I was keeking my bloody whips. They call him the Starshyna, the Sergeant. The boy's a vet. He's a fucking hero of the Chechen wars. He's worked in Mexico. He's a pro, Killian. There's me looking at him, remembering his play in Ballymena, thinking Mary and me are for the cold cold ground and you're sorry? You're fucking sorry? Do everyone a favour, mate, go for a long bloody drive somewhere and when you're well away tell us where she fucking is."

"Look, the game's changed, the laptop's gone forever, it's all over now. Finished."

"That's not how Tom sees it."

"How does Tom see it?"

"Call him. Call him now!"

"I will."

Dead air.

A sigh of disappointment.

"How could you do this, Killian? After all I've done for you?"

Killian shook his head. How could he explain? He had tried the legit universe and failed, his confidence broken, his faith in himself shattered along with the Irish economy. He'd taken one step backwards to work with Sean again, but coming here had transported him not one year but decades. Sean might be a surrogate father, but these were his people.

This was a different world.

This was a world that lived in a web of obligations, duties, lore, folk wisdom, tradition.

This was a world where honour was not a concept heading for obsolescence.

He liked Rachel and he liked the girls. He had taken them under his protection and he had given them his word.

"I better go then, Sean, I'll try Tom."

"Do that," Sean said. "I wish you luck. Please don't call me back until this is resolved."

Killian was more than a little upset by this…this *betrayal* from an old pal, but as if to an unseen familiar he said aloud: "Ach, he's only protecting himself. Do the same thing myself more than likely," which he and the ghosts and the familiars knew wasn't true at all.

He shook his head, took the wallet out of his pocket and found Tom's number. He got through a secretary by saying "I'm Killian, Mr Eichel's been waiting for my call."

"Killian," Tom said.

"Hello Tom," Killian replied.

"Where are you?"

"I can't tell you."

"Like fuck you can't, you're working for me."

"Not any more."

"You gave me your word. You made an agreement. Now, where are you?"

Macau seemed a long, long time ago.

"How about a new agreement," Killian said.

Instead of exploding, Tom hesitated. "I'm listening," he said cautiously.

"I take it our friend told you what happened to the computer?"

"He did."

"As I see it that returns things to the status quo ante," Killian said.

"How so?"

"Well, just like before, we've got nothing on you and you've got stuff on us, so why not just let things go back to the way they were?" Killian said.

"It's 'we' now is it?"

"Cut that out, Tom, you're a fucking grown-up. We're talking business here."

Tom said nothing for a while.

"You don't have a backup of the computer's hard drive?" he asked.

"No."

"How do we know that?"

"You can give me a lie detector test if you want. Why would she need a backup when she had the machine itself?"

Killian could hear Tom pacing on the hardwood floor of that fancy office of his on Royal Avenue. Killian got to his feet and walked down to the water.

Sue came running past him and made it to the den yelling, "One, two, three, I'm in free!"

Killian stood in the wet sand, watching his army boots sink. The ferry had long since vanished into the pink haze and the seascape was empty but for a couple of gulls.

"The way they were?" Tom said at last.

"Yes."

"She'll keep her mouth shut?"

"She'll keep her mouth shut and you'll keep the stuff you have on her under wraps. She and he will agree to share custody with the girls. I can make her see that our friend's predilections were all in the past and a long, long time ago."

"What about her parents?"

"What about them? I've been watching the news. It's still a blank sheet there, isn't it? The cops are still treating Rocky as a missing person's rap."

"Aye, but for how long? Five days? It's not going to go a week."

"She'll talk, I know she'll talk. She's the type."

"She won't."

"This isn't just about C. It's about me, too. My life!"

"I know. I'll explain it to her."

"And then there's our other friend. He thinks the films were burned up in an incendiary attack in 1982. An attack which him and his friends carried out. C has been lying to him and me for twenty years."

"Tell him that."

"No! I'm not telling him fucking anything. We'd all be fucking dead."

"Tom listen—"

"No, you listen. I never trusted you, Killian. But I had heard you were a man of your word. You made a deal with us. Keep your end of it. It's the right thing to do. You know it's a ticking clock. As soon as she hears about what happened in Ballymena she is going to fucking squeal," Tom said dismissively.

"She won't. Not if it's to protect herself and her kids. And if she did say something she wouldn't have the proof to tie our friend to it."

"She doesn't need proof. The innuendo would be enough to destroy the share price, and my friend's reputation. My whole fucking career. Our lives. It would be fucking catastrophic. I'm not prepared to take that risk."

"I'll fix her," Killian insisted.

Tom coughed. "And there's a third fucking problem isn't there?"

"What?"

"You. You know about Ballymena. And she showed you the laptop. What do we do to keep you quiet?"

"Are you kidding? I'm cheap, Tom, I'm cheap as dirt. A couple of grand will keep me happy. You can spare it."

Silence.

The waves on the beach.

Children's laughter.

Tom's brain churning gears.

"Well?" Killian asked.

"Let me get this straight, you fix her, and everything goes back to the way it was?" Tom asked.

"Aye."

"And the guarantee is what?"

"Make her sign something. Something legal. You're a lawyer. If she ever bad-mouths our friend or you in any publication then blah blah blah…"

More silence.

"Tom, I need to ditch this phone."

"Okay. It might be doable. Allow me to talk it over with our friend, will you?" Tom asked with less edge in his voice than he'd had all conversation.

"Okay," Killian said.

"I'll call you back in a couple of hours," Tom said.

"No, no, I'll be trashing this phone as soon as we're done here. I'll call you back in a couple of hours."

"Our friend's in London, I'll have to track him down, why don't you stay on the line and I'll see where he is."

"Come on Tom, don't play me—"

"I'm not playing you, Killian, I'm a fucking glorified PA based in fucking Belfast; when he's across the sheugh our friend has a million things to do, half the time his mobile's off for an interview, I'll have to call Paula and get his itinerary."

"I'm not holding on, Tom, I'm trashing this phone, I'll call you back later," Killian insisted.

"Okay, okay, keep your hair on. Call me at five, okay? I'll have our word by five."

"Five o'clock it is."

"Just to be clear: you'll square your girl, I'll square my boy and we'll shake hands in the middle?"

"That's the plan."

"Okay. Oh, and Killian?"

"What?"

"Don't fuck it up this time," Tom said and hung up so that that would be the last word.

Killian smiled.

"Well, that certainly wasn't a no," he said to the ghosts. There might, actually, be a way out of this muck that didn't involve bashing heads.

Killian *had* topped people in his career as a heavy. He had also six-packed a few people and beat the shit out of a couple dozen more, some of whom had been guilty of nothing more heinous than forgetting to pay their protection money on time.

But over the years he had gained a rep as a man who could convince people to pay their bills and keep their beaks shut without the necessity of having to shoot them in the kneecaps. He had gained a rep for diplomacy, as the Tallyrand of the Tinkers.

He was competent with a gun, but he preferred not to work with one.

That's why Enniskillen had been so satisfying.

Clean. Neat. Apart from that poor bastard ferry operator that Ivan had obviously topped.

And perhaps this could be finessed too. No one else need die.

The hard part would indeed be breaking the news of her parents' murder to Rachel, but Killian knew that if anyone could do it, he could. He would put on his serious face and *explain*. As nice as it was here, this was a fantasy, a holiday, and it couldn't go on forever.

He walked a little further into the surf, flipped the phone shut, cocked his arm and skimmed it into the sea. It bounced four times before it sank.

"Not bad," he muttered.

He strolled back through the Kick a Tin game, over the dunes and up to the Pavee camp.

He nodded to Katie who was feeding scraps to the chickens outside her caravan.

She gave him a smile and jerked her thumb behind her which meant that her old man Tommy was inside. Killian nodded.

He walked to Donal's caravan.

"Hi," he said to Rachel.

She looked up from her book.

"Hey," she replied, grinning.

She too had put on weight in her three days here. She'd slept well and the wind and sun had caught her face and brought out her colour. She looked great. Beautiful.

"Whatcha reading?" he asked.

"*The Catcher in the Rye.*"

"I missed that one. Any good?"

"So far. He wants to know where the ducks go in the winter."

Killian rubbed his chin. "Well, the teal go to Spain and the mallard go to Morocco."

"These are New York ducks."

Killian shook his head. "Oh. I don't know. Mexico?"

Rachel put down the book and smiled. "I don't think we're going to find out. That's not really the point."

Killian cleared his throat ruminatively.

Rachel recognised his ticks by now. "What's up?" she asked.

Killian squatted beside her and his mind filled with the image of Rachel's cigarette-burn tortured stepmother and dead father.

"Well?" she insisted.

Killian shook his head. She was so pretty and happy that Killian couldn't bring himself to mention it at the moment. And there was no hurry on it anyway. He had all day. "Oh, uhm, I was wondering if you…if you'd mind…I was thinking of going to help Donal out this afternoon at his wee job. I feel I should give him a wee hand you know."

Rachel looked concerned. "Because we're imposing on him?"

"God no. He would mortified if you thought that. No, I'm just a bit bored."

"Oh okay, yeah sure."

"You're comfortable here? You'll be okay by yourself?"

She pulled the hair back from her face and tied it in a ponytail. She grinned. "I'm comfortable here in a way I've never been comfortable in my whole friggin' life," she said. Killian repeated her remark to Donal two hours later in the small, ancient, Mill Bay graveyard on the Larne Lough side of Islandmagee.

"Oh aye? I'm glad to hear it," Donal said, pleased.

Killian had been waiting for Donal to hint that they might want to look for a caravan of their own or something like that but no hint had come. And wouldn't come. Donal had given them his place for as long as they wanted and that was all that needed to be said.

Killian paused on his spade.

"How do you like the work?" Donal asked.

"It's nice to build up a wee sweat," Killian replied.

They had taken their coats off and were digging a grave.

It was a navvy job and Killian had had plenty of those over the water.

He moved onto a new square and pushed in the spade. He lifted the spade out and turned the edge perpendicular to the first cut and dug, the shovel again meeting no resistance in the soft grass. He withdrew the spade and cleaned the muck off the bottom and then he dug again, perpendicular to the previous cut, parallel to the first. A final cut completed the shape and when he had made four incisions in the moist earth, he stepped back and looked at the rectangle he had created in the ground. He paused only for a moment and then shifted his weight on the shovel, hooking his left hand over the "t" of the handle and his right hand firm on the metal staff, and then in one motion he scooped up a cube of turf and dropped it a few feet away to his left.

He grunted and looked with satisfaction at his third square-foot done.

"Aye, it's not too bad," Killian said.

After ten minutes with sweat running along the sheugh of their arses they were done with the first part of the job. All the surface grass was turned over and stacked in a neat triangular pile.

They could be less careful with the rest of the task, as it required only a raw labouring against the ground. They got big snow shovels from the gravedigger's shed and commenced hoiking out the soil. It was moist, with the texture of chocolate cake, and they scooped it out easily.

"Doing well now," Donal said.

They shovelled on in the musty heat until the rain clouds came and filled the western part of the sky.

"When's the funeral?" Killian asked.

"Ach we've a wee while yet, I think," Donal said.

"Who's it for?"

"Some old boy. This cemetery is officially full, I was told. You have to be from an old family to get in here. Nice wee ground though," Donal said. Killian agreed. There was a view of Larne Lough and the green Antrim hills beyond, and it was quiet. Sheep fields and wee lanes choked with nettles and blackberry bushes.

As the rain began to fall gently on the outlying houses of the peninsula the grave was nearly done. They were working in the hole now and Killian paused to wipe the sweat off his hands on the back of his trousers.

Water was pooling underneath them and it was getting slippy.

"What do you think? Enough?" he asked Donal.

They were a good five feet down.

"Aye, I think that'll do," Donal said.

They climbed out, covered the hole with tarp and retreated under an oak to wait.

Donal produced a bottle of red wine, thick Irish batch bread, a wrapped package of butter and homemade raspberry jam. They drank the wine and ate jam pieces and watched curlews and oyster catchers on the mudflats of the lough. Red wine and horizontal attitudes made Killian think of the *Symposium*. Was Rachel the other half of his splintered self? It didn't seem likely. She was her own other half. And *they* could never be. These days with the tinkers had shown him that.

She wanted certainty and an end to the madness and a return to the steady life. But that was the world Killian had failed in. He saw an older world which Donal and the others had shown him still existed. A world where the past wasn't a dead story in a book but was a living history in the mouth of a storyteller or a bard, where paper rules were trumped by the older principles of natural law and justice, where family and clan mattered more than money, where your name was everything, where the landscape was teleological and every hill and stream had a legend, where the great thing was to *move*. He grinned and joined Donal in a pipe and finally around four when the rain had eased once again the funeral arrived. Six or seven cars led by a black Daimler.

The two men went over and lifted the tarpaulin from the grave, folding it over like a bed sheet, water slithering onto their hands. They carried it across to the next grave along and set it down. The minister came in a white cassock, nodded to them and stood patiently at the head of the grave. The mourners, coughing and fixing their hair in the wind, formed in a polite semicircle around him. Killian listened to the words respectfully for a while before his mind drifted back to the curlews and the other birds. He watched the lough water fill back in again and wondered if the tide ever got so high that Islandmagee actually became an island rather than a peninsula. Maybe in the distant past.

The bearers brought the coffin, the minister gave Donal a nod and Donal whispered, "Give us a hand mate." While the minister ended the Psalm they took cloth ropes and slid them through the brass handles and lowered the coffin into the ground. The widow threw in some soil and a boy too young to know what was going on was lifted up and carried, and the whole procession walked sullenly back to their vehicles.

A windy burst of weather was rolling in from the hills, conjuring up an outcry among the crows and ravens. "Let's finish up quickly before the storm comes," Donal said.

They shovelled the earth back into the hole, perspiration pouring down his back and the rainwater falling on his head. With the big snow shovel he slid the earth in over the coffin and buried it forever under the thick and inky soil.

It took them fifteen minutes to refill the grave and when they were done they replaced the sods and put soaked wreaths on the small mound that was a good two feet above the level of the ground. They put the tools back on the cart and wheeled it over to the shed.

They locked the shed and took a well-needed drink from the standpipe.

"What now?" Donal asked.

"Do you have the time?" Killian wondered.

"A quarter to five," Donal said.

"Need to make a phone call, is there somewhere around here I can do it? A payphone."

"Might be one at the pub," Donal suggested.

They walked to the Mill Bay Inn and Donal got a couple of pints and Killian called Tom.

Tom sounded cagey and maybe a bit annoyed. "I'm sorry Killian, I haven't been able to reach him," he said.

"You've got to tell him that this the best and only way out of our difficulties," Killian said.

"I know! But it's another big clusterfuck Monday for him. They're closing all the Manchester routes, it's a big thing over there, he's having a hell of a day."

"This is more important than anything else in his bloody life, don't you think?" Killian said, irritated at this runaround.

"Who are you arguing with, mate? I agree. For me, too. Look, I'm sorry. I know what you're saying. He's flying back tonight. I'll speak to him in person. Call me first thing in the morning. I'll have it sorted by then. Okay?"

"Okay," Killian agreed reluctantly.

"And you worked on our girl? Is she okay with everything?"

"She'll agree if your boy agrees. No press, no peelers, no fucking Russkies, no nothing. Status quo."

"Status quo. Call me in the morning, Killian."

"I will."

Killian hung up, pissed off. Sure he had a million bastard things to suss: an airline, a casino, a fucking trip to space, but only Rachel could destroy him. That boy needed to get his priorities straight.

They drank their pints and dandered along the Millbay road the seven miles from the graveyard to Brown's Bay.

It was pleasant walking along the single lane B90 and then the Brown's Bay Road.

When they got back to the Pavee camp a tall Pavee kid with blond hair took Donal by the arm and led him away for a barney.

Killian watched them with a growing sense of concern and sure enough when the parley was over Donal's face told him something was up.

"What?" Killian asked nervously.

"A man came taking photographs, asking questions," Donal explained.

"Shite. Did he have any accent? Was he Russian?"

"No. Irish guy. Short, with black curly hair, glasses."

Killian shook his head. It didn't ring any bells.

"He said he was a tourist but everyone gave him the runaround anyway, acting thick, pretending not to speak English."

"Could he have been a tourist?"

"Maybe. Probably not though. Almost certainly the DSS, the benefit fraud people, they're always snooping around."

"What are you going to do?"

Donal sighed. "Nothing for it. Better safe than sorry. It's a nice spot here, but it's probably time for us to move."

"When?"

"First thing in the morning."

"Where do you think you'll go?"

"Probably Lough Swilly in Donegal, we haven't been there for ages and there's fishing and we can get into Derry to sign on."

Killian nodded. "Is it okay if we tag along? Just for a couple more days. Our wee difficulty is – hopefully – in the process of getting itself sorted out."

Donal shook his head. "Mate, look, you're family, what's ours is yours. Stay as long or as little as you like, okay?"

"Okay," Killian said.

They walked through the horse field and Donal gave sugar lumps to a couple of favourites and Killian tried to remember the last time he had ridden a horse. Eighty-six? Eighty-seven?

When they got back to camp they found that a tent had been rigged between the two lines of caravans for the ceilidh.

"See, you couldn't have escaped work today even if you hadn't come with me," Donal said.

The ice-cream van had appeared again and sausages and hamburgers, clams and lobsters were grilling on a barbecue pit.

"Listen, I better go tell the lads we're heading out tomorrow, I'll see you later, okay?"

Killian returned to his caravan.

The girls were there and he said hello.

"We're having a party tonight! A cay-lee," Sue informed him. Her face was painted to look like a cat.

"That's great," Killian said.

Claire was holding a tambourine. "They're letting me play the tambourine," she said excitedly.

"Can you play anything, Mr Killian?" Sue asked.

"I'm afraid not, I can't even whistle," Killian told her.

Rachel kissed him on the cheek. "That's a shame, Mr Killian, I suppose it will be my chance alone to shine," she said mysteriously.

"Oh, really? Why, what do you play?" Killian asked.

"Yeah Mum, what do you play?" Sue asked.

Rachel touched her nose. "That's for me to know and you to find out."

"Well, I better go shower, I can't go anywhere looking and smelling like this," Killian said.

"Wait a minute, the girls have been asking me about knives," said Rachel.

"Yeah Mum, we want knives," Sue exclaimed and even Claire nodded.

"I'll see what I can do to rustle up a pair," Killian said.

Rachel shook her head. "No, you don't understand – I want you to talk them out of it. Knives are dangerous."

"All Pavee kids have knives, they're not dangerous if you know what to do. I'll ask Donal to get one of the older kids to show them the ropes."

Rachel folded her arms.

"Come on, Mum," Sue insisted.

"It's a spiritual thing with us," Killian explained. "Iron from the heart of a sun, turned into an blade which is an extension of your hand."

Killian pointed at the leafy deciduous woods on the hills of Islandmagee. "With a knife you could live out there indefinitely. You need to learn how to use it. You need the woodcraft. It's important stuff. As important as letters in your world. My dad made my first knife on a forge. The hand is the cutting edge of the mind."

Rachel wasn't completely convinced. Still keeping her arms folded she turned to the girls and muttered: "We'll see."

Killian excused himself and went into the caravan's tiny but extremely well-designed bathroom. He stripped off his dirty clothes and put them in the laundry basket that hung on the wall.

He turned on the shower, set it for cold and got in. Under the water he rubbed the stiffness out of his joints and the dirt off his skin. Washing away the black muck of the surrounding country. He opened his mouth and drank the water. It was fresh and good. Brown's Bay had a freshwater well. He wondered if the Lough Swilly site would be so well set up.

Probably not, but at least Donegal was a good bit further away…

He turned off the water and grabbed for a towel. He looked on the rack but all the towels were out there on the washing line.

"This is all your fault," he told the reflection. "Poor planning."

He smoothed out his black hair with his hand and tried to dry his legs and chest with a facecloth.

"Come on!" Rachel shouted. "It's starting."

"I'll see you out there."

He lifted a T-shirt and dried himself with that and then put on some more of what must be Donal's clothes. Blue jeans, yellow socks, sneakers and a hoodie that had one of the guys from *The Big Lebowski* on it.

He tided the caravan and before stepping into the world stopped to look at the barometer on the wall. For some reason, almost every tinker in his clan had a barometer glass in their caravan, as if being able to predict the weather was an essential part of being Pavee. The hand dial on Donal's barometer was pointed at STORM. The sky was telling a completely different story, but somehow that seemed about right.

When he got outside he was surprised to find that the sun had set over the water and pink fairy lights had been strung between the caravans.

A ceilidh band had formed, with Donal on the accordion and assorted others on fiddle, bodhran and mandolin.

A posse of kids were dancing like lilties on the grass as the tune switched from "Ghost Riders in the Sky" to "Whiskey in the Jar" to "Waltzing Matilda".

Rachel was nowhere to be seen, but Katie found him in the throng and gave him a hamburger and a can of Harp. Katie was wearing emerald earrings of such Celtic Twilight gaudiness that they could only have come from a safety deposit bank job of the seventies.

"Do you still not dance ya big hallion?" she asked him.

He laughed and shook his head. "I never picked it up," he said.

"There's nothing to pick up, you just go for it," Katie said.

"I'm too afeard of looking like an eejit," said Killian.

"Honey child it's too late for that," Katie laughed.

"Hey!" Killian protested.

"Oh, I wired the money to Karen. She was thrilled to bits. She was asking a million questions about you."

"What did you say?"

"I told her you were an international man of mystery."

"That sums it up nicely."

"Well, I'm away so I am," she said and grabbed a fourteen-year-old kid and wheeled him into the throng.

After three more songs and a round of poteen almost everyone was dancing. Killian got another burger and another beer and walked a little bit away and sat on a dune and watched them.

Was it only a fortnight ago that he was worrying about his houses and his term paper at UU? How silly. How trivial. Where he was from money and property weren't things to be worshipped.

He lit a cigarette and lay back on the marram grass.

More songs.

More dances.

The meditating sea.

The cool sedge.

Music rippling in the night air.

Killian saw Tommy Trainer carrying a double bass.

"How do you get that thing under your chin?" he asked.

"Hilarious and original. Listen mate, you better get over there sharpish, your bird's up next," Tommy said.

Killian followed Tommy back to the camp.

Tommy set up his double bass next to a solitary fiddle player. The dancing area was cleared and people were sitting in a semicircle.

There was an expectant lull before Rachel came out in a long golden red dress. Her hair was curled and had daisies in it. She sat on a stool and when the violin played an A she sang as haunting a version of "She Moved Through The Fair" as he had ever heard. Her voice was elfin, haunting, old, as if she was an eyewitness to the events in the song.

She finished the final chorus and the hush of the crowd was followed by applause.

Donal stepped into the jerry-rigged spotlight.

"Okay folks, sorry to be the bearer of bad tidings, but we've an early start in the morning, so finish your drinks and get the weans to their cots after one more round of 'The Star of the County Down'."

The crowd groaned and heckled but after the "County Down" finished they did as he said.

Killian found Rachel and kissed her.

"You were wonderful," he said.

"Ten years training, so I'd better be. Me da's money wasn't completely wasted," she replied.

"No, it wasn't," he agreed and kissed her again.

The girls were exhausted and went to bed without a fight.

They shared a cigarette on the deckchairs outside.

"I like it here," Rachel said.

"Me too," Killian agreed.

Rachel stared at him and smiled. "What was *that* look?"

"Nothing," he said.

"Come on, what?"

"Oh, I don't know. I think you romanticise this life. What do you see when you look at these caravans and these people?"

"Why, what do *you* see?"

Killian didn't answer but he shook his head ruefully. The truth was that he romanticised it too. It was his childhood and he was an adult now.

She didn't belong here.

He thought back to his decision at the graveyard. They'd part soon. Him and her. There was no other way.

"I don't know, Killian, I'm just a wee, middle-class girl from Ballymena, you know? I didn't want to be in a big flipping melodrama."

Killian laughed and finished the cigarette. "You don't know the half of it. My whole life has been about melodrama."

They went back inside.

The girls were safely down.

They lay together on the bed.

Her song and the moment and the remark about her da killed another opportunity to tell her about the murders in Ballymena.

It would have to be in the morning then.

He was annoyed at his cowardice but not that annoyed. He was lying with the star of the ceilidh and the most beautiful girl he knew.

He kissed her and she held him. It was the more perfect because of the bitter sweetness of the moment. He told her of the Pavee, of their passions and their belief that the great enemy Death was conquered only if you lived, really lived when you breathed the world's air. You fought and you ate and you breathed and moved under the stars and that was enough…

They made love until they were drenched with perspiration.

Exhausted they fell asleep in one another's arms.

He dreamed of fire and woke up in the cold.

The tide was out.

The rain had stopped.

Everything seemed fine.

The dogs however were telling a different story.

Two of them were barking and Cora, the next door neighbour's border collie – the smartest of the lot – was growling. Killian shook Rachel. "What is it?" she asked groggily.

"Trouble. Where's the gun?"

"In the dresser. What's the matter? I don't want you to shoot anyone."

"Let's hope I don't have to. Wake the girls, get shoes on them, I'll go see what's happening."

He pulled on the hoodie, jeans and sneakers and slipped outside the caravan. It was a clear night and the moon was so bright you could see the hills in Scotland. The hairs on the back of his neck were up.

He found Cora who was still growling into the darkness. She was rigid and her tail was high above her body and her bright eyes were staring at the dark meadow next to the horse field.

He went two caravans down and banged on Donal's door.

Donal answered it immediately. He was fully dressed and carrying a twelve-gauge. He looked at Killian.

Killian shook his head.

"Aye," Donal agreed. "And I have a feeling it's going to be a bad one."

chapter 17
the killing of the tinkers

KILLIAN SNIFFED THE AIR. THERE WAS AN ACRID TINGE AS IF from an oil slick or a chemical spill out at sea.

"What's that smell?" Donal asked.

"I was going to ask you the same question."

"I don't know," Donal said.

"Cora seems to know," Killian said.

Donal broke open the shotgun and loaded a couple of shells.

"It's only birdshot," he said. "I don't think we'll be in the business of trying to kill anyone."

Killian wasn't so sure about that. He took the clip out of the Hechler and Koch and counted slugs. Thirteen out of a possible fifteen max which wasn't bad. He reloaded the clip and chambered a round.

Donal stepped out of the caravan and went over to Cora.

She was straining at her rope, desperate to go.

"Not a fox?" Killian suggested.

"We'll see," Donal said.

He let Cora go and she ran across the car park into the overgrown meadow next to the horse field.

Nothing happened for a beat.

Two beats.

Three.

Then there was a scream. A man's scream and another man yelling, and a gunshot.

"Everybody up!" Donal yelled and starting rapping on caravan doors.

"What's going on?" Killian asked.

"Women and children onto the beach! Men and boys by your houses!" Donal yelled. "What is it?" Killian asked, straining to see into the meadow.

The dogs were all going crazy now and the horses panicking.

Before Donal could give him an answer, the first of the petrol bombs came sailing out of the darkness in an arc of white phosphorescence. It smashed short of the caravans in a whoosh of flame.

"What the fuck?" Killian said.

Three more molotovs came tumbling from the night, two also landing short but the third hitting a caravan roof and bursting into flames.

There was a cheer from the field and a man deep within the meadow yelled: "Tinkers go home!"

"Fuck off gyppo thieves!" another called.

From the cheer Killian guessed that there could be twenty of them.

There was chaos in the camp now. Children were screaming, dogs barking and half the adult men and women were still drunk from the ceilidh. No one even attempted to fight the fire incinerating the top of the caravan.

"Rachel!" Killian called and he saw her standing at the entrance to Donal's caravan with a red shawl around both girls.

"What's going on, Killian?" she yelled.

He ran to her. "Get the weans down to the water."

"What's happening?"

"It's an attack."

"Is this about us?" she asked.

"I don't know."

The girls were trembling.

"Is it going to be okay, Mr Killian?" Sue asked, looking at him sternly.

"Aye, it's going to be okay," he said patting her on the head and gently shoving Rachel towards the beach. Rachel picked them both up and ran with them to the water, congregating on the strand with the other mothers with children; the women without kids were going to stand by their men in the camp.

"Go back to fucking Poland, ya gypsy bastards!" a man yelled in the dark as another round of molotovs and petrol bombs arced through the air. Two exploded short in the field, one went long into the sand, but one hit the side of a caravan stowing in its window and exploding inside.

"Was there anyone in there?" Donal asked.

"Nah, I think wee Connie's on the beach," someone said optimistically.

Two more molotovs came gultering in, one hitting a car, another going straight into a chicken coop, setting it on fire.

"They've got the distance now," someone said.

A burning vodka bottle curved a steep parabola through the night air and smashed a yard from Killian's feet. He was knocked over and he hit his head on a plastic oil drum and, dazed, he swatted at the constellations and the sickle moon.

Fire surged across his ankles.

The moment elongated itself as those moments do: children screaming, men cheering, the smell of the sea and of burning.

"I'm on fire!" he yelled as the yellow flames shot up his leg, but Donal already had his coat off and threw it on him.

The smothered fire stopped immediately.

Donal pulled Killian to his feet. His trousers were scorched, his head was throbbing, but he was almost completely unscathed.

"Are you okay?" Donal asked.

"I think so," Killian said.

"Are you sure?"

Killian had moved on from his own needs to the needs of the clan, to the needs of Rachel and Katie and the girls. "We've got to do something. They're murdering us," he said.

Donal looked at him. "Will you come with me into their lines?" he asked.

"Aye, I will," Killian said. "Let's go, we've got guns," a little Pavee fellow said next to him.

"They'll have guns too more than likely," Donal said.

Of course they will, Killian thought, fucking skinhead cowards. But there was no choice; to stay here was death.

"Come on lads!" Killian shouted.

"No, after the next wave," Donal said and grabbed him by the arm.

Killian halted and nodded. He wasn't thinking straight.

He looked around him. Perhaps only half a dozen of the Pavee men were sober enough to go with them and only one other had a shotgun, the rest armed with tent pegs, kitchen knives, baseball bats. Big Tommy Trainer was with them though and he had a tyre iron which Killian wouldn't like to be on the other end of.

A barrage of six molotovs tore through the air, two hitting caravans and setting them ablaze, the other four dropping into the dunes.

Now four caravans were burning and the men in the field gave a mighty cheer.

Donal released the camp dogs from their ropes and they ran fearlessly into the attack.

Donal turned to them. "Now's our chance, lads, let's go!" he shouted with a wild sort of glee about him.

"Come on, lads! We'll have to run!" Killian called.

With their dogs ahead of them they sprinted between the burning caravans, across the car park and into the meadow.

Tommy Trainer began screaming like a banshee and the scream got taken up by all the others including Killian himself.

"Fucking hell!" someone shouted ahead of them in the darkness and they could hear some of the attackers turn and leg it across the fields.

There was scuffling and confusion ahead but before the Pavee could close the gap completely a shotgun tore the air between them, flame shooting from the barrels and lead careening past them like white lightning.

"Keep going, lads!" Donal shouted and now they were close enough to pick out individuals.

Killian could see maybe ten or eleven men who had stood their ground. Four of them were armed with shotguns. One had what looked a lot like a pistol.

All were wearing balaclavas.

"Fire!" someone called and the four shotguns fired together, two sprayed wild, but a Pavee man fell to Killian's left and he felt a pellet strike his shoulder that burned like hot fat.

Killian and the remaining Pavee kept running.

Two more of the men ahead of them turned and bolted. Four were desperately reloading their shotguns.

The odds seemed more even now.

A man on the far left of the meadow lit a molotov and with practised form leaned his body well back to throw it.

On the fly Killian took aim at him, squeezed the trigger and got him in the shoulder; the bottle dropped and landed on something sufficiently hard for it to break. It exploded in a lovely jet of horizontal fire that must have caught a jerry can or a plastic jug filled with petrol.

There was a bang and a simultaneous flash and the man and the bloke next to him were tossed backwards through the air.

"An rud a lionas an tsuil lionann se an croi!" Donal yelled.

"Aye," Killian agreed.

But one of the men ahead had done a fast reload and from a crouch pulled one barrel of his shotgun getting another of the Pavee in the legs.

He went down next to Donal with a horrible scream, which left just four of them racing against double that number.

But Killian was close now, close enough to make every shot count.

"Thieving bastards!" the man directly in front of him yelled, which gave Killian sufficient warning to hit the dirt.

Both barrels sailed over the top of him.

Killian shot the man's legs from under him, taking him kneecap style in the left patella.

"Jesus!" the man yelled and Killian scrambled to his feet, walked to him and shot him in the right kneecap.

He grabbed the man's shotgun and tossed it away.

To Killian's right Tommy barrelled into another of the shotgun boys, knocking him down and beating him with his own gun.

Donal fired his old birdgun at another assailant who was preparing the last of the molotovs. The pellets hit him in the back, sending him flat on his face. He got up and without looking back, ran – or rather, hobbled – away.

"I'm out of shells," Donal said.

"Only three armed men left," Killian said. "Poor fucks don't stand a chance."

His eyes had adapted to the moonlight and he knew the idiosyncracies of the gun.

He crouched, aimed and shot the nearest of the attackers in the fleshy part of the thigh. The man screamed and fell backwards in the grass. His companion accidentally discharged his gun right in front of himself catching his own shoes with a terrifying eruption of white fire and sparks. Before he'd even hit the ground big Tommy Trainer was on him, clobbering him with the tyre iron.

Only one gunman left and that fella wasn't daft. He had dropped his weapon and was legging it Usain Bolt style for his auto. "Stop and get your hands up or you're a dead man," Killian yelled, took careful aim and sent a shot whizzing over his head.

The man stopped and put his hands up.

"Lie down in the grass and don't move a fucking muscle," Killian shouted. Killian patted the man down, confiscated his wallet and went to see the other

"I think that's it," Donal said, looking about the meadow.

"The armed men are all down. Get their guns and we've won it. The others won't bother us for a bit," Killian said to him.

Donal grabbed two shotguns from two of the prone men.

Tommy lifted a third shotgun.

Among the attackers everyone who wasn't shot was running or crawling for their lives.

They were amateurs.

He went to all the other attackers lying in the field, searched them, ripped their ski masks off and, with what was left in his clip, put a bullet in each of their right kneecaps. Disabling them and maybe teaching them a thing or two about social iniquity, if not the quality of mercy. He emptied the Glock and nodded with grim satisfaction.

"Come back, you fucking cunts!" Tommy was yelling at the others who were distant forms in the far pasture.

Donal was looking at his new shotguns with grim satisfaction.

But still it had been ugly.

Six men were moaning in the field, four caravans were burning, the horses were running wild, the children in hysterics.

"It's finished," Donal was saying.

Killian nodded but it didn't feel quite right.

It was the old proverbial.

Too easy.

"We've got prisoners!" Tommy shouted.

"Fuck that, let them go, we've got to get out of here," Donal said.

He turned to Killian. "None of those boys are gonna die, are they? We don't need that trouble."

"I don't think any of them will die and it was your actual fucking self defence—" Killian began.

"Even so, Aidh. Better to do a quick triage on the fuckers, mate."

They did a twenty-second walk around. It was as Killian had thought. Kneecappings and shotgun pellets were painful but rarely fatal and all of them were making a lot of noise which was a good sign.

"I think we can leave them. Their mates'll come for them after we scarper," Donal said.

"How long will it take you to get on the road?" Killian asked.

"Could be moving in half an hour. You'll come with us?"

"I don't know, I—"

Killian froze.

Wait a minute.

There'd been five men with shotguns, but one guy with a semi-automatic. In all the excitement he'd forgotten about him.

Where was the guy with the pistol?

He wasn't here.

And he hadn't run.

Where was he?

Killian knew.

He was going for the beach.

He had outflanked him.

Again.

"Fuck!" Killian said and ran back towards the Pavee camp.

Glass was buckling and exploding in the four burning caravans, metal warping and bending in on itself. The smell of the melting plastic furniture caught him and made him retch.

But it didn't stop his pace.

He kept going towards the surf.

Fifty Pavee waiting around the beach, trying to calm their crying kids...

Fifty Pavee under the bright starlight.

Where were Rachel and the girls?

Where was she?

Killian made it through the dunes, stumbled, got up and saw Sue playing leapfrog with another girl.

"Where's your mother, Sue?" he yelled at her.

"She's over there with Claire," Sue stammered, a little frightened of him.

Killian looked to where the shaking little white hand was pointing. Further down the beach, almost in the blackness, Rachel was sitting on the sand with her arms around Claire, both of them staring out to sea.

"Thank you, Sue – go back to your game, everything's fine," Killian said quickly and stood.

Killian scoped the crowd for a man wearing a ski mask.

"Where are you, asshole?" he muttered.

But he wasn't here.

"Where the hell are you?"

Not one person in a balaclava, not a single…

But of course he would have taken it off. The Pavee would have jumped him if he'd still been wearing it, even with a gun.

Killian started eliminating individuals. He knew him, he knew him, he knew her, she was the mother of those kids, he knew that guy, who was that – oh yeah…

And then there he was:

It was Ivan, of course, or the Starshyna, as Sean had called him. The balaclava was rolled up to the top of his bald head so that he could spot Rachel, pull it down immediately, shoot her and run for it.

Killian understood it all now.

Tom had planned everything.

Hired or rounded up the thugs through his paramilitary contacts.

Probably UDA or boys from the British National Party. People who would enjoy it.

Tom had hired a crew, paid them and sent Ivan with them.

Let's scare the shite out of some fucking gyppoes…And oh dear, tragically something goes wrong and a woman gets shot dead.

By bizarre and tragic luck, the woman, unfortunately, was Richard Coulter's ex-wife, who was in the middle of a month-long methamphetamine-induced nervous breakdown.

Killian filled in the rest of the pieces as he ran.

It had to be Sean.

Tom must have found out where they were from Sean.

Sean knew him better than anyone.

"Tell me, Sean, if Killian was going to hide somewhere, where would he hide?"

Sean knew there were only a dozen Pavee campsites in Ulster. From then on it was merely a process of elimination. Tom had known from this morning and he'd sent his boy posing as a DSS officer to confirm it.

And now he'd sent Ivan.

It was clear that Ivan's mission was only to murder Rachel.

He himself was irrelevant.

After she was dead Sean had probably told Tom that he would play ball.

"Killian? Nah, he isn't in the grudge business, mate."

Fucker. But now was not the time to think about the insult.

He had foolishly emptied the Heckler and Koch's magazine after kneecapping the other attackers, but he checked it just in case.

Nothing.

"Shit."

This would have to be hand to hand.

Rachel was hugging Claire tightly, both of them wrapped in a crimson shawl, her back to him.

Her back to Ivan.

Ivan was twenty feet away. Walking deliberately so as not to draw attention to himself.

His instructions would be to spare the kid.

He would shoot her in the head from point-blank range.

Killian was sprinting.

Ivan was fifteen feet away.

Ivan's big cannon was equipped with a silencer.

Deliberately pacing the way a tiger might, paw in front of paw, head completely still.

"Rachel!" Killian screamed but there was too much chaos. Too much noise.

Ivan heard something though and looked to his left and right.

It was okay, no one was nearby.

Ten feet away he pulled down the ski mask, raised the .45 ACP and pointed it.

Eight feet away he sighted her along the barrel.

Six feet away he began squeezing the trigger and Killian slammed him into like a Samoan prop forward into a visiting scrum half.

While they were still in the air Killian smacked the gun out of Ivan's hand and the Russian stuck a finger in Killian's eye.

They landed hard on the wet sand.

Searing pain along Killian's cracked ribs and, still on the ground, the Russian headbutted him.

"The game's up, pal," Killian said, pushing him off. "It's all over."

Ivan got to his feet and scrambled for the gun.

Killian grabbed his ankle and pulled him down.

"Give it up, Starshyna," Killian said, attempting to engage him.

"My name is Markov, remember it," Markov said, ripped his ankle out of Killian's grip and kicked Killian in the chest with a full-force round-house kick.

Killian winced and rolled away, attempted to stand, lost his balance and sat backwards on the sand.

Markov attempted another roundhouse to Killian's neck but this time Killian got up a block.

With his big powerful hands Killian grabbed Markov's calf and wrenched the Russian off his feet, punching him in the gut with two quick right jabs before he could recover. Very fast for a big guy, Markov thought, as he rolled to the side and got to his feet again.

Rachel saw everything and began yelling for the others but no one could hear her over the fire. Markov launched a crescent kick at Killian which he dodged.

"We don't need to do this," Killian muttered, scrambling to his feet.

"You talk too much," Markov said, kicked Killian in the shin, grabbed the drawstrings of his hoodie and pulled Killian forward into an elbow punch that broke his nose. Markov hit him again with a right hook and a left uppercut.

Killian reeled.

Blood poured from his nostrils.

He gasped air and breathed more blood.

His eye was partially closed and couldn't see but he could feel the punches raining in.

He put his hands over his head, stepped back, pulled the hood from his forehead and tried to open his eyes.

Markov did a knifehand strike to Killian's throat and if it had connected properly that might have been it but Killian got up a partial block on pure instinct alone. His heart was racing. He was in full panic mode.

This guy was destroying him.

In a second or two he'd think to look for the gun again while Killian couldn't see. And if he had a blade Killian was a dead man.

Killian had one play.

It was it or nothing.

He ran at Markov, picked him up bodily in a bear hug and kept running until they reached the sea.

Markov punched and hit him but Killian kept going until he could feel the surf about his knees and then he dumped the Russian in the water.

Killian shoved Markov under the breakers and pushed down on his shoulders.

He squeezed with those big butcher-boy fingers, holding Markov just beneath the surface while Markov punched and kicked and even screamed.

Killian began counting in his head.

Ten, twenty, thirty, forty.

Markov looked up through the waves.

He didn't want to die here.

In Ireland.

So far from home.

So cold.

With this horrible man's face the last thing he would ever see.

He didn't want to die.

"Marina!" he screamed.

So cold.

So very cold.

Like Volgograd in winter.

Like Grozny.

That stupid Irishman, so slow, so old.

Look at him.

Look at him.

I should never have killed that priest.

So cold.

Marina…

When Killian reached 150 in his count he pulled Markov out of the water.

A crowd had gathered.

Killian dumped the dead Russian on the beach.

Rachel was up on the dune with Claire and Sue. As soon as she'd been able she'd gathered her girls and run. Good lass. He was proud of her.

"Is he dead?" Donal asked from behind him.

Killian turned, nodded.

"I suppose now we'll have to call the peelers," Donal said.

"Or just leave. Now," Killian said.

"Was he local?" Donal asked.

"Russian. He was an iceman. He was going to kill Rachel. This whole attack was just cover for him," Killian said.

Donal nodded and said no more.

Pavee didn't pry. Killian fished out Markov's wallet which contained a Nevada driver's licence.

"You think we should up sticks and go?"

"Leave him here," Killian said, his brain cooking. *If I'm fast enough I can pin it all on Markov. This and what comes after.*

"Aye. We'll go," Donal said. "We'll go to Donegal right now."

Donal gave him a handkerchief for his nose.

"Thanks, mate. I'm sorry for all the trouble," Killian said.

"Brother, think nothing of it, we're all still alive and more or less in one piece," Donal said.

"More or less," Killian agreed.

Killian offered Donal his hand. Donal shook it, smiled.

"I'd be grateful if you'd take Rachel and the girls and look after them," Killian said.

"What about you?" Donal asked.

Killian spied the Russian's gun and used Donal's handkerchief to pick it up out of the sand.

"I'm going to finish this."

Donal nodded and pressed his forehead against Killian's forehead.

"God and Mary and Patrick," Donal said.

"Aye," Killian replied.

He walked over to Rachel.

She was hugging her girls and crying. He kneeled beside her and wrapped his arms round all of them.

"I can't take much more of this," she said.

"Don't worry," he said. "You're not to going to have to."

Rachel looked at him and she looked at the gun. "What are you going to do?"

"I'm going to end it. Tonight."

"Tell me."

Killian shook his head. "It's best that you don't know."

Killian knelt next to Claire and Sue. "Goodbye girls," he said and kissed first Claire and then Sue on the top of the head.

Claire politely said goodbye and Sue looked at him oddly and hugged his legs.

"I'm going to miss you, little one," he said in Irish.

"Me too," she replied in the same language and burst into tears.

He could feel his throat crack. "Now, now child," Killian said and to Rachel: "Go easy on this one and she'll be just fine."

"Girls, give me one moment," Rachel said, stood, took Killian by the arm and walked a little bit away.

"Where are you going?" she asked when they were out of earshot.

"It's like I said, I'm going to finish this."

"You're going to see Richard? What are you going to do, Killian?"

"I'm going to take care of it. Come on, Rachel. Trust me," he said and smiled.

She looked at him. Those dark eyes, that lunk jaw. He looked like a B-movie villain.

But he wasn't a villain.

He had brought the best out of Sue.

And Claire liked him.

And he had saved their lives.

And now he was going to go and risk his life again.

For what?

"What have you got from all of this?" she asked.

Killian breathed deep and looked at her and the girls and he thought of the photo in his wallet. "I got plenty," he said.

"I don't think I understand," she said.

"That's okay," he said.

"Kiss me," she said.

"I can't, I'm bleeding," he said.

She grabbed his shoulders and pulled him close and kissed him and held him and burst into tears.

She knew that this was it for them.

One way or another.

But then it didn't matter.

He had already given her everything he had. He had given her his time and his patience and he was offering up his life on the altar of her and the children's future. And she was changed by him, changed for ever. Never again would she put the gun barrel in her mouth, never again would she surrender to despair or to fear.

As he said the great enemy was death.

The great enemy was death and as long as you breathed you were his master.

You could never forget that.

To live at all was miracle enough.

"I'm never going to see you again, am I?"

"If it all works out…no," he said and kissed her on the cheek and walked to the car park, hot-wired the Merc, and headed south with the burning caravans and the crowd on the beach and the men loading horses into horseboxes fading quickly in the glass of the rear-view mirror.

chapter 18
once upon a time in belfast

IN PAVEE SOCIETY, LIKE AT ILIUM, A MAN AND HIS ACTIONS WERE identical. You didn't think one thing and do another. If you ran, you were a runner. If you abandoned someone to their fate, you were a coward. You acted and the gods observed and Fate turned her wheel.

It was time to act.

Killian drove the Merc to Belfast along the A2.

He pulled into a BP station and bought paracetamol, a balaclava and WD40. He gulped the paracetamol and cleaned and oiled the .45, being careful to leave Markov's fingerprints on the grip.

He drove to the Malone Road in leafy, wealthy south Belfast. He parked the Merc a street away from Tom Eichel's house and put the gun in his pocket.

It was a comparatively modest Georgian three-storey affair with black, cast-iron railings and a door that opened onto the street. It was all location of course and around here it was two million five, easy.

Killian walked up the steps and rang the doorbell.

There was a pause before Tom opened it. He was dressed in a purple nightgown and holding a cup of tea. He should have thrown the tea and slammed the door immediately – his only chance, Killian thought.

Killian pointed the .45 at him. "Turn slowly, and put your hands up."

Tom's eyes were yellow and glazed. He seemed out of it.

"Turn slowly and put your hands up," Killian repeated.

He set his teacup on the hall table and put his hands in the air.

Killian closed the front door behind him.

Tom was unmarried but you never knew who might be around. He made Tom walk him through the house and they finally retired to a book-lined living room where a peat fire was burning. They sat in leather armchairs on either side of the hearth. Killian made sure Tom was well away from pokers or fire irons.

There was a strangeness to Tom's face and his movements were like a man drowning in molasses.

Killian looked into those yellow, beady eyes and noticed that the pupils were dilated. His face was flushed and there was sweat on his upper lip.

"Are you high?" Killian asked.

"Yes," Tom said simply.

"On what?"

"H. Dragon chasing. Over tinfoil. Nothing too serious."

"You're a drug addict?"

"Oh, no, nothing like that. I have rigid discipline. Only in times of great stress or on special occasions. Half a dozen times a year at the most."

"Which one's this? A time of great stress or a special occasion?"

"A little of both."

Killian leaned back in the chair and examined him. He wasn't on top form. He was like a melted candle with his hair draped over his face and perspiration on his face. He looked haggard, tired.

"So," Tom said at last.

"I need to ask you something, Tom," Killian said.

"What?"

"It's about Richard. I know that *you'll* never stop but I would really appreciate your honest assessment of Richard. I've killed Markov and I'm afraid I'm going to have to kill you but what will Richard do? He's an unknown quantity. Can I let him live or will he keep going after her?"

Tom's eyes widened but he didn't flinch.

He thought about it.

"I've put the fear of God into him. She's a junkie, Killian. She's capable of anything. If she told the cops or the papers there would have to be an inquiry. It took a while but I finally explained just how serious this all was to him. One of the girls in the house died during an abortion. She might be one of the ones in the tape. Jesus! It would be the end of everything."

"So you think Richard will try and top her?"

"I do. There's so many angles. We could blame her junkie pals, the IRA…And she's silenced."

Killian nodded. "That's what I thought. It's a real catch-22. If she says nothing she'll never feel safe from Richard, if she goes to the police, the IRA will see to it that she never makes it to trial. At the very least she'll never feel safe."

Tom shook his head. "No," he agreed.

"The only way is to take Richard out of the picture, you out of the picture and never mention the laptop or what was on it to anyone."

They sat while the turf logs cracked and spat and the grandfather clock in the hall ticked.

"I suppose there's nothing I can say to dissuade you," Tom offered with a thin smile.

Killian shook his head.

"She got her hooks into you, huh?"

"It's not like that," Killian said.

"What about money? I have a lot of money," Tom tried.

"No."

Tom swallowed hard.

"So you're just going to kill me?"

"I have to kill both of you."

Tom nodded.

"Did Richard know about the attack on the tinkers?" Killian asked.

"Not a thing. Plausible deniability."

"So he's not sitting up waiting for a phone call?"

"No. Although that place is a bloody fortress."

"Yeah, I know. It's going to be tricky."

Tom sniffed and bit his lip. He repressed a couple of sobs. He had a German father and an Ulster Presbyterian mother. Not the most demonstrative of combinations. "There's really nothing I can say?" he asked.

"No."

"Please."

"No."

"Please, Killian."

"No."

Killian didn't want to torture the man. He lifted the .45.

Tom put up a finger. "Wait! You don't have to actually shoot me, do you?"

"Yes, I do."

"What if I overdosed? What if I injected myself," he asked.

"You take it intravenously too?"

Tom laughed. "Not since the bad old days, not for years, but as you'll find with your lady friend the hunger never leaves you."

Killian walked him to a compartment in the floorboards. An iron lock-box with a passport, money, bags of unrefined heroin and cocaine, a bag of sterile needles.

"I've been saving this. For a rainy day," he said.

He was excited now.

All he could think about was the hit. The adrenalin would make it all the sweeter.

"Do you need any help?" Killian asked.

Tom shook his head.

He cooked the heroin with a lighter, made a speedball with the cocaine, sucked up a dose to kill an elephant, tied off an arm, lay down on the sofa and injected himself.

He closed his eyes and a look of ecstasy passed across his face.

Fatal respiratory depression occurred when the cocaine wore off and the heroin was felt in isolation. His breathing became laboured and finally he stopped breathing all together. There was no death rattle, no heave.

Killian checked for a pulse, found nothing and left the house.

He drove the Merc back to Whitehead and parked it on a side street just before the Bla Hole cliff.

It was half a mile from here to Knocknagulla.

He got the spare tyre from under the cloth in the Mercedes' boot. He put the tyre under his arm, turned up his funny-looking raincoat, rolled up the balaclava until it was just above his eyebrows and walked along the road.

The night was clear.

The Bla Hole cliff afforded a view over all Belfast Lough, North Down and Scotland as far as the distant town of Girvan.

Belfast itself was stretched ahead of him under the surrounding hills like an upturned mirror. The old girl winking at him through the lights at the shipyard and the Cave Hill.

Killian carried the tyre to the lodge at Coulter's house.

It was a one-storey, pokey wee building right on the road. He must have driven by it a hundred times, never once considered it.

A light was on. He didn't have much of a plan. If he could get in and out without a positive ID or camera angles – the peelers could, maybe, pin this on Ivan. It was *his* gun. His fingerprints. Maybe.

Killian knocked on the lodge window.

No answer.

He knocked again. Someone moved apart a Venetian blind and looked at him. A young guy running a bit to fat and baldness.

Killian lifted the tyre.

"What's the matter?" a voice said over a concealed intercom.

"I've got a puncture. And you are not going to believe, but spare has a puncture too. Could let me use phone?" Killian said in an vague Eastern European accent.

"Why are you carrying the tyre?" the voice asked. He was a Brummie, which pleased Killian. He liked Birmingham and he liked Brummies. He wouldn't kill this guy if he could help it.

"I thought I would leave car here. I park it up road at corner. I call for taxi to take me to hotel in Belfast."

"You're going to leave your car?"

"I get sleep, have spare fixed in morning and get taxi back tomorrow," Killian said with an embarrassed grin.

"Where'd you park your car?" the man asked.

"On corner, at cliff," Killian said, catching the man's drift.

"Are you mental? That's a blind corner. Someone ploughs around there, hits your car and they're over the fucking edge!"

"Oh no," Killian said, sounding foreign and clueless.

"You're a bloody idiot!" the man said and Killian watched him leave his perch behind the bulletproof glass. A moment later he came out of the lodge. He was a chubby fellow but then a lot of ex-blades piled on the pounds after their military service was done. Eliminate that ten-mile run every morning and suddenly all the sausages, chips and beer took their toll. "You're going to get somebody fucking killed mate. You're gonna have to move your car."

Killian took Markov's silenced Colt .45 from behind the tyre and pointed it at the man's heart.

"Let's go inside and talk about this," he said in his normal north Belfast burr – maybe the most unlovable and menacing accent on the planet.

He pulled the balaclava down over his face. The Russian accent and the funny games were over. "Take it easy mate, take it easy," the Brummie replied.

"Hands on the top of your head and if you squeak the wrong way you better hope that the atheists are wrong."

The man put his hands on his head.

They went inside the lodge.

It was a small single-room affair with a lot of camera monitors, a desk and a set of pigeonholes for the mail. There was a door to a toilet, a microwave and a kettle for making tea and Cup-a-Soup. Some of the monitors were infrared which impressed Killian as did the man's Heckler and Koch MP5 assault rifle which was lying on the desk.

"Nice place you've got here," Killian said.

"Mate, please, please, don't top me. I'm just a fucking lackey. You know?"

Killian looked about the room for rope or string or a long piece of electrical cord that he could strip.

"I'm lucky to be alive, I know that, I was fucking blown up in Mosul. RPG in the side of the Rover. Fucking Sergeant Halder bought it. I have burns on me left arm, to this day it hurts in the winter and..."

Killian couldn't see anything that he could use.

He remembered the play of his mentor, one Michael Forsythe. "What's your name?" he asked.

"Viv."

"Well, Viv, you don't have any gaffer tape do you?"

"What?"

"Gaffer tape, duct tape, you know the stuff I'm talking about?"

"I think we do. Top drawer." Viv said.

"Great. Now, tell me where all the other guns are."

"No other guns, just the MP5," Viv said with a depressing attempt at cunning.

Killian shook his head and tutted. "And I thought we were getting on famously," he said and shot Viv in the left ankle.

Viv crumpled to the floor. He didn't cry out – which must have been that vaunted SAS training – but instead groaned and said between gritted teeth: "In the black drawer, under monitor number one, there's a police special .38, a Smith and Wesson 9 millimetre semi-automatic and you can see the MP5 for yourself."

Killian opened the drawer and took out the handguns. He shoved them into his coat pocket. They were useful but without question the MP5 was going to be his weapon of choice.

"What about that duct tape?" he asked.

"Drawer next to the kettle."

"Next to the kettle? Ahh, I see."

Killian strapped the MP5 over his shoulder, inserted the long 9 millimetre magazine and got the duct tape.

He bent over Viv. "Flip over on your stomach, there's a good chap," Killian said.

Viv flipped. "Please don't kill me, please…"

"I suppose you've got a wife and kids?"

"No, I don't, but I've got a season ticket to Villa Park. Mr C lets me go every home game. This is going to be our year," he said.

Killian was impressed by this piece of bullshit. It was just the sort of thing that the guy thought might impress someone like Killian.

"Gimme your paws," Killian said.

He rolled up the man's sleeves and duct-taped his wrists tightly together. Killian had a look at Viv's ankle. It was nasty. Bone sticking through the skin and the bullet had awkwardly travelled down through the man's foot.

"This is going to hurt, I'm afraid," Killian said.

He rolled up Viv's jeans and duct-taped his ankles together, wrapping the tape around a dozen times.

Viv grunted but was still flying with this stiff-upper-lip stance.

Your standard Mike Forysthe move now would be to hog-tie him or beat him unconscious or lock him in a cupboard, but Killian reckoned that that was going overboard. Viv would just need a good talking to near the end of the convo, to impress upon him what kind of a man he was dealing with.

"You did well, Viv. We're done," Killian said.

Viv grunted and lay there on the floor blinking back the waves of pain. And he wasn't alone. Markov had given Killian a good beating and anything around the ribs smarted for a long time.

"Okay now, this is how it's going to go: I'm going to ask you a series of questions and you're going to tell me all the answers. If I find out that any of your answers were incorrect or incomplete I'll come back here and put a bullet in your brain. Fair enough?"

"Fair enough," Viv said.

"Okay. Let's do this fast and I'll get you a smoke. How many other guards are on duty tonight?"

"Two. Ginger's in the grounds and Bobby's in the house. Ground floor."

"Where on the ground floor?"

"There's an ante-room off the entrance hall. Little cubby. He sits in there, reading, wanking."

"You must have a plan of the house, somewhere," Killian said.

"Over there on the noticeboard, there's a fire exit evacuation plan, that's got the whole house except for the greenhouses and the hangar."

Killian looked at the plan, memorised it.

"Now you fellas must do a radio check or a shift change or something."

"Radio check every hour, shift change every two hours."

Killian nodded. "Go on," he said.

"Go on what?"

"When's the next radio check? When's the next shift change?"

"What time is it now?"

Killian didn't have a watch but there was a clock above the microwave.

"Two-twenty if that clock's right," Killian said.

"It's not right, check my watch," Viv told him.

Killian rolled down some of the duct tape and found that it was actually two thirty-one.

He took the watch off and slipped it on his own wrist.

"Two thirty-one," he said.

"You better move fast if you're going to burgle the house," Viv said. "Ginge is supposed to come and relieve me at three and then I go over and swap with Bobby."

Killian nodded grimly. Did he really think that this was all about a burglary? A man would take on the three ex-SAS types just to steal some pictures or antiques or whatever? Well, maybe if they were really valuable, which they probably were.

"Do you talk on the radio before you do the shift change?"

"Well…"

"Well, what?"

"We talk on the radio all the time. All night."

Shit. That was a fucking fly in the ointment.

"Viv, that causes me some difficulty doesn't it?"

"How so, mate?"

"Well, if they give you a buzz on the radio and you don't answer they're going get all Red Alert on me, aren't they? Red alert, this is not a drill, call the fucking peelers."

"I suppose they would," Viv admitted.

"Where is this walkie-talkie of yours?" Killian asked, looking around the surfaces and not seeing anything.

"I may have left it in the toilet," Viv said.

Killian went to the toilet and the radio was indeed there sitting on the spare toilet rolls next to a copy of *Viz*. He picked it up and carried it back.

"When Ginger calls, you'll just act natural, you won't try and fuck me will you?"

"No way," Viv said.

"Cos whatever else happens you'll be for the memorial wall at Hereford," Killian said.

"I know. Don't worry."

Killian sat down in what turned out to be a comfortable, leather swivel chair.

"Who else is in the house?"

"Mr C, Helena, Mrs Lavery, Paul," Viv said.

"Who the fuck's Paul?"

"Butler type. Must be seventy if he's a day. He's in the right front bedroom on the ground floor."

Killian looked at the chart. Right front bedroom. Check.

"Mrs Lavery?"

"She's all the way at the back of the house in the other bedroom."

"And how old is she?"

"I don't know. Fifty-five?"

"Okay."

"She might have her niece staying with her. Sometimes she does. It'll be on the visitor's chart in Bobby's room, but I haven't checked it."

"Niece. Christ. How old is she?"

"Eleven, I think."

So that was another maybe seven people to deal with.

The radio crackled. "Joke for you," a man with a London accent said.

Killian held the radio up to Viv's mouth and pushed the Talk button.

"Go on then," Viv said.

"Don the Brummie lorry driver's been on the road for thirty years, always local. He gets into work one morning to find that he has to drive to London for the first time with a big load of timber. He sets off down the M1 and after a bit he's on the Edgware Road."

"I've heard it before, a million times," Viv said to Killian.

"Let him tell it," Killian said and pushed Talk again.

"Go on," said Viv.

"He's in the Big Smoke, traffic, tall buildings, people. He pulls over at a bus stop, winds the window down and shouts across the road to some bint waiting for the number 17: 'Oi love, is this London?' he asks. 'Yeah,' she says. 'Well, where do you want this wood then?' he asks."

Killian looked at Viv. "Laugh and tell him that's a good one," Killian said. He pushed the Talk button and Viv laughed and said, "Oh mate, that's a good one, ya cockney bastard, ya."

Laughter. Laughter right outside the lodge door.

Killian checked the watch. It was only 2.40. Ginger was twenty minutes early.

But he was laughing and completely at ease.

Killian looked at Viv, put his finger to his lips, held the MP5 in his right hand and put his left hand on the door handle.

The door opened outwards. Ginger would see it opening, but he would be expecting Viv so he wouldn't be in a weapon-ready stance and it—

As Killian turned the handle Viv suddenly yelled: "Ginger, look out! There's a fucking cunt in here with a gun!"

Killian kicked the door open and forward-rolled out of the lodge into the Belfast night. A drizzle of automatic fire and Killian kept rolling until he reached a mature palm tree that must have been here long before Coulter.

Every single second would be precious now.

If they called 999 immediately the nearest peelers would be coming from Carrickfergus, Killian's own manor, and Killian knew those boys well – yeah, they were slow and a bit thick but they wouldn't take half an hour. Maybe not twenty minutes.

Killian stepped from behind the tree, gave himself a covering burst and ran for the house – not the obvious escape route of the front gate. He reached the portico before Ginger fired back at him.

He dived for the marble steps and Ginger's MP5 9 millimetre bullets carved holy hell out of the front door, a line of splinters making its way at a thirty-degree angle up the wall. He was firing the MP5 on full auto and Killian waited for the silence. When it came he stood up and took aim. Killian saw Ginger switching clips with remarkable speed and proficiency.

It wouldn't save him.

Killian squeezed one well-aimed single round into Ginger's chest, topping the poor bastard immediately.

Killian had no time for remorse.

He shoulder-charged the front door and burst into the hall.

Pistol fire from the side room.

Killian hit the deck. Crawled behind a pillar.

Pistol fire.

Killian took a quick look: a hand connected to a wrist from behind a door. No person standing there exposing himself, just the pistol and maybe a mirror on a piece of stick.

No. 3 was being cautious.

"The cops are on their way!" No. 3 shouted. He was called Bobby or something, right?

"Bobby, I don't want to kill you, close that fucking door, don't come out, and wait for the cops!" Killian yelled.

"Fuck you, arsehole!" Bobby yelled and shot at him.

Killian looked at No. 3's door. Some kind of dark expensive tropical hardwood no doubt, and sleekit old. No. 3 knew that 9 millimetre slugs wouldn't penetrate it.

However Killian also had Markov's ACP.

He let the MP5 hang on its strap, took out the Colt, removed the suppressor and gave No. 3 four .45 rounds through the door.

Killian heard nothing. No scream, no moan, no cry of defiance. Nothing.

He hesitated. Go on into the house? No. Couldn't have this sneaky character behind him.

Holding the .45 ahead of him he ran to the No. 3's ante room and entered FBI-style, clocking corners and blind spots.

Bobby was lying on the floor, his skull cracked in half like a broken egg. Blood, brains, bone all over the floor.

"Jesus," Killian muttered and ran back out into the hall.

A woman was standing there with a walking stick.

"Ye dirty baste!" she screamed at him and advanced on him at a shuffle-run.

Killian smacked the side of her head with his closed fist and she went down like a thirteen-year-old lassie during a Justin Bieber concert.

Killian ran into the foyer, saw the venerable butler, nodded to him, didn't see any niece and ran upstairs taking the steps three at a time.

He had forgotten the floor plan and he tried three bedrooms before finding the master bedroom at the back of the house.

Stupid place for a master bedroom – no view, he thought, as he kicked the door in and dived for the floor.

The expected shotgun blast did not come.

Killian opened his eyes.

Helena was standing by the bed, clutching her swollen belly.

"Everything okay?" Killian asked.

She looked terrified. Petrified, to be more strictly accurate.

"Everything okay?" Killian repeated, checking the blind spots.

"What? No."

"I mean with the baby, is everything okay with baby?" Killian asked, looking under the big four-poster.

"I think so, I don't know."

"Cops will be here soon. Where is he?"

"I don't know, I—"

Killian walked towards her and nudged the barrel of the MP5 against her stomach.

"Where?" he asked quietly.

She pointed at the balcony.

"He's right out there? I don't believe it."

"There's a staircase to the garden," Helena said.

Killian was cruising on adrenalin now, he touched an imaginary forelock and said, "Much obliged, ma'am," in a good ol' boy accent.

He opened the French doors and walked out onto the balcony. There were indeed steps down to the garden.

Down to the massive garden that had sheds, a rosary, a couple of different greenhouses and a bloody orchard.

"Shit," Killian muttered.

If he was halfway smart Coulter would just find a quiet corner and hold his breath, knowing that rescue was roaring to him along the Belfast Road.

"Coulter!" Killian screamed.

No answer.

"Coulter, you motherfucker!"

Surf.

Wind.

Sheep.

"Damn it," Killian said. He looked at Viv's watch.

3.00.

How long did he have before this jig was well and truly up?

"Coulter, I'm going to shoot her if you don't come out!" he yelled.

Killian waited but Coulter did not come out.

"Coulter, you can't hide forever!" Killian yelled.

But Coulter was no mug.

"Come on, man, we can talk about this!" Killian yelled.

Killian caught something on the wind.

Far off in the distance he could hear a siren tearing along the coast. Them boys had got their dicks out of each other's arses faster than he'd been expecting.

Killian drummed his finger on the balcony rail.

And then he slapped his forehead.

Did an actual Buster Keaton forehead slap.

He ran back into the bedroom where Helena was sitting on the bed and talking on the phone to someone.

Killian touched his imaginary forelock again and ran along the corridor and down the sweeping staircase.

Mrs Lavery had recovered sufficiently to call him a "filthy heathen Turk" which was a nice anachronistic insult.

Killian ran past the butler who was also on the phone to someone.

Again no niece.

He sprinted out through the wrecked front doors onto the gravel driveway.

He ran back to the lodge where Viv was trying to cut the duct tape off his hands with the meal edge of the chair."Now, I have to blow your brains out, don't I?" Killian said.

Viv flinched and Killian flipped him over and ran another couple of lines of duct tape around his wrists.

How do I get these frickin' cameras to go to infrared? he wondered, and then noticed a switch on every single monitor that said "Heat".

He found the camera overlooking the back garden and flipped the "Heat" switch.

"I can hear the sirens," Viv said. "You better leg it, mate."

Killian examined the infrared camera and sure enough there was a massive red human-shaped heat source coming from inside the longer of the two greenhouses. It was Coulter and he was hiding up in a corner behind some bushes or trees or something.

Killian grinned and leaned over Viv. "I'm not your mate, mate, and by the way Villa are fucking shite," he said and sprinted back across the gravel and ran around the side of the house.

He held the MP5 in assault mode and keeping a low posture ran to the larger of the two greenhouses. He turned the handle and went inside.

Crouching he made his way along a line of fruit trees towards where Coulter had been hiding.

Gunfire.

Glass bursting above his head.

Two shots. A third.

It wasn't Mrs Lavery, was it? Or Helena, god love her. Nah. It was coming from *inside*. Coulter had very sensibly armed himself.

Killian hit the deck and belly-crawled between the trees, which were housed in red terracotta pots.

Two more shots, just above him. They were big heavy slow slugs as if from a .38 revolver.

There had been what, five of them? Five shots?

Killian lifted his hand and waved it in the moonlight.

Another shot, a window splintering and then a distinct click. And Coulter would not be reloading that thing in two seconds SAS-style.

Still, there was no point hanging about. Killian sprang to his feet and ran to Coulter's corner.

Coulter was scrambling for a back exit.

Killian put an MP5 round in the door to get his attention.

Coulter turned and dropped his gun and put his hands in the air.

"You wouldn't shoot an unarmed man," Coulter said.

Killian walked towards him holding the MP5's pistol-grip in his right hand and its curved magazine in his left.

A wave of depression passed through him.

He was getting the post-action blues before the action was even over.

He took a deep breath.

How lovely it would be just to have a wee lie down.

The sirens, however, were distinctly closer now.

Coulter was standing right at the greenhouse door, where Helena or Mrs Lavery or anyone else could see him and maybe help.

This next act needed privacy.

"Have a seat," Killian said.

Coulter sat on the ground with his head against the door handle. Killian squatted in front of him baseball-catcher fashion.

"What are you going to do?" Coulter asked, trembling. His face was pale, his blue eyes nearly black under the moon. He had cut himself on the cheek and the blood was dripping onto the ground. He was dressed in a plain black T-shirt and blue pyjama bottoms with racing cars on them.

"What are these, orange trees?" Killian asked.

"Lime and lemon," Coulter said.

"Lime and lemon."

The two men looked at one another.

Killian shook his head and raised the MP5.

"Wait a minute!" Coulter screamed. "Why are you doing this? Why?"

"I'd like to say I was sorry, Richard," Killian said. "But I saw the video. I heard about the abortions."

"Hold on. Hold on a minute, Killian. They were all older than you think. They were all fucking willing participants. There was no rape. We fucking paid them. We got them presents. We bought their silence."

"I'll bet you did. I'm sure you and your good friend Dermaid McCann did indeed make sure that no one fucking talked."

"It wasn't like that, Killian. It wasn't like that. Do you remember the seventies in Belfast? It was a fucking war. There were different rules. It was Berlin 1945. There were no rules. Bombings every day. Firebombings. Shootings. Do you remember? Running a fucking brothel in all that madness. In all that madness. A wee bit of fun. That's all it was. It was a good thing. A coming together across the divide. Me and McCann and a couple of others."

"Fun was it?"

"Don't be such a fucking choirboy, Killian. This is Ireland. Far fucking worse was happening in orphanages and fallen girls' homes and fucking convents. This is old news, mate. Special Branch knows about it and you don't hear them fucking blabbing."

"So that's why you've never been granted a knighthood," Killian said, as the sound of a helicopter now got added to the sirens.

"It's all bullshit, Killian, it's water under the bridge, it's a fairy story. Nobody's interested. You see?"

Killian shook his head. "Why did you get the film transferred from Super 8? Why did you keep it?"

"Insurance. McCann wasn't a player back then, he was just a fucking muckety-muck who controlled a local racket. He got me a couple of contacts and then both our stars started to rise. He got onto the IRA Army council. That's a fucking useful chip to have. What would you do? Just insurance, that's all. I didn't even think about it anymore. It was on some old bloody computer that I didn't even think about."

"Does he know you have the film?"

"Aye, he remembers us filming it, but he thinks it was destroyed ages ago. He's never brought it up with me. Nobody knows about the footage. Just you, me, Tom…and Rachel of course."

Killian nodded. That helped clarify things.

"See? It's all over. No harm done. All fucking over, mate. Nobody gives a shit about that old nonsense. Belfast has changed. Ulster has changed. Ireland has changed," Coulter continued.

"Yes."

Coulter laughed. "And the laptop's at the bottom of a bloody lake! Did you know that?"

"I was there," Killian said.

"Aye. So you get it, right? It's all bullshit, Killian. Once upon a fucking time in fucking Belfast…"

Killian stroked his chin, looked Coulter in the eyes.

"I've been a force for good, mate, and I've worked bloody hard. I didn't get any breaks."

"That's not strictly true, is it? Your little self-protection society. You and McCann. You never had to worry about the IRA blowing up one of your offices. Yours was the one building company people knew could get the job done even during the darkest years. How was that? Luck? Hard work? No, now we know what lay at the back of the Coulter miracle don't we?"

"That's bollocks. The fucking seventies you're going on about? It's old news, Killian. Those were the bloody days. It's 2011! The century's turned, the decade's turned. Listen to me, mate: Nobody. Fucking. Cares!"

"I do see what you're saying, Richard, and maybe you're right about that, but I am going to have to shoot you," Killian said. "Tom told me you won't stop until she's dead. Her existence threatens everything."

"I'll give you a million pounds to put down that gun right now. Come on, you're smart, you're a tinker, what does one wee doll matter against a million quid? Every man for himself, right?"

"That's your philosophy? That's your accumulated wisdom?" Killian asked as the sound of the chopper thudded off the lough water.

"Aye. Look, it's not a bad thing. Remember Mrs Thatcher said that there was no such thing as society, there's only individuals. Remember that?"

Killian kneeled in front of him on one knee, like a bridegroom before a bride.

"I remember, but you see, that doesn't work for me. I say life is given meaning by context. There are no individual selves. There are only humans embedded in practices, places, cultures. And in my culture on the other side of the criminal line, the world of The Life, there are heavy bonds imposed upon you. To be a Pavee, to be a tinker, is to wade through a sea of mutual debts of hospitality and loyalty."

"What are you fucking talking about?" Coulter asked, his mouth dry, his hopes of rescue increasing as he heard the brakes of a police Land Rover squeal outside his front gate.

"It's very simple. I promised Rachel I'd take care of this tonight and that's exactly what I'm going to do."

This was Killian on firm ground at last. He had left that confusing straight world of real estate and banks and mortgages. He had left Sean's world of smart hoodlums exploiting the weak for financial gain. He had even left the Northern Ireland he had grown up in, that place Coulter had spoken of, that odd non-country in the midst of a low-level civil war, indulging its sectarian passion in a way no other place in Cold War Europe could.

No, he was back in the land of his fathers and forefathers. The world of men who shook hands on horse deals and debts and kept their word in the face of the abyss.

And he knew he had been fair. Even in the labyrinthine world of tradition and obligation that made up Pavee society there were ways out. There had to be. Tradition was not meant to be moribund. It was a living argument. You were not a puppet following a preset script. You were a live actor with permission to improvise.

There were one or two things that Coulter could have said that would have saved his life.

He had, however, said none of them.

The glass was falling.

His time had run out.

Killian sighted the MP5 on Coulter's forehead and pulled the trigger once.

Coulter was killed instantly.

From existence to black non-existence just like that.

Amazing really.

Killian unstrapped the gun, let it drop, walked out the back of the greenhouse and across the garden.

He climbed the garden wall, jogged to the exterior fence, climbed that, and then ran deep into the Antrim hills, running until he reached the high bog – an ancient and traditional place of refuge for men seeking shelter from the authority of kings.

epilogue
on gog magog street

ICHAEL FORSYTHE WALKED THROUGH THE GREEN CHANNEL of Heathrow's Terminal 5 and was not stopped by the Customs inspectors. He was wearing a charcoal grey Armani suit, black Testoni Norvegese shoes and his luggage was a Floto men's garment bag. He didn't look like a heroin mule, although heroin smuggling was a residual part of the criminal empire he shared with his wife Bridget.

He took off his sunglasses and scanned the chaotic arrivals area for his contact.

A pale, cuddly-looking character in a uniform was holding up a sign that appeared to say: Michel Fireside. He was a curly bap, only about twenty-three or twenty-four. He was listening to something on an iPod and you could just tell it was Coldplay.

Michael approached him.

"Are you waiting for Michael Forsythe?" he asked.

"Are ye he?" the man asked in a friendly Scottish accent that should have been a voice on a cartoon.

"Yes."

"I'm Douggie. Gimme yer wee bag and we'll gay outside, Mr Paulson is weeing in the car."

Michael gave him the bag and followed him to a black limousine where

Mr Paulson was not, alas, "weeing". He was a tiny but not unimpressive character in a three-piece suit with scarred knuckles and DM shoes.

He was listening to the cricket and fiddling with *The Times* crossword. He shook Michael's hand with un-English enthusiasm.

"Pleasant flight?" Paulson asked.

"Very," Michael said. "On time, no problems."

"I love Virgin. They treat you well," Paulson said in an accent that Michael now realised had a touch of Geordie in it, which perhaps explained the handshake.

"They do," Michael agreed.

"I booked a hotel room if you want to go freshen up," Paulson said.

Michael shook his head. "No, I feel fine. Let's do this."

Paulson looked about the car park. "I've a few things to give you, let's go inside the limo, okay?"

"Fine," Michael agreed.

Once inside Paulson opened a Sainsbury's bag and gave Michael a ski mask, a map, a mobile phone and a Biretta 92 FS with an ambidextrous manual safety and an AAC Evolution 40 pistol suppressor.

Michael took the Biretta, stripped it and put it back together.

He took off the silencer, blew through it and reattached it.

"Everything okay?" Paulson asked.

"Spare magazine?" Michael asked.

"Two in the bag. Forty-five rounds all together."

Michael nodded.

"Everything's okay?" Paulson asked, sensing that something might be up.

"We're not going there in this, are we?" Michael asked.

Paulson nodded nervously. "Uh, Douggie knows the road and we've got satnav and—"

"From what I understand it's a small English village, right?"

"Yes."

"Don't you think a big honking limo's going to look a wee bit out of place in a scene like that?"

"What do you want me to do?" Paulson asked.

Michael yawned. "I'll go inside, get something to eat; you get me another car, programme the satnav and I'll drive myself."

"Are you sure? I thought Douggie would be your backup. He's got experience."

Douggie's "experience" had *resumé inflation* written all over it. He was somebody's nephew or little brother.

"I'm sure he's very capable, but I'll be fine. I'll meet you back here in an hour."

"Yes, of course," Paulson said, a little chastened.

Michael left his gear, went back inside Terminal 5, had breakfast at Gordon Ramsey's and read the English papers. He too tried *The Times* crossword but he had been so long out of the UK that he got few of the contemporary references.

When he returned Paulson was standing beside the limo and smiling.

"We got you a black BMW 5 series. Common as muck up there," he said.

"Great," Michael replied with satisfaction.

"And Douggie's programming the satnav right now, he's taking you the easiest route, i.e. not through London, is that okay?"

"That'll be fine."

"Did you get breakfast?"

"Went to Gordon Ramsey's. Got the Spanish omelette."

"It was okay?"

"If you want to eat well in England you should have breakfast three times a day," Michael said, attempting to diffuse the tension a little.

It didn't work. "You want another breakfast? Ramsey's famous for his small portions. You know there's a McDonald's on the slip road. The last thing you wanna be is hungry on a job like this."

"Where's this Beemer?" Michael said with a little inward sigh.

He resisted the temptation of the McDonald's and had no difficulty finding the M25.

He listened to Radio 4 until the satnav's saucy female voice began warning him about the turn-off for the M11.

He took the M11 to Duxford and then almost immediately took the A505 and finally the A1301 to Sawston.

He found that he was in East Anglia. A part of England he had never been to before.

Flat: wheat, barley and rapeseed fields.

It was attractive countryside.

At the village of Sawston he let the satnav take him onto New Road, Babraham Road, Woodland Road and at last Gog Magog Street.

He parked the car, got out, stretched.

The street only had houses on one side. Nineteen-thirties-style Mock Tudor mansions that looked across the fields to a small set of hills to the north.

It was drizzling.

His watch told him that it was five past five in the morning, which meant that it was 10.05.

The scouting reports had been consistent and at this time of the day he was not expecting trouble. Killian worked at the Royal Mail sorting office in Cambridge. He cycled the eight miles into the city each morning at five and came back around one.

And the traveller camp itself was not difficult to spot. A line of a dozen caravans on the common next to the wood.

The field looked boggy.

Michael winced.

It would play havoc with his shoe leather but there didn't appear to be any actual road so there wasn't much of a choice.

He stood for a bit and let the warm English drizzle coat him. The rainwater slowly reservoired in his sandy hair, awaiting a critical mass when it would pour down his face in baptismal streams. "This is stupid," he said and got back inside the car and texted Bridget:

ARVD SFLY NO PRBS LUL M.

He put the silenced Biretta in the specially cut pocket of his jacket, got out of the BMW and locked the car.

He stepped over the sheugh onto the common and walked gingerly across the field to the traveller camp.

A dog came and kept him company. Thinking he must have food or something, a goat began following him too.

He reached the camp without adding to his menagerie.

There were a few people pottering around. Michael nodded a good morning to a kid and looked for the caravan with the blue door.

He found it a little apart from the others on a small rise near the wood. It was tiny and dented but on a good site, protected from the easterlies by an ancient oak tree and with a view to the north and west. There was a goat outside it too on a long tether. A nanny goat that Killian obviously used for the milk in his tea.

It nuzzled at the pocket of his trousers and he had to shoo it.

Michael looked for a spare key under a breeze block and a rubbish bin and finally under a spare tyre. There was no key.

He went round the back to see if any of the windows were open, but they were all locked.

"It's the old skelly then, isn't it?" Michael said to the goat. This was not his field of expertise and it took him nearly ten minutes to get the door open with the wire and the skeleton key. If any of his boys had ever taken that long he would have fired them on the spot.

He was fortunate in having not drawn any serious attention or, worse, comments from any of Killian's neighbours.

He'd had a yarn prepared – "I'm a cousin from Belfast, I'm here to surprise him, don't say anything" – but he was glad that he didn't have to use it.

Killian's caravan was uninteresting.

A fold-out bed. A TV. A radio. A tub of rice. A bag of new potatoes. Cans of mushroom soup. A couple of paperback novels. A distinct aroma.

Michael sat on a rather grubby-looking sofa, set the Biretta on a

Formica table in front of him and rifled through the novels, finally selecting a bruised copy of *Nine Stories* by J. D. Salinger.

The first story was about a newly wed couple who were on holiday in Miami – she was uptight and he had mental problems. Michael had never read Salinger before though Bridget and Siobhan swore by him; that was perhaps the reason why he'd avoided him, he reflected: the girls, God love them, did not share many of his tastes.

He pushed open the rear caravan window and let in a more pleasant odour of cut grass. He could hear kids talking to the billy goat in Irish and there was birdsong from the oak tree.

If Killian had decided to cut across the fields that particular afternoon, which he did sometimes when it wasn't raining, he would have seen the open window and Michael would have been rumbled; but as it was he stuck to the road.

He liked this job. Delivering letters on a bike to the villages of South Cambridgeshire was like a profession from the sepia fifties that never were. The person who had had the route before him had obviously been some kind of slacker genius who had convinced the Royal Mail that it took you seven hours to do what you could have done hopping on one foot in half that time.

Killian got to know his customers and they him. It was a mutual admiration society and everyone liked a bit of craic.

A third of the way through his round he stopped to drink a pint of Greene King at the Pickerel which had been serving working stiffs like himself for half a millennium.

After the pub it was a very light load and he'd stop to chat to anyone who wanted to talk. On this particular day he'd gotten the brief histories of concrete, colonial Simla and Dutch Jazz and listened to an unpatriotic attack on Lord Nelson, who apparently could have caught Napoleon with his pants down if he hadn't been so hasty at the Nile.

Killian was feeling good. He wheeled his bike into the tinker camp and nodded to the Coaghs, new arrivals from Donegal, who only spoke Irish.

"A good afternoon to you, Eamonn," Mr Coagh said to him in pure

Gaelic, adding nothing about the visitor he had seen go into Killian's caravan.

"And to you a good afternoon, Seamus," Killian replied.

He wheeled the bike on. He didn't really like the name, Eamonn, which he had assumed on hopping the ferry to England, but it was way too late to change it now.

Of course he could never go back to Killian or even his real name. The Ulster peelers would be after him forever and he'd heard rumours that Michael Forsythe had a contract out on him too.

He leaned his bike up against the caravan and rubbed the beard which the Communication Workers Union had fought to let him keep in the face of management's displeasure.

Molly was looking at him nervously and he could tell she had a guilty conscience about something.

"If I find you've been at my carrots I'll be furious," he said.

Molly bleated and shook her head as if she'd understood.

Killian put the key in the lock.

Michael was on the last paragraph of the Salinger when he heard Killian's voice outside.

He picked up the Biretta and slowly clicked off the safety.

Killian came in, clocked Michael, tensed, thought about a sudden move.

Michael disabused him of the notion with a shake of the head.

"Close the door, sit down," Michael said.

Killian closed the door and sat opposite him in the rickety wicker chair he had found in a skip.

What a bloody shitty chair to die in, was Killian's immediate thought.

"I'll be with you in one minute," Michael said. "Don't, you know, fucking breathe."

Michael kept the gun trained on Killian, picked up the Salinger again and finished the story about the newly weds.

He put the book down and shook his head. "Dear oh dear," he said.

"Which story?" Killian asked.

"'*A Perfect Day for Bananafish*'."

"Ah," Killian agreed.

Michael dog-eared the book.

"So," Killian asked. "Why you?"

"Why me? Me in person you mean?"

Killian nodded.

Michael sighed. "It'll sound a bit old-fashioned."

"I'm all about old-fashioned."

"It's my debt of honour, isn't it? I recommended you to Dick Coulter. I told him you were the right man for the job. In a way it's all my fault."

Killian rubbed his chin. "I take it you're not of the school that believes everything worked out for the best?"

"How so?"

"Well, Markov took the fall for the hit on Rachel's parents – which he did do, incidentally."

"I know," Michael said, his eyes narrowing.

"You want me to continue?"

"Sure."

"Okay. So Markov takes the fall for that, the press loves it, blames the Russian mafia or the FSB, case closed on that. Tom dies of an overdose. I take the fall for the hit on Coulter, but nobody knows who the hell I am, except that I'm either Russian or Irish and probably involved with the FSB too. The upshot is that you're not involved, Rachel inherits a chunk of change to provide for the girls, Helena inherits the bulk of the estate."

"Is that it?" Michael asked.

"No. Dermaid McCann doesn't get his name dragged through the mud, the IRA doesn't erupt in civil war, the Northern Ireland Assembly doesn't collapse, peace reigns in Ulster."

"So everybody wins?"

"Everybody wins," Killian agreed.

"Except for poor old Tom and poor old Dick Coulter," Michael said.

"They were kiddie fiddlers. Pimps. Poor old Tom Eichel and Dick Coulter should be doing ten years."

Michael pursed his lips. "You've got proof of that, of course."

"Seen it with my own eyes," Killian replied.

"And now conveniently lost forever," Michael said.

Killian knew that Michael was smart. You didn't get to be where he was without being extremely intelligent. So it annoyed him that Michael was being a prick.

"Michael, Tom already told you all this – you don't need the proof, you know it's true. If you're looking for an additional reason to top me, be my guest – add the fact that I'm a liar if you want, but I'm not lying and you know it."

"The Dick Coulter I knew—" Michael began but Killian interrupted him.

"Aye, the Dick Coulter you knew was as pure as the driven snow, it was all a terrible misunderstanding. Rachel and me got the wrong end of the bloody stick…"

Michael coughed. "All right. Let's say I believe you. It doesn't really change anything does it?"

Killian smiled. "How many years since you've been on a job, Mike? Since you've been in a position like this?"

Michael leaned back in the sofa. "Must be seven years now since I even picked up a gun. I wouldn't have done it this time either, but for the fact that it was all so bloody personal."

"Okay if I smoke?" Killian asked.

"I'd prefer it if you didn't. Can you hold off? Are you desperate?" Michael asked.

"I can hold off," Killian said.

"Where was I?" Michael asked.

"It was all so personal…"

"Yes, I mean, I liked you, Killian. You had a rep. You were a quality closer. A first-class pressure man who could do the job without breaking a little finger. You were a bit of a wee local star and the fact that you were so conflicted about it made you even better. You were a class act. I heard about your Uruguay story. Genius."

Killian smiled. "You liked that?"

Michael laughed. "I did, aye. And in many ways I'm sympathetic to your point of view. Avoiding the rough stuff. Using the old noggin…I dig it. But you've crossed a line here. What you've done cannot be allowed to stand."

Killian looked Michael in those blue-grey eyes, now a little greyer than blue.

"No one cares, Michael. Coulter's dead and buried and on his way to being forgotten. Everybody's rich. Nobody gives a shit," Killian said.

"Not no one. *I* know and *I* care," Michael said, his voice rising, becoming a little shrill. Killian's eyebrows shot up. The Northern Irish house style was understatement. You didn't get all shouty at the drop of a hat. Michael had been in New York too long.

"Why don't you have that cigarette now," Michael said. "Maybe I'll riff on the smoke."

Killian was wearing a light jacket over his blue post-office shirt. He reached in the outside pocket for his Marlboros and his lighter. He'd been easing off. He was down to five a day, not that that would matter much now.

"Are you okay for one?" Killian asked.

"I gave up," Michael said.

"I'm in the process, or was."

Michael sighed again. "Ach, I mean, what kind of a life is this anyway, eh? Always looking over your shoulder, stuck here in a dull wee corner of England?"

Killian took a drag on the cigarette and blew smoke at the ceiling.

"It's not dull. Nowhere's dull if you look hard enough. Take a gander at yon book at the end of the shelf there. Take a wee look, you might get a kick out of it. I know I did."

Michael picked up a book with the title *Where Troy Once Stood* by a Dutchman called Iman Wilkens. He flipped the cover, read the back, was completely uninterested, put the book down.

"It's this guy's thesis that all the events of the *Iliad* took place in East

Anglia. The whole of the Trojan War took place in Britain during the Bronze Age. It was so famous that the story got spread across Europe and adopted by the Greeks and so became part of their mythology."

"It sounds nuts."

"Oh, it is. Completely. Wilkens got the idea because it rains so much in the *Iliad* but not very much in Greece or Anatolia. So where does it rain a lot? England, of course. It's so loony it's kind of brilliant in a way. Anyway, you see that hill behind you through the window?"

Michael smiled. "You think I'm gonna fall for that?"

Killian chuckled. "Okay don't look, but anyway that hill behind you is called the Gog Magog, we're on Gog Magog Street and according to Wilkens's theory that hill, that very hill is the hill of Troy."

"That's why you moved here?" Michael asked.

"No. We moved here because of the common land, but I found that book in the Oxfam Shop and started reading it and thought it was great," Killian said and then in the voice of the preview guy at the movies: "Here we are in the shadow of ancient Ilium."

"Or not," Michael said, laughing.

Because of who he was and what he'd done Michael didn't have many friends. He liked Killian. Killian could have been a pal, once. But, of course, not now.

The laughter died on Michael's lips. "Look, Killian, I don't want to give you false hope. I don't want you to be labouring under any illusions. You realise that, right? This isn't a debriefing. I haven't come here to get your side of events, I've come to end this sorry episode."

"I thought there might be a reason for the fancy-looking piece of equipment in your right hand."

"I mean, you see where I'm going with this? It's for honour and, if you will, professional reasons."

"What if I put up a fight?" Killian asked

"Do whatever you have to do, but only one of us is going to walk out of this…" Michael's voice tailed off.

"*Caravan* – you're allowed to say the word, you won't turn into a tinker just by saying it," Killian said.

"I wasn't shitting on your accommodation, I was just trying to think of the British term. We call them trailer homes in America," Michael said.

"Aye, I know, trailer trash and all that malarkey."

"No, you don't know. That's got nothing to do with it. I'm not prejudiced. I've been through the mill myself a few times as well, mate."

Killian put his hand on his thighs and smiled. "By 'put up a fight' I didn't mean fisticuffs. I meant me using my skills, what I've got, to make you change your mind," he said carefully.

Michael nodded.

There was not a soul in the pasture behind him and it was beautiful out there: a golden sea of rapeflowers, an azure horizon, carnation-shaped clouds. The light was bending through the perspex making a halo in the dust thermals above Michael's head.

Killian liked that. An angel, even an angel of death needed a halo.

"As I was trying to say, only one of us is going to leave this caravan alive. I know you're good, mate, but you're not talking your way out of this one," Michael said.

"You're not going to fault me for trying though, are you?"

"No."

Killian's smile broadened. What more could you ask than to be given a chance to do what you did best.

"Well then," Killian said and out poured the words, which, of course, are deadlier by far than bullets in the hands of an expert practitioner.

Killian was a little rusty, but eventually he warmed to his theme and Michael listened, and the goat outside listened, and even the Trojan shades in Hades listened. He talked and talked, and shadows fell on the tinker camp and on the rapeseed fields and on the Gog Magog; and Venus rose in the vermillion sky, and the moon lowered her pointed keel, and in the background, in the broad limb of an oak tree, a wheatear was singing.

www.serpentstail.com

Visit serpentstail.com today to browse and buy our books, and to sign up for exclusive news and previews, interviews with our authors and forthcoming events.

NEWS

cut to the literary chase with all the latest news about our books and authors

EVENTS

advance information on forthcoming events, author readings, exhibitions and book festivals

EXTRACTS

read first chapters, short stories, bite-sized extracts

EXCLUSIVES

pre-publication offers, discounted books, competitions

BROWSE & BUY

browse our full catalogue and shop securely

* FREE POSTAGE AND PACKING ON ALL ORDERS WORLDWIDE *

follow us on twitter • find us on facebook